PERSONS LIVING OR DEAD

THE AUTHOR

Nia Williams was born in Cardiff in 1961 and studied History at Exeter University and European Studies at Reading. Her first novel, *The Pier Glass*, was published by Honno in 2001. She now lives in Oxford where she works as a freelance writer and pianist.

PERSONS
LIVING
OR DEAD

by
Nia Williams

HONNO MODERN FICTION

Published by Honno
'Ailsa Craig', Heol y Cawl, Dinas Powys
Bro Morgannwg, CF6 4AH

First impression 2005

British Library Cataloguing in Publication Data.

A catalogue record for this book is available
from the British Library.

ISBN 1 870206 71 1

Published with the financial support of the Welsh Books Council

Cover design by Chris Lee
Cover photograph: Nicola Schumacher

Typeset and printed in Wales by
Dinefwr Press, Llandybïe.

Acknowledgements

'Build A Little Home' (words by Al Dubin, music by Harry Warren).
© 1933 M. Witmark & Sons and Warner Bros Inc, USA.
Warner/Chappell North America Ltd, London W6 8BS.
Lyrics reproduced by permission of IMP Ltd.
All Rights Reserved.

'I Don't Want To Set The World On Fire' (words and music by Bennie Benjamin, Eddie Durham, Sol Marcus and Edward Seiler).
© 1940 (renewed) Bennie Benjamin Music In., Ocheri Music Publishing Corp and Eddie Durham Swing Music, USA. (83.33%) Warner/Chappell North America Ltd, London W6 8BS. (16.67%) Redwood Music Ltd, London NW1 8BD.
Lyrics reproduced by permission of IMP Ltd.
All Rights Reserved.

'In The Moonlight' (from *The Kid from Spain*, words by Bert Kalmar, music by Harry Ruby).
© 1932 Harms Inc, USA
Warner/Chappell North America Ltd, London W6 8BS.
Lyrics reproduced by permission of IMP Ltd.
All Rights Reserved.

'Pick Yourself Up' (words by Dorothy Fields, music by Jerome Kern).
© 1936 TB Harms & Company Incorporated, USA.
Universal Publishing Limited (50%).
All Rights Reserved. International Copyright Secured.

JANUARY

1

'You know who this is!'

The removal man stops in his tracks and stares at me. He's carrying a cardboard crate full of crockery. He's got another job in two hours. It's not a good time for my mother-in-law to start telling him he knows who I am.

Gill nods towards me, watching his reaction. She's wearing her little smile. Her 'I'm about to tell you something that'll knock you for six' smile. I stand there in the hall, scrunched newspaper in one hand, a bedside lamp in the other, trying to look like someone worth knowing . . . Trying to look like my mother.

The removal man looks blank. His cardboard crate is slipping. Gill delivers her punchline:

'This is Marian Westwood's daughter.'

The removal man adjusts his grip on the crate and searches for clues. He assesses my woolly hair, my acne-scarred cheeks, the stains on my sweatshirt, and the bagging knees of my jeans. He says, 'Well, I'll be buggered. Where d'you want this lot?'

He hasn't got the foggiest idea who Marian Westwood might be. I could hug him.

At six that evening the removal man and his mate finally finish unloading, three hours late. He has to ring the office and arrange another van for the next client. I give him all the cash from my purse as a tip. He twitches his head in the direction of the hospital, making his jowls tremble.

'Nice neighbours,' he says. 'Catch *me* living next to that lot.' He leans against the bannister and seems ready for a chat. 'They've just shut that evil bastard in there, haven't they? The Face-Slasher? Saw it in the paper.' He lets the coins dribble out of his hand into his overall pocket. 'Nurse, are you?'

I shake my head. 'No, I'm not on the staff.' The removal man looks slightly alarmed. 'My mother-in-law used to work there,' I say, to reassure him, but he's suddenly eager to go.

When they've gone I rest against my new front door and look at the fallout of boxes and bags and heaped coats on the floor. I wonder whether the Face-Slasher had any belongings to unpack when he moved in up the road. Gill is in the living room, ferreting through a crate.

'I *told* you to do a big chuck-out before packing up,' she calls. She appears at the door, wiping her glasses on her shirt. 'Can't find the kettle. Didn't you put it on top?'

'Forgot. Sorry.'

'Ne-ver mind!' she sings, extending the last vowel with an impressive vibrato. 'We'll nip across to my place for tea.'

My life has stalled. Three months ago it was mayhem; unpaid bills, unopened envelopes, unsold stock multiplying across every surface and into every space. Our business in a state of collapse, my husband in a state of denial. Life lurched and staggered from one day to the next. One morning Bobby sat drinking coffee among the detritus and said, 'I've got a few ideas . . .contacts. I might go and chase them up . . .

'Gareth,' he called over his shoulder, 'do you want a lift to school?'

He drove our son to the school gate, called goodbye and U-turned away, narrowly missing a bus. That afternoon Gareth came home on the tube.

'Didn't Dad pick you up, then?' I asked, but my son doesn't bother answering stupid questions.

Bobby didn't come back. He phoned late that night and told me not to worry.

'It's all going very well,' he said.

'What's going very well?'

'We're going to be fine,' said Bobby. 'I'm on the move,' he said. 'I'll phone you when I can.' Then he said, 'Don't worry,' again.

So I didn't. I didn't throw his belongings into the street, or report him missing, or send out a search party. Why would I? We were going to be fine. But each day that Bobby didn't return lost a bit more momentum. Sounds stretched and slowed to a growl. Blood settled and congealed in my veins. I sat on my bed or at the table while hours passed around me. My limbs forgot to respond to my brain, then my brain forgot how to instruct them. After 10 days Gareth phoned his grandmother and asked her what to do. Gill took charge. She spoke to the creditors. She spoke to valuers and agents. She put a deposit on a cottage that was up for rent on the hospital estate. She arranged for Gareth's transfer to another school. She rang me with a progress report.

'But his A-levels . . .' I whined. 'He can't change schools now . . .'

'Gareth will cope' announced Gill. Gareth wasn't the problem.

As she opens the door to her house, Gill says, 'Don't bother to take off your shoes. The place is a mess.' Until she says that it hasn't occurred to me to take off my shoes. I check the soles of my disintegrating trainers and wonder what to do. If I start fumbling with the laces now she'll lose her patience altogether. I keep the trainers on.

But of course Gill's place is never a mess. It's comfortable, mildly shabby, stylishly cluttered, but never a mess. Bigger than my new home, but designed along the same lines: one long sitting room and a kitchen downstairs, two bedrooms and a bathroom upstairs. A huge armchair bleached with sunspots gulps me up in the corner. Gill bustles into the kitchen, door-keys jangling.

'I don't know why you gave that guy such a huge tip,' she comments. 'They weren't up to much if you ask me.'

I hate the way she says 'guy'.

'We'll start on the crates tomorrow,' she calls from the kitchen. 'Get things straight for Gareth. Three days – should be plenty of time.'

Gareth is staying with his friend Zek. Short for Ezekiel. His parents aren't particularly religious, apparently; they just fancied the name. They're good people, decent, sympathetic. They offered to let Gareth lodge with them for the last two years of school, but Gareth turned them down.

I lever myself upright as Gill brings the tea. It's piping hot but soothing; my muscles begin to relax. I ache all over from physical effort – a refreshing change, after months of stagnation. Maybe Gill was right, and this move was the sensible thing to do. Maybe I'll get used to it. After all, Gill has lived here for years, even after retiring, and seems almost fond of the place. Bobby had an uncle, a bit of a wild card, who spent some time here many years ago. I suppose that gives it a sort of family feel.

'Gareth will be fine,' says Gill, imagining she's read my mind. 'Term will kick off soon and before you know it he'll be in the swing of it – new crowd, new girls, new vices to try.'

She makes it sound perfectly normal. As she keeps pointing out, we're better off here than surrounded by uncharted cranks and their nasty habits, masked by the city scrum. Here, at least, the criminals are under triple lock.

Sorry – not criminals. Patients. Gill corrects me every time. These are troubled people. Not monsters. And besides I never need to set eyes on any one of them.

2

I've made an early start. I want to unpack as much as possible before Gill gets here, but within an hour I'm ready to drop. Instead of filling shelves and hanging clothes, I find myself floating around with my mother's photograph under my arm.

There are lots of photographs of my mother. Baskets full. Shoeboxes, albums, drawers full. But the framed picture under my arm is the one we always mean when we talk about my mother's photograph. She faces the camera with her head tilted downwards, as if she's about to charge. She looks up, delivers that insolent glare – 'take me if you dare' – and the inkling of a vulnerable squint. Her hair is tied back, but a single S-shaped strand has escaped and undulates sexily across her forehead. Her eyes are outlined in long, shallow curves of kohl. We can see just a hint of black dress between the lower edge of the frame and her perfectly curved, perfectly symmetrical shoulders. She is absolutely gorgeous. Her name is signed diagonally across the lower corner: Marian Westwood, 1954.

I hang it in the hall, next to the living room door. I polish the glass frame. It's an uncertain day, more like spring than winter. Sunshine ebbs and flows in a heavy sky. As I work at a sticky mark on the glass, a wave of light washes through the landing window and into the hall, projecting a sharp image of my quarried, scowling face across Marian Westwood's monochrome beauty.

What would she think if she saw all this? She'd probably think: typical. Jayne spoils the show again. Just as it was all coming together – Bobby and Jayne, the perfect romantic comedy couple, hand in hand, singing jaunty tunes from a bygone age. That's what she'd think: Jayne couldn't hack it. All her sympathies would be with poor, carefree Bobby, driven away by his stodgy wife.

Sorry, Mum. Sorry, Bobby.

I resist the urge to buckle onto the floor, and return to the packing crates.

Radio, kettle, mug, coffee. Time for a break . . .

I stand in the kitchen between a hill of crockery and an island of cans and wait for the kettle to boil. There's a programme on the radio about survivors. They talk about Nine Eleven, Omagh, the *Hindenburg*, the *Titanic*.

I inspect the garden through the window. 'Garden' isn't really the right word. It's a shoulder-high tangle of mare's-tail, bindweed, thistles, goose-grass, dock. At the far end a hedge spills over its own boundaries. There's a dark mass of something half-hidden in the greenery a couple of feet away. It might be a tyre.

A woman on the radio is recalling the cries of *Titanic* passengers left to drown. Gradually, she says, they all died away into the night, except one: the last voice, a man's voice, calling: 'Oh, my God. Oh, my God.'

The phone rings. I fling myself into the living room, scale crates and up-ended chairs, bark my shin against an edge. Don't stop ringing, I'll find you, don't stop. Over the easy chair, behind the boxed-up telly, under a computer key-board . . . It's still ringing. I nearly drop the receiver.

'Hello?'

'Jayne. Hello. It's only Natalie.'

I wish she wouldn't say 'only'.

'Natalie!' I'm sure I don't sound disappointed.

'How are you coping? Seen any nutters yet?'

I brace myself for a lecture. Natalie disapproves. She thinks I should have stood up to Gill. Yes, she understands we had to sell up, but why not move to a market town, a squat in the Hebrides, a caravan in the Pennines – anywhere, a million miles from the interfering in-law? When I tried pointing out that Gill was doing me a favour Natalie lost her temper.

'How can you talk about *favours*? How can you even *think* of taking your own son to live in some godforsaken hole with raving maniacs on the loose?'

Not on the loose, I explained. I repeated Gill's assurances. Only one escape in 30 years. A man who'd carved up his cousin with a bread knife. And he only got as far as the bus stop; he didn't have the fare. He was trying to get back to his mum's.

Today Natalie's being diplomatic. 'I might have some free-lance work lined up for you. Not a huge project, I'm afraid, but still . . . It'll do for starters, won't it?'

'That's great.' I know I sound phoney. 'Thank you. Just as soon as I get straightened out here . . .'

'No problem,' says Natalie. 'It's here when you're ready.' No ticking off. 'Take your time to settle in,' she says. 'Take it easy. That's the main thing.'

Natalie's supportive phone call leaves me sapped. I decide to leave the unpacking and explore my surroundings.

You couldn't honestly call it a cottage. It's a brick-built house in a row of 24 other identical brick-built houses with small, brown-framed windows. The front door opens onto a strip of green, which runs unbroken from the first house to the 24th. Every third house has a regulation horse chestnut tree blocking out the light. As far as I can tell, nobody uses the front door except for deliveries. Strange, that, because from the front you could imagine you were living in an unremarkable, remote wedge of rural Britain. The strip of green ends at a hedge, and then the road. This is the only road between Berriford and Acreston, so occasionally it's quite busy. Traffic builds to a climax just before and after hospital shifts, when there's a constant moan and roar as the staff rein in their cars at the pillar-flanked entrance. Across the road are private houses, aloof and detached.

Gill's house, long and low, is to the left. Beyond them the
view breaks into a run of broad, flat fields and sky. I stand
at the open front door and contemplate my choice of routes.
This is a world of horizontals. Hedges fussing in the breeze.
Gates cross-stitched with shadow. Crouching shrubs and
dwarf conifers, nervous of the winds. Mostly sky, though,
which makes it difficult to plot any kind of journey. A
paper-grey sky, taking up two-thirds of the picture.
Scratches of telegraph wire; a diagonally low-flying plane.
Nowhere to go.

I pick my way back to the kitchen. From here I can hear
the tap of heels, see heads bobbing past my drunken hedge.
Nurses, assistants, caterers, social workers, admin' staff, all
issuing from their back doors to disappear into the maze of
hospital routine, to feed and restrain and record and
question and study and drug. I kick open the swollen back
door and head for the hospital grounds.

Not as bad as I'd feared. At first it has no suggestion of
hospital – or prison. Our back garden faces other back
gardens across a narrow street: child's swing, a mouldering
football, an empty washing line – ordinary family leavings.
My overgrown plot is the only abnormality.

At the end of the street I turn right along the main estate
drive. On one side there are solid houses that wouldn't be
out of place in an affluent suburb. No toys and fripperies
here, though, no curtains or flowers. Just official plaques:
'Personnel and Finance', 'Social Work – entrance through
side door'. On the other side of the drive there's a car park
and a pleasant stretch of green, framed with trees. Ahead
are the staff accommodation blocks, low, mellow-bricked
buildings scribbled with Virginia creeper. Two young
women clack past, giggling. Both carry files and papers
under their arms. It could be a university campus. Sunlight
cuts briefly through the chill and pauses on the back of my
neck.

I turn the corner and there's the hospital itself. The main façade has a civic grandeur. Automatic doors buzz open and kiss shut, over and over again. Members of staff go in and out, each with a plastic tag swinging from a belt or pocket. Some of them have keys attached to their belts, like Victorian housekeepers. The doors have tinted glass, but I can see when they open that there's another door almost immediately beyond them. I walk away from the entrance and along the perimeter fence. Just a wire fence, about 15 feet high, with wisps of barbed wire at the top. It doesn't seem very robust; I imagine Natalie's horror. Probably electrified, I assure myself. Behind the fence there's a ditch, and behind that a stone wall. After the corporate pomposity of the main entrance this seems stark and medieval: fences, ditches, walls.

I walk on for a while and try not to stare through the wire. Visible above the stone wall are the upper floors of separate blocks – 'villas', Gill calls them. Like my cottage, they have small, dark-lined windows. No bars, as far as I can tell, but I don't stop to check. I have the sense of envious eyes monitoring my progress. Ludicrous, I know but, nevertheless, I veer away from the fence and stride across the green towards the far corner of the estate, which is bordered by more family homes. As I approach I can hear children arguing and a dog's bark. Thank God, I think. These houses have no horse-chestnut trees, no grassy strips; the walls are blank, grey, concrete. The last three in the row come into sight, with thick, ridged metal clamped over their windows and doors . . . Hannibal Lecter . . . I falter, and my pace slows.

A man in a suit, carrying a briefcase, has come out of the car park and is skirting the green. He catches my eye and immediately looks at his shoes. I feel like a fool, standing there at a loss, unnerved by a couple of derelict houses. Speak to him. I work up saliva in my dry mouth. Go on. Make the effort.

'Excuse me,' I call.

I want to explain myself, present my credentials of sanity. I ask him whether there's a shop on the estate.

'Yes, of sorts,' he says, gesturing towards the hospital. 'Just for the bare essentials. If you're after a shopping spree . . .' I laugh. He doesn't. He's got a public school drawl, scuffed with estuary. 'They do sandwiches, though' he says. And, since I've already fallen in step, adds with resignation, 'I'll show you where it is.'

He's young. Late twenties, maybe. I wonder whether there's anyone Gareth's age around. 'I've just moved here. Into one of the estate cottages,' I say.

'Staff?' he asks, more brightly.

'No. Oh no. But my mother-in-law lives just . . .' I point vaguely, meaning 'outside', and add, to avoid misunderstandings, 'She used to *work* here.'

The young man doesn't ask any more. He tells me there's a farm shop half a mile up the hill. He says there's quite a nice pub in Peccam village, a couple of miles north. He makes it sound like the kind of place you might choose to live, and I'm grateful. As he directs me to the shop and swerves towards the hospital entrance, he says, 'Welcome to Disney World, then. Enjoy!'

Again, I laugh; he doesn't.

The shop has a bow window with a dusty display of dried flowers and faded ribbon. Inside, two-thirds of the shelves lining the walls are empty. A make-believe shop. A movie set. Only the section that's in shot, behind the counter, seems real: the bubble-bursting noises of the till keys, two assistants bustling about and, behind them, cans of baked beans and soup, packets of loo rolls, instant coffee, tea bags, cigarettes, chocolates, bleach, tampons. There's a stand of cards at the end of the counter: 'happy birthday'; 'get well soon'; 'what do you give a man who's got everything?'; 'sorry'. I'm at the end of a short queue. The man at the front is broad and extravagantly muscular under his clerkly shirt. He's teasing the woman at the till, who's keyed in the wrong price for something. Next to the till, a blackboard with 'Menu' etched in loops and scrolls at the top has a chalked pricelist: 'ham and cheese', 'cheese and pickle', 'tuna mayo', 'bacon and egg (5 mins)'. I buy a cheese and pickle sandwich to take home.

3

'Bigotry,' says Gill. She slams the wine bottle back down and makes the glasses rattle.

'A guy slaps burnt cork all over his face and cavorts around like a lunatic. It's offensive. It's bigoted.'

'Singers wore blackface in those days,' I say. 'It was a different kind of—'

She takes a wide mouthful of wine. Drinking wine is a statement, like everything else she does. This is the kind of pointless, dead-end argument I'm always having with Gill, usually about my mother. Gill has the devoted fan's capacity for storing useless information. She knows far more about Marian Westwood than I do. She knows, for instance, that her burgeoning movie career was scuppered by a third-rate director who went on to make the Saturday Minstrel Parade for TV.

'Anyway,' I say, 'my mother admired Johnny Dunville. I remember her talking about him. She said he did a lot for charity . . .'

'Jayne, dear, there's nothing to stop bigots doing a terrific amount for charity.' She's chastened, though. I've played my ace. When she backs me into a corner, all I need is 'my mother said'.

After another swig, Gill rallies and points at me across the table. 'Besides, she said he was a great *man*. That doesn't stop him being a crap director.'

And so we go on, talking about someone else's past, because it moves so much more easily than the present.

Gareth clatters down the stairs and peers through the living room into the kitchen. He'll have to pass us to get there. Is it worth the effort of communication? Or will he turn on his heel and dash back to the safety of the computer screen?

'We're having a full and frank discussion in here, Gareth,' announces Gill. 'I'm trying to get your mother to face up to the big, bad world and its harsh realities.'

She's tying the ends of her words with exaggerated care. Gareth answers by lifting his chin a fraction. Gill says, 'All sorted about school tomorrow? The bus picks you up more or less at the doorstep, doesn't it?'

'I'm going to run him in,' I say, hastily. 'Just for the first week—' But Gareth is already raising his voice over mine.

'No, I'll get the bus,' he says. 'I don't want a lift. I'll get the bus.'

'He'll be fine,' Gill assures me. She sounds as if she's calming a horse. 'There are other kids catching the bus from the estate – he'll get to know them.'

Gareth mooches into the kitchen. After a moment of opening and shutting cupboards he calls, 'Mum, where are the crisps?'

'Still calls you "Mum", then?' Gill lowers her voice. 'Funny, isn't it? Bobby never called me anything but Gill from the age of 10.'

I long to say, 'That's what *you* think.' Unfortunately, though, she's right. Bobby never did hang that millstone around her neck. She was never 'Mum'. She was 'Gill', his equal, his pal.

After Gill has gone home and Gareth has closeted himself in his room, I spend a couple of hours unloading one of the last boxes. This one is full of Bobby's videos, cassettes and CDs. I dig out his only copy of Marian Westwood in *Leaving Town*. My mother in a pencil skirt and a tight blouse, wrapping her tongue round an East End accent . . . I discard it and choose one of Bobby's old favourites – a preposterous 1932 musical with stagey sets. I make room on the sofa and run the video with the sound turned down, gazing at the Busby Berkley girls as they open and close their chubby legs like flowers.

4

When Bobby and I first met, Gill was living in London, in the house where he'd grown up, a quick tube ride away from our student block. He went to see her every day or two, and it never struck me, or any of our other friends, as odd. That's how Bobby was: he made everything seem natural and easy.

'Join you later,' he'd say, as we were gathering to go to the pub. 'Just off to see how the old girl is.'

He used terms like 'old girl', 'mater', 'the duchess', within audible quotation marks. In ordinary conversation, as she rightly maintains, he always called her Gill. I couldn't imagine having a mother who was available for casual visits, who could prattle and tease and say, 'Right, best get on,' when she'd had enough, without a hint of martyrdom or suspicion.

I made excuses to stay with friends over the summer; during the shorter vacations I simply stayed where I was and worked in the library. I was fascinated by the idea that you might visit your mother by choice. I didn't fall in love with Bobby. I fell in love with Bobby and Gill – friends, who happened to be mother and son.

I never asked him what their private gossip sessions were about. Sometimes, when he came back from her house and settled next to me in the pub, his eyes would be shining with left-over laughter. Other times, he'd be peevish and preoccupied, continuing a debate in his head. He never returned untouched.

'You know who this is, don't you?'

The first words Gill ever said in my presence. We were standing in the front room of their London house. She gripped my arm and shook it, as if to spark a faulty connection and light up my true identity. Bobby's father lowered his newspaper without shutting it.

'This is *Marian Westwood's daughter.*'

Bobby's father had been better value than the removal man. He slapped the open newspaper onto his lap and sat forward.

'Good God! Marian Westwood? Good grief! Now that takes me back . . .'

I'm not sure he ever asked my name.

Bobby's father was a man who sat on the margins of a room, who made responses rather than conversation. He was often away, and when he did pass through the house he and Gill greeted each other like strangers in a country lane. But for Marian Westwood's daughter he became young again, a man who spent all his spare cash on the theatre, who went to the matinée and stayed on for the evening performance, who reflected the intensity and affection in his wife's eyes. Their first real date had been a trip to the Carlton Playhouse to see Marian Westwood in *Daisy Chain*. The first memorable compliment he paid was for her 'husky Marian Westwood voice'. Bobby saw me in his mother's grasp. He saw their memories swarming around my head. He heard his mother say, 'This young woman's mother was one of the greatest actors of her day.'

That night was the first he spent in my bed.

I loved their house. It was a 19th-century terrace, tall and narrow, each floor stacked precariously on the one below and bulging with brick ruffles and protrusions. The rooms were large, high-ceilinged and furnished in Gill's trademark style – big, blowsy sofas, banks of cushions, low tables piled with newspapers and arty clutter on the shelves and surfaces. Gill must have been in her forties when I first met her. Her husband – Robert Senior – was much older. He looked out of place in that house. He was a large, egg-shaped man – a narrow, bald head, wide girth, small feet. He wore suits in various shades of stone. Gill was slight and quick, with an explosion of aubergine hair. She wore crocheted smock-tops and jeans that faded disturbingly between the thighs. They'd been an odd couple from the start. Robert Senior, a desk man, something in insurance, and Gill the do-gooder, the secular missionary. He took her to restaurants and theatres; she took him to public lectures. Their tastes rarely overlapped, with the one notable exception of Marian Westwood.

Much to my relief, they didn't fish for introductions or invitations. I certainly wasn't about to offer any. Marian Westwood was already a caricature of herself by then, and wasn't in the habit of receiving callers outside her own narrow circle. Besides which, you never could be sure that she'd behave.

I don't remember Bobby ever talking with affection about his father. All his childhood memories – playing on the wet sand in Margate, going to the reptile house at the zoo, that sort of thing – they all involved Gill. Little adventures shared by mother and son. Robert Senior was an occasional presence, an irritant, defined by a gap in years. When he died, when Gill phoned from the hospital, Bobby was clipped and efficient. As he replaced the receiver I tried to put my arms around him but he shrugged me off. He said, 'Oh, you know. He was so much older than Gill . . .', as if that explained everything. He had a few disturbed nights; I'd find him brooding, dry-eyed, at the end of the bed, or standing over Gareth's cot, watching him sleep. It wasn't what I'd expected: it wasn't what I'd have called grief. I guessed he was worrying about his mother. He received other people's condolences with a sweet, sad smile and a pat phrase: 'Life goes on,' or 'Time heals,' that he probably wholeheartedly believed.

Bobby assumed we'd be moving into his parents' house. At that time we were living in a tiny flat in Archway. I'm not sure how I felt about taking up residence in the family home – like an intruder, I suppose. Anyway, it never came to that. Not long afterwards Gill announced that she was selling the house and taking a new job at Emmett Park. There was no discussion – there rarely is with Gill. Robert Senior had bought that house for tuppence-ha'penny, as she said, and it made a mint. Gill gave us a sizeable chunk of the profit to buy a house of our own.

'It's healthier to make a fresh start,' she told us. 'All this hoarding up of possessions, passing them from one generation to the next – there's something stifling about it.' Unlike me, Gill was good at clear-outs. Within a fortnight of her husband's death she'd bagged up all his clothes and shoes, his books, his briefcase, his watch, and given them to Oxfam. She binned his letters and old diaries. If Bobby hadn't insisted on keeping the photographs – his father as a child, his grandparents walking on Brighton front in 1920, Robert Senior and Gill in a park, in Trafalgar Square, on their wedding day – I've no doubt she'd have got rid of them too. There's nothing acrimonious about it. She simply doesn't invest the same emotions in objects. To me, throwing away a photograph or a letter is like obliterating a smile or a voice. Letters particularly. A snapshot is random, accidental, but a letter is deliberate. A statement, delivered specifically to me. That's how I feel about it. But Gill is different. She throws things away to free herself of their weight.

'I can't move, with all this *stuff* tripping me up,' she says. 'I need room to move.'

So out it all went. The house was hollowed out and sold, and Gill took up her new post on the staff of Emmett Park secure hospital.

We dutifully bought our house – a smooth-faced '70s semi: no frills, no protrusions. 'Gill can't stand this bland architecture,' Bobby said, with disgust, as we studied the details. But Gill was encouraging.

'Space and light, no nooks or crannies to collect the dust,' she said. 'That was always the trouble with the old place – too many nooks and crannies.' It was already 'the old place'. Gill had moved on. 'That's why living there would be so suffocating for you two,' she explained. 'All those corners gathering memories and associations . . .' It didn't occur to her that none of them would be mine. I heard her brisk voice on the phone as she galvanised Bobby into action.

'Put in an offer, Bobby. You can't afford to hang around these days. And anyway, that's exactly the sort of house I'm hoping to get up here, as soon as I can get out of this bloody awful hospital accommodation.'

Poor Bobby . . . He missed her so much. He talked, half seriously, about finding a job in Berriford, or Acreston, somewhere within reach of her. But he couldn't deny the distance Gill had put between them.

5

Gill has spent her entire working life calculating needs and risks. It's a phrase she trots out, stripped of sense by its coupling. Needs-and-risks. Bread-and-butter. Law-and-order. When Bobby's father was alive and Gill was working in a breeze-block social services office every day, she used to contrive a connection between them, maintaining that their jobs were essentially the same.

'He balances the need for security against the risk of disaster. And that's exactly what I do too.'

Whenever she met a new client, they would 'have a chat'. She would ask questions, the client would answer, the conversation would meander on, and all the while she'd be weighing up these two sides of the problem sitting opposite her. What kind of help was needed? What would happen if it wasn't provided? Would this one throttle the landlady? Slash a wrist? Or just blunder on from week to wretched week, alive and alone? When she transferred to Emmett Park the same process applied. Woman slices her innards with broken bottle. Does she need counselling? Sedatives? A big fat lock on the door? Her scars heal and her panic subsides. Is she ready to join the crowds, find a flat, hold down a job, get through the nights? If not, will anyone know the difference?

Gill wasn't meant to talk about her clients but every now and then, when she stayed with us on occasional weekends, she'd let off steam. I remember her telling us about a patient who'd 'worked his way through the system', as if he'd been on a career path. Had an unfortunate habit of rubbing himself against women's buttocks in queues or on the tube. Started his progress on a psychiatric ward, where a couple of patients who disapproved of 'pervs' picked a fight. Absconded a couple of times. Earned promotion as an awkward case. Ended up behind the perimeter fence.

There was Gill, sitting in our open-plan, nookless room,

legs swung over the chair-arm, feet braced against the radiator. We had no fireplace to interrupt the wall; the house was freezing even in summer. Bobby topping up her glass with white wine, Gill holding forth. 'This one guy attacked his brief, held her hostage, jammed a penknife against her throat, said God had told him to do it. Very sad. He's a real sweetie when God leaves him be.'

She never identified anyone: she was very careful about that. Everyone was 'this guy' or 'that poor soul'. Nobody had a name.

When Gill retired in 1997 Bobby and I assumed she'd come back to London. We were still in the same house, though we'd had an extension tacked on. Bobby wanted to offer her the spare room, 'Just to get her out of that hole while she looks for a permanent place.' He wove it all in to his latest plan. He'd become obsessed about opening a shop. Gareth was 12, settling well into his secondary school, and I was worried. I knew it was no good trying to dissuade Bobby once he'd got a bee in his bonnet, so I urged him to wait a while, at least until Gareth had his GCSEs. It was useless. Every evening over supper, every morning over breakfast, he subjected us to a catechism of schemes and requirements. The small business loan. The fantastic stockist he'd found. The perfect retail site. Eventually Gareth joined forces with him, for the sake of some peace: 'Go on, Mum. Don't be such a wimp. Just go for it.'

Bobby had it all worked out: the family business, the family home – Bobby, Jayne, Gareth and Gill embarking on our great adventure.

'We're leaving our jobs,' he announced to Gill on the phone. 'Yes – both of us. Come on, Gill, you know how soulless they are. We're only doing what you've done, after all: moving on.'

He laid it out before her in simple, logical steps. We get a loan. We open a shop. We sell movie nostalgia, theatrical bric-à-brac, videos, posters, publicity stills, programmes – memorabilia of all conceivable types. We already had a loft full of the junk my mother had left.

'That's enough to fetch a good price before we even *begin* to stock up,' Bobby told Gill. 'You should be proud of us, clearing it all out *and* making a profit.'

He developed his theme. We'd invite people to sell as well as buy. We might even experiment with a bartering system. 'I've already got a name,' he said. 'We'll call it The Great Escape.'

Gill spoke for a while and he looked a little crestfallen. I hoped she was talking him out of it; at the same time I was infuriated with her for spoiling it all.

Bobby said, 'I know all that. I've done my homework. There are plenty of advisers who . . .'

Another long pause while Gill's voice fizzed through the receiver. Bobby turned away from me and said, 'Well, of *course* he'll be OK. Do you think I'd jeopardise his future?' He was irritated now, and defensive. He told her he'd done his sums (though he didn't mention what the results had been). Eventually he said, 'Look. I have to do this. You'll be happier about it when you're here and I can show you all the . . .'

So then Gill had to explain that she wouldn't be leaving Emmett Park. Somehow, she'd put down roots in that weird place. And anyway, she added, wherever she went from now on, part of her would always be behind that perimeter wall. She might as well stay put.

I had orders from Gill to make contingency plans before handing in my resignation.

'For Christ's sake don't shut off all the options' she said. 'You know Bobby's never been great at foresight.'

Natalie promised me she'd put me on her list of freelance editors. 'I'll make sure there's plenty on the backburner' she said, 'in case it all goes horribly wrong. And believe me, it will.'

In Natalie's eyes, anyone strolling away from a decent job was heading for disaster. Natalie and I had occupied neighbouring desks on the 8th floor of Morgan Tenniel Publishers for about four years. In office terms, that made us a devoted old couple. I sat facing the photocopier and the coffee machine; her desk was latched on at a right angle, with a clear view of the emergency exit. Every morning she would approach her desk, still wearing her tailored coat or jacket, and stand for a moment behind her chair, scan the immaculate town plan of paper stacks and files, figure out the tasks ahead – first, second, third – and then, as the pattern of her day locked into place, give a quick sigh of satisfaction and preparation, and get down to work. Natalie likes her job and treats it well, snipping off its loose ends at the end of each afternoon. In return her job keeps itself to itself, waiting while she goes out to the pictures or enjoys a relaxed dinner, allowing her the privacy of her own dreams in bed, knowing that she'll be back, fresh and focused, at 8.30am sharp.

Work was never like that for me. My job and I slouched along in a fog of mutual resentment. My desk was a muddle of unfinished sentences, buried telephone numbers, half-full notebooks and curling Post-it notes. My job and I got on each other's nerves; I overstayed my welcome, frantically trying to finish overdue proofs after everyone else had gone; slunk back early the next day to find that new tasks had maliciously appeared overnight. I was forever having to ring Bobby to ask him to collect Gareth even though it was my turn. (Not that he cared. Bobby and his job were already practically divorced.)

My life had its own plodding motion. Deadlines marched by. Authors failed to deliver, designers refused to compromise, managers went to meetings, the books got published despite everything. Timesheets marked the hours, production sheets the season. Colleagues and working methods came and went. Department heads were given 'offices', fenced off with glass partitions. A new director preferred transparent government and the partitions were spirited away. A recycling policy was introduced and I threw my waste paper into a special sack; the policy petered out and I threw my waste paper into the bin. My old desk was removed, revealing my legs to the photocopier. A new desk was put in its place, with holes for computer wires. We wrote corrections onto page proofs; we keyed corrections onto images of page-proofs. I didn't enjoy my job, but I could live with it. Across town, Bobby sat over a page of accounts and wondered how much longer he could bear this before jumping from the canteen window.

Bobby had negotiated terms for a loan, but nothing was signed. We hadn't reached the point of no return. He wanted us to resign on the same day, to make it a milestone.

'Imagine going in to work on Monday' he said, 'and handing your notice in. *Imagine* it.'

'Nice thought, but it's a fantasy', I said. 'It's just running away from real life.'

'Fine. OK. Let's run away. Why not?'

He had leaflets about partnership and sole ownership, shop-fitting, retail law, marketing and advertising. He'd seen the perfect site, not too costly, in a tired 1930s flat-roofed row – newsagent, bookies, off-licence, launderette – in Fulham.

'Why shouldn't it work?' he said. 'People make their schemes work all the time.'

Gareth chimed in again, 'You're always telling *me* not to give up.'

'Exactly!' Bobby clapped him on the back. 'And you want to give up before we've even begun!' They presented their alliance to me in two identical grins.

I began to believe them. I began to consider breaking my own rule (keep your head down and minimise the risks). Why shouldn't it work? Why should I seize up with anxiety at every turn? Why shouldn't a shop make a living? This is

a nation of shopkeepers. People have been raking it in from
trade for centuries. Bobby went ahead with the loan and put
in an offer for the shop.

'Maybe if I go part-time . . .' I said.

'All or nothing, Jayney. One door closes, and all that. And
let's face it, that job is no great loss to you, is it? It's not
what you might call a vocation, after all.'

That was true enough. I drifted into publishing. I didn't
want to be an editor. I wanted to be a dancer. Of course, I
never learned to dance. My mother would have laughed me
out of town. Lumpen Plain Jayne, cutting a rug? Splintering
the floorboards, more likely, she'd have said. The point is,
though, I had no desire to *learn*. I didn't want to *learn to
dance*. I had no urge to heave on a leotard, go to a rehearsal
room, lever and twist my limbs, spin myself into a sweat.
Even dancing at parties and weddings holds no appeal for
me. What I wanted was *to be a dancer*. Fully formed, fluid as
music, easy-breathing and seamless. Flung round a room
and caught by my partner without a bruise or a gasp. I
wanted to be a work of art. A performance. I wanted to
waltz in swing-time.

This was the greatest gulf between me and Bobby. Every
fantasy of his became an impulse, every impulse an action.
He was one of those types who mystify me, people who
freeze-frame their dreams, spool back for a proper look,
figure out how to reach that scene and proceed to Step One.
To me, these are people who want to straddle two planes of
existence. It simply wouldn't occur to me to take that leap
from imagination to reality. If I want to waltz in swing-time,
why on earth would I spend long evenings shuffling
my feet in three-four time? If I want to be Bette Davis,
reminding Paul Henreid that we have the stars while he
lights my cigarette in his sexy mouth, do I take up smoking?
Dreams and life are entirely unrelated and cannot be
merged. I should have made Bobby understand that. But his
desperate optimism wore me down. He was terrified that if

he took his eye off time it would sneak past, and he did his utmost to instil that fear in me too.

'Imagine catching your reflection in the coffee machine one day,' he'd whisper, in bed, 'and seeing an old, old woman, and realising you've spent your entire allotted span correcting and copying other people's words.'

I should have told him there were worse fates than that. I should have insisted that I was prepared to accept my lot. That sanity is acceptance. Instead I handed in my resignation first thing on Monday morning.

'Don't expect me to wish you luck,' said Natalie. 'You know what I think.'

'Yes, I know.'

'I think you're off your head. If you're sick of this job get another. Don't throw everything away on a whim.' She tried another tack: 'You'll miss the office more than you think. After a couple of weeks on your feet behind the counter you'll realise how civilised office life is.'

For the first three weeks after leaving work I was aimless. Bobby was seeing through all the necessary transactions, painting the shop, planning the fittings and ordering stock. Meanwhile, I stepped into the outside world for the first time since Gareth had been a toddler. I was vaguely surprised to find it heavily populated: young mums, small children, OAPs, the unemployed, students and other unplaceable people all moving around outside the office walls as if this were a perfectly normal way to behave. It was mainly a universe of women, and it bustled in daylight with the kind of energy that had leaked away under strip-lights. It operated to its own rules, sharing rotas, keeping appointments, booking and shuffling playgroup sessions and aerobics classes. Libraries were visited, meals planned. These outsiders knew how to handle life: they knew bus routes, ticket zones, café tokens, discounts, peak and off-peak. They spoke to each other – not petty coffee-machine

mantras or photocopier back-biting, but grown-up, incon-
sequential small talk, exchanged with whoever happened to
be there, whatever their age, sex, colour, faith, accent or
dress sense. This was a world of equals. Nobody deferred or
threw weight around. Nobody made speeches, or pretended
they mattered. Instead of the murmur of air-conditioning,
the humming lift, the discreet purr of phones, we strode
about to a fairground din: pneumatic drill, baby's wail, car
exhausts, laughter, argument, buskers, the cry of a *Big Issue*
salesman. I was reminded of the contracted triumphs and
tragedies of Gareth's early years. The happiness of his soft
head bowed over plastic bricks, his hands clapping to a
Thomas the Tank Engine video, his confused versions of
songs and sayings. And I recalled the blanket of anxiety that
was wrapped around those years. Every night, as he slept, I
had veered between relief at leading him safely through
another 18 hours and terror of the monsters and malefactors
creeping over his cot. At least now I could roam among
strangers without that cold clenching around my heart.

When Gill called to see how we were getting on, I was
radiant on Bobby's behalf.

'We'll be up and running in no time' I told her. 'He was
absolutely right, you know – this is the best decision we've
ever made.'

Four days before opening, we had a batch of posters
delivered: fresh and glossy blow-ups of my mother's photograph. There was stock heaped all over the floor, pushed
against the walls, languishing on the sofa. We made a space
on the table and opened the box. Gareth pushed us apart for
a better look and peeled a poster from the top of the pile.

'Cool,' he said, drawing a sticky hand across Marian
Westwood's face before Bobby could nudge him away.
'Lush.'

In my dream that night, Marian Westwood's throat had
sprouted a coat of short grass. I put my hand against it and

felt it, moist and springy and strong and delicious. All at once it was horrific: her face, putrefying in turf and soil; my hand rooted fast, and green fronds writhing around us, claiming us for the earth. Bobby found me downstairs at dawn, wild-haired and bleary-eyed, staring at one of the posters, trying to dispel the vision with my mother's silvery poise.

6

When Bobby and I met we were both in the first year of the Ancient History and Archaeology course. He's two years older than me; I have his indecision to thank for bridging that gap. He took a year out after leaving school, started work on a building site to see what Real Life was like, then decided to pursue the Spiritual Life instead and set off around India, came back after three weeks and did some work experience in his mother's office (his contribution to the community), and then in his father's (always useful to have a good, solid desk-job in the final analysis). At university he studied English Literature for nearly a year before concluding that one must ground oneself in the past before true art can flourish. It took six months for boredom to set in again; he talked wistfully of dropping out and trying for drama school, but I managed to dissuade him.

After graduating he worked in a Pizza Express, a petrol station, his father's office again; meanwhile he was a budding actor, director, writer, inventor, entrepreneur and archaeologist. That was OK as long as I had the security of my own career. When I got pregnant, Bobby's father put his foot down. He paid for him to take a part-time accountancy course and practically frogmarched him into a job. Surprisingly, Bobby stuck at it. Gill's theory was that being a father himself had been an injection of responsibility. But I always knew Bobby's office job was just background noise, a way of staving off our impatience while he plotted his escape.

There were plenty of schemes in the meantime. He bought a metal detector and enquired into the possibilities of setting up a local archaeology museum. He would open a second-hand bookshop with a stage, where actors could perform or read from the works on sale. After I complained about backache while washing my hair, he spent months working on designs for an extendable basin. He suggested selling the house and travelling round the world, all three of us, in a campervan. He was going to re-train as a teacher. Or maybe a midwife . . .

Some of these schemes evaporated while they were still trapped in his head. Others went as far as research, business plans, getting the house valued. The Great Escape was the only one that really took on a form of its own. Finally, I thought, he might have found a good fit.

Incidentally, we sold most of the posters of my mother. She would have revelled in that. I don't think many of the customers actually knew who she was, but it's a striking image. Movie posters were another success: *Casablanca, The Curse of the Cat People*. And Jane Russell's cleavage evidently still provokes the odd adolescent stir. It was all tacky, ten-a-penny stuff – artists' impressions of publicity stills, touched up in livid colours. The videos sold fairly steadily, but too many customers turned on their heels after asking where the latest blockbusters were. A few were disappointed that we had no private stores 'out the back'. Others were after even more specialised stock. One man complained that we didn't have any early documentaries and newsreels.

'You've left out everything important and kept the kind of crud that gave cinema a bad name,' he said.

Instead of apologising and promising to see what he could do, Bobby discovered a point of principle.

'I'm an escapist,' he said with pride. 'As far as I'm concerned, the further removed from reality, the better.' His conviction evolved as he argued. 'You can get realism anywhere!' he insisted. 'You can't get out of bed of a morning without falling over it!'

The man propped his elbow on the counter, settling down for a debate. He was dressed in a faded suit and had a neat, grey pointed beard and glasses. He looked like Freud's shrivelled ghost.

'Since when,' he asked, 'has it been the role of cinema to

escape from life? Surely it's there to show us what life is?'
He spoke with precision; I may have invented the Austrian
accent.

'This shop,' announced Bobby, 'celebrates an era when
films *didn't* claim to show life. They didn't *want* to be life.
They wanted *more* than that.' He gazed into the middle
distance. 'They wanted to be magic.'

The man laughed. I groaned. Bobby beamed. I served
three other customers while they continued their argument.
Eventually they agreed that the pure escapism we were
peddling was better than the pseudo-realism of modern
cinema.

'These are the people who are truly deluded,' the man
mused. They were both leaning on the counter by this time,
like two old wives nattering over the fence. 'These half-wits
who want to *believe* their fiction.'

Bobby nodded solemnly. Together they poured scorn on
the vogue for natural lighting, faithful flesh tones, scripted
hesitations and inarticulacies, sickening violence, squelchy
sex.

That's not reality, either they concluded.

'So why not ditch reality altogether and have girls in
their scanties dancing on the ceiling?' said Bobby.

They shook on it. But the man left empty-handed.

The point is that we gave it our best shot.

This is the line I rehearse while Eddie Cantor skips back
and forth across the screen in *Roman Scandals*. 'The point is,
Bobby, we had a go. That's what we meant to do, and we
did it.'

Here I am at 5.30am, drinking cold tea and watching
another soundless video, crooking my eyebrows in
reassurance at an absent husband. Before too long there'll
be a prickling of light through the curtains. Dawn breaks so
early round here, even in midwinter. Start digging out
another daft film to watch on a restless night, and by the

time the credits roll it's almost daylight again. No time to languish in the quiet hours, no chance to listen to your thoughts before they're scrambled by the sound of those wretched birds, and Gareth going to the bathroom. Maybe it's the size of the sky. There's such a lot of sky in this part of the country. You can see the weather coming before it hits. No hills to cushion the sun – no hills, no trees, no roofs or chimneys: just miles of untramelled view. I wonder whether it's a comfort to those nameless inmates, or an added torment. Gareth creaks back to his room and I feel the house shift and shudder as he twists himself into the duvet. If I stand at the window and stare hard enough at the sky and the fields, maybe I could break through that horizon. Maybe I could see where Bobby has gone.

My husband is away on business, seeking new opportunities.

He's making contacts, networking, preparing the ground.

He hasn't disappeared.

I prove it to anyone who's interested, waving his irregular, untraceable letters. He hasn't bailed out. The letters flap before my son's resigned face, under my mother-in-law's flaring nostrils. He hasn't done a bunk. He's hatching one more scheme. He'll be back.

I keep faith with Bobby's excuses for Gareth's sake, and Gareth accepts them, for mine.

7

It's Saturday and the post has arrived. I stand in the hall
under my mother's photograph, reading the latest letter.
My hair is scraped back under a wound-up scarf. The
banisters cast crisp shadows across the floor, across the
opposite wall, across my body and face. The house waits for
an outburst. I'm aware of my own stillness; I'm the figure in
a Dutch interior. I have to break out. I stuff the letter into the
pocket of my jeans, put on Bobby's overcoat and leave,
slamming the door.

I probably shouldn't go to Gill's. I tell myself to keep this
letter to myself, not to stir anything up. I can't shake off a
certain smugness: he's written to *me*. My name, our old
address. Gill must have remembered to redirect the post.
I'm sure I didn't. A young girl clops past and shoots me a
quizzical look. I realise that I'm standing at my front gate,
smiling. I should go somewhere, out of the house, out of
Gill's range, and consider his words. Squeeze anything I can
out of them. Where shall I go? The options are limited.
Berriford is out of bounds today: Gareth is meeting new
friends there. He wouldn't let me give him a lift in. It'll take
him an hour on the bus – wandering through half-dead
villages, skirting vast, flat, stripped fields, so that he can
spend an afternoon loping around Woolies and HMV and
eating Big Macs on the corner with people he hardly knows.
But he had to go somewhere too, I suppose. Acreston is too
far away to bother, and anyway it gives me the creeps. It's
one of those normal, 21st-century towns – market square,
Marks and Spencer, library, ring road – with a dark, medieval
settlement skulking behind the mask.

I could just go for a walk. Cross the road, walk along the
edges of fields, find my way to Peccam and explore the
church, that good pub the bloke mentioned. But I don't
think I know quite how to do that. Not on my own. It seems
such a presumptuous, proprietary thing to do, and I don't

belong to or own this landscape. We have no relationship at all. I need Gill as my guide.

I'm trapped.

She's got the *Sun* and the *Mirror* spread over her kitchen table. This is Gill's angry hour. She claims it's good for the soul, exercising your temper to keep it in trim. For an hour every Saturday she reads the tabloids; broadsheets on Sunday. She sits there stoking her fury about the idiocy of statistics, the distortion, the triviality, the injustice.

'Name and shame, name and shame,' she fumes, 'there's always got to be a scapegoat, no such thing as accidents or bad luck.' Then she has a go at the named and the shamed for good measure. When she's built up a head of steam and yelled it off, she folds the papers away, takes a full intake of breath and faces the day. I've arrived too early: she's still flushed and tetchy.

'All this crap about one in five teenagers being law-breakers,' she shouts, ushering me in. 'What does that *mean*? Bugger all, that's what. It means *four-fifths* of our maligned youth *haven't* broken the law. Have you ever committed a crime?'

'Er . . . speeding, maybe . . .' I'm fingering the edge of the letter in my pocket.

'Exactly. We've all done it. So why isn't the big story "80 per cent of teenagers better behaved than us"? And I dare say it's all based on some random sample of two-dozen liars, so it's bollocks whichever way you look at it.' She whacks the offending newspaper with the flat of her hand. 'Where's Gareth?'

I tell her he's gone to meet his new friends and add: 'I hope they're nice lads.'

'"Hope they're *nice lads*?" *Suitable*, you mean?' Mimicking me with a vicious sneer. 'Honestly, Jayne, I sometimes think *you* should be the in-law, not me. Your head is 25 years older than the rest of you.'

She thinks I'm a closet snob. Once she told me I was like her father – 'A man who'd spend a fortune to help the needy, but couldn't spare two words for anyone who "wasn't quite the *type*".'

I protest weakly. 'No, I just mean I hope they're . . . nice. That's all.'

Grouchily, she opens the coffee jar. The scent lifts and comforts me. Gill's homes always have those convivial aromas – real coffee, baked cakes, delicate flavours sizzling in a clever sauce. They were a revelation to me, after my mother's flat and its captive air of sugary perfumes, unwashed tights, stale wine and cigarettes. I continue to defend myself.

'I don't care about their accents, or what they wear, or what their parents earn, or anything. All I care about is that they're nice to Gareth, and don't get him into trouble. That's all.'

Gill rolls her eyes. 'Just because Gareth's friends live beyond the tube line, doesn't mean they're all savages, you know,' she says. 'I hear some of them have even been known to read the odd book.'

I sit down to drink my coffee and immediately stand again to wrestle the letter from my pocket. I hand it to her and she releases a long, exhausted sigh.

'Postmarked Carlisle,' I say.

'At least we know he's still in this country,' mutters Gill. She sits in her bright kitchen by the window and eases the page into focus.

I look at her garden, plain and neat, wide and low. Through Gill's windows the fields become a view. My windows are small and scared; to them, this flat expanse of land is a threat.

Gill bends over the letter to read it again, screwing up her eyes behind her John Lennon specs. Her face droops towards Bobby's writing in tiny stalactites of flesh. She's trying to read clues, going over and over his four curt sentences, tracing them with her lilac fingernail.

I feel sorry for her. Today, Bobby has reduced his assertive, independent mother to old age and loneliness. 'You won't find anything in there – no more than he's written,' I say. '*I* couldn't. He might as well have sent an e-mail. At least that wouldn't risk giving anything away with punctuation and capitals.'

I'm a traitor; trying to ally myself with Gill, trying to whip her back into life, into rage, by denigrating her son. And I'm an idiot. I should know it's useless slagging him off to his own mother. I back-track a little.

'He *is* thinking about us, though . . .' I begin, and I'm horrified to hear the strain in my voice. Gill stops reading the letter and looks elsewhere, willing me not to cry. Why do I have to be so pathetic? No wonder he won't come home. No wonder her son walked away. Name and shame, name and shame . . .

Hardly opening her mouth, Gill says: 'He doesn't even *mention* Gareth.'

This takes me by surprise and I lose the urge to sob. This is what we should do, Gill and I: join forces, join the force of our fear and anger and hope and grief and send it screeching after him like a missile. But of course, I miss my opportunity. Instead of backing her up, I switch sides.

'Yes, he does!' I insist. 'He *does* mention Gareth—' I'm overwhelmed by a surge of faith. She can't throw that one at him. It's *all* for Gareth. Isn't it?

Gill quotes from the letter: 'Making progress,' she reads. 'Made some useful contacts. Things definitely looking up.' She enunciates every word without mercy, crossing every 't' and dotting every 'i' of Bobby's delusion.

Then she hands me the letter in one swift, slicing move, like drawing a sword.

'Contacts,' she says. 'Progress. Has he started to believe his own lies? What is this – a fact-finding trip? He doesn't have to go looking for facts anywhere else. There are plenty of them here, where he's left them. A failed business. A stack of debts. A wife. A son.'

She's still holding me at letter-point; it wilts at my chest. I take it from her. Gill's eyes sizzle through her hippy glasses and burn my cheeks.

'He doesn't even mention his own son,' she repeats, slowly, as if I hadn't understood. I scan the letter.

'Love to everyone!' I shout in triumph. '*Everyone!*'

Gill actually spits on her spotless pine table. (I don't think this is deliberate.) She tugs a tissue from her sleeve and immediately dabs it away. For a long time we both wait for the morning to shift. She turns to the window and stares, searching the infinite fields for her only son. Her breathing grows slow and heavy. I think: oh, God. Surely Gill doesn't cry?

MARCH

1

Gareth is in school and I've been working on that job for Natalie. It's a mindless, tedious piece of work. They're cobbling together a coffee-table book on historical buildings from several smaller editions. My job is to tailor the old text – slice off paragraphs, mix in sentences, squeeze and stretch it until it fits. If there's a white space at the end of a column, fill it up with words. It hardly matters which words, as long as there are no uncomfortable silences at the bottom of the page. I'm working in Gareth's room. Gill has hinted that she might help me buy a computer of my own, but for the time being my files are lurking on the edge of his desktop. I feel as if I've wandered into a foreign land. His screen-saver casts a disturbing veil across my folders. It features a scuttling creature with bulging eyes and a fat, priapic tail, and the words 'Badass' and 'Muddafucka', which slither endlessly from left to right. CDs are stacked in towers around the machine. To reduce the glare of sky, I work with his curtains drawn and the desklamp on. Beyond my greenish halo are mounds of Gareth's clothes, tiers of his belongings. I don't feel welcome here.

I need to cut 70 words from a description of Portchester Castle but I can't concentrate. A shared computer is like a shared room: it harbours secrets. All it takes is the press of a key, the soft click of plastic, and I can go exploring. A mother nosing through her son's files: Gill would be outraged, I'm sure.

The first files I open are pretty innocent. Assignments and essays, folders and documents titled 'History'; '19th C – Industry. Disease and Poverty'; '20th C – Depression.

Holocaust.' I shut my eyes briefly. My boy, not yet old enough to cast a vote, already making casual notes on misery's furthest extremes. Suddenly I'm longing for the day when his education comes to an end and he can shove his head into the sand with the rest of us.

Back to work. 'Extra floors were added to the keep to house French prisoners of war. Over 500 men were crowded together in the cold and filth; water streamed down the walls and disease was rife. In one year alone, 93 died in these wretched conditions'. I highlight everything from 'over' to 'conditions' and 30 words vanish.

I slump back in the chair.

Gareth's room smells of feet and Fanta.

The e-mail icon stares at me from the top of the screen.

He's in the middle of composing an e-mail to Jinx, his great friend from our former life. No capitals, no punctuation: it's a monotone, machine-gun scattering of in-words and nicknames and jokes that I don't understand. He's added an attachment and I open it. It's a recipe for the ideal babe. Britney Spears' thighs; Kylie's arse; someone called Mandy's breasts, Penelope Cruz's mouth.

Bobby once told me I had a mouth like my mother's. I was pleased, although I knew it was a lie. Marian's upper lip was thicker than the lower; it gave her a look of petulance, a childishness at odds with her knowing eyes. My lips are thin and straight, like my father's. Bobby was being kind.

I finger the outline of my mouth and close the e-mail window.

What sort of a mother pries into her own son's private correspondence? At the moment I don't particularly feel like anybody's mother. I'm just a woman with a headache, a woman with thin lips and a teenage stench in her nostrils. I need some fresh air.

Gill has upped her order at the estate shop from one daily

copy of *The Guardian* to two. I never used to read a daily paper but it gives me a reason to get out of the cottage. While I'm at the shop I buy a tuna mayo roll for my lunch. You'd think a journey to the brink of bankruptcy would teach me not to waste my money on ready-made food, but I tell myself it's only this once. Next Tuesday I'll start the regime recommended by Gill: a weekly trip into Berriford with a carefully prepared list of basics and economical retailers: the Co-op for household items, the market for fruit, veg and fish. I won't have to spend much. Gareth's already taken to calling at Gill's after the school bus drops him off and filling himself with egg on toast and home-made malt loaf. At least twice a week she asks us round for 'a proper meal'. As Bobby always assured me, 'Whatever happens, Gill won't let us starve.'

I'm trying to organise myself at the shop door, paper under my arm, mayonnaise and grease seeping from the bread roll, through its tissue-paper bag and over my wrist, when a voice says, 'Discovering the local delicacies, I see.'

It's the young man in the suit. My face blossoms in an outrageous blush and *The Guardian* drops onto the floor. I scrabble to pick it up; he doesn't. We shuffle around each other. His briefcase knocks against my leg.

'Settling in?' he asks.

'Oh, you know . . .' I say, but he's already turned to greet someone in the queue.

An hour later I'm leaning against the kitchen worktop with the paper spread out and the remnants of my lunch pushed to one side. The back gate shivers and I see the top of Gill's head bobbing above the long grass. I chuck the evidence of my shop-bought lunch in the bin and open the back door.

'This garden is a disgrace,' says Gill. She's carrying a Co-op bag; I can see the fat fingers of a gardening glove pointing over the rim. 'I'm going to borrow a strimmer from Ted in the next house and we'll make a start on it this weekend.'

I make tea.

Gill sees the newspaper and peels back a couple of pages. 'Our latest celebrity,' she says, indicating a story headed 'Life for "Devoted" Killer'. 'It says they're sending him to Crafford Gaol, but you mark my words, he'll be in here like a shot as soon as they've done the reports.'

I skim the story for a second time. Marcus Peters, loving husband, caring father, beavering away at a plumbing job in the bathroom one morning, suddenly lost it and bludgeoned his wife of 19 years with a piece of piping.

'What happened to him?' I ask, mashing a tea bag into the bottom of her mug with a spoon. 'What made him flip like that?'

'If you ask me he didn't,' says Gill. 'Have you followed this case at all? They'd left the door open downstairs. According to the police Peters went barmy, thundered into the parlour, walloped her to death and then sauntered back to his DIY. Does that sound likely to you?'

I gape at her. 'You think he's innocent?'

She touches my hand to stop the mashing and retrieves the tea bag. 'I suppose,' she says, in that resigned way. 'I suppose *you'd* say the police must have a reason for bringing him in.'

'Well, don't they?'

'Oh, yes!' She laughs theatrically before taking a wary sip at her tea. 'Yes, they've got a reason. They need an arrest. Why not the husband? That's who it usually turns out to be in *Morse*, isn't it? For Christ's sake . . .'

I follow her into the sitting room, clutching my own mug of tea. She's wittering on about the garden again but I'm in a cell with Marcus Peters, dazed by the treachery of events. So many years slotting into predictable order, so many routines allowed to weave themselves into a life and then – bam. An open door, a roaming psychopath and you're minus a wife, minus a home and locked in a building full of crazy people behind a prison wall.

'What's the matter with *you*?' Gill's voice splits the thought and I register the sparks of hot tea on my legs. She takes the mug from my shaking hands.

I grasp at a stray wisp of logic: 'Anyway, if it wasn't the husband, where did the piece of piping come from?'

Gill studies me through her circular specs. I can see her choosing to humour me.

'Well,' she says, 'I guess we might not know the whole story.'

We sit down. I cast about for a new subject. I nearly mention the young man in the shop – to show that I'm capable of ordinary human intercourse – but I decide against it. Instead, I tell her I've had a letter from my dad.

'He's sent a cheque,' I say.

Gill makes a cynical face which means 'finally'. As usual, I grow defensive.

'He's not a wealthy man,' I protest. 'And he's got his own family to support . . .'

Gill's raising her hands in concession. 'I haven't said a word! I'm sure he's been a great—'

She fans away the rest of the lie. As far as Gill is concerned my father proved his inadequacy the day he left home. Just another mediocre sap who couldn't live up to my mother's magnificent flaws, that's how she sees it. Marian Westwood couldn't have put it better herself. When my father moved to Australia, with his shy, kindly wife and their baby son, my mother's only comment was: 'That man's a fucking coward.' As if he were trotting the globe to get away from her. Well, maybe he was, but who could blame him? If I hadn't been grown up and enmeshed in my own romance at the time, I might well have run with him to find shelter from her storms.

'It might be as well,' Gill is saying, 'to put it into a savings account.'

And make the most of a bad job – that's what she means. As though it were my father's place to bale out her useless son.

'Anyway,' she says, after draining the mug. 'I won't stay. Thanks for the tea. I'll let you get back to work. And this weekend we'll tackle the rainforest.'

She's on her feet. I'm thanking her for the gardening gear, and firing silent salvoes. My father may be a bore, I rant, but at least he hasn't run up a catalogue of debts and buggered off. If Bobby had been more of a bore, I bellow, we would still have a proper family.

Gill waves from the path and calls, 'Here's to the strimming!'

And I call back, 'Can't wait!'

When she's gone I slog back upstairs and restart the computer. It taunts me with a cheerful fanfare and I wait for the screen to compose itself. While I'm waiting I revise my charge against Bobby. He *was* a bore. He was probably the biggest bore of all, with his schemes and dreams and false starts and happy endings. Nevertheless, everyone, including Marian Westwood, fell under his spell.

2

Marian Westwood grew up in the area of Cardiff still called The Docks by older locals, though its new brand name is The Bay. Her childhood home, the terraced house where we occasionally visited my grandmother, was demolished to make way for the marina development. Both my grandmother and my mother were long gone by then, of course. My grandmother would have been baffled by the glass hexagons, swooping roofs, hotels, high-windowed eateries and flickering yachts that now constitute the view from her old neighbourhood. She would have been upset, I expect; she lived all her life in that place and knew everyone until the last few years, when her increasing bulk and bad heart confined her to two downstairs rooms. Those streets were her story; every house had names and pasts attached. She would have grieved over their loss, mourned the passing of their narrow spaces and dank pubs, blinked in consternation at the alchemy that changed black cranes and mudflats into glinting lakes and towers. My mother, on the other hand, would have shed no tears for the old way of life. She got out as soon as she could.

To celebrate her second great success in the theatre – in *After Silence* at the Monarch – she rented a tiny flat in Bayswater. And that's where she stayed until her death. For nearly 40 years she doled out her rent money once a month; for nearly 40 years she arranged her paranoia, her moods, her tempers and passions around the same four rooms. She had no more space and no more property rights than her mother had in Cardiff. In the Dockland house the wallpaper flowered with damp stains and curled at the corners; in the Bayswater flat the plaster grew long cracks and smaller tributaries to mirror the wrinkles travelling around my mother's face. She was never sensible with her money, my mother; never saved or invested. Every Christmas she would address an envelope to Cardiff with her mouth set in distaste, and post off a modest cheque – 'just in case', as she put it, 'the old lady ever goes to the papers to moan'. There was no thought of buying the old lady a clean, dry house on a hill, clear of the marshes, even at the height of my mother's success. The old lady wouldn't have wanted to move, but that wasn't the point. The point was that Marian Westwood felt no obligations to a woman who, to her mind, had done no more than keep her alive and leave the door ajar for her departure.

And yet I remember the look on my grandmother's face when our rare visits came to an end. My mother would be fidgeting, taking staccato sucks at a cigarette, turning and shifting on her stiletto heels. She never seemed to sit down in that house. My grandmother would sit at her little square table, 'puffing like a horse', as my mother said, fingering the edge of a threadbare tablecloth laid in our honour. The moment would come after an hour, two at the utmost, and mother would yank my arm and say

'Well, time waits for no man . . .' and my grandmother's eyes would swivel up at her, wary and puzzled, and then at me in my pink anorak, and back down at the tablecloth, and she'd say nothing.

'Charming, isn't it' my mother would explode as soon as we were safely in a taxi. 'All this way and she can't even be bothered to say goodbye.'

I never met my grandfather. He was killed in an accident while working on the dockside in 1938. All I knew of him was his exotic name – Aloysius – and a creased snapshot of him in baggy overalls, arm flung over a comrade who's half out of shot. He was what my mother still called 'half-caste': black father, white mother. The photograph shows a handsome, slightly pudgy face, wavy hair; he's laughing, so his eyes are half-shut. Maybe he looked completely different with a straight face.

I never really felt comfortable in the Bayswater flat. It

was always too full of my mother's friends, music, cigarette smoke to allow me any particular claims. What I hated most of all was the kitchen. It was even smaller and pokier than my grandmother's, with bulbous, exposed pipes running above the skirting board and a grimy window over the sink. Opposite, on a slightly higher level, was the kitchen window of a flat in the next block. We had no blind or curtain; as soon as dusk fell and she switched on the light, we were on display. I preferred to blunder around in the dark, watching my feet, sure that if I glanced up I'd meet a stranger's eyes. I'd nag my mother to hang a curtain; when I was older I offered to do it myself, but she gave a pained expression and said, 'Do you really think our neighbours are remotely interested in our culinary activities?'

It didn't bother her, the idea of a private audience. She moved between icebox and cooker, cupboard and sink with self-conscious grace. She performed the washing-up, danced the preparation of a meal, hummed to herself and struck attitudes of reflection or forgetfulness. There may have been someone observing it all; there may have been noone at all. She was too much of a professional to check.

It was strange to see her circling that flat in just the same way that her mother had padded around her house, as the years closed in. The furniture, once perky and stylish, sank imperceptibly out of date. My mother swelled and shrank like the ocean tides, according to her state of body and mind. She felt her way through the diminished spaces of her den, where once she had bustled and offered drinks and laughed at the mess, just as, in some lost era, my grandmother had perhaps been slim and quick and sociable within her own walls.

Gareth is like me: he hides away. Like me and like my father, scuttling out of the spotlight into the wings. Gareth was a child when Marian died, and maybe it's just as well. I doubt whether she'd have had any more to say to him, as he grew up, than her own mother had to say to her. A bashful boy, struggling for words, huddling behind a bolted door with his beloved PC. I've nagged him about it, of course – he'll ruin his eyesight, lose the power of movement, fry his brain. Get outside, I used to urge him; play some football. But when I was a child I was exactly the same. I had my scrapbooks, my magazines, the telly; the few friends I had were an intrusion.

Marian Westwood had no time for shrinking violets like me and Gareth. We bored her. We could provide an audience, which was all well and fine, but even an audience has to give something back. Bobby, on the other hand, affable, good-looking, head-in-the-clouds Bobby – he was the son she should have had. As far as Marian was concerned, Bobby was my greatest, perhaps my only achievement. Between our marriage in 1983 and my mother's death 10 years later, Bobby was the court favourite. She was reluctant to meet him at first. She didn't come to our wedding – public appearances were absolutely out of the question by then. I'm sure Bobby's parents were bitterly disappointed, but they put a good face on it. After all, they didn't want their illusions shattered. Another year went by. And then we had our summons: an invitation to drinks on Boxing Day 1984. I was astounded. Horrified, in fact. I'd foreseen them ignoring each other indefinitely, and that wasn't a problem for me. I was quite happy to straddle two worlds – the everyday existence, with Bobby and Gill and the open-plan house, and, when necessary, occasional forays into Marian's galaxy of past glories and present afflictions. But I suppose even Marian must have reckoned a woman should set eyes on her son-in-law at least once in life. It seemed a very pedestrian conclusion for Marian to draw. Maybe she just wanted to play the bride's mother.

Anyway, I warned Bobby about the mess, her appearance and possibly bizarre behaviour, and Gill stoked him up with questions about past productions, technique, trivia and celebrities of the day. The lift up to Flat 7a was its usual vacillating self, adjusting its position at each floor with a jolt up and a dip down. I gripped the bottle of champagne and battled with nausea. Bobby was holding a parcel by the ribbon and I worried that it would snap and deposit *marrons glacés* all over the floor. I heard them rattling with every surge of the lift and announcing our arrival like amplified castanets. The ribbon held, though, and my mother was there, opening the door, before I could fumble for my key. She'd obviously spent hours recreating an approximation of Marian Westwood. She was 54 at the time and looked a good 15 years older. I was glad to see that she hadn't overdone the make-up. The lipstick was a touch too vivid but not freakish, and her eyes were mercifully free of kohl. She was wearing a voluminous black dress – no cleavage, no bulges of puckered flesh. Thank God, I thought. Thank God. When she ushered us in to the flat there were more surprises in store. The sofa and leather chair were visible: we could sit down without clearing away newspapers, towels, underwear and plates. In fact most of her sheddings had been swept into reasonably inoffensive dunes around the sides of the sitting room, and apart from half a fresh cigarette leaning in her stand-alone ashtray all the fag-ends had been thrown away. A fog of perfume covered the permanently sticky smell of old alcohol and smoke, and it was bearable. I was deeply moved. I thought: she's done this for us, for her daughter and son-in-law. She's done it for me. I kissed her on the cheek and she clutched my arm and steered me away.

'Nice to see you, dear,' she said, and fluttered a hand towards the sofa. 'Now, then, Bobby.' She remembered his name. 'You come and sit by me while Jayne finds the glasses, and we'll make up for lost time.'

As I took the champagne into the kitchen I could hear her apologising for being unable to attend the wedding – 'My health is unpredictable, you know . . .'

As I wiped three greasy champagne flutes, she was cooing: 'Ah, *marrons glacés*, my weakness, you clever boy!'

She was coherent and pretentious and word-perfect. I was proud of her. ·

We stayed for three hours. Marian sipped her champagne slowly and answered all the questions Gill had supplied, complete with tittle-tattle and lucid anecdotes. She asked Bobby about his work and he told her about his ambitions. At the time – on that morning, at least – they involved becoming a theatre director. She patted his thigh and said, 'Whatever I can do, my dear . . .' as if she still had an address book full of the living and the active. 'So refreshing to meet a young man with vision. Never settle for less than the best, Bobby, dear. Always want more, never just enough.'

He lapped it up. I refilled the glasses.

We emptied the bottle and she didn't suggest finding another. When she'd had enough she placed her hands on her lap and straightened her back, inhaling deeply, and I recognised the signal. I said, 'Well, Mum, we'd better get going', and she said, 'Yes, indeed, time waits for no man', and encouraged us to call in again soon.

As we left Bobby said, 'I don't know what all the fuss was about. She's a charmer. She's an inspiration.' He held the lift door open but looked at the door of 7a, not at me. He was wondering how a woman like that could have given birth to his frumpy wife.

Fair enough, I thought. Under my winter coat I was sweating with relief. Well done, Marian Westwood. What a trooper.

3

'We're opening this story
By giving you a peep
Into the dormitory
Where all the co-eds sleep!'

Three am. Curled on the sofa, watching another woman in bed in 1932. *The Kid from Spain* – another one of Bobby's silly films. Another one starring Eddie Cantor. The volume's turned down low again, for fear of waking Gareth. Curvaceous women in lacy nighties are stretching their lovely limbs and dropping their smutty hints.

'I'll be here till I'm twenty –
I'm only seventeen.
By that time I'll know plenty.
Of course – y'all know what I mean!'

Oh, yes, we know what you mean.

They go into their dance, skipping in circles, like children. And like adults we're allowed lingering close-ups of the knickers under those lacies.

Half an hour ago I woke out of a dream that is still moving among the dancers and making my tired muscles twitch. I woke gaping, drooling onto the pillow, one hand squeezing the flesh inside my thigh.

In my dream I spoke again to the young man in the shop, but our conversation was charged with certainty and anticipation. He led me out through a tunnel and into a place moist with shrubbery. He pressed me against a wall; its stones vibrated with the unseen lives on the other side. I have never used the word 'fuck' to describe the act of sex: I've always found it an ugly, arrogant word, but in my dream that is what the young man did. He fucked me. Hard, rhythmic, purposeful and detached. And behind the wall a thousand hands felt the stones hum, a thousand hearts beat, a thousand men watched and listened.

I drink strong coffee, trying to banish the dream's hang-over. I thought a musical, a bubbly, innocent, whimsical song and dance would do the trick. More fool me.

Now the girls are in a pool and we're looking down on them from high, as they form their kaleidoscope patterns, legs spreading and shutting, buttocks bobbing and dipping.

Oh, yes, we know what you mean. You mean slapping and panting, thrusting and pumping, but we won't let on. We can't let on. It only works if we're *all* pretending, all the time.

I'm not unduly worried by the young man's appearance in my dream. It doesn't mean anything. That's the whole point of fantasy, isn't it? To break the banks of meaning and intention, to flow into all the hidden corners, the ridiculous and appalling corners, while we tread our careful path through the middle of the room. Don't be true to your fantasies: that's not what they're for. Ignore them. Deny them. That's what keeps you sane.

Gareth has grown to detest these escapist films. He prefers movies with a high and gory head-count. That's *his* escape. That's his relief from the tedium of a routine that will probably deliver him alive and unmaimed to the end of each day. Bobby enjoyed music and romance in his leisure hours; Gareth prefers fear and horror. Serial murder, the undead, alien experiments. God knows what *his* dreams are about.

There's a nightmare that I've had from time to time, since moving here. I'm standing outside the cottage and I can see my son, a speck of movement miles away across the flat fields. Even from that distance, with nothing to block my view, I can tell he needs help. Sometimes he's being attacked; sometimes he's sinking into quicksand. I can see atrocity unfolding, miles away, and then I'm toiling across the fields, trying to get to him, but knowing it will all have happened by the time I reach him. As I lunge and wade across the slow earth, I pray: not for Gareth, but for streets, for crowds, for hills and corners to hide my son's fate.

Stern matron has entered the giggling co-ed dorm.

'Say "I'm a naughty girl" twenty times!'

Naughty girls. Bad children. Matron slaps a mound in one of the beds and up pops Eddie, all wide eyes and fluttering lashes: 'I'm a naughty girl! I'm a naughty girl!'

'How is it, young man, that I find you in the girls' dormitory? *How is it?*'

''T ain't bad!'

Naughty, naughty. They roll their lascivious eyes and flash their fleshy bits and wink. Eddie's been in the girls' dorm all night. All night, under the covers, in his jim-jams, alone. He hasn't done anything unspeakable. He's only a naughty little girl.

All about sex and nothing to do with sex. All about race and nothing to do with race. You can read what you like and omit what you like – that's the magic of the movies. If Gill and Gareth and I watched any number of films together we'd all see something different. She'd see bigotry, he'd see aggression, I'd see sex. There's nothing mystifying about that; we'd all be right in a way. It's what human beings do: they find subtle ways of hating each other, hurting each other and wanting each other. So it's bound to end up in the movies.

4

At 8.30 on Saturday morning Gill arrives bearing a strimmer and shears. For the next three and a half hours we tear and heave at the weeds and by noon we've cleared a path to the back gate. Every time I shut my eyes I see bobbly negatives of goose grass. My hands are sticky, red and smarting.

After lunch Gill fetches a stepladder from her shed. While I strim the hedge, she balances on the top step, slicing away the overhanging branches of next-door's conifer.

'There's an old flower bed dying in the dark under here,' she grunts. 'If we can let the sun get at it we might manage a splash of colour before the end of the year.'

Her arms flap in time to the shears above her head.

By leaning over the hedge and straining to the right I can see the fields beyond the end of the estate: strips of yellow and green, clouds, slivers of birds. I picture a transformation: rosebushes, meandering gravel paths, petals dripping over bulbous glazed pots. It could happen. From one of the houses opposite comes the tinny sound of a radio, and a child singing out of tune. I could make this into a real garden; I could make the cottage into our home.

'Hey, come on – get your arse into gear' says Gill. I brace myself against the strimmer's power and lay into the hedge again.

'If we really get stuck in,' says Gill, the next time the engine pauses, 'I reckon we can make a halfway decent display out of this lot.'

'That would be great,' I say. 'Imagine Bobby's face when he turns up and finds a little Eden out the back.'

Snip, snip, snip.

I'm stung by her lack of response. She's not playing the game. I attack the hedge with new vigour. Between the strimmer's rasps, I can hear branches crackle and fall around the ladder.

When, eventually, I run out of steam, I notice that Gill has stopped snipping, and is squinting through the branches towards the house next door.

'Thought so. We're on *Candid Camera*.' She waves a cheerful hand, and there's a minor commotion at the upstairs curtains. 'Can you credit it? Someone with a camcorder. Of course, that's what everyone does now. Instead of coming out and *speaking* to you – "excuse me, but why are you decimating our tree?" – oh no. Instant evidence, do-it-yourself litigation . . . They're like Nazis. Recording every crime. What's the matter with *you*?'

I let the strimmer bury itself in the hedge and goggle at the next-door cottage. I've never seen my neighbours, and they're making films of me.

'Oh, don't *worry*,' says Gill, and returns to her task. 'They won't sue you. We're well within our rights. *Leylandii* are fair game. If they show this to the authorities they'll probably get a visit from a council man with an axe.'

My domestic visions fade into a mist of paranoia. My neighbours hate me. I wonder whether they've heard Eddie Cantor clowning into the small hours. I wonder whether they've heard Gareth's video games and evenings of blood-lust. I say,

'Maybe we should leave the tree for now.'

'For *God's sake*!' The step ladder rocks, steadies. Gill heaves a branch free and skims it across the garden. 'For God's sake, Jayne, we're not doing anything *wrong*. We're just trying to get sorted out. You can't give up at the first sign of a nosy neighbour.'

'I'm *not* giving up!' My voice peaks and drops. I wrestle to untangle the strimmer and get back to work. '*I* am not the one who gives up!' I say aloud, but she doesn't hear me over the engine's noise.

By four-thirty, we've reduced most of the growth to ankle level. The abandoned tyre has re-emerged, stuffed in the middle with sludge, dead leaves and spiders. There's one patch of jungle left in the far corner. Gill looks at her watch and flaps her sweatshirt to circulate the air.

'Shall we call it a day?'

'You put the kettle on,' I say. 'I just want to finish this off.'

'You don't have to prove anything to me, you know' she says, lightly. I burrow my way into the green mess. Behind me, I hear her say,

'Have it your own way. I'm knackered. I'll start the tea.'

I lose myself in the chaos of goose-grass, bindweed and wild fennel. A watery-green insect scuttles over a leaf, inches from my face. There's a riot of unheard movement all around me. I squat to enjoy this diminished privacy. Like many children, I would often retreat from the wider stage and reduce my experience to the smallest, closest focus. I was shy, but not in an endearing way. I was hideously, stubbornly, paralysingly shy. When my mother exhorted me to do a curtsey for her friends, or show off my 'pretty little voice' with a comic song, I froze with the effort of willing myself to drop dead. When her friends had coaxed and wheedled and were losing interest, I removed myself to the bathroom to crouch in a corner and follow the route of a red spider as it meandered over grouting and skirted drops of water on the wall. And here I am again, 35 years on, drawing my world around me as closely as I can.

Around its edges is the comfort of irrelevant sounds: cars passing the end of the road; another neighbour's hedgecutter, groaning and whining in the late sun; a dog scampering and yapping alongside brisk footsteps. Unwillingly I get up, brace myself, gather an armful of clamminess and heave. Rye grass tickles my cheeks and neck. I tighten my grip on the thick rope of weed and give it another tug. One of those sounds has grown louder. Just ahead of me, at the foot of the hedge, is a bank of leaves and dead matter. It ripples and fidgets. It hums. Terror glows in my throat and chest. Quietly, I drop my cargo and back away. I can see quite clearly, now, the dense layer of wasps quivering and fretting over the heap. A sudden crescendo in my ear makes me toss my head; a needle-jab burns above my left elbow, another, almost simultaneously, in my right arm, under the sleeve of my T-shirt. A third. A fourth. I'm hobbling and hopping out of the long grass, holding both arms stiffly away from my body, drawing in a slow, shocked gasp. Something is fiddling with my hair. I hear myself shriek: 'Get off, OFF!'

The neighbour's hedgecutter pauses. The dog hurls back a torrent of little screams. The back door thuds open and Gill is there, leading me up the path to the house, making wide sweeping gestures around my head, issuing calm orders to me and to the wasps.

'In my . . . they're in my clothes,' I whimper. Carefully, cleanly, Gill pulls the T-shirt over my head and shakes it out, yelling, 'Sod off, you buggers!' while I run for the kitchen door, stooping to hide my threadbare bra from next-door's camcorder.

'I hate to say it, but you'll have to get Rentokill in.'

Gill stands over me as I perch, trembling, on the kitchen stool. She's brought an armful of pots and pads from her house, and is rubbing antiseptic cream into my blotched arms.

'I suppose so . . .' I'm eyeing that last corner of long grass through the kitchen window.

'Such a shame about that garden,' murmurs Gill, shuffling round to attend to a new sting. 'Leaving it in that shocking state. I've got a good mind to call the estate manager and give him a bollocking about it.'

The front door slams and Gareth rustles around out of sight, until Gill calls:

'We're in here. Come and salute the wounded soldier.'

He emerges in the doorway, startlingly tall, and surveys the scene, eyes flitting to the window, the shorn grass, back to his shirtless mother hunched on a stool.

'Wasps,' I say, and smile stupidly. 'I got zapped.'

He tuts. He regards my stings dully; his lips part very slightly, but enough to indicate scorn and disgust at the idiocy of middle-aged women. Then he's gone, and we listen to the percussion of feet on stairs, door opened and shut, computer-chair trundled into place above our heads.

'Oh, not to worry,' says Gill, partly to herself.

That's right. There's nothing to worry about. These are simple matters. A wasps' nest in the garden; call Rentokil. Stings on arms; apply antiseptic. Teenage son brimming with contempt; allow a few more years to pass. These are all manageable, run-of-the-mill problems. So why am I stunned by indecision? Why does the next move – every move – seem impossible?

That garden should map out a lifetime, if necessary, of waiting for Bobby's return. First the heavy-duty stuff, while I'm still relatively young and fit: sledgehammering the concrete path, levelling the lawn, building walls and raised beds and rockeries. Then the long, slow, sheltered slide into fragility, limiting myself to a little pruning here, a bit of dead-heading there. By the time Gill's kicked the bucket – if people like Gill ever do kick the bucket; by the time Gareth's got his three kids and rambling farmhouse in Surrey, that garden should be solid and structured enough to sustain me in my lone vigil. For a few hours all that was feasible. One encounter with wildlife later, and I can't believe anything will ever change.

From the corner of my eye I'm sure I can see the rattling of the swarm. I turn to check and suddenly my nose is streaming, my mouth drops open to release a phlegmy moan. Without a hint of surprise, Gill reaches for the kitchen roll, spools off a wedge of paper and starts mopping me up.

'Don't mind Gareth,' she says. 'He's scared. Seeing his mother getting hurt scares him. He's young enough to be disappointed when events aren't under your control. I'll leave the antiseptic in here, shall I?'

She puts the bottle in the cupboard under the sink. She snaps off a fresh square of tissue and pinches my nose clean. She smears away a fresh tear with her thumb. Her voice is more tender than I've ever known it before.

'That's just the way it goes,' she says. 'Bobby was exactly the same.'

I'm grateful, but I don't believe her.

5

Bobby must have been an easy child to love. Bright, fair hair and brown, lithe limbs, powered with optimism and delight and invention. He smiled his charming smile and wove his make-believe and was exactly as a child should be. No wonder Gill indulged his pie-in-the-sky notions for so many years. Who'd want to narrow those guileless blue eyes with misgivings?

It was difficult to glean much from Bobby about his upbringing. There were intermittent flashes of action, sketches of mood, but no narrative. You never could pin him down to dates or sequences. Was he happy at school? Oh, yeah, school was a laugh. Did he hanker after girls? Oh, yeah, always besotted with someone or other, but (a quick, firm hug) none of them would ever match up to you, Jayne. He forgot his friends' names; whose teacher's-pet he'd been; which subjects he'd preferred. But he did recall, in faultless detail, the plot and cast of every musical comedy he'd ever watched on Sunday afternoons and bank holidays; TV matinée specials, BBC 2 seasons, Saturday morning cine-slot. He would shine and expand like lamplight as he described Fred and Ginger gliding among polished floors and feathers, cheek to cheek. He could sing all the lyrics of 'Shuffle off to Buffalo' or 'Meet me in St Louis' or 'Keep Young and Beautiful'. To Bobby these joyful frivolities captured something essential. Not a promise, not a wish, but a profound truth – just as his childhood storybooks were more than words on paper, and his toys more than foam and cotton, and his invisible friend was infinitely more than an empty chunk of air.

Wherever he is now – in a guesthouse or a hostel, in a gutter, a prison cell or a pub – I can't help picturing Bobby breaking into a soft shoe shuffle to keep his spirits up, sweeping a passer-by into a waltz, jigging along in a personal carnival parade.

I've seen photos of Bobby at Gareth's age, posing with his schoolfriends round a swimming pool, or grinning at the camera with Gill at his side. Bobby was easy to love even then, even in his teens, and I hate myself for drawing comparisons with our sullen son. It's not Gareth's fault. It may even be Bobby's. After all, *he* never had to cope with an absconding parent.

I suspect that the hardest fact for Bobby to deal with wasn't the failure of our shop but the absence of sympathetic rescuers. Nobody stepped in to put it all right. No anonymous benefactor appeared just in time for the credits to roll. No cuddly angel thanked Bobby for contributing to the general sum of cheerfulness. No bells rang on our Christmas tree. Bobby wasn't used to being stranded. He was used to being loved.

Marian Westwood loved him with proprietorial passion. When we visited 7a, after that first time, she would grab him at the door and lead him to the sofa, where she sat close, wrapping herself around his arm. The cleavage reappeared, the make-up was random and desperate, but Bobby didn't seem to mind. And it didn't seem to bother him that being loved by Marian Westwood meant giving up your own identity and history. Marian Westwood soaked it all up – Bobby's carefree past, his dismissal of the present, his absurd schemes. She wanted to captivate, own and become him. I'd handed him over, and I was no longer involved.

Am I over-egging the pudding? What would Bobby say? He'd say, 'Steady on, Jayne.' He'd say, 'You're getting a bit gothic now'. He'd give me a cuddle. There's no one to match up to Jayne, he'd say – not even her mother. Marian was no she-devil, he'd scoff. Self-obsessed, frustrated, thoughtless, progressively crosswired by drugs – all that. But she was not a fiend. If he were here Bobby would clasp my shoulders, press his forehead against mine, fix me with a blue gaze and tell me to leave my worries on the doorstep. Lighten up. Watch a movie. But Bobby's not here, so Marian and I can be as infernal as we bloody well like.

6

Gill is back at 10 o'clock the following morning. She's been up for hours, of course, but she knows how idle we are at weekends. She's taken aback when I tell her I've been up since five. I was woken by another weird dream, about terrier-faced insects scampering up my arms. The stings were itching like fury: my right arm, especially, is swollen and raw. I roll up my sleeve and Gill inspects it solemnly. She tells me I got away lightly, all things considered.

'Good job they didn't get your face.'

Anyway, the itching kept me awake and in the end I went downstairs and made myself a cup of tea. It was peaceful, standing in the kitchen, holding the cup to my cheek for warmth and comfort, watching the light broaden over the garden. In the wasps' untouched corner, rye grass swayed with slow confidence, rosy in the early sun. I listened hard, and was sure I could hear their indifferent, evil drone. I squinted at the greenery, checking every disturbance. Then a hiccough in the water pipes brought me back to my senses. What a fool. It was the water-heater I could hear, not the wasps.

Gill bats my hand away as I rake at the flesh around the stings.

'First thing tomorrow,' she says, 'ring the council. Ask for pest control. And, listen,' raising her voice to address Gareth, who's just slouched past in his T-shirt and boxers, smelling of bed, 'make sure you don't go poking around in that long grass. You don't want to provoke them any more.'

Gareth, sloshing milk over his cereal, mumbles something incoherent, but the rise and fall is enough to convey his indignation at the very suggestion that he might.

'In the meantime' Gill says to me 'we can always carry on with the rest of it.'

I shake my head. 'Let's leave it for now,' I say. 'Until these stings die down a bit.'

'Shall I find the number for pest control, then?'

Gareth, who's been leaning against the cooker, shovelling cereal into his mouth, looks up and says 'Pest control?' through a swill of milk and cornflakes.

'It has to be done, I'm afraid.' Gill retrieves the antiseptic and cotton wool from the cupboard and starts tending to my wounds.

'You can't just *kill* them,' says a man's voice.

Gill and I gawp at Gareth. He's pressing the cereal bowl against his chest. There's a faint moustache of milk on his upper lip.

'You can't *wipe them out* just for *being there*,' he goes on.

Gill blows air through her nose impatiently. 'If we don't deal with the swarm, it'll get bigger. I don't want to kill them any more than you do, but if we leave them be they'll take over.'

'Christ!' hisses Gareth, and skims his half-empty bowl into the sink. Milk spatters across the draining board and floor.

'Gareth . . .' I raise my blotched arm. 'It's not safe to leave them there . . .'

But he's already storming out. I hear him say, 'Why do you—' before the door slams his sentence in half. Gill pads at my stings as if nothing happened.

'"They fuck you up, your mum and dad . . ."' I mutter, miserably.

'Oh, that's just poetry. Not truth' says Gill. My nose wrinkles in a spasm of resentment.

'I bet *you* never fucked *anything* up.'

Gill begins a smile and says, 'I've messed up somewhat with my son, though, wouldn't you say?'

I don't contradict her. I sit there enjoying her guilt. Without looking up she goes on: 'Have I ever told you about the first time I saw your mother on stage?'

Here we go.

'Some day,' I say, 'I'll tell you some *real* home truths

about Marian Westwood. Great star, crap mother. That must be where I got my parenting skills from.'

'You're not a crap mother,' says Gill.

'There must be *something* wrong with me.' My skin seethes with antiseptic and self-pity. 'I drive everyone away.'

Gill becomes headmistressy. 'Listen to me. You haven't driven anyone away. Gareth hasn't gone far. And Bobby . . . well, Bobby's not your fault.'

'Well, he certainly can't be *yours*,' I insist, angrily. 'You and Robert were Mr and Mrs Perfect Parents, as far as I could see.'

Gill stops padding. She's cradling my hand in hers, resting the damp cotton wool on my wrist, considering something. Then she looks at me, stares until I have to look away. It reminds me of Bobby's intent expression before he kissed me for the first time. Working up to it. Steeling himself.

Eventually, Gill says: 'OK. You're right about one thing – it's time for some home truths. So, fair exchange. You tell me about Marian Westwood, and I'll tell you some truths of my own.'

7

Bobby wasn't the first of my family to run away. There was my father, fleeing from his past to the furthest point of the globe; and there was Marian herself. At Gareth's age Marian Westwood had already made her escape from Cardiff and was living in a guesthouse in Brighton with her 'manager', Alec Blessing. They first met a couple of years earlier in the Ship's Bell on the dockside, a pub run by a captain's widow and universally known as the Ship's Tits. It was nearing the end of the War, a period of lethargy between the fear and the euphoria. The Ship's Tits stood alone in a wasteland of bomb sites. Marian, who'd just started work as a shopgirl in town, had gone there with her mother's boyfriend, a GI with cash for drinks. She was 14, but capable of gaining several years with a touch of make-up. So there she was in her knee-length utility skirt and stockings courtesy of her escort, sitting at the end of a wall-seat with a fag in one hand and a glass of port wine in the other, legs crossed at the knee and tucked at an angle away from the table. Two old lags were telling the American dirty jokes further along the seat; she ignored them all and pouted through the smoke. She caught Alec's attention as soon as he entered, and he couldn't fail to catch hers. Alec Blessing didn't have the look of a regular. He was a small, nifty, dapper man in a pale grey suit and gold-coloured tie. His hair, a shade greyer than the suit, was slicked back from a high forehead. He wore a signet ring on his left hand. Alec Blessing had made a bob or two from the black market. He could afford to drink in better watering holes than this, but he was generally drawn to places where girls like Marian were liable to be found. He bought a beer, leaned on the bar and exchanged a few pleasantries with the landlady. He drummed his fingers and let his eyes roam in every direction except Marian's. After an hour or so the old lags left. Shortly after that the GI, tired of the unresponsive daughter, left in search of the mother. Marian stayed put, striking sultry attitudes over her drink. Alec lingered at the bar. He was waiting for her to come to him. He had underestimated Marian Westwood. Doubt was an unfamiliar emotion to Alec Blessing. He liked to think that in settings such as this he exuded spending power. Now, as the minutes ticked by, he began to feel ordinary. He wondered whether his clothes were too flashy. He asked himself whether the spark of connection between him and this girl had been no more than an accidental collision of glances. As last orders approached and the landlady moved down the bar to serve another customer, he was left without a companion. He fiddled with his signet ring. The loner was beginning to look lonely. Stranded in a teenager's neglect, Alec Blessing began to feel his age. Finally, when the bell rang and the landlady prepared to bolt the door for a lock-in, Alec Blessing was obliged to make his way over to Marian's table and introduce himself.

Alec Blessing came to visit us once at the Bayswater flat. It must have been about 1968. My father was still around. I remember him and Marian having a fierce argument about it beforehand. Marian stood in the middle of the room, leaning forward to project her voice, arms at her side, hands angled outwards – 'the penguin act', my father called it. She yelled at him:

'He's an old man, Harry. Have some respect, for Christ's sake.'

But there was humour in her eyes, and I knew this wasn't dangerous. My father, shifting from foot to foot behind the sofa, threw back his head for an incredulous 'Ha!'

I piped up, '*Who's* an old man?' and my father's answer wasn't directed at me.

'Mr-inappropriately-named-Blessing is, the man who's been fleecing your mother for the past 20 years.'

Marian went into one of her mimes of inexpressible fury. I shrank into a corner and watched. Her posturing had a beauty of its own – the star-spread hands, the arms flung wide, the elegant throat exposed. It was like a ballet. Harry watched, too, from his safe place between sofa and door, and then shrugged and said,

'Do what you want. *I'm* not hanging round for him, though. I'll go to a show.'

I longed to go with him, but didn't dare take sides. Come to think of it, he probably didn't mean the sort of show a six-year-old could see.

Alec Blessing certainly was an old man. His hair had receded halfway down the back of his skull, but the remainder was still grey and oily. His face hung in folds. He sat curved forward like a letter 'C' at the edge of the chair. When Marian indicated my presence he nodded with an embarrassed wheeze. I withdrew behind the sofa with my dress-doll, lulled by the rise and fall of their voices and the chime of glass.

Phrases returned again and again, in a comforting, meaningless adult litany:

'Well, my dear, you're doing all right.'

'Thanks to you, darling.'

'Beautiful as ever . . .'

'You're too good to me, Alec . . .'

When he left (extending a claw to tousle my hair as he passed), my mother stood with the door ajar for several minutes, overseeing his departure.

'That's the man who set me on the right track,' she said, 'whatever your father might say.'

But my six-year-old instincts told me she was making quite sure he'd gone.

In 1944 the right track was any route that took her away from home. Marian hung on to her new friend and as soon as the war was over she flounced out of Cardiff on his arm and practised calling herself Mrs Blessing. On her 16th birthday Alec bought her a silver bracelet. As she turned her slim wrist to and fro, admiring the sheen of metal against her brown skin, Alec made a confession. Another Mrs Blessing – the real Mrs Blessing – was bringing up his two lads in Leicester. Marian pushed her lips out indifferently and said, 'Thought as much.'

Marriage wasn't part of her plan.

Several decades later, she was still astonished that Bobby and I chose to go through all that nonsense, 'especially' as she declared down the phone, 'when there's no call for it these days.' She had no truck with sermons and statistics lauding the stability of wedded life. 'Take it from me' she said. 'It's all a bloody great lie and it always was. Even when I was a girl. They might have been Mr and Mrs till death, but half of them weren't even under the same roof. Nobody made a big deal of it, that's all; nobody bothered with divorce or separation or what the hell. They just waited till the middle of the night and buggered off.'

That, apparently, was what Alec Blessing had done. And that was what Marian Westwood intended to do as soon as he'd grown too old or useless. In the meantime she sat in a Brighton guesthouse, watching the rain on the seafront or rehearsing sexy poses in the cracked dressing-table mirror. Alec went out on unspecified 'business' and brought back magic gifts, hauled in from a pre-war world: a skullcap hat with a feather; a pair of butter-soft leather gloves; silk underwear; pearl earrings. In return Marian let him pet her and stroke her, comb her hair and wash her, expend his energy on her in short, frantic bursts at night. She didn't pretend to enjoy it: just lay there, listening to the rain on the window and the headboard knocking against the wall. And afterwards she would let him tell her how lovely she was, what a star she could be-the best and most beautiful and brightest star; she should be a fashion model, a countess, she should go on the stage.

Alec took her for disgusting meals in dingy restaurants. She was pleased: she hadn't eaten in restaurants before, and besides, there was hardly any other kind just after the war. He took her to the pictures. They saw Lana Turner in *The Postman Always Rings Twice*. Marian kept her eyes fixed on the screen for 115 minutes, while Alec pawed her leg and nibbled her ear. As the lights went up and the national anthem creaked through the speakers, she turned to him and said, 'I could do that.'

'What's that, sweetheart?'

'Act. Like Lana Turner. I could do that.'

'Of course you could, baby girl. You're the brightest star. You could do anything you like.'

'No,' said Marian, clearly and seriously. 'But I *could* do *that*.'

There's a picture of Marian and Alec taken on Brighton seafront by a street photographer. Marian's wearing that feathered hat and an A-line dress; her feet are turned out in fourth position, right heel against left toe, her hands clutch Alec's arm, her face is caught in a grimace, as a ribbon of hair is whipped across it by the wind. Alec's left arm is flying, mid-gesture, issuing some direction to the camera. On the back of the photo, written in capitals in pencil that's faded almost to nothing, are the words 'GOODBYE BRIGHTON – 1949'.

That was the year Marian persuaded Alec to take her to London. He wasn't keen. Alec had contacts in Brighton, friends and ex-lovers. As Marian told me many, many years later, 'He had a wide range of tastes. A sweet body was a sweet body to Alec, never mind what equipment came with it.'

But Marian got her way, and by 1950 she and Alec were in rooms with brown furniture and mustard-yellow walls over a Soho club, and Marian was working as a 'tray girl', serving drinks to the punters downstairs. It was the best Alec could get, and that was only because he'd known the club manager in Leicester.

'Ordinarily,' the manager had muttered, as Marian strutted between tables on her first shift, packed into a frilly bodice, 'I would have said no. She's a bit . . .' his chubby hand chopped up and down before his chest '. . . a bit *petite*. Wouldn't you say? But since it's you, Al.'

'Very decent of you, old man,' said Alec, eyeing the customers as Marian's bottom swung past their chairs.

'And I will say this, Al. She's got style. Knows how to make the most of what's there. Wouldn't you say?'

Within three months Marian had wheedled herself a place on the edge of the stage show. She was one of the 'standers', who arranged themselves in a semi-circle as a frame for the dancers and comedy acts. Hour after hour, night after night of mincing, standing, shifting on cue (hand on hip, hand under chin, hip tilted, knee bent), changing costume and doing it all over again. She wore three-inch, razor-sharp heels, fishnet stockings, an assortment of sequins, tassles and slightly grubby white feathers across her torso. She was shorter and slighter than all the other girls. Everything had to be taken in, and one of the friendlier dancers showed her how to pad out her costume at the front.

No more petting and stroking for Alec. Marian hobbled upstairs at 4 every morning and disappeared under the sheets until noon. Sometimes she would surface as he left to do whatever deals he did, and aim a hoarse word at his back: 'Audition'.

'Yes, yes,' he'd say. 'I'll fix it up for you, baby girl, don't you fret.' And he'd yank the door behind him.

She was 20 years old, wilful and ambitious, but she didn't know how to go out into the city and make things happen. She'd been with Alec six years by now, and still believed he could sort it all out. Standing on a low platform, making patterns of herself every night, escaping upstairs to the brown and yellow rooms – that was one thing. Venturing outside and claiming to be an actress, when she'd never spoken a public line in her life – quite another. She was scared. But she was also impatient. So Marian Westwood made the most of what she had.

Billy Smith, one of the club's comedians, did a routine as Julius Caesar, which required a girl to step forward, kneel before him and pretend to eat from a bunch of papier-mâché grapes. (They were the only kind of grapes most of those girls had ever seen.) Marian begged the club manager to let her have a go.

'Just one night' she coaxed, with her lowered, sideways look. 'One night is all it takes.'

The manager mused that the kid had filled out a bit after all. She stood very near him, letting her breast press lightly against his arm. She got her way. Sure enough, one night was all it took. Kneeling at Billy Smith's feet, she accepted the grapes in her cupped hand, tested their weight, raised her eyebrows at the meagre audience. A rumble of laughter. She put her tongue to the grapes, then her mouth, mimicking ecstasy so that Billy did a double-take: 'Hang about. I thought these were paste. Who slipped *these* under the counter?'

Marian didn't push her luck. She didn't upstage him completely. As he left the club that night Billy took the manager aside and issued instructions: 'I'll keep that one. Tell her not to go over the top and she can have a nightly spot.'

By the end of the year she was feeding him gags and clocking off at 2am.

Billy Smith had once dreamt of being a hermit. Three times a night he went on stage to tell dirty jokes and ogle show-girls' cleavages, and three times a night he returned to his closet-sized room, read a verse from the good book and knelt in prayer. His hobby was abstention. Outside working hours he abstained from profanity, alcohol, cigarettes, gambling and sex. He offered to give Marian some tips on technique-boom, boom! But in fact that was exactly what he gave. In the girls' dressing room-a partitioned corridor lined with sweating pipes and streaming walls and dubbed 'the boiler room'-one of the standers gave Marian a tip of her own: 'Get any leg-ups you can from Billy, love. No leg-over involved. He'll show you the ropes and nothing else.'

When Billy's club contract ended he went to do panto on the east coast and Marian Westwood went with him. She refused to let Alec chaperone her.

'Your job,' she told him, jabbing his chest, 'is to fix me up a proper, honest-to-God audition. With all your contacts you *must* know *someone* who can help.'

Alec nodded hopelessly. By now she should have stopped believing in his contacts, but Marian Westwood was a stubborn woman. He saw her off on the train, kissing her mournfully as she leaned through the window.

'Don't forget,' he called as the engine gathered steam, 'to send a Christmas card to your mother.'

Mother Goose played for four months to half-empty houses. It was a cold, wet winter. The audience coughed and rustled. The Good Fairy forgot her lines every afternoon and came on pissed every evening. The costumes stank of mould and there were fleas in the dressing-rooms. Marian was having the time of her life. Each morning she sat bolt upright in her narrow guesthouse bed; each morning she washed in icy water from the basin in her room; each morning she drew back the curtain to a foggy drizzle and she wiggled her hips in a private dance to greet the afternoon show. At 2.15 she would be backstage, listening to the chorus tittle-tattle, slapping on the pancake as Billy had taught her, soothed by the clatter of activity beyond the

door. Technicians, stagehands, orchestra, cast, all busily sure
of their tasks; and Marian, too, knew where to go, how to
move and what to say from then until curtain-down. After
that there were only a couple of hours to survive before
everything fell back into place for the 7.30 show. She stood
in the wings as happy as Larry, confident of the moment
when she would step forward into the warm, gaudy light
and speak to a clownish dame in a painted village.

During rehearsals her words had fallen short of the
fourth row and she was hoarse from the strain.

'We're not on the platform in the High Kicks Revue now,
missy,' said Billy. 'You're going to have to sing for your
supper.'

He showed her how to deepen the pitch, lift the palate
and float the lines to the back. He showed her how to
exaggerate her turns and gestures without hamming them
up.

'It's got to come natural,' he said, 'and up here, natural
means big.'

He taught her to respond to other players, even when she
had nothing to say.

'The art of acting,' he said, 'is in *re*acting.'

In return, Marian calmed his pre-show nerves with
readings from the Old Testament, and before leaving the
theatre every night delivered two hard blows to his back-
side with a leather belt, as penance for the gag about the
Bad Fairy's wand.

Sometimes the cast would crowd into a greasy spoon in
town for a late-night meal. They scraped tables together,
shared seats, sat on each other's laps and created enough
noise and hilarity to serve instead of conversation. Everyone took on an extra role for these outings. There was
Richard, who played the dairy maid's father on stage and
the ponderous pedant at table. There was Good Fairy Kay,
who played the ditzy drunk. There was Paul from the

chorus, camp and bitchy, and Frances Dee, 'a villager', butch and raucous. They all stayed in offstage character until they were safely back behind their boarding house doors. Billy Smith was the only one who never joined in.

One such night they were feeding each other the usual lines in the usual order. They'd related, with exhilarated pride, their missed cues and bungled moves. Richard had pointed out a flaw in the plot. Kay had spluttered and twittered about the rhyming couplet that she'd ruined, and Paul had told them yet again that the director 'may be a cretin but believe me, he fucks like a sewing machine.'

Somebody complained about Billy's protracted comic monologue. 'I mean, what's the big idea, padding it out with new gags, when we're all panting to get off home?'

'He could cut out the filthier ones, at least for the matinee,' agreed Paul. 'It's not as if they're getting big laughs. Two old dears and a tramp out front and Billy droning on about the size of Mother Goose's dumplings – what's that going to get him?'

'Five Hail Maries and six of the best, lad,' said Marian, imitating Billy's lugubrious delivery to perfection.

There was an explosion of genuine laughter, heightened with the relief of a fresh line. Marian had cast herself as the jester. The Life and Soul. When Alec came to town for the weekend, booking (at Marian's insistence) into a hotel down the road, she found his presence a hindrance and banned him from their meals.

'Never a good idea to bring the home comforts along,' agreed Paul. 'They're as much use here as a queer in a nunnery.'

When *Mother Goose* came to an end Marian was as tearful as the rest, embracing and cooing and swapping addresses with the best friends she'd ever had. But her tears were more desparate than sentimental. Billy had no immediate prospects of work and was going on a retreat in West Wales.

Her only option was to slip back in among the standers-if there was any room left. On the morning after the cast party Marian sat on her bed with a pendulum in her head and a rock in her stomach and glared at her bags, propped in a huddle in the middle of the room, over-packed with presents from the other actors, copies of the programme-souvenirs that she would never throw away. Grey, ordinary daylight blanked out the window. Instead of orchestra and beginners, the only promise 2.15 held was a laden walk to the railway station. Instead of cartoon companions in the greasy spoon, there'd be Alec Blessing at King's Cross Station, neat and obsequious and offering nothing. By the time she tottered queasily onto Platform 3 of King's Cross, she was too depressed to notice Alec's triumphant, dentured grin. She endured his hug and ordered him to take the bags.

'You can't get a bloody porter for love nor money.'

'I've booked a table tonight,' said Alec with infuriating emphasis. 'To celebrate.'

Her bad mood had set like cement, and she was at the door of their flat before understanding what Alec had done. He'd arranged a reading. She was going to be heard – 'and it's only a formality, baby girl, a sure-fire thing' – for a minor role in a play. A real, grown-up, po-faced play, by a young talent just out of National Service; 'a friend,' explained Alec, 'of a friend.'

The play was *I Can Hear You*. It was about a woman plagued by the voices of her father and son, both killed during the war. Marian played a nun who tried to console her. *I Can Hear You* opened in The Attic, a tiny theatre rigged up over a pub on the edge of a bomb site, in May 1952, and closed seven weeks later. The playwright complained that he should have written a musical, 'or a tetchy little piece about the tenements'. Everyone was tired of war victims.

During those seven weeks Marian learned to break all Billy Smith's rules. No 'natural means big' when most of the audience was close enough to feel her breath and spittle.

She watched the other actors, groped for the same fine balance of artificiality and truth, copied the muted, graceful gestures of their arms and hands.

She loved it. She loved coming in from the rain or the sunshine, shutting the door on the traffic and bounding up the stairs to this insulated, clandestine place with blacked-out windows and dense air. She loved the sounds of backstage preparation, the knock and scrape and laconic instruction, each one muffled and isolated like voices in a snowscape. There were no in-jokes or pally gatherings in this show, but still, Marian Westwood felt perfectly at home.

8

Gill has brought the number for an infestation control officer.

'I'm not pushing you. Obviously it's up to you. If you want to try some other method . . .' She makes a great show of placing the piece of paper next to the phone. 'But this is the quickest and the most thorough way, and it's got to be dealt with if we're going to get on with that garden.'

'Well,' I mutter, 'I'm not doing anything for a couple of days anyway. Not until my back's recovered . . .'

'What's wrong with your back?'

I rub the tired muscles round the base of my spine. 'Just the usual,' I say. 'Just sitting at the computer, that sort of thing.' Just that my backbone barely seems able to hold me up. Just that I've forgotten how to walk without effort.

'How are the stings?'

'Not so bad now. It's the itching that gets me.'

'Well, there you are. We've got to sort them out.'

'I know.'

This morning I stood in the kitchen, long before Gareth was up, and watched the long grass. The weather was clear, and the garden was at a standstill. I forced myself to go down to the back gate and put the bin out, and as I lolloped along the path with the putrid-smelling bag knocking against my leg a solitary bee looped round my head and flew off. I froze. I almost screamed for Gareth. An aeroplane moaned overhead. Two streets away, a motorbike was revved and released. I had to resist a perverse urge to creep into the grass and see the wasps again, mumbling over their nest, to test how close I could get before the cloud shattered into a thousand angry shards. Eventually I dumped the bin-bag impractically inside the gate and retreated to the house, step by step, like a cat backing away from a fight. I thought: this can't go on. Have the damn things killed. Clear away their ugly little corpses, hack down the long grass and plant a suburban paradise, as planned. Gareth will just have to lump it.

A low groan starts up outside and my heart lurches.

'Is it that time already?' says Gill. 'I'll shut the window, shall I?'

The groan rises and inflates into a wail that blankets the whole estate and the fields beyond. I should be used to this by now. Every first Tuesday of the month they test the escape siren at Emmett Park. Ten o'clock sharp. As Gareth has pointed out, 10 o'clock sharp on the first Tuesday of the month would be a damn good time to make a break for it. He hasn't heard it much himself: he's 15 miles away in a classroom at Berriford Comprehensive. Gill doesn't seem to mind it-after all these years I suppose she'd only notice if it didn't go off. But I detest this sound. After reaching its plateau it howls on for another 2 minutes that seem more like 20, vibrating behind my eyes, pressing against the walls and the windows. I wonder what it's like for the patients, listening to this monthly proclamation of captivity. I put my hands over my ears until the din subsides. Gill waits till her voice is audible and then says,

'I presume you know Gareth's got himself a girlfriend.'

I didn't.

Apparently her name is Hannah. A gentle name; a nostalgic name, that makes me predisposed to like her. Gill knows her parents, but not very well.

'He hasn't mentioned anyone to *me*,' I grumble.

'Well . . . I suppose that's how most sons are with their mothers. They keep their cards close to the chest.'

Most sons, but not hers. She seems to attract confidences-from Bobby (even now, I suspect) and, it seems, from Gareth. I long for her to go. After 20 minutes without the offer of a coffee she takes the hint and leaves. I go back to the computer, close down my work file and enter 'Hannah' in the 'Search and Find', with no results.

When Gareth gets home from school I'm in the kitchen making toast. He swings his schoolbag into a corner and rummages for biscuits.

'Gill came round this morning,' I say, 'with a number for the wasp-killers.'

He glares at me as he's gouging biscuits from their packet.

'You're going to do it?'

'No, I put her off. Have some toast before you binge on those biscuits.'

He munches a Jammy Dodger without fully closing his mouth and watches me butter the toast.

'Just tell her,' he says. 'It's nothing to *do* with *her*.'

I'm smiling despite myself. I hand him his toast and he shovels it in before the remnants of Dodger have had time to clear. I say,

'They *are* spooking me out a bit, though. I don't like going past that patch . . .'

'Move them, then. It doesn't mean we have to dump chemicals on them, does it?'

We're doing well. We're exchanging comments in a fairly conventional way. I chatter on, treating my son as another, incidental adult in the house.

'It does seem a bit drastic. I remember my mother putting ant powder down in the flat-that used to upset me, too, though I don't know what else she could have done, I suppose . . .'

He's losing interest. I start to ad lib. 'It was awful – I remember – she was scattering this stuff round, and it stank, and I'd brought a boyfriend home from school for the first time . . .'

I'm making it up on the hoof. As if I'd ever have dreamt of bringing boyfriends back to my mother's home, even if I'd had any. Gareth stiffens, then forces in the last of the toast and wanders towards the living room. I follow, shackled to my own wittering voice.

'It was one of those awkward situations, you know, where I didn't really know how to introduce him, and I didn't know whether my mother would disapprove . . .'

He turns on the telly and flings himself back on to the sofa. There's an advert on for sweets; a woman in a violet wig is licking her lips, chin smeared with sugary paste. A voiceover says: 'They're quite good. Don't tell mum'. Gareth's throat makes a noise that substitutes as a laugh. I struggle on, reminiscing about the agonies of adolescence, as if he's passed it all by. Before I know it, I'm talking about sex. How we thought about it all the time, how we didn't know anything, how the boys were always staring at the girls' chests, and the girls always trying not to stare at the boys' crotches . . . Gareth turns briefly from the screen to deliver a look of utter horror, as well he might. All I can do is stumble on.

'Worst of all was knowing I would look, and trying to stop myself . . .' Shut up! Shut up! He thinks I'm warped, degenerate . . . 'It wasn't really *sexual*, I suppose – not *dirty*, I mean . . .' (Gareth gurns at the telly in consternation) '. . . only a kind of curiosity . . .'

Abruptly, he gets to his feet.

'I'm going to do my homework,' he says, and disappears upstairs.

I knew I shouldn't have done it. I knew it would all go wrong, even as I sat at the computer during an endless afternoon's editing, concocting our fictional exchange. I'd sketched out a chummy chit-chat, leading to a sheepish announcement.

('Mum, I've got something to tell you. I've got a girl-friend called Hannah. I only hope you'll like her.'

'Son, all that matters to me is your happiness . . .'

'Oh, Mum, there'll never be anyone to match *you*.')

Instead I've sent him fleeing to his room, where he's probably sending a surreptitious e-mail to social services. To keep the line busy, I phone Natalie. I want to double-check that I'm normal.

'Natalie, you remember that stage when we were always looking at crotches?'

'Oh, Jayney, you haven't been at it *again*?'

Gareth doesn't come down for supper. I sit in front of the telly for a while, then go and heat up some frozen veggie lasagne. In the background I hear the adverts repeated on their endless loop. 'They're quite good. Don't tell mum.' 'Have you seen our prices? We've never stooped so low.' I deliver Gareth's food to the door and eat mine out of the foil tray in my own room. I can hear the tinny explosions and screeches of his computer game through the wall. I wonder whether he'd ever bring Hannah here. I try and see the cottage, and myself, through her eyes. A fly picks its way across the remains of my meal. Would things look any better from its glitterball point of view? Idly, I try and envisage 4,000 lasagnes, one for each segment of the eye. I reach forward to brush the fly away; it circles the room and lands on the curtain, where it grooms itself ready for the next circuit. I'm sure Gareth would point out that a fly doesn't actually see 4,000 versions of the same thing. More like a mosaic, maybe. I might even ask him, if I can ever face him again.

His door opens. 'Mum?'

I leap up and tread in the leftovers. 'Yes?'

'Are you going to Gill's on Friday?'

I hesitate, assessing the most useful answer, while cheese sauce oozes between my toes.

'I'm not sure . . . Why?'

'Doesn't matter.'

Then, after a long pause, 'If you do, can my friend come for supper here?'

Forewarned is forearmed. On Friday I linger long enough to meet 'the friend' before being exiled across the road. Gareth hovers and tuts, but I won't be ousted.

'I'll just say hello,' I promise. 'They'd think it was rude otherwise.'

'No they wouldn't. You might be away. On business or something.'

We still haven't specified gender, though we're both aware that he wouldn't have tidied the living room or splattered chilli sauce over the worktop for Zek or Jinx. He's cooking her a meal. Apparently he knows, by some sort of osmosis, how to make chilli sin carne.

'I'll be on my way out, literally on the doorstep. Just 'hello' and I'm off. How are they getting here?'

'Parents.' He's stamping back into the kitchen when he stops, spins round and commands: 'DON'T SAY HELLO TO HER PARENTS.'

Her parents. We're making progress.

She arrives at seven, all blow-dried hair and earnest toothiness, and seems to want to be liked, which I take as a good sign. She's slightly taller than I am but has the face of a child. We shake hands and I brandish my bottle of Berriford plonk as assurance that I'm on my way to dinner myself, actually –

'Oh!' she gasps, 'I hope you enjoy it as much—' and her pale skin blossoms red, and her eyes dart around, on the lookout for faux pas and rescue. I squeeze her hand hard and giggle with her. Gareth is clattering in the kitchen, waiting for me to go. Hannah spots the photograph of my mother and blurts,

'That's a nice picture!'

'My mother. She was an actress – Marian Westwood?'

'Oh!' Shrill embarrassment.

'She was in a few films in the late 50s, 60s . . .'

Hannah risks the fraction of a laugh. Of course it means nothing to her. I somehow thought a Hannah would know about the past, about the years before her own, but evidently she lives entirely within the brackets of her life, just as the rest of them do. That's as it should be. Bobby and I, wallowing in escapism, singing of a million little stars that would decorate our ceiling, dreaming of swirling dancers on limpid ballroom floors – we were the freaks, the anomalies, towing the wrong histories behind us.

Gareth has appeared and I make my excuses. Hannah's parents will be picking her up at 12. It's all very safe and very civilized.

'Personally,' says Gill, 'I can't abide the girl. False. Nothing underneath, you feel.'

'That's a bit harsh. She hasn't had time to grow into her own personality yet.'

'I wouldn't hold my breath if I were you. Her mother's just the same – false as the old man's pearlies, as an old boyfriend of mine used to say. You never get the genuine article. Just a succession of dramatic parts. All you can do is play to them.'

Sounds like Marian Westwood. So at least I'll know what to do.

We're having a Moroccan dish – couscous, carrots, apricots, raisins – with a vast hanch each of crusty bread. Unusually, we eat off our laps in the front room. Gill leaves the curtains open; we can see the light in my cottage window gain strength in the dusk.

'A romantic meal and home by midnight. He's a very conventional boy, really, isn't he?' she says, but I notice that she's allowed herself a clear view and keeps glancing towards the cottage.

'She's his first proper girlfriend. As far as *I* know.'

Gill says, 'Hannah's parents might yet put him off, I suppose. Who'd want to be lumbered with in-laws like that?'

When I'm breadwiping the last blobs from my bowl she says, 'We still haven't decided what to do about the garden'. My stomach gurgles apprehensively. 'You need a project.

Something to get you away from that computer. Something to motivate you again, something that's interesting as well as functional.'

The word 'motivate' immediately sucks all the moisture and energy from my body. I droop over my empty bowl.

A shift in the darkness attracts our attention: my front room window has grown dimmer. Gareth must have turned off the overhead light and switched on the standard lamp. Gill waggles her eyebrows.

'Smooth operator, huh?'

Blackout. Suddenly I can't see the cottage, Gill or the bowl on my lap.

'Oh, *shit*!' Gill's voice swells as she heaves herself from her chair. 'That's the third time in a month. And I've left the candles in the garage.'

I can hear her groping about in a corner, then her face appears, red-shadowed and ghoulish in a beam of torch-light. I say,

'I'd better just see if Gareth knows what to do . . .'

'Nonsense,' she says. 'He's not an idiot. I'm sure they're loving every minute of it. Power cuts are no hardship at that age.'

The phone rings.

'Well, at least the phone lines are open. That'll be him, I expect, seeing if the wrinklies are scared of the dark.' She shines the torch towards the phone and I stumble towards it, but the beam wavers, then suddenly swings full into my face.

'No,' she says. 'Tell you what – I'll get that. You find the candles. I know exactly where they are.'

Her instructions are precise; they leave no margin for error, despite being rattled off at high speed while she reaches for the receiver. She hands me the torch and I'm at the front door before I hear her say, 'Hello?'. She's waiting to hear the door slam, so I slam it.

When I get back Gill is about to put the phone down. The torchlight catches her in the act, so she waves the receiver in the air, instead, and says,

'It's Bobby.'

I pass her the candles and the torch. I have to take a couple of long breaths to stave off the urge to throw up. I make my shoulders and voice smaller around the receiver, and Gill pads off to find the matches.

'Hello,' he says. His voice is subdued and controlled.

'Hello.' My throat crackles. I wait.

'I tried the house,' he says, and I'm not quite sure whether to believe him. 'I got someone else's answerphone. I thought I was . . .' He's going to joke about it, but changes his mind. 'Anyway. Gill told me you're renting a cottage there.'

'Yes.'

It's all I can say. My jaw refuses to work.

'Good. That's a good idea.'

'The house . . .' I clench my teeth, release them, and start again. 'We had to sell the house, Bobby.' I'm surprised by the venom in his name.

'Of course. Of course you did. I wasn't thinking.'

I feel as if I might cry; I'm battling, furious, knowing that I might waste this opportunity to – to what? Tell him that I love him, miss him, hate him, want to kill him? To beg him to come home or order him to stay away?

He says 'Gill tells me there's a bit of a love scene going on at . . . at the cottage.'

I cannot answer him. I cannot tell him conversationally that his son has acquired a girlfriend while he's been away. I remember what I need to ask, though Gill's probably asked already.

'Where are you?'

'I'm in Liverpool.' As if it's a casual question and an easy reply. 'I met some very interesting people here. They run a dot com company. I've been doing a bit of work for them-there'll be a cheque in the post this week. Now that I know your address it should get to you fairly quickly.'

I understand. This is the fantasy we have to play out. All at once I'm composed and professional.

'That's good news,' I say. 'Well done. Why don't you take a break?' I say. 'Come and see how we're fixed up.' Despite my calmness, I'm clutching the phone so tightly that he won't be able to hang up however hard he tries.

'Soon. Very soon. Just a few people to see. I've got some proposals for you to look at. Nothing iffy. The real McCoy. Foolproof. We're on the up and up.' He sounds relieved. Then he says, 'I hope Gill's not giving you any grief.'

As a matter of fact Gill has saved our bloody bacon. Gill has been clearing up your mess. But I say, 'No, no, she's been fine. It's nice for Gareth to be near her.'

'Of course it is. Well . . .' He's had enough. He rounds things off. He says he'll take that break soon. He says he's got great hopes for this new plan. He says there's no reason we shouldn't make it work.

'No,' I say, 'there isn't.'

He says goodbye. I listen for several seconds until I'm sure his voice won't break through the dialling tone. Then I set down the receiver with exaggerated care. I feel like the butt of a joke.

Gill comes back with a carriage lamp, humming too heartily.

'Has he gone?' she says, unnecessarily.

She sets the lamp down. In the safety of its diffused beam, questions form. I'll ask her what she and Bobby talked about. What they didn't talk about. What I should do. Whether I should want him back. But the lights come on again, and the questions scuttle away with the shadows. Instead, I say:

'He's in Liverpool.'

'Yes.' Her mouth droops at the corners.

'I suggested he might want to take a break from work soon.'

I start laughing. Gill laughs too, but neither of us is hysterical.

We sit and watch a programme about gardening make-overs. Then some terrible sci-fi film starts. Gill turns the volume down and alters her position on the sofa to face me.

'I never did tell you, did I? About the first time I saw your mother act?'

She launches into a long account about playing truant and spending the afternoon in a pub theatre. Maybe she needs to do this: backpedal to a time before Bobby was here, or there, or anywhere else. So I nod and wrinkle my forehead and make listening noises, while on the TV space explorers blunder soundlessly into a parallel universe. Blood explodes against a spaceship wall; someone is blown apart in a decompression chamber; Gill chunters on, about her school, her parents, her first boyfriend. At midnight, on the dot, we hear a car draw up and Gill lets her story trail away. She gets up to draw the curtains and reports:

'Yep, it's them. Parents are staying in the car. Hannah looks unsullied. Maybe there was no reckless behaviour after all.'

Later, in bed, I find Gill's musings revolving around my tired brain. I've had enough of screens, so instead of watching another musical I lie on my bed and think about her tidy past, its signposts and outcomes and steps on the ladder. Hour follows hour, year follows year, time follows its inexorable course, and so it goes on, despite the impression that it's screeched to a halt in my cottage in Emmett Park. Changes will occur even if I do nothing. Gill's strength and vitality will evaporate, little by little. My hair will grow grey and coarse, my back will seize up in habitual pain, my flesh will dry and rumple and weigh me down. Gareth will grow taller, broader, will love someone, leave someone, love someone else, will father children, start to gain flesh and lose hair . . . Only Bobby will stay suspended in his own delusions, outside time and space.

I drift off and dream that Gareth, Hannah and I are waiting, hand in hand, outside the entrance of Emmett Park. Gareth is excited. I'm afraid. Bobby is about to emerge and I'm sure that something in his appearance will be unbearable. The doors swish open and Bobby emerges, but it's the young man in the suit. He reaches for Hannah's hand to lead her back into the hospital, which is now an immaculate formal garden, open to the sky, and I am Hannah as well as myself, following the man who is himself and Bobby and may also be Gareth, although I check and double-check constantly that Gareth is by my side. It's so easy, in dreams, to break the boundaries of identity and absence. When you wake up, you have to pause and remind yourself of the daylight rules, if you want to stay outside that perimeter wall.

9

In the third week of its run, Gillian Parker skived off school and saw the Wednesday matinée of *I Can Hear You*. She'd caught the morning train into Victoria, ducked into the ladies to change out of her uniform and set out to see the first event she saw advertised. A torn flier for the play had been slapped on a wall near the station entrance, half-obscuring a poster for the Big Top Circus on Clapham Common. Gillian memorised the details and cantered down the steps to the tube.

During the interval Gillian Parker moved to one of the empty seats in the front row. She sat in the twilit Attic on that sunny afternoon, soaking in her surroundings: the desultory clinking of the downstairs bar; the scuff marks on the black stage; the smell of dust and rubber and nervous sweat. Gillian was 16 and had never been in love, had never been inspired or intoxicated until now. In five minutes' time there would be a mumbling and shuffling and a clacking of seats as the audience returned (probably in diminished numbers). There would be a descent into blackness, and then two men and two women would trudge into eerie spotlights, an arm's length away, two feet above, and tell Gillian Parker what she needed to know. There would be revelations, questions of vital import and their solutions. Four characters would speak to her, provoke her tears, and show her who Gillian Parker was destined to be.

Marian Westwood crouched beside the distraught leading lady and took her hand.

'God?' quavered the woman, nostrils flaring. 'You offer me God, as if He's alive and well?' She directed her anguish to the auditorium and enunciated roundly. 'Don't you know God was shot down in flames over the English Channel? All I hear are the voices of the Dead!'

Gillian could see the tip of Marian Westwood's tongue moistening her lips ready for the next line.

'Maybe we *have* killed God,' said the nun, and a low tremor passed through the audience. 'But faith survives even death itself. Faith in life.' She went up a semi-tone with each phrase. 'Faith in renewal. What can we do—' she gazed soulfully at the middle row – 'but try and understand, and hope for a better day?'

The play was dire but Gillian Parker didn't care. She'd never seen anyone like Marian Westwood. The long, catlike eyes; the fronds of black hair slipping sinfully from the confines of the wimple; the mouth, that passionate, innocent, top-heavy mouth, its full upper lip vibrating to every exaggerated consonant. When the cast linked hands for their bows and Marian's line of vision passed for an instant across Gillian's, the shock hurtled through her body from skull to heels.

All the way home, as she swayed and jolted from the strap on the tube, as she tugged on her school uniform in the loo, as she rattled against the train window, Gillian was trying to retrieve every scripted word Marian had spoken. She mouthed the lines. Her lips seemed to take on the form of Marian's as they curled and circled around the syllables.

'What can we do,' she asked her reflection in the glass, while back gardens and building sites unravelled in the gloom, 'but try and understand, and hope for a better day?'

At school the following day Gillian sat straight-backed and alert in every lesson. She was sure that her new sense of purpose radiated through her skin. She treated her friends and hangers-on with even more disdain than usual. Gillian had never quite been a rebel, but she was the kind teachers dreaded more: the quiet pupil at the back, monitoring, mocking, pinpointing every weakness. Her nicknames for the staff were the most accurate and consequently the cruellest: Ice Maiden. Mummy's Boy. Last Chance Saloon. Her sly quips earned the loyalty of a little gang but masked a private truth. The truth was that Gillian was a zealot in search of a cause. While she slouched in her seat and doodled on the desklid, piano-wires hummed in her brain, ready to snap under the pressure of undirected passion. She longed not for heavy petting and french kisses but for belief, ambition, obsession.

If the bill-posting boy hadn't pasted his last leaflet across the Big Top, maybe Gillian Parker would have resolved to go on the trapeze. If *I Can Hear You* had provided a better script and a better cast, maybe she would have come away stagestruck and determined to act. As it was, Marian Westwood left her mark another way. Gillian toyed at first with being a nun, unable to disentangle the role from the impact of that Wednesday matinée and Marian herself. She could be an atheist nun, perhaps; she pictured herself delivering those thrilling words to horrified companions: 'Maybe we *have* killed God'.

That notion soon gave way to a more practical goal. Like the stage Marian, she would comfort tormented souls. She would listen to their voices, take their hands, gaze at the middle row and try to understand. She would lead them to a better day. Tears sprang into Gillian's eyes and the algebra master, turning from the blackboard, stopped mid-explanation.

'Gillian, are you quite all right?'

Gillian sniffed imperiously. Heads turned, eager for distraction.

'Yes, sir,' she said, blotting her eyes with the back of her hand. 'Just carried away with the beauty of your equations.'

Elvira and Maurice Parker had an unconscious knack of arranging themselves as if for a studio photograph. In 28 years of marriage they had rarely been apart. Gillian's mother had been her father's secretary, and continued to work alongside him in the small back room known as the study, where he worked on translations of reports and manuals. Whenever Gillian came in there they were, framed together in a snapshot of gentility: Elvira seated, pen poised over her notebook, Maurice standing behind her, one hand resting on the back of the chair. Maurice at his desk searching for a reference, Elvira at his side, extending a bony finger towards the appropriate line.

The Parkers had married late and Gillian had been a late child. By the time she was verging on adulthood, she felt like an intruder from another time. She came in to confront them one early spring morning in 1952, dressed in a light sweater and figure-hugging slacks, her hair scraped back into a ponytail. They turned towards her from their sepia circle of starched collars and hairpins and demurely folded hands. Gillian had come to tell them that she intended to leave school and find work with the disturbed and the destitute. She had decided not to waste any more time sitting exams, while her missionary fuel burned away. She would seek out a shelter or a refuge, find out where she was most needed, and take it from there.

Elvira sat in the leather chair by the bookcase. Maurice had taken up his position, resting an arm on the high headrest while she read to him from her notes. As usual, they beamed at their daughter when she entered the room. She was home. She was safe. Gillian's breathing quickened as their love closed around her and threatened to draw her into their frame.

She told them her decision and watched as they settled into a subtly different arrangement. Maurice dipped his head with a frown. Elvira swivelled in her seat and faced Gillian with wan alarm. Her face was a plea for mercy. Gillian's anger rose.

'I'm not *asking* you about this. I'm *telling* you.' She was infuriated by the petulance in her voice. 'I've *got* to do it. I *can't possibly* stay in school.'

'You're so young to make these far-reaching decisions,' said her gentle father. 'There's no call to rush headlong into—'

'I am NOT staying in school.' Gillian could feel the lava in her cheeks. Her father flinched at the interruption. In his family voices were never raised and sentences never cut short.

'It's not as if I'm running away to be a whore,' said Gillian, flinging the word at them with calculated ease. 'I want to help people. Even *you* should approve of that.'

She was inventing opposition as she went along. Her parents hardly ever expressed disapproval of anyone-only flickerings of fear and hurt.

'We think it's an admirable idea' said Elvira. Gillian's parents always spoke collectively. Gillian refused to look at her mother's moon face. 'An idea to pursue, in due course . . .'

'In *due course*?' yelled Gillian. 'People need help *now*, not in *due course*. There are desparate people, people who . . .' – she summoned a line from the play – 'people who look into the abyss every hour of the day. And all we can do' – she gestured at the bookshelf – 'is read poetry and learn futile facts and do long division and . . . and wait for *due course* . . .' Unsure of the sense of her words, Gillian succumbed to the silence of the room. Silence was the natural condition of the Parkers' house. There was no radio, no telephone and only a few old gramophone records that were never played. Just the rustle of pages to disturb its warm air; just a faintly sour odour of carpets, overstuffed chairs and the rose-water that Elvira sprinkled on her arms.

Maurice waited a moment for the stillness to absorb Gillian's bellowing, then said, 'Don't get upset' – possibly to himself. Gillian let out a roar that brought tears to her eyes, and stomped away before they could fall. She slammed herself into her own room, which she kept bare-walled, open-windowed and cold.

Eventually Gillian compromised. She agreed to stay in school and reconsider her future after sitting her exams. In return she demanded the right to find voluntary work that would stand her in good stead for 'a career in welfare'. This was the term she had recently adopted to lend solidity to her ambitions. 'A career in welfare' was a sound and feasible plan, a modern plan for a modern era. War and its dreary afteryears, childhood and the stuffy gentility of her home – they were all so much dust clinging to Gillian's clothes. She would brush it all away.

Nevertheless, for a few months Gillian was at a loss. She had no idea how or where to offer her help, and she was more daunted than she cared to admit by the prospect of wandering the streets in search of people to understand. Elvira and Maurice allowed their fears to subside, though they said nothing to Gillian. Acutely aware of their diplomacy, Gillian lay on her bed for hours on end and imagined herself hunkering down with the meths-drinkers under the railway bridge, accepting the burden of their sodden minds, oblivious to puddles of piss and vomit.

A notice appeared in the local paper asking for volunteers to run a shelter for ex-servicemen. Gillian told herself it wasn't the kind of thing she'd had in mind, and turned the page. It appeared again the following week. Gillian was sitting at the dining room table; her mother was fussing over the mantelpiece clock, which was losing time. Gillian knew, from the intensity of her mother's concentration, from the curve of her mother's back, that her parents had spotted the notice and were relying on her apathy. She drew a thick, black ring round the address and signed herself up, that afternoon, for three nights a week.

Gillian learned the first lesson of her career in a pokey church hall with three long tables and a tiny, fenced-off kitchen. She learned that however hard she listened, there was no guarantee that others would talk.

'Maybe,' she suggested to Mrs Harris, the hefty shelter-manager, 'maybe I could sit and chat with them for a while. Keep them company.'

Mrs Harris was checking the tea urn. She glanced from Gillian's pony-tailed hair down to her white socks. She glanced at the half-dozen frozen-faced men slumped randomly around the hall, smoking, hawking, mumbling into their chins. She wiggled the urn tap, released a puff of steam and said,

'Best hand round the brew for now. Plenty of time for chats.'

In due course, thought Gillian, bitterly.

Some of the men who came to drink tea or soup had fought in the Great War. Gillian thought they might want to tell her their stories, but most ignored her altogether. Occasionally one would thank her, or raise an inscrutable, rheumy look. A few younger men attended, cast aside by the '39-'45 war; they wouldn't meet her eyes. They seemed to find the presence of a plain 17-year-old uncomfortable and puzzling. After a couple of weeks Mrs Harris restricted Gillian's duties to the kitchen.

'I don't feel very useful,' complained Gillian.

'Nothing more useful in life,' said Mrs Harris, 'than keeping a man's stomach filled and warmed.'

Gillian was bored. She was bored with Mrs Harris. Bored with the tea urn and the shelter, with its aura of stale flesh and caustic soda. Bored with men who guarded their memories and wounds like honours. Men who hardly acknowledged her scrap of life. Men damaged by wars that were fought and finished a million years ago. She would have given up the whole idea, if it hadn't been for her father's stoic concern and her mother's frightened eyes, issuing a fresh challenge every time she came home at the end of a shift.

She needed a sign. According to Gillian's system of omens, there had to be a moment or a word of portent, guiding her in another direction, before she could leave the shelter. She would recognise it if it came. This wasn't an excuse for doing as she pleased: Gillian followed her system assiduously, testing her reactions for sincerity. She was waiting for the involuntary, the spontaneous crackle of energy that would force her existence into a higher gear. Lines spoken in The Attic on a Wednesday afternoon; an advert in the paper two weeks running . . . Gillian believed in no gods, but she waited nonetheless for some nameless, remote will to be done.

She waited until half past ten on New Year's Eve, 1952, and then Lenny walked into the hall. No, he didn't walk. Lenny swaggered. He was a cowboy, entering a new saloon. Gillian was stationed behind a makeshift counter – three tables set end to end – ladling out chicken stew for the latecomers. The hall was quite full that night-as it generally was on public holidays and special occasions, when the outside world expanded in celebration and squeezed out the drunks and madmen. Gillian had been here on Christmas Eve too, though she'd taken pity on her parents and joined them for the midnight service. This shift was less painful to them as they never welcomed in the new year, hoping only that each one would resemble the last. So Gillian endured the shuffling queue without even the satisfaction of defiance. She'd given up greeting her customers and sloshed stew into bowls in a dull, unthinking rhythm. A movement of the door at the far end of the hall caught her eye. Lenny stood with his thumbs in the pockets of a pair of overalls scored and splattered with paint. He scanned the room. He was smirking; his eyes were wide and his eyebrows high, anticipating laughter. He had thick black hair in loose, long, shaggy-dog curls. Something about him, about the shimmer of hair, the arrogance of movement, the sly eyes, brought a vision of Marian Westwood flashing into Gillian's mind and made her catch her breath.

The man at the head of the queue said, 'Yes please, darling,' and jiggled his tin bowl at Gillian. She resumed her rhythm – scoop, slosh, scoop, slosh – but her shoulders and neck and stomach ached with tension. This was it. The sign. She didn't yet know what it would tell her. At her side, Mrs Harris muttered,

'Oh-oh. Here's trouble. Hold on to your hats' – as if she could read Gillian's thoughts.

He jumped the queue, and the men didn't mind. He clapped their shabby shoulders and greeted them as old pals, without using a single name. They grinned and wheezed and passed him a bowl.

'Found a new hobby, have we?' said Mrs Harris, directing a look at his overalls.

'Mrs Harris, I'm proud to announce my latest commission.' He spoke like an actor. The vowels were narrow and affluent. 'It's my singular honour to be recreating the glories of the Tuscan landscape on one wall of the Vita Nuova coffee bar.'

Gillian couldn't tell whether he was serious, couldn't raise her eyes to check. She ladelled out his ration of soup and willed Mrs Harris to keep him talking.

'Won't last you very long, though, will it?' said Mrs Harris.

'O, ye of little faith. Something will come along. Just as the last golden blob of sunlight plops on to the last vine-clad hill. You mark my words.'

The other men were shambling forward, pushing him on. Gillian wanted to ask him whether he was an artist, but she couldn't speak. Luckily he answered her anyway. He said – and she knew he was looking at her – 'I paint, you see. I paint and I plaster and I potter about.'

She managed to lift her eyes in time for his outrageously broad and overcrowded grin. He seemed to have two mouths'-worth of teeth.

Instead of trailing off towards the trestle tables, he moved round to stand behind the counter, slurping his soup, chattering to Mrs Harris and the men, telling them about the owners of the Vita Nuova, imitating their London-

Italian accents, adopting a different falsetto pitch for each of the five daughters, gesticulating with his spoon and splattering the floor with fat globules of stew.

'You'll be wiping that lot up, I hope,' said Mrs Harris.

Occasionally they added footnotes to the conversation for Gillian's benefit.

'Mrs Harris thinks I'm a wastrel,' he said.

'This young feller has missed more boats than I'll ever see sail,' said Mrs Harris.

'Mrs Harris thinks I've disgraced the family name, you see, Gillian.'

The sound of her name hammered against her spine. She summoned the courage to ask: 'What *is* the family name?' and cringed when he laughed at her, an engulfing, full-chested laugh that set off an echo along the queue.

Mrs Harris leaned towards her and said, 'Just call him Lenny. He won't be called anything else.'

'That's right!' He was still laughing – too hard, thought Gillian, suspecting a joke at her expense. 'I mustn't drag the old name down!'

After finishing his soup Lenny wandered off towards the trestle tables. Gillian helped Mrs Harris clear away. From the galley kitchen she could hear him whipping up a chorus of Auld Lang Syne. Then he was there, behind her, grabbing Mrs Harris for a New Year's kiss. Gillian's hands shook and knocked bowls together in the dishwater. His hands on her shoulders; his kiss clumsily on her cheek, just in front of her ear. She flushed; the dishwater was cool around her wrists.

'I'm off' she heard him say. He tapped her arm, and added, 'Come and see the work in progress if you like. Vita Nuova, Acre Street. Know it?' Before she could lie he'd gone.

School term started on the Monday. On the Wednesday Gillian caught the tube to Covent Garden and asked her way to Acre Street. She was nervous but determined: this, after all, was meant to be.

The Vita Nuova's windows were blocked out with sheets of paper but the door was propped open. She peered round it into a mist of paint fumes and cigarette smoke and strong coffee. The floor was covered in tarpaulin, planks, paint pots, cups, saucers sprouting cigarette ends. A storage heater glowed orange in one corner. Three people argued at a table in another. Lenny was halfway up a stepladder, leaning heavily against it and stretching to reach a patch of wall, which he was rubbing with a rag.

'We're closed,' called a voice from the table, and Lenny turned. He launched himself off the ladder, which lurched backwards before steadying itself, and bounded up to take her hand.

'Gillian, oh, Gillian,' he sang, 'My guide and postilion . . .' Gillian felt ridiculed. 'Exclaim at my brilliance, oh Gillian!'

He swept an arm along the mural and she nodded, solemnly. He guided her to an empty table near the others, who'd resumed their argument. He sang low and privately, 'So now we'll decamp and drink coff-ee, and you'll tell me half your life sto-ree . . .'

She talked all afternoon. Most of the time he listened; sometimes he'd interrupt with a burst of song and she wondered whether he'd heard anything at all. Nobody seemed to mind that he wasn't working. Maybe she was just his excuse for a free afternoon. But Gillian talked. She talked about the refuge and her frustrated ambitions. She talked about school and her shallow friends.

Lenny said, 'Shouldn't you be at school today?'

She hoped the others hadn't overheard. She snorted. 'It's a waste of time.'

He frowned at her. 'You mustn't play truant, Gillian. If you've got somewhere to go, you must go there.'

She was impressed. He was living up to his oracular role.

She told him about seeing the play; she told him about her parents. She complained about the house and its suffocating comforts, about her mother's anxieties, her father's caution . . . Lenny sat up and threw his arms out. That cluttered grin again.

'They *love* you, Gillian!' he hollered. She decided he was like a foreigner, compensating for his lack of vocabulary by investing too much emotion into every simple phrase.

'They just want to keep me under house arrest,' she moaned.

Lenny lit up a cigarette and shared it with her, touching her fingers with his, every time he handed it over.

By half-past three it was growing dark. Someone switched on the light and Lenny rallied everyone's attention, insisting that they admire his half-finished mural 'in its electrically illuminated aspect.'

'We bask in an Italian summer,' he yelled, 'while London freezes outside the door. Incidentally, why don't we *shut* that bloody door?'

Gillian waited for him to calm down and return to her. She had plenty to say yet.

Lenny had a way of changing expression as she spoke, as if he'd marked some detail of her skin or hair. For the first time in her 17 years, Gillian began to wonder how she appeared to the outside world.

At ten past six he told her to go home. 'Don't break your poor mamma's heart,' he trilled, steering her across the café floor. She was wearing her shapeless winter coat, with a pair of woollen mitts poking from one pocket. He snatched them out and put them on her hands, giving each one a neat, final snap into place. He said,

'When's your next shift with the estimable Mrs H?'

'Next Wednesday,' said Gillian, and her pulse stuttered in her neck.

'I'll pick you up there,' said Lenny, and scraped the door shut behind her.

10

Lenny had a key to the Vita Nuova coffee bar. On a Wednesday night in January 1953 he collected Gillian at the end of her shift and drove her to Soho in a very old Ford 8 saloon. The seats had virtually no padding-their frames bit into Gillian's thighs and buttocks and left long scarlet weals. There was a stink of petrol, which she would associate with sex all her life, and she had to cling to the door to keep it from swinging open.

Lenny locked the coffee bar and put the light on. He manoeuvred her by the shoulders, placing her in front of the mural to show its progress: he seemed to have painted over the finished section and started again. He marched her behind the counter and through another door into the staff wash-room. He turned her round and grabbed her face in both hands to kiss her. Gillian had never been kissed before and was taken aback by the violence, the taste, the saliva and the clash of teeth. It all looked so well-fitting in the movies. Lenny was impatient, silent, urgent; Gillian was silent, curious, resigned. She'd known that he would want this, and was more than willing to gain the experience. She found his excitement puzzling, and intercourse painful, but she was glad to get it over with quickly, and glad that, afterwards, he found a bottle of wine in one of the staff cupboards and wanted to drink and chat.

Then he wanted to paint.

'I'll show you why it was all wrong,' he said. 'I'll put it right. I know how to put it right.'

It was nearly 3am. Gillian put on her winter coat and watched him set up the ladder, unroll the brushes from their cloth. He was talking all the time-about the colours he would mix, the details he would add, referring with self-deprecation to his 'masterpiece' but preparing to work on it in a frenzy.

'Lenny,' she said, finally, 'I'll have to go home.'

'Go home? After our first night of love, and a chance to see genius at work, you'd abandon me to—'

'Lenny. My parents.'

She'd told them it was a double shift, assured them that her co-volunteer would bring her back, made them promise to go to bed. It wouldn't cross their minds that she was lying, but she knew they'd be awake in their hump-backed bed, in the dark, each one breathing shallow breaths to avoid dislodging the eiderdown, each one waiting for her key in the lock. Lenny started to sing.

'Gillian, oh, Gillian, a child in a million, her parents vermilion with worr-ee . . .'

He was crouching over a wooden box, fingering half-squeezed tubes of paint. He looked up suddenly and said, 'Off you go then.'

'Lenny . . .' She wondered whether he was punishing her. 'Lenny, I can't walk home. It would take hours . . .'

He caught the rise of panic and his face closed down. He stayed there, on his haunches, hoping she would go away. Gillian controlled the waver in her voice and said,

'You told me if I had somewhere to go I should go there.'

A smack of wood made her jump back as Lenny slammed the paintbox shut. He was on his feet, striding to the door. She heard the splinter of a brush under his foot; he deliberately kicked the wine bottle aside and it rolled to a corner, spurting its dregs along the floor. By the time they were in the car and he'd managed to start the engine his temper had vanished. He treated her to the grin and said, 'It was a good night tonight, wasn't it?'

She was exultant with relief, with the way he gave the question added meaning by looking into the centre of her eyes. As the car bucked and growled into movement he was singing again: 'Gillian, oh, Gillian, she's not such a silly 'un; she wants more thrilling fun with Lenn-eee . . .'

11

At about the time Gillian was losing her virginity to Lenny, Marian Westwood was entertaining Russell Mitchell in the rooms above the High Kicks Revue. Russell Mitchell hadn't expected to be entertained. His approach had been quite innocuous. He'd seen Marian in *I Can Hear You* on one of his talent-spotting rounds and remembered her feline presence when he started casting for *The Affairs of Men* at the Davenant Theatre. He asked around and that January night, after the early show, tracked her down to the boiler room. Marian assumed that a deal was being struck, and sent a message up to Alec telling him to make himself scarce. She sat touching up her make-up while Mitchell introduced himself and paid his compliments, then told him what time she finished work.

'Come up the back stairs and knock.'

Russell Mitchell was startled, but he managed not to show it. He'd enjoyed a drink or two; he'd spent the evening studying Marian's upholstered physique; he wasn't about to look a gift horse in the mouth. After the last show Marian hurried upstairs to find some decent underwear and comb her hair out. She examined herself in the shaving mirror, powdered the crevices and hollows, licked her teeth, blew her nose. In an undertone she told her reflection a riddle she'd seen scratched on the wall of the dressing room toilets: 'What do you call a tart with a runny nose? Full.'

Russell Mitchell arrived 10 minutes later, sucking in his paunch and reeking of tobacco and nerve-steadying scotch. Marian had to do most of the work; the whole episode was mercifully quick. Afterwards she took a hip bath while he rumbled into sleep. Her first words to him the next day were: 'Is there anything we can sign?'

So Marian Westwood got her next break – her biggest break, as it turned out – thanks to one impressive performance, and always privately attributed it to another.

I've read the reviews and heard the personal accounts and I can only conclude that my mother's time had come. She was a sensation. *The Affairs of Men* was a sound play; Mitchell was a competent director; the cast was an interesting mix of bright new unknowns and grand pre-war names. And Marian Westwood stole the show. The part was ideal: Mitchell knew his stuff. She played an ambitious working girl from Liverpool (close enough to her reconstituted Cardiff accent), combining naïvety and cunning to make her way in the world at the expense of various other lives. The only sour note was from the *Standard* critic, who wasn't convinced by Marian as an ingénue and griped that she 'hasn't an innocent bone in her body'. He was the only one who cared.

On that stage, eight times a week, Marian Westwood perfected and paraded her trademarks: the panther movements, easy and sleek; the tilted head and sideways glance; the slide from brazen trumpet notes to throaty purr; the stance – hands on hips, chest thrust out – that promised a fight and made men shift in their seats. First thing in the morning, last thing at night, she practised it all in the bathroom mirror, while Alec sat smoking on the loo seat, doling out advice: 'That's right, baby girl . . . not too much . . . don't let them think you're cheap . . .' and she let him believe, as usual, that she was taking it.

Gillian Parker didn't see *The Affairs of Men*. Later in life she regretted it; she would have liked to say she'd witnessed my mother's coming of age. But at 17 she had other things on her mind.

Everything was changing for Marian Westwood. Autograph-hunters waited for her at the stage door, letting the big names pass without a second look. There were post-show dinners, this time at decent clubs and restaurants, and there were post-show friends who were going somewhere other than panto. Marian bought herself a snugly fitting dress, sharp high heels, a fur stole; she bought Alec a new suit and

new dentures. Alec spent most of his time in the rooms
above the High Kicks, snipping out reviews to paste in her
scrapbook. During the day he wandered through markets
and slipped into back-room bookies, occasionally settled
himself in a pub and made conversation, searching for ways
to introduce Marian's name and mention that he was her
agent. She wouldn't allow him to claim anything else.

She was cast to type in *After Silence*, and it worked like a
dream. She was interviewed for the *Daily Express*. She was
asked to endorse a brand of lipstick. She had that publicity
shot taken, the picture that hangs in my hallway. Notes
were delivered to the dressing room from a lovesick youth
who'd been to nearly every performance of *The Affairs of
Men* and who was spending all his wages booking ahead
for the run of *After Silence*. She was pursued by several
members of cast and crew. She was young and sexy and she
knew it. It was time to find a more suitable place to live.

So Alec stayed on above the High Kicks and Marian
Westwood rented her Bayswater flat. I can only guess, from
my father's comments, that at some point she also started
paying the Soho rent on Alec's behalf. The role reversal was
complete.

In 1955 Marian had a flat-warming party almost every
night. There were always enough friends and admirers to
create an atmosphere. There was always a willing companion
to take to bed if she didn't fancy sleeping alone (and she
usually didn't). There was always someone or other to
appreciate her, tell her how appealing she looked off stage
as well as on, how adorable she was in her bathrobe, how
sweetly she made love. And on the bad nights, when a critic
had expressed reservations, or another actor had objected to
being upstaged, or nobody wanted to stay and laugh at her
jokes, she would take a cab to Soho and knock on Alec's
door, and let him comfort her and pet her as he had in the
old days, and tell her she was the best and most beautiful
and brightest star.

12

For a while after we moved here I jumped out of my skin every time the phone rang, thinking it might be Bobby. But how could it be Bobby? He wouldn't have our number. He'd have to ring Gill before contacting us. I must have known that all along, somewhere in the back of my head. It should have been the first thing I said to him, as soon as I heard his voice: Bobby, this is where we are. Here's where you can reach us. And yet it wasn't until the day after his call, until a passing comment from Gill, that I realised I hadn't told him.

Gill said: 'By the way, I made damn sure Bobby was writing it all down. Your details, I mean. The new address and number.'

I just nodded, and tried not to show my dismay. I wasn't sure what disturbed me more: the fact that I hadn't remembered to tell him, or a sudden sense of exposure. Bobby knows where we are now. He really can turn up at any time. And then I'll have to decide where we go from here.

'What's the matter?' says Gareth.

He's sprawled on the sofa, muddled up with cushions, schoolbooks, chocolate wrappers, his eyes slithering to and fro, following the thunk and blare of the TV.

'Nothing, why? I'm just reading the paper.' I turn a page pointedly.

'No you're not. You keep looking at the phone.'

'No, I don't. Anyway, how would you know? You're transfixed by the telly as usual.'

After another 10 minutes he says, 'Why didn't you tell me Dad rang?'

'When?' I ask, stupidly, and his whole body convulses in a sneer. The newspaper sags in my hands. I don't answer him because I don't know the answer. Why *didn't* I tell him?

Because I didn't want to spoil his romantic evening with Hannah. Because our paths didn't cross, because days went by, because it seemed easier not to bring it up. Because I'm a coward.

All I can come up with is: 'He didn't have much to say. He's in Liverpool.'

'I know. Gill told me.'

'Well, there you are. I knew she would.'

It's not enough and we both know it. But Gareth doesn't throw a tantrum or berate me for being a useless mother. He searches between the cushions for the zapper and channel-hops for a while, before leaving the room to seek refuge with his PC.

There's a woman behind that perimeter wall whose case made headlines at the time. She killed seven children. Three of her own, two of her husband's by another marriage, two of her sister's. She spent a quiet hour that evening, when the children had gone to their room, grinding sleeping pills into a fine paste, mixing chocolate milk, measuring out portions, calling up the occasional admonishment as the kids giggled and fought in their shared bunk-beds. She went upstairs with their drinks on a tray and passed them round with goodnight kisses. She waited in the kitchen, counting the hours, until they were all unconscious, hauling vast breaths from a great depth, and she carried them, one by one, into the bathroom and finished them off in the bath. Her husband found them the following day, towelled and brushed and lying tidily in their beds. One newspaper dubbed her the Mother of Evil.

I consider barging up to Gareth's room and reminding him of that case. You think *I'm* a bad mother? You think *we're* dysfunctional? Well, think yourself lucky. I may not tell you things I ought to tell you; I may tell you too many things I should keep to myself. But I'm not the Mother of Evil. At least you can bank on outliving me. All I did was make an ill-judged career move. All I did was mislay my husband. I watch cheesy old films into the early hours. None of this makes me the Mother of Evil. I don't run from reality, like your father. I don't pretend I can keep you safe from the world – with love, or with fairy tales, or with a spiked bedtime drink.

I turn another page and it rips noisily along the crease. Here's another idea. I could go up there and fling my arms around him. Take the initiative, croon my love in earnest soap-opera phrases and break down the barriers between us. But I won't do that either. I'll settle down for another evening of police dramas and doctor dramas, and an old video, and a vague and improbable daydream about the young man in the suit.

I try and imagine the young man loosening his tie, unbuttoning his shirt, but the scenario refuses to develop. Bobby is in the way. I'm thinking about the way he's aged, about his middle-age gut and pasty thighs and wobbly upper arms and burgeoning boobs. I'm missing him. Missing the alleys that have trailed deeper and further into his face with every year we've been together. Missing the retreat of his hairline. Whatever I did or didn't say to him, whatever fleeting panics and doubts I suffer, I want him back. I want his restless night-sweats dampening and rucking the sheets. I want to thump him when he snores and moan at the scree of stubble pattering down the sink after he's shaved. I don't want to make do with half-hearted fantasies and long-dead films.

With a thousand little stars,
We can decorate the ceiling . . .

Hello again, Eddie, my old friend. Eddie's lilting songs and eyes, his camp gestures and his double-takes – all familiar, all for me. And my son – my son and his sulks and silences, his foot-smells and fart-smells, his croaking, crackling voice, his man-voice, his sleepy child-voice, the moods that ripple in his eyes, his smooth cheeks and fingers and elasticated legs; my son, whom I know as well as I know my own curled warmth when I wake in bed – my son is as distant and mysterious to me as a movie star.

At 11 o'clock on Thursday morning I'm making myself a second pot of coffee when I hear the back gate clang. There's a man in a white boiler suit on the path, scrutinising the patch of long grass. I know immediately why he's there. I open the back door and call: 'Are you the wasp man?'

'That's me, love.'

'Who called you?' As if I didn't know. I fail to muster any fury at Gill's interference.

'I don't like the idea of killing them all,' I say, feebly.

'I know, love, but there's nothing else for it' says the man. He's used to queasy sentiments. 'You pop back indoors and stick the kettle on and when I'm done you won't even know they were there.'

So I carry on making coffee and think about the wasps' mesmeric dance; I think about acrid fumes seeping through their papery honeycombed walls, into their wings and segmented bodies, into the larvae, suffocating their young.

After he's gone I snip my way gingerly into the wasps' blasted den, cutting the shoulder-high foliage with a sewing scissors, seedhead by seedhead. I brace myself for the first sight of corpses melting into mush. There's nothing. Not so much as a wing. Gareth will detest me for this, of course. He'll spend even less time at home and more on the bench at the junction where the local village kids hang around smoking and counting the cars. Nevertheless, relief seeps through me as I finish clearing the patch. This is how to make peace with yourself and the world, as my mother could have told me years ago. Chemicals to nudge us from day to day. Chemicals to evaporate the bugs and the bites and the headaches. Now I can get on with making my garden. And when Gareth brings his indignation home I can put the blame on Gill.

13

There was a story my mother liked to tell about herself. She used to recite it to her friends in a coy way that never quite disguised her pride. It happened when she was rehearsing her part in *After Silence* at the Carlton Playhouse. The director wanted to cut one of her speeches.

'Not a great speech, I have to admit,' she'd concede. 'But it was *my* speech.' (Appreciative murmurs.) She sulked in her dressing room. She threatened to walk out on the production. The director paid a visit to the Bayswater flat, to try and talk her round.

'Why he didn't just sack me on the spot I'll never know,' she'd insist, with a flourish of false modesty. 'There was any number of actresses baying for that part, all better than me, I'm sure . . .' (Howls of protest.)

Rather than sack her he reasoned with her. The speech held up the action, he explained. It was too sluggish.

'You can rely on me not to be sluggish,' said Marian.

He lost his cool. He asserted his authority. 'Nothing in your delivery will inject the necessary drama into these lines. They have to go.'

Whereupon Marian went into the kitchen, took the dirty plates from the worktop and – watched, no doubt, by the neighbours – hurled them on to the floor, one by one, until there were no more to throw. She shoved her hair back over her forehead and drew herself up.

'Is that dramatic enough for you?'

(Wild applause, cheers, cries of 'encore'.)

In Marian's version she swept past the open-mouthed director and tossed a pay-off over her shoulder: 'The speech stays.'

I told Gill about the plate-smashing episode, but it did nothing to tarnish my mother's image. If anything, it increased Marian's standing as an out-and-out diva. As I related it, with mounting disgust, Gill sat there with a beatific smile. When I'd finished she said,

'Remarkable.'

'What's remarkable about it?' I snapped. 'It's just bully-ing. Emotional blackmail.'

Instead of answering Gill made some cryptic comment about parallel lives. She loved this story that's always left me uneasy and frustrated, even when I was a child. What *was* the speech, I wanted to know. *Why* was it sluggish? How *did* she deliver it in the end? My questions buzzed around my mother like gnats. She swatted and winced and refused to remember. Why did I have to ruin her anecdote? Why couldn't I stick to my part and applaud the punchline? I was threatening to crumple her pretty face into frowns. She would turn her back on me, turn to her friends and leave me standing in my cloud of questions until I became invisible and could sneak away.

I hated spoiling it all for my mother. I hated to see her fidgeting under my interrogation, losing the impetus and the audience. I didn't want to do that to her, but I couldn't help myself. I wanted to know the truth. I never quite lost my suspicion that the speech *was* cut, despite my mother's antics.

Many years later she related it all to Bobby. He showed me the correct way to respond. He knew better than to ask who'd tidied away the mess, or what the director had said before he left. He just said, meaninglessly, 'That's the way to do it!' and she clasped his hand and rocked him back and forward, taking a bow.

'When I look back on it, he probably thought I was stark staring mad,' laughed Marian, and gave Bobby's hand a squeeze. 'But I knew what I was doing.'

'There was method in your madness' agreed Bobby, and she shook back her dyed hair with girlish satisfaction.

I asked Gill whether she remembered any sluggish speeches in *After Silence*.

'I assume you did go and see that one?'

'Oh, yes. I went on my own again.' But this time she couldn't recall any lines.

14

As she approached her 20th birthday Gillian was still living with her parents. After leaving school she found work at a National Assistance Board reception centre. She carried on with her shifts at the refuge, and added more shifts for the British Red Cross Society. She filled her hours and kept away from her parents' house as long as she possibly could.

Sometimes she stayed the night with Lenny. He had a bedsit on the floor above the coffee bar. Apparently the mural was supposed to have been in lieu of a couple of months' rent, but two and a half years after Gillian's first sight of it the Tuscan landscape wasn't finished. He'd painted over it and started it again several times in the interim, always running out of steam before reaching the end. Eventually the owners called it a day and covered the bare patches with mirrors and Italian film posters. Gillian liked the owners. The Tambinis were a wonderfully noisy, brash, easy-going family, always coming and going with various children, spouses, dogs and friends in tow. They treated Gillian with cheerful indifference and she ached to be caught up in their swirl of relationships. But Lenny always hustled her straight up the back stairs to his room.

One night she asked him, 'Why didn't we come up here in the first place? You could have had me on the mattress instead of the washing-room floor.'

Lenny shrugged. 'Couldn't wait that long,' he said.

She didn't often ask him questions nowadays. She was used to the evasion, the sudden huffs if she pestered him too much. At first Mrs Harris had offered some information. She said he came from 'a good family.'

'Rich, you mean?' asked Gillian with a hint of scorn.

'Not badly off. They'll see he doesn't waste away-lucky for some. But they won't touch him with a bargepole, other than sending the necessaries. As far as they're concerned Lenny has gone to the bad and that's that.'

'What do you mean, "the bad"?'

Mrs Harris eyed her carefully. 'A bit wild, our Lenny. A bit moody. I hope this is only a *passing* interest, girl. Not a reliable feller, our Lenny, if you're thinking that way.'

So Gillian stopped asking, and when Mrs Harris realised that her suspicions were justified, she stopped gossiping.

Over two years since they'd met, and all Gillian knew was that Lenny's real name was Leonard Hall; that his parents lived in Norfolk and sent him money; that he painted and plastered and pottered about. She didn't know his age, whether he was old enough to have served in the war (she didn't think so), whether he'd done or dodged his National Service (she guessed the latter). She snatched up any spare titbits of information with relish, but made it a point of honour never to beg. Apart from the Tambinis, he seemed to have no friends. But then by this time neither did Gillian.

She lay on his mattress, wearing his shirt to protect her skin from the scratchy blankets. She talked as he painted the walls in his room. He'd decided to paint a thunderstorm at sea-'to surround us while we cling to our bedship' – and he worked at it obsessively, day and night. Deep red skies appeared, and black swags of rain, while Gillian told him about the people at work, the characters who turned up off the streets, her plans to work with refugees in Europe or villagers in India; the possibility of applying for a course at the LSE. She broke off to fry eggs on his camp stove or to pour terrible coffee. When Lenny did speak, it was in an accusatory tone:

'Don't your parents *mind* you staying here?'

'They don't know. I've told you before, Lenny. I fob them off. I'm staying with one of the volunteers, or doing a double shift-whatever comes to mind.'

'But won't they find you out?'

'Not a chance.' Gillian balanced his plate on one of the lower rungs of his ladder, shielding it against paint splashes with her hand. 'If I wrote it all in gruesome detail and left my diary open at the right page on the breakfast table, they simply wouldn't read it. Prim's more likely to find me out than *they* are.'

This provoked one of his magnificent laughs, as she had known it would. 'Prim' was the pet name for her parents' housekeeper, who'd helped maintain their sealed world since Gillian was a child. For some reason Lenny found Prim hugely entertaining – her existence, her role, the fact that Gillian couldn't call her real name to mind.

They ate, and Gillian talked on until she finally talked herself to sleep, and in the early morning, as she rushed about getting herself ready for work, Lenny was still assaulting the walls.

'I wish you'd give yourself a rest now and then,' said Gillian as she left.

'If I were a Great Artist you wouldn't say that,' said Lenny. Then he grinned at her, wiping his brush. He was livid with energy. 'Anyway,' he said. 'I've picked up a little job in Bethnal Green this afternoon. Change is as good as a rest.'

Gillian believed him. Lenny could cope. He was indefatigable. He was invincible. To Gillian, this was the stuff of life and love.

And on her 20th birthday everything changed.

15

He'd arranged a party. When Gillian arrived she found Mr and Mrs Tambini, their eldest son and youngest daughter and the daughter's friend, seated on chairs from the coffee bar around Lenny's room. He'd propped the mattress against one wall and hung a sheet on it, painted with 'Happy Day, Gillian, One in a Million', with a different colour for each letter, and stars and flowers splotched into every available gap. In the centre of the room was one of the café tables, laid with Italian cake and biscuits, glasses and a bottle of wine. Lenny was hopping on hot coals. He led her in, gripping her arm painfully tight, and listed every item on the table and its individual ingredients.

'*Panatone*,' he said. 'Panatone for you, it's your birthday cake, it's delicious—' He paced between her and the spread, gesturing at the food with a conjuror's flair.

'Well, thank you, it looks . . .' Her voice sank under his frantic commentary.

'It's made with raisins and eggs and sugar and flour and we used them all, all the right ingredients, no cheating. Delicious. Italian birthday cake. For your birthday.'

Her appreciation must be lacking, somehow. She thought he must be pushing her for the right response. She cursed her parents for burdening her with these bound-up manners, wished she could fling her hands out and clasp them together in wonder at a Tambini cake.

'We've got wine,' he was saying, 'we've got to toast you, toast you on your birthday, you've got to drink some . . .' He bundled a glass into her hands. She had to juggle to keep it in her grasp. Mr Tambini was pouring wine. They all sang. They weren't troubled by Lenny's excited state and Gillian rebuked herself again for being so easily scared, just like her mother. Lenny was stabbing the cake, stacking it on to a plate, trying to shove it into her midriff.

'Wait a minute!' she forced herself to laugh. 'I'll drop the lot at this rate!'

She hadn't taken off her mac yet – a neatly buckled, sensible mac that her parents had given her that morning.

'Eat some. Try some. Panatone. Delicious. It's made with eggs, lots of eggs, and sugar and raisins . . .'

He spoke so rapidly but with such clarity that Gillian thought time itself had speeded up and left her lagging behind.

She was never sure, afterwards, how long the party lasted. Sometimes it seemed an eternity: Gillian perched awkwardly on a chair, still in her mac, trying to balance her plate on her lap while Lenny shovelled more and more food on to it. The high-pitched percussion of the Tambinis' chatter, broadening into laughter or stretched into chords of debate and dissent. She couldn't detach Lenny and his dervish dance from the mayhem around her and in her head; couldn't separate the cawing and rattling, the scales and grace-notes into words or meanings. Gillian sat in the eye of the storm for hours and hours. Or it may have been just a few minutes before Lenny swept everything off the table and threw them all out.

She watched it happen. She'd been watching him the whole time, hoping for a wink, a knowing glance, a clue to the joke he'd become. She saw him stand suddenly, momentarily still. She saw him breathing hard, focusing on his thoughts, withdrawing – an athlete on the blocks. Good, she thought: now he's coming back to me. She saw his arm stiffen, draw back and swing forward, saw him bend his knees for an accurate aim, saw an accumulating wave of plates, cake, biscuits, glasses, bottle, wine – building and tumbling against him, breaking at the table's edge. She saw the others spring to their feet and back, flinch from the shatter of glass, and she heard his voice, loud and steady over the shrieking and the shouts.

'Everybody go. Time to go.'

Mrs Tambini stooped towards the mess and he pulled her away.

'*Time to go.*'

They crowded out. Mr Tambini's hands were on Gillian's back and he was moving her on with low, urgent directions. Gillian was reminded of hurrying into the underground with her mother during an air raid. As they were pushing her down the stairs she heard the crunch of glass and china, followed by an almighty crash as Lenny kicked over the table.

They took her downstairs and sat her down. The Tambinis' son started up the coffee machine. Nobody called for help or rang the police. Gillian became aware of discomfort in her stomach and realised that she was still pressing her plate against the buckle of her mackintosh belt. In her other hand she was holding her glass up, clear of danger. She was a caricature of a party-goer. Mrs Tambini appeared with a hanky and wiped Gillian's face with efficient force. Gillian deduced that she must have been crying.

'Don't worry,' said Mrs Tambini, and she sounded genuinely cheerful. 'This is Lenny. This is how he is. Moody. This is the artist's way.'

But Lenny isn't an artist, thought Gillian, and admitted to herself the sour truth that his painting was as third-rate as he'd always claimed it to be. Somebody eased her party food away from her. Somebody gave her a coffee. People bustled about and left her alone, and presently the door scraped and jangled and they were open for business again. Gillian stayed in her corner while customers drifted in and out. The Vita Nuova had a juke box by this time, and every now and then music filled the spaces. There was no sound or movement from upstairs. During a quiet spell Mrs Tambini returned and took a seat next to Gillian.

'He had furniture when he moved in, you know,' she said, smiling. 'Gave it all away in one of his moods. Asked people in off the street to pick whatever they want.' She laughed at the recollection. 'And he broke up his bed with an axe and gave it as firewood!'

'All your things . . .' Gillian stopped, afraid of more tears.

'*His* things.' Mrs Tambini gave an extravagant shrug. 'He gives his things away and what is he? An idiot? Or maybe a saint?'

'But, today . . .'

'Oh, *those* things? Ah!' Mrs Tambini slapped away the idea. 'We have plenty more. Never mind.' She patted Gillian's hand. 'He'll be very sorry about your party. Very sorry about the glasses and the plates. He will hate himself. He'll think you hate him too. You'll forgive him and . . .' Her face lit up with comic anticipation. 'Ah! It will be very sweet to make friends again!'

Gillian stayed away for a week to punish him. She stayed away for another week to see whether he would approach her first. She told herself he was self-obsessed, melo-dramatic, petulant and puerile. She told herself he was dangerous and cruel. She told herself he was tired of her, that she'd driven him to distraction with her inane views and sheltered upbringing. She went back to the coffee bar to tell him he needn't worry: she would never impose herself on him again.

Mrs Tambini was wiping cups behind the counter. She called a greeting and added, as Gillian headed for the back stairs,

'Not yet, my sweetheart. The door is still locked.'

Gillian pretended not to hear. She climbed the stairs quietly. I should march up here singing, she thought, and give him every chance to blockade the door, or open it. But she didn't want to give him chances. She tapped at the door. She said his name. A shuffling inside the room stopped her breath. She waited, then rapped harder. There were scrambling sounds, like an animal taking cover. She gave up and went downstairs.

Mrs Tambini's eyebrows were saying 'I told you so'. Gillian leaned across the counter, needing to cast blame.

'Is he eating?' The accusation was clear. 'I mean, is he looking after himself? Should we call a doctor?'

'I leave a tray every morning, every evening.' Mrs Tambini was offended. 'Some food he takes, some he leaves. I suppose he eats what he takes. If not, it's too late for the doctor.'

The two women avoided each other's eyes, shaken by this unexpected frost. Mrs Tambini served an old man and followed his laboured progress to the window table. Then she murmured, more softly, 'This is the way Lenny is. Winds himself up, works like a lunatic day and night. Tires himself out. Hides away and gets better. When he's ready he'll unlock the door.'

'But how will I know?'

Gillian was staring at her fingers, spread out on the counter. She resented these pocket lectures about the man who'd been her lover for the past three years. She suspected Mrs Tambini of being in league with him, helping him dump the girlfriend just as he'd dumped the furniture.

'He'll be back,' said Mrs Tambini. 'In time. Back to his old self. He'll come and find you.'

But in the end Gillian had to go and find him. She took to visiting the Vita Nuova before her late shifts. She didn't try his door again, didn't even ask about him-just sat and drank her coffee and relied on the Tambinis to let her know when the right time arrived. Five weeks after the party, she drained her cup, stubbed out her cigarette and left the café. She was standing outside, tucking her cigarette packet into her bag, when she saw him sauntering along the other side of the road. It was June. The dust and haze of the day had settled. Every brick and paving stone and every passer-by glowed in the twilight. She couldn't be mistaken. He was wearing his overalls, strolling with his hands in his pockets. He crossed the road and she said,

'Hello.'

He looked up without surprise, without regret or pleasure, and said, 'Hello, Gillian.'

He entered the coffee bar and shut the door. He hadn't even slowed his pace.

'It's the way I am.'

'That's exactly what Mrs T said.'

'She's right. It's me. I can't help it.'

'Oh, of *course* you can help it. *Everyone* can help it.'

They were standing in the middle of his room. She hadn't intended to pursue him. She was going to be late for her shift.

His room was completely bare. No stove, no mattress. The floor was clean and the walls stark white. All trace of the thunderstorm had gone. Lenny tried a smile.

'That's your mother talking,' he said.

Her jaw was set. She was bloodless and taut with anger. For an hour she had nursed her coffee downstairs; for an hour the Tambinis had given nothing away. For an hour Lenny had walked the streets, and there'd been no sign that he was ready.

He looked terrible. Shadows dragged at his eyes and cheeks. She faced him in the bleached room and refused to answer. Eventually he said,

'I understand why you despise me.'

'*No.*' She'd squeezed her hands into hard, bony fists. 'That won't do. Too easy.'

He reached forward and enclosed one of her locked hands with both of his. He said, 'I'm sorry. It'll be all right. I promise.'

16

Gillian went alone to see *After Silence*. Marian blazed. Once again, Gillian stayed in her place during the interval. People tripped over her feet and tutted, but Gillian was lost to them, immersed in a vision of Marian's fierce eyes, her top-heavy, crimson mouth; Marian's legs, her hips and arms and neck and their fluid dance; Marian's angrily tossed head and the ripples of reflected light writhing along her hair. The house lights were fully up now and threatened to weaken the image. Gillian leaned forward and caged her face in her hands. She pressed her fingers into the tops of her eyelids so that blue veins split the darkness. Marian's white cleavage clamped in her black dress. Marian's wide, white smile and wild, black mane. A charge of excitement and distress filled Gillian with thoughts of Lenny. She tried to block him out but it wasn't possible. He and Marian were two merging demon spirits, making her throat ache with misery and her hands tremble with desire.

A male voice, so gentle that it seemed to emerge from her mind, asked whether she was all right. Gradually Gillian returned to herself. She noticed the pain behind her eyes and eased the pressure of her fingers. Her nose was running; she gave a long, surreptitious sniff before lowering her hands. In this suddenly small auditorium, among suddenly close conversations, Gillian was seized with terror. Had she spoken aloud, moaned, sobbed? She had no idea at all.

'I beg your pardon. I thought you might be feeling faint.'

He was sitting in the row behind her. She turned and tried to answer but had to interrupt herself with another sniff. She fished for her bag but he was already offering a hanky: a vast, plain, man's hanky which obscured her whole face. It had a clean scent of fresh cotton. The man smiled at her. Like the handkerchief, he was large and plain and comforting. Gillian thought she must look a sight. Her hair was unfashionably pinned up; loops and scribbles were struggling free. She wasn't sure what to do with the hanky. She said, 'I'll wash it and send it back . . .'

But he raised a dismissive hand and said, 'Absolutely not. Please, keep it.'

He was wearing a dull suit and had oiled-back hair. He was ageless. He must always have looked this way, like a man who had set his life in order, a man who knew who he was.

That was Gillian's first meeting with Robert. He soothed her with polite small talk. He asked her opinion of the play, praised my mother's performance, asked Gillian whether she often went to the theatre. When she said no, it was too expensive, he nodded again. Not for me, though, his smile seemed to imply. Leave the expense to me. But Robert wasn't a man to push his luck. He was cautious. He waited until the end of the play, until they were queueing for the exit, before asking casually where she worked. He had a coat over his arm and was carrying a briefcase. He'd come straight from the office. As the queue loosened into the foyer he waved and said, 'Maybe we'll bump into each other at Miss Westwood's next triumph!'

And that was that: another sign for Gillian to follow.

17

Their first date was to see my mother in *Daisy Chain*. That's what Gill and Robert used to say. The first milestone in their romance. It wasn't quite true: just part of the mythology of marriage, of any relationship that lasts long enough to relate its own history. He came to find her at the reception centre with an offer of good seats and dinner. She declined the dinner but couldn't resist seeing Marian Westwood again. And as it turned out they did go on for a late meal. Robert was a patient listener and Gillian needed to talk. She didn't need a new lover; she had Lenny.

The touching prelude to their date was true enough-Robert did, indeed, attend two matinées and an evening performance of *Daisy Chain* in the hope of seeing her there, before plucking up the courage to go to her place of work. Even then he made sure the tickets were refundable. Robert was a man who hedged his bets.

Sitting in a restaurant, eating a bland meal, talking to her bland companion, Gillian tried not to enjoy herself. This was a situation that her parents would recognise and probably condone. This was a situation familiar enough to anyone, any normal, civilised passer-by. Robert listened and responded with all the appropriate murmurs and shadings of expression. He didn't burst into song. He didn't stare at her hair or her collarbone or into the dark centre of her eyes. She knew the china would be intact and the knives and forks neatly coupled in their place at the end of the evening. Gillian answered his mild questions about her work. She told him her plans to apply for the LSE's new applied social studies course. She chattered about the play, about Marian Westwood's charisma, and her unexpected gift for light comedy. Gillian was eating a more substantial meal than she'd had in several days. The wine expanded her veins and massaged her muscles. She told him of the friend who was brought to mind every time she watched Marian Westwood on the stage. She was drawling slightly. She told him how unpredictable this friend could be, how puzzling; she told him her friend made her nervous, these days, and tears quivered in her eyes and voice.

Robert nodded, hummed, and his forehead crinkled in sympathy or surprise. He paid the bill. He helped her on with her coat. He escorted her back to her parents' house. At the front gate he kissed her on the cheek and shook her hand.

When Gillian woke the next morning with a pounding head, and let her mind adjust itself to the duties and tasks ahead, she didn't think about Robert. She gave a passing, automatic thought to the blighted lives that would file past her table at the reception centre that day. Then she thought of the Vita Nuova, of Mrs Tambini's flamboyant words and secretive smiles; she thought of the blanket on the bare floor that now served as the bed. She thought of the bread and jam Lenny would bring her, singing, from the café kitchen. She thought of the questions she'd be half afraid to ask- about the job he'd held down for two months for a builders' firm, and whether he'd offended the foreman yet, or succumbed to boredom and absconded from the site. She prepared herself for all this, for a day of the desperate and a night of Lenny, with clenched body and sinking heart.

18

Natalie has hinted about coming to stay for a long weekend. Out of the question. Where would I put her? What would we do? But Gill seems to think it's a fine idea. It'll do me good, apparently. I mustn't isolate myself from my friends. Even Gareth reckons it's OK.

'Where will she sleep?' I say, to test him. 'I'll have to put her in your room and you'll have to stay at Gill's.'

'No way,' he says. '*She* can go to Gill's.'

We start arguing. Then he says, reasonably, 'You don't want your friend in *my room*, do you?'

No, I don't. He's right. Natalie is far too crisp and fragrant to inhale male teenage air. Billeting her at Gill's isn't a bad solution: comfort and cleanliness and only enough mess to put her at her ease and, if I can wangle it, at least a couple of well-cooked meals. It begins to seem feasible, and I begin to look forward to seeing her.

It's also an incentive to get on with my work, and to get on with the garden. This morning the sun came out and for the first time in weeks there was no rain, and only a moderately high wind. It seems barely credible that a shift in the weather front could have such a profound effect on my general outlook. But when I step out to survey the stubbled lawns and lean against the wall in my pyjamas and Bobby's ample dressing-gown (losing some of its Bobby-smell every day), with my hair sticking out to all points of the compass, hanging on to my mug of tea to hold me upright-I can honestly say I'm in a more positive frame of mind than I have been since . . . Well, let's be exact: since opening the doors on the first day of trading at The Great Escape.

This back garden is 75 feet long. When the hospital built these estate cottages in the 1930s it economised by making the buildings as small and cramped as practicable and leaving the rest of each plot as garden. Maybe the nurses and cleaners and security staff and ward staff were expected to spend their enforced leisure hours much as the patients did, growing vegetables. Some of the gardens have been covered in concrete or paving; next-door has erected some kind of small pavilion; one or two of them are dizzy with flowers, twisting paths, bubbling fountains, nooks and dells, stone squirrels and miniature windmills. The previous occupants of our place used their patch to bury plastic bags, fag packets and ash from the fire. Their dog used it to bury alarmingly large bones. All these treasures have been unearthed by heavy rain in the muddy area next to the kitchen door. But this morning I slurp my tea and plan my next task, and it doesn't look that bad.

Gareth comes shambling out and stands a yard away, far enough back to avoid my eyeline. A couple of white butterflies hesitate over the goosegrass. I say, 'Oh, look! It must be spring!'

A snuffling from behind me may be laughter. I decide it's affectionate.

19

I seem to have lost the knack of falling asleep. My mind is baked hard. It refuses to let my thoughts drift or my body rest. Gareth turns in his bed next door; a neighbour's cat grumbles outside, and my mind calls itself to attention. I reason with it, distract it, try and fool it. My mind has split away from my self and become my enemy.

It's odd that on these nights I have an instinctive urge to call for my mother. I was always a light sleeper, a grizzler, but this was one fault that my mother endured with patience. The door would open briefly to a gust of strangers' conversation, my father's laughter skipping over it, and my mother would be there, bright with adrenalin, noting my tears with bemusement. She'd shut the door, shut out the others and swish across the room to my side; sometimes, on the best nights, she'd kick off her shoes and climb in beside me and gather my clamminess to her with cool hands. I'd burrow my snotty face against the sweetness of face powder and perfume, touched with a thrill of alcohol; I'd snuggle against the curves under her clothes. There she'd be, in her cocktail dress and pearl necklace, relating the gossip as if I were her equal, her friend: telling me who'd said what, who was chasing whom, listing the new compliments paid to her, asking me-*me*-how I thought she should wear her hair to the next party. She seemed to enjoy my company on those nights. She made consciousness a treat, an adventure. She made my distress irrelevant. I knew she would stay there, crumpling her dress, until I didn't need her any more.

I sometimes think that's really what it's all about – the fixation with sex and attraction, the endless anxieties of love and intercourse that weave their way around every structure of life. I sometimes think it's all about having a call to answer your own. When you come into your house and call hello; when you call for comfort at night. That answer is all we're after. On nights like this Bobby's absence swells and spreads, obliterating every presence, sweeping it all over the edges of existence. Every part of my mind reaches out for a touch, seeks a response, and there's nothing there. Is this what it's like to be released from gravity and to float into space, like those poor sods in the film? Is this what it's like to die?

I watch videos, and I listen to chapters of Gill's life. She talks about Lenny, about Robert, and I'm on tenterhooks, waiting for the moment when Bobby arrives. It's as if her account of his birth, his boyhood, his wanderings, will draw him closer to the present day; as if her account of the past and our stalled life will eventually meet, and at the appropriate point in her tale there'll be a knock at the door, and there he'll be. The only trouble is, as Gill's story carries her forward, closes the gap between then and now, she grows more reluctant to tell it. Maybe recalling her first lover's behaviour has upset her more than she anticipated. She keeps making excuses. There isn't anything else to tell, she says. Just the tedious minutiae of an unremarkable life. Why don't I dredge up more anecdotes about my mother? Now *there* was a remarkable woman.

And then, after putting me off for so long, she suddenly resumed her story. I wasn't even prompting her, this time. We'd been discussing Gareth's school, and how well he's settled in, and how he's knuckled down to his work – as far as we can tell – despite everything. And I felt a quick, reflex kick of anger in my stomach and I said, 'All this – changing schools, mocks, A-levels looming, and he just takes it in his stride. And his father can't even be bothered to ring and wish him luck.'

Gill was perched on the arm of her chair, waiting for the oven timer to pierce the air. She kneaded her lower lip between her finger and thumb, folding and turning, folding and turning, sending a spurt of wrinkles across her chin. Then she placed one hand neatly over the other, palm upwards, on her thigh and regarded the creases and lines and pouches of flesh cupped by her fingers. She said, 'Shall I tell you about when I married Robert?'

'Yes,' I said, cautiously, afraid that she'd change her mind.

The timer let out a staccato shriek and she leapt off her perch. Damn. But she was back almost immediately.

'I've turned it down,' she said. 'It can wait a while.' She sat on the chair seat this time, took a deep breath and tugged her T-shirt straight, as if she was about to deliver a speech. She said, 'I need to go back a bit further, though. Let's see . . .' She looked at the ceiling, calculating, 'back to spring, 1959.'

20

On a spring evening in 1959 Gillian Parker sat with her lover on the windowsill of an upstairs room, looking down over a Soho street. They were held in a temporary silence; her questions had run out. Lenny leaned against the windowpane and rubbed a circle in the murk.

'Gillian, oh Gillian . . .' he sang, softly, then said: 'I'm not a problem for you to solve.'

Gillian watched as his circle of clear glass widened.

'I know that,' she said. But she was thinking: you're wrong. A problem is exactly what you are.

Gillian often lied to Lenny these days. When he promised they would be all right she agreed with him. When he lost his jobs she claimed he'd get another, and assured him he'd hold it down. She didn't lie about Robert Gilbard, though. There didn't seem much point. He was just a man who took her out once a week and listened. Lenny said he was glad she had a real friend to turn to. He said, 'Your parents will be glad too.'

He was right. To Gillian's parents, she and Robert Gilbard were as good as engaged.

Gillian was now a fully trained social worker. She'd moved out of her parents' house and was sharing a flat with a telephonist in Clapham. Her life had changed. But still there was Lenny. Oh, yes: Lenny was a problem. During the past four years, Gillian had discovered just how much of a problem he was. She'd discovered that his apparent non-chalance disguised a limitless introspection. She'd discovered that everyone who cared about him was drawn into the game: the constant second-guessing of what might trigger a mood. Every sentence was a calculation. Every tranquil day was a step towards the next day of frenzy.

He lost the building site job. He turned up at midnight, put the concrete mixer to work and started building a wall that wasn't on the plan. A policeman turned up to investigate the noise, listened to his gibbered explanation and carted him off to the station to 'sober up'. Lenny called the desk sergeant a moron and was put in a cell for the night. He had some stubs of coloured chalk in his overall pocket and passed the time illustrating two walls with progressively more obscene drawings of police officers in nothing but their helmets.

Gillian found him a temporary job painting the walls of a health centre. He grew bored of beige and cream, and added a vast, pink nude with luminous orange nipples and a gash of fiery labia.

A stint with the bin men ended when he started upending the bins in the street and kicking through the rubbish, pocketing the occasional soggy piece of packaging or torn letter 'for future reference'.

'Why did you have to do that?' asked Gillian, leading him away from the council offices after his dismissal.

'Why do people throw things away?' he asked, with real interest.

'*You* should know that, of all people,' muttered Gillian, and he performed a happy buck-and-wing, shrieking: 'That's right! You're absolutely right! – Gillian, oh Gillian, My perfect logician . . .'

'Shut up,' said Gillian. Passers-by were altering their pace and staring. She seized his wrist and tugged him after her like a child. 'Stop that asinine singing,' she said. 'It doesn't even rhyme.'

His mood swings grew more frequent. The Tambinis were cool with Gillian: they seemed to think her presence made him worse. Sometimes Lenny thought so too:

'Always keeping watch on me. Always waiting for the next slip-up. You make me anxious, and that sets me off.'

More often he castigated himself and shut himself in his room with his guilt for several days. Gillian had managed to obtain a copy of his key and took him food and bedding, ignoring Mrs Tambini's rolled eyes and clicking tongue as she hurried through the café with her boxloads of provisions. Mrs Tambini thought it best to let him be. 'He's sorry for himself' she said, once. 'He'll have his sulk and then – all better.'

As Lenny rolled away from her again, cocooned in his blankets and self-pity, Gillian fought to keep her temper. She didn't always succeed.

'If you're mortified about the way you behave, well, so you should be,' she snapped. 'If you feel so bad about it, *don't bloody do it.*'

Some nights she shook him and told him to pull himself together. Some nights she slept sitting up against the wall, because he wouldn't let her hold him. And every time she decided she couldn't bear it any more, Lenny broke free of his chrysalis and came back to her, singing, joking, swearing it would be all right.

She complained about him to Robert during the worst periods.

'He's worse than some of my clients,' she said. 'Some days it's a relief to go to work and deal with normal problems.'

Robert never asked her to explain the relationship with Lenny. Gillian assumed, by this time, that he understood. Every so often a question would niggle at the back of her mind: should I tell him, clearly and explicitly, that he can expect nothing more from me than this? But whenever she tried, tentatively, to introduce the subject, Robert dismissed it.

'Let's muddle on for the time being' was his stock reply. And Gillian was grateful for it. She wasn't sure that she could manage without Robert any more.

Robert had been to visit her parents. She knew they were reassured by him, that they hoped he would entice her away from her dangerous occupation, and she was on her guard against hints and enquiries. In fact they didn't press her on the question of marriage. They seemed to trust Robert to act when the time was right. Gillian trusted him not to. Once, during one of Lenny's bad weeks, she leaned against Robert to sob and let him support her with his arm.

'I don't know why I go back,' she wailed. 'Why don't I just leave him there and walk away?'

'Well,' said Robert, in his matter-of-fact way, 'I suppose it must be because you love him.'

She wasn't convinced that she did love Lenny on that spring evening in 1959.

'I know you're not a problem,' she told him. 'I'm not trying to solve you. Just to understand.'

His finger slid from the circle on the glass and left a long trail jabbing into the corner of the windowframe.

'You should take a leaf out of your parents' book,' he muttered. 'Respect a man's privacy. Don't try and read his mind.'

'I'm not, Lenny, I'm . . .'

'Trying to understand, yes, so you said.' He looked up and she failed to answer him, defeated by his contempt. 'You're trying to understand my madness.'

'Not *madness* . . .'

'Oh, yes. That's what it is. You want to sneak into my head and look around, cast judgement, make decisions . . .'

Gillian hoisted herself off the sill angrily.

'Well, if you don't want to be judged, stopped buggering life up for everyone else,' she said. 'And if you *do* think you're mad, there are . . . treatments.'

She turned, reluctantly, to see him grin.

'Mmm, I know all about *them*,' he said, then shrieked and stiffened in a parody of electric shock before lungeing, claws extended, eyes bulging. They grappled; she couldn't help laughing as he clamped his arms around her.

'What a farce,' he said through her hair, mouth against her ear. 'What a great big bloody sham.'

'What's a sham?'

They were swaying with each other, rocking from foot to foot.

'Oh, you know. Everyone scrabbling around, bellyaching about social welfare and the common good. And here we are, two run-of-the-mill people, and we can't even agree on a normal state of mind.'

He steered her back to the window. The sky was deepening, sinking into its most intense blue before darkness. Lenny said,

'Trying to understand each other is a waste of time. We're not rational enough, Gillian. We see what we see. The sun sets, the stars shift in the sky – how many of us really, *really* believe, with our hearts and souls, that's not the case? How many of us really believe this is just a thin layer of gas and air, and we're a crust on the surface of a spinning ball of muck in a cold, black space? Jesus! Never mind all that. How many of us *really* believe that everyone we ever set eyes on will die?'

Gillian took steady breaths, hoping to guide his words at a manageable pace. But he was fine this evening. He was himself.

She taunted him gently: 'I suppose *you* know who we are and where we're going then?'

'Of course. I know lots of things. I know despair isn't a disease, to be cured by . . . *treatments*.' He squeezed her until she yelped. 'I know we're none of us on firm ground. *I* can see the planet spinning. Can you ever understand that? I see the earth spinning, and I spin with it.'

He turned them about in a clumsy circle, around and around again. He was teasing her, playing his game. He was fine. But Gillian decided, nevertheless, not to tell him quite yet that she might be pregnant.

21

Timing is everything, my mother used to say. If Gillian had told Lenny that night, or the following night, or within the next 10 days, it would all have been different. A whole fistful of little lives, including mine, would have taken another course. Lenny was OK. He'd gone several months without a 'mood', apart from the odd fit of mischief. He was cheerful and busy; he had work; he'd allowed Gillian to furnish his room with second-hand chairs and a fold-up table. She let herself consider the possibility that he was mellowing. Maybe this was how he would be from now on: slightly eccentric, but under control. After all, just because things had happened before didn't mean they would happen again.

She was sketching a future – a future in which her child grew up, a future set in a small and shabby flat full of games and songs and oddities. A future in which Gillian provided the income, the security, the rules, and Lenny provided the fun. She would have to find a delicate way of explaining matters to her parents, but they would be the best kind of grandparents – reliable, long-suffering, devoted. She would have to persuade Lenny to marry her: that would soften the blow. One night, two nights, 10 days went by and this future took shape, seemed workable. She rehearsed ways of breaking the news. On the morning of the 11th day Lenny got into his old Ford Saloon and drove it at high speed all night until it somersaulted into a cornfield.

She sat by his hospital bed and told him she was going to marry Robert Gilbard. She told Lenny before telling Robert, but there was no doubt in her mind. One future had hurtled out of that car along with Lenny, cut clean across like the bone in his leg. Gillian promptly arranged another.

A nurse had taken Gillian aside when she arrived on the ward.

'Please ask Mr Hall,' she said 'not to try and stand on his bed.' He'd been hauling himself upright, hanging on to the metal frame above him and balancing on one foot while his bound leg hovered on its pulley.

'It's not a good idea,' said the nurse. 'The friction might break his support cord. And if Matron finds out we'll all be for it.'

Lenny, propped against the pillow with his leg suspended in traction, asked Gillian for a cigarette. His hands were shaking. Gillian didn't want to tell him her news while he was in this state, but she had no choice. She wasn't planning to come back.

'Good idea,' he said. '*Great* idea. Marry Robert Gilbard. Make your parents happy.'

He rattled off the words so fast, she couldn't tell whether he was being sarcastic.

She said, 'You need someone to keep an eye on you. In case you do anything stupid.'

Lenny grinned. 'Me? Stupid? Don't you worry. The Tambinis will keep me on the straight and narrow.'

A shock of jealousy went through her. They'd won him back, after all.

'Why did you go off like that?' she asked. She might as well ask, one last time.

Lenny shrugged. He was wriggling around, searching the bed with his hands. He said, 'I was stifling in that room. I needed to get out and go somewhere. I needed to *move*. Gillian, where are my cigarettes?'

She hadn't told him she was pregnant. She sat there while he fumbled and stuttered, and the clock above the ward entrance ticked away her visiting time. She sat and waited for the next moment, the next prompt. Maybe he'd guess. Maybe she wasn't pregnant after all. The bell rang. Along the ward people kissed and whispered, packed and waved; the door squeaked and thudded as each visitor passed back into real life.

'I'll say goodbye, then.'

'Goodbye,' said Lenny. 'Good luck. I'll come and make a speech at your wedding if you like.'

She thought: he doesn't believe me. She put her hand to his head and twined his hair through her fingers, and said: 'Promise me you'll eat Mrs Tambini's food.'

He nodded, distracted. At the end of the bed she stopped, remembering something: 'Lenny, don't try and stand up in bed. The nurse doesn't like it, and you might hurt yourself again.'

Then she left without turning back. As the door banged behind her she said to herself: I'll never see him again. But it was only a phrase, a touch of drama, and she was already preoccupied with other plans.

JUNE

1

I've mapped out Natalie's visit with military care. After picking her up from Acreston station on Friday morning I take her shopping. She insists on buying me lunch. We find a decent enough pizza place and she flirts outrageously with the waiter.

'What?' she says, making innocent eyes at me as the boy sashays away with the peppermill.

'He must be about Gareth's age,' I hiss.

'So?' says Natalie through a mouthful of Four Seasons. 'I bet Gareth enjoys the odd flash of chemistry outside the school lab once in a while.' She swallows and fingers a dollop of cheese into her mouth. 'Anyway, you're too hung up about age altogether.'

'It's embarrassing. It makes us look so . . . desperate. He's only humouring us, you know.'

Natalie shrugs. 'Well, that's fine,' she says, loudly. 'We do it nostalgically, he does it professionally, and everyone's happy.'

Her hair is rich brown, expensively and immaculately coloured, with a few strands of grey to add authenticity. As she witters on about the office scandals and management cock-ups, her slim shoulders move under a silky blouse. Her make-up is soft and flattering; her skin is perfect. No wonder she flirts with teenagers. I smooth back my wayward, shadeless hair and think for the first time about the clothes I'm wearing. Baggy sweater. Clean jeans. An anorak, for God's sake. I thought it might rain.

Late in the afternoon I drive us back to Emmett Park. Natalie gazes through the passenger window as the road bends regretfully away from town and wanders further into the treeless plain. After a while she asks, 'How can you tell your way without any landmarks?'

I gesture vaguely to my right, where a trio of power-station stacks squat on the horizon. Natalie starts to laugh.

'I did warn you . . .' I say, and she interrupts: 'No, no – I'm looking forward to it! A weekend with Gauleiter Gill on the margins of the loonie bin-what could be more relaxing?' Then she pats my thigh reassuringly. 'I'm here to see *you*, Jayne, and the rest is incidental. And to take you home with me, if I've got anything to do with it . . .'

I'm surprised to find myself resenting her condescension; she becomes an irritant, an irrelevance, as we drive on into the great, still sky.

Natalie and Gill shake hands in the middle of Gill's sitting room and challenge each other with their broad, no-nonsense smiles.

'How long have you lived here?' Natalie is saying. Her hand glides towards the front window. 'It's a hell of a view.'

Gill beams. 'Better from the back. Come into the kitchen and have a look while I put the kettle on.' Gill marches out and Natalie flashes me a look before following. I hear her in the kitchen saying, 'Look at that. Nothing, as far as the eye can see. Remarkable.' She's using the snipped accent generally reserved for recalcitrant authors. Roll on Monday.

When I call to collect Natalie on Saturday morning she and Gill are drinking coffee and Gill is having her rant over the newspapers. Natalie murmurs assent and looks amused. I know she's waiting for an opportunity to take the piss, and I don't want to get into all that. So as soon as we leave Gill's I start waffling about my plans for the day.

I drive her to Berriford and we wander around. I hear myself picking out highlights like a travel guide: the hand-some Victorian town hall. The only bookshop, where they will order copies for you or do a booksearch on the internet. I take her for another coffee at a new place that's just opened, with bare floorboards, square leather sofas and angular mugs. Natalie manages not to pass comment on the sullen waitresses and lukewarm coffee with UHT milk. She even says Berriford 'isn't so bad'. She calls it a 'cute little town' and I hurry off to pay the bill, hoping the other customers didn't hear.

I wonder what else I can show her.

'They seem to be putting in the effort, anyway,' says Natalie, nodding at the pedestrianised centre, where shiny cobbles have recently been laid. Cafés and cobbles – a desperate cover-up. Berriford is worn out with facelifts, and still the decay continues. After our coffee-break we trail through reconstituted alleys full of empty shops. Natalie wants to buy a gift for her sister, so we look round the Old Ironmongery, an olde-worlde knick-knackery store. While she inspects the handmade candles and soapstone cats I read a leaflet about the shop's 'heritage'. Apparently, since its ironmongery days, it's been a tearoom, a clearing house, a florist's shop and a 'drop-in centre' for crackheads and tramps; now it proudly displays an old mangle and a firescreen, salvaged from the original stock. There's nobody else in here. When we leave empty-handed the shopkeeper glowers from behind her *Home and Lifestyle* magazine.

We peer into windows as we walk. Nobody in the already faded tapas bar; nobody in the tile centre. Nobody reading the haikus carved into paving slabs in the high street. Nobody sitting on the sustainable wood benches engraved with symbols of the town's economic past (a cow, a train, a cogwheel). Nobody looking at the public art – *Mother and Child Reunion* – by local artist Amanda Stott, in the old wreckers' yard. Residents skirt their relaid streets and avoid the refurbished gift shops and stick to the Mr Pastry bakery and caff, where they can smoke, where old men can sit and chew their dentures at the plastic tables, where the waitress calls them darling and ignores the spilt pools of cold tea. The busiest place is the indoor mall, where shoppers shoulder through Peacocks and the factory-price shoeshop and the Co-op, and the cracked new stained-glass ceiling rings with children's screams and parents' rebukes, and the floor rattles with old Coke tins and ciggie packets.

I lead Natalie through the town square; the old department store, Beech and Maystick, is boarded up.

'That had quite a good café' I say, by way of compensation. 'They're knocking it down to extend the Safeways car park.'

'Oh, there's a Safeways?' says Natalie, brightening. 'Well, that's something.'

She smirks at me and I laugh despite myself. I know that's one of the places where Gareth and his friends spend incomprehensible hours straddling a low wall, pulling each other around and waiting for adolescence to pass.

'It's a shame,' I say. 'Beech and Maystick was a real museum piece. You know, one of those stores where you have to be drawing a pension to go in. Carpets and wooden counters, you know the sort of thing.' I remember the creak of the floor as customers padded between stands quivering with useless glass ornaments and paperweights.

'An Edwardian emporium,' says Natalie. 'Ladies' separates upstairs.' I warm towards her again. She says, 'What about the local museum? There's *always* a local museum.' So we shuffle through a room on the ground floor of the town hall, where there's a grimy dummy huddled at a cotton loom, a letter from Dickens to the local inn-keeper, a piece of Roman pottery and a plaque saved from the demolished home of Elijah Trewett, antiquary, 1778-1850.

Then I summon my courage and say, 'Come on. I'll show you the hospital grounds.'

It starts to spit with rain as we're walking up the hospital drive. Natalie's face changes as we pass the ivy-league accommodation blocks and turn left. She's seen the perimeter fence and the upper windows of the villas.

'Are they in there?' she whispers.

'Yes, but they can't hear us, Natalie.'

She stands still for a moment, appalled, then grasps my elbow and turns me round.

'It's awful,' she mutters. 'I can feel them looking at me.'

As she's hurrying me back down the drive I turn my head to check.

'There's no one there,' I assure her. 'They're probably eating lunch, or seeing visitors . . .'

But she's right: those windows are never empty, even when no patients are in the rooms. There is always a pair of watching eyes, monitoring our progress beyond the wall. Everyone sees them. Everyone. The difference is, I suddenly realise, that Natalie sees them as a threat; whereas I search for the movement, the shadow across the glass, with a kind of yearning.

We turn off the main drive and there, ahead of us, are Gill and the young man in the suit. They're laughing a conspiratorial, playground laugh; Gill is clutching his arm and covering her mouth with the other hand. She spots us and waves.

'Don't listen to us,' she bellows as we approach. 'We're being very naughty.'

I've never seen Gill being coquettish: it's quite disconcerting. From the corner of my eye I see Natalie's back lengthen and her shoulders straighten, and I know she's fixed her sights on the Suit. He acknowledges her with an interested sideways nod, and Gill makes the introductions. His name is Patrick and she describes him airily as a colleague, quickly adding,

'Former colleague, I mean, since I'm defunct now. Pat's still wet behind the ears – we only just overlapped, didn't we?' And she taps him playfully on the back. I can't imagine Gill flirting like this with Lenny, or with Robert. Then it occurs to me that she did behave this way, sometimes, with her son. Mothering evidently brings out the lighter side of

Gill. She chats away, even puts a friendly arm about Natalie's waist, and now she's inviting us all – including the Suit – to dinner. Tonight.

'I'll make something hearty and hot' she promises, and to my amazement Patrick the Suit jumps at the idea. Natalie rears and her expensive hairdo shimmies. Well, good, I think: she might be glad she came after all.

2

That evening, Natalie comes over to advise me as I get ready. She's wearing a sage-green dress that shows off the lines of her hips and breasts. She leans on my bed and crosses her legs. 'Gill's cooking up a storm,' she says, languidly stroking her thigh. 'I thought I'd better leave her to it. She's OK, actually, isn't she, Gill? I mean . . .'

She means it's me who's the wimp, not Gill who's the bully. I grope at buttons and Natalie says, 'Why don't you wear that nice orangey skirt? You know, the one that's cut on the bias?'

'I can't get into it any more.'

'Don't be ridiculous. Try it on,' she commands, and I do. And it fits, and it looks presentable.

'You see? You're just too down on yourself, Jayne. You could be a very sexy woman if you let yourself.'

'I'm too old to be—'

'Phah!' She launches herself off the bed and grabs my shoulders. 'If you stand there scowling into the mirror, of course . . .' pulling me away. 'We're *all* too old, if we look too closely. The trick is not to dwell. You'll only see things nobody else has noticed yet. Come on – defy the tyranny of reflection. Let me put your lippy on.'

I never wear lippy and I haven't got any. Natalie produces a stick from her bag. I submit to her attentions, despite knowing that by the end of the evening the colour will have leaked out in sad rivulets. When we finally troop downstairs in all our glory, Gareth is parked in front of the telly with his homework on his lap, watching some man in a cravat pricing antiques. There's a close-up of the man's hand caressing a hideous gilt box warty with jewels and cherubim and other baroque growth. A caption runs across the bottom of the screen like ticker-tape: 'current demand high . . . £2,500 at auction . . .'

'What do you think?' says Natalie. 'Couple of foxy ladies or what?'

I see Gareth note my make-up and my pathetic, ridged mouth, and I wait for some crack about over-priced antiques. Natalie doesn't give him a chance.

'Don't wait up for your mother' she says, breezily. 'Once she gets cracking into that wine . . .'

'Yeah, I know, no stopping her,' agrees Gareth, to my astonishment and delight.

Now Natalie will think we have a teasing, pally relationship. I take my cue, and tell Gareth not to trash the place while I'm gone. We exchange a glance of grateful complicity before I shut the door.

Patrick is there when we arrive, draped across one end of the sofa. He's wearing a sky-blue shirt and grey jacket and trousers – a suit without the tie. He stands up as we come in, and excuses himself before shedding the jacket. Natalie settles herself next to him and twinkles.

He compliments her dress, and she tells him he's looking very smart.

'In fact,' she adds 'I've never seen a social worker so smartly dressed!'

'Actually,' he says suavely, 'I'm a psychiatrist.'

Natalie lights up as if she's won the jackpot. I cringe into an armchair.

'Pat's the dandy of the team,' says Gill, emerging from the kitchen with a tray of wine and tapas. Pat moves forward to help; she fends him off with a flick of her head. 'Such a gentleman. And he calls his patients Mister too.'

'My parents always told me to show respect,' says Pat. Natalie stares.

'Do you respect the patients, then?' she asks.

'Some of them,' Pat answers, simply.

'I don't think *I* could respect someone who'd done unspeakable things to someone else . . .' Natalie looks around for support.

'Some of them,' says Pat, 'are battling the kind of demons

you and I will never know.' He grins at her discomfiture. 'Then again, some of them are right royal pains in the arse.'

Right royal. He talks and behaves like a fugitive from some older generation. Bobby would like him, I think.

Natalie's making a little speech about the work he does, how she could never do it, how grim it must all be. Gill perches on the arm of my chair. She reaches for an olive and pops it into my mouth. The uncharacteristically intimate gesture takes me aback.

'Oh, I don't know,' she's saying, 'every job has its upside.'

'Well, I could see that from the mass hysteria this afternoon,' says Natalie, on surer ground, now. 'What were you two giggling about?'

After a bit of coyness and mutterings about confidentiality, they confess that they were having a laugh about one of the patients.

'A nice guy, very gentle,' says Gill. 'Tied an iron to his dick.'

She enjoys the effect on Natalie, who splutters over her wine. Pat ministers to her, laying a tentative hand on her back.

'He reckoned it was a DIY extension job.'

'It's not funny,' insists Pat, but they're both chuckling again.

'Must be a riot,' says Natalie, 'your office chat.'

We eat well, of course, and we drink too much. As the evening progresses Gill and Pat try to outdo each other with gruesome accounts of anonymous clients, past and present. Some of the stories are terrible. With each new misery we laugh more helplessly. Every so often, like a pause in conversation, I feel the presence of the patients behind the wall; I feel them listening to this betrayal. But I suppress it easily enough as Natalie howls with protest, 'This is awful! What kind of bastards run this place anyway?' and the laughter starts another round. I'm befuddled with alcohol, exhilarated with the breaking of taboos, benevolently marking the crackle of attraction between Natalie and Pat.

At the end of the evening we call loud farewells to Gill and Natalie, and Pat walks me back to my gate.

'You're not driving?' I say, and blush furiously, aware that it might sound like an invitation to stay. He shakes his head.

'Dossing down with a friend,' he says, 'at the accommodation block.' Then, as he's waving and walking backwards, 'A male friend, you understand.'

In case Natalie wants to know, I tell myself, and snort with laughter, though I don't know why.

3

Natalie turns up mid-morning on her last day here, attractively jaded. I don't mention Patrick's parting shot. Gill has told her about a nice pub about 10 miles from here, and Natalie announces that a hair of the dog and a big unhealthy lunch will do us the world of good.

Before we leave I show her the garden and start telling her my plans for it. She looks at it with dull eyes, which I assume to be due to her hangover until she shakes her head with finality.

'You mustn't do this,' she says. I stare. 'Planning your plot, arranging your territory, putting down roots – you *mustn't*.'

'Gill thinks a project will do me good . . .'

She makes a guttural sound of annoyance. 'Never mind Gill. She's a great cook, great company, but she's not the bloody oracle. This, here, is *not* your life, Jayney. Those poor sods over there,' her head stammering in the direction of the hospital, *'they're* the ones who are stuck here, behind barbed wire. *You're* not. Never mind landscaping the wretched garden. Let it choke itself to death – what the hell? You'll be well out of here by then.'

We drive to the pub and order a full Sunday roast and Guinness. The aimless Sunday chatter and the smoke and the smell of beer and potatoes lull my headache into the background. I settle comfortably into the corner of a bench.

'So,' says Natalie, snuggling over her drink. 'What about that Patrick, then? He's worth a second look, isn't he?' She watches me intently. 'I bet you—'

'I *don't* fancy him,' I snap and Natalie sits back in triumph.

'Actually,' she simpers, 'I was just going to say I bet you don't meet many nice young men like that in the middle of nowhere . . .'

She sets about haranguing me. The stronger my denial

the more she insists that I'm lusting after Patrick. There's a hint of nastiness in her cross-examination, a touch of anger. She's always like this about men. She wants me to review the evidence in her favour, to state the perfectly obvious and bear witness to Patrick's interest in *her*. I will not do it.

'No one would blame you,' she wheedles. 'The abandoned woman, in search of a little consolation. . .'

'Don't be childish.' I shift on my bench and dust erupts from the cushion. The smoke is beginning to sting my eyes.

She says, 'It sounds quite catchy, doesn't it – Jayne and Pat.'

'It's Jayne and Bobby,' I say, in a tone that makes her shut up.

The food arrives and we tuck in with relief. After a while Natalie says, 'Anyway. He's a damn sight better quality than the geeks in the office at the moment.' She gives me a sly look and adds, 'Don't mind me. I'm just bitter, twisted and single.'

We re-establish friendly relations by making fun of Gill. I tell her about our gardening sessions and about the wasp man and Natalie says, 'Really, Jayne, you want to watch this garden business. People can get seriously obsessed with potting up and pricking out. It's dangerous stuff.'

'She means well. And it's not such a bad idea, if only to make the place presentable. Less depressing.'

She regards me with concern and compassion, then says, 'Jayne, it's none of my business, but are you ever going to say No to Gill's grand strategies?'

I put down my knife and fork and trace a sticky beer stain on the table. I say,

'What's that supposed to mean?'

'Well, just look at yourself. You don't want to live here but Gill summoned you, so you do. It wasn't the only option, surely? It's like she's using you as bait to retrieve her son and—'

'No. You're way off the mark.'

'Maybe,' she says, doubtfully. 'But the fact remains that – pleasant as she is – Gill always calls the shots.'

'The Great Escape wasn't Gill's idea' I say defiantly.

'No . . . and I bet she was thrilled to bits when it went down the pan. You really got your come-uppance there, didn't you? I bet she was hugging herself. *Wetting* herself . . .'

'Don't be ridiculous. You think she *wants* to pay our bills? Manage our lives?'

'Frankly, yes. And I think she wants to feed you little tasks to keep you sweet and stop you running off in despair like her son did.'

I shut my eyes. There's hardly any point in arguing. Natalie's written the script and cast the parts. She senses another impasse and softens her voice.

'All I'm saying' she says, giving me a conciliatory nudge, 'is: do what *you* want to do.'

'OK,' I agree. 'So – how do I find out what that is?'

I take Natalie to the station to see her off. Come again soon, I say – very soon. And I mean it. We hug.

'You're a tonic,' I say. 'I can face another week at the screen, thanks to you.'

Suddenly she releases herself and grips my wrist.

'*Don't* face another week. Don't face another *day*. Come back with me. Now. Come on. Go home and pack some stuff and we'll get a later train. Or drive down, if you like. You're not a prisoner. You can just up and go. *Now*.'

I groan. 'Of course I can. Easy, isn't it? If Bobby can do it, so can I. Except there's the small matter of my son to consider . . .'

'No problem. He can come, too. Or, if he doesn't want to come, he can stay with Gil – she'd love that, wouldn't she? Taking charge. Gareth's a big boy, now. He'll understand, and you can send for him when you've sorted yourself out. Go on, Jayne – drive home and pack a bag. Couple of hours, and we're off.'

I shake my head, and try not to take her seriously. 'I appreciate the offer, but . . . apart from anything else, Bobby—'

'*Bobby*! Oh, *Jayne*!' She chucks my wrist back at me, then resumes more kindly:

'Are you going to wait for Bobby indefinitely? What will you do – stay here the rest of your days? Just in case he decides to pay you a call?'

'Well . . .' I'm begging the train to appear. A sheaf of empty railway tracks converges on the horizon. Helplessly, I say, 'What choice have I got?'

'Jayne, you've got to face the fact—' She fixes me with a look. Her eyes are so black that the pupils disappear. 'You've got to face the fact that he might *not* pay that call. You've got to move on . . .'

All at once I can read her thoughts. I clamp my hands to my stomach as if she's shot me.

'Natalie! He's not . . .' I gasp. 'He's still – We get *letters*. We talk to him on the phone. Bobby may be useless but he's not . . . Look. He hasn't *topped* himself!'

I release a laugh that's more like a scream. Natalie nearly smiles.

'Well, good,' she says, giving up on me. 'Good,' in that open-ended way that expects worse to come.

4

He was standing on the doorstep, trembling. An injured animal, thought Gillian. His hair was even longer than usual, matted and dirty. He was painfully thin. He'd come out of hospital the previous day, and was walking with a stick.

'You married him,' he said, with incredulity that was verging on laughter. As she opened the door a little wider his eyes travelled to the mild swelling of her belly, and he giggled.

'I did tell you, Lenny,' said Gillian. 'I did *try* and tell you, months ago.'

'Nine weeks, to be precise,' he said. Despite his appearance his words were steady and articulate. 'People don't get married in nine weeks. Not people like you.'

His eyelids lowered as he focused on his thoughts. She waited for the accusation, but none came. He stood where he was, propped lightly against his stick, shivering. His shirt and trousers were too big; a tie was knotted round his waistband and the shirtcuffs were rolled back. Mr Tambini's hand-me-downs. It was summer, but there was a cold wind blowing.

'You must be freezing,' said Gill, at last. 'You'd better come in.'

He sat in Robert Gilbard's front room and accepted a cup of tea. Gillian sat opposite him, keeping her distance. Robert wasn't due home for hours, and anyway she had no qualms about them meeting. She simply didn't want to get too close.

Lenny didn't refer to her pregnancy. He didn't even mention the wedding again, until Gillian brought it up herself. After asking him about his leg (mending) and his job prospects (uncertain) she watched him gripping his teacup, controlling the tremor in his hands, and then said: 'I *did* try and tell you, Len. As I remember you said it was a good idea. You said it would please my parents.' He slurped at his tea. She added, 'And you promised to make a speech at my wedding.'

Lenny grinned at her, the old, crowded grin, and her throat closed.

'I should have done that, shouldn't I?' he said. 'But you didn't even wait until the bone had fused.' He looked away, at the mantelpiece, at the curtained window, anywhere except at their growing child.

'It wasn't a speeches kind of affair,' said Gillian. 'It was very low-key. I'm not at all sure it qualified as a wedding at all in my parents' eyes. In fact it was all so quick that I hardly felt . . .' She shrugged-a Tambini shrug, with shoulders, arms and hands. She hardly felt married herself. But she was married enough not to finish the sentence.

They both sat in silence for a while. She could hear the juddering of his lungs. He finished his tea and set the cup carefully back into its saucer, with only a minimal rattle. They exchanged a look.

'I know,' she said. 'Robert doesn't have mugs. And this is just the second-best china.'

'I'm flattered,' said Lenny. Then he smiled at her with such affection that she had to dig her fingers into her palms to ward off tears. He said, 'It's a very nice house.'

Gill composed herself and said, 'Makes a change from sidling round my flat, trying not to tread on other toes.'

Lenny nodded.

'And quite an improvement on my padded cell,' he said, softly. 'Which isn't to everyone's taste.'

Soon afterwards he struggled to his feet, refused the offer of a jacket and left. As he hobbled down the front path Gillian stood at the door and called, 'Does it hurt a lot?'

Lenny waved without looking back. 'I can bear it,' he said, in a mock-tragic vibrato.

Gillian should have been relieved as she shut the door and turned back into Robert's comfortable, spacious house. She wasn't. She knew too well that Lenny's answers were never final.

5

In 1959 Marian Westwood was appearing in *Promise Me* at
the Three Arches Theatre. The critics were half-hearted but
the house was filling well. Five weeks into the run and she
was coasting, hurling lines to the back of the theatre like
tennis balls, catching them, playing with them, lobbing
them to and fro without bothering to watch. It was an
evening performance, a Friday. The audience was receptive
but restless; there was an atmosphere, an expectancy –
someone whispering, others shushing him, a break in
concentration. But it was going reasonably well. Ten
minutes into the second half Marian was delivering a
lengthy speech to her stage husband when she was cut
short by a scream from the auditorium. She faltered,
resumed her lines automatically, then petered out as
everyone on the stage and in their seats turned to see the
wild-haired man who'd gone stark raving mad in the
middle of the stalls. There were words within the scream:
something about lying, something about faith. Hands
grabbed at the man but he was already crabwalking along
the row, heading for the aisle, where he stood and pointed
towards his companion, and shouted, loud and clear: 'If
that's what you wanted why didn't you take it, instead of
wasting my time?'

He was led away; the audience hum subsided; they
turned back to Marian, seeking rescue and resumption.
Marian glared. She had forgotten Billy Smith's lessons: how
to see through, beyond and above the audience, how to
twitch its leash, calm it, drive it . . . She was seeing
individual faces: an old woman picking at her teeth; a man
shuffling in his seat to get comfortable; a pregnant woman
with her head in her hands. Her stage husband ad libbed a
prompt and she garbled half a line. It should flow from
there, like music: each phrase should deliver her painlessly
to the next. She could hear the rhythms, the rise and fall, the

suddenly detonating accents, but she had no words to fit around them. Marian had dried. She swivelled on her high heels and stalked offstage.

Gillian blamed herself. She blamed herself for letting Lenny have his way in the first place. When he turned up at her office, only just containing his mood, she should have talked him down and taken him back to the Vita Nuova. Only three weeks had passed since his visit. Gillian was on the phone, searching for solutions as usual. Her current problem was a long-running dispute between a woman and her elderly father. A voice was warbling with emotion down the line: 'Everyone thinks I'm hard on him, but they don't know what a swine he was all those years . . .'. Gill raised her eyes and saw Lenny fizzing through the office like a fuse. She should have taken charge there and then, wrapped up her phone call and escorted him home. Instead she indicated the chair by her desk and Lenny sat there, seething at the edge of her vision, until she'd finished her conversation. Then he began. Gill listened to his monologue, delivered through gritted teeth, occasionally leaping into a fierce bark. She knew he was using all his strength to keep control.

He said he needed to see her. He said he wanted her to do one small favour-not much to ask. His eyes darted to her stomach and she turned her chair to try and shield it. She should have spoken to him sharply, as she had so many times before. But something – guilt, perhaps – made her agree to his request, ring Robert with an excuse, fetch her coat and walk with Lenny down to the Three Arches, where the tickets were already booked.

Lenny was wearing a borrowed suit. He'd made an attempt at tidying up his hair. He handed her the ticket and said, his cheeks burning with success,

'Your idol. Marian Westwood. Bet even Mr Gilbard hasn't brought you to *this* one yet.'

Gillian didn't answer. She and Robert had seen the show in its first week.

'This is what you like, isn't it?' He was a drowning man, holding her arm so hard that she feared the fingers might plunge through the flesh. 'Theatre, wine and dine – we can do that too afterwards, I'm flush today . . .'

'Where did you—?' Gillian began but decided against it. She might not want to know where the money had come from.

'Theatre-wine-and-dine-smart-clothes-comfy-house . . .' he went on. She recognised the acceleration, the mounting aggression, and pulled back against him.

'Let's go somewhere else and talk,' she suggested, and he flung back: 'NO, let's not go somewhere else and talk, let's go in here and watch your heroine and cuddle up and hire opera glasses and do all the crap you thought crazy Lenny couldn't do for you . . .'

Safer to go along, thought Gillian, and wished she'd told Robert the truth about where she was going. He would have understood. He would have been there at the end of the show to make sure she was all right.

Of course I'm all right, she reminded herself. This is Lenny. And Lenny would only ever hurt himself.

They sidled into their seats. Lenny had forgotten to buy a programme. He stood up to sidle back out and half-a-dozen seats clattered grudgingly upright as their neighbours stood to let him pass. Gillian grabbed his sleeve.

'Never mind,' she said. 'Sit down. It'll start soon.'

'No, you need a programme. I'll get you a programme.'

'It's a bit late for that now,' she said, crossly, and saw disappointment flit across his face. He sat down and twisted his sleeve from her grasp. And then he started to giggle. The high, astounded, idiotic giggle that made her skin prickle.

'Quiet,' ordered Gillian. 'Or I'm going home.'

All through the first half, though he managed to rein in the volume, Lenny's chin was on his chest and his shoulders were shaking. Disapproving heads turned next to him and in front of him. Somewhere in the far distance, in an ethereal haze, the play took its course. As the curtain went down on the first half Gillian encouraged herself: halfway there. One more hour and I can get him out of here.

She blamed herself for speaking to him at all during the interval. She blamed herself for ticking him off, when she should have let it be. As the first bell rang and people drifted out of the foyer and bar her nervousness got the better of her.

'I've come here when I should have gone home,' she said, close against his ear, a mother issuing her charge with a private warning. 'If you're going to play the fool in there I will get up and leave you to it.'

All her fault.

She could sense his simmering anger as the play recommenced. Anger and fear, thrumming through his body in the half-darkness. Once again, she had threatened to abandon him. She filed away every minute that passed without incident.

The dialogue bounced off the walls. The audience noted its progress with barely audible currents of sound. Framed by the proscenium arch, far off in the footlights, Marian Westwood shouted and gestured, a scripted version of the energy at Gillian's side.

For a moment, when the explosion came, Gillian saw the two of them together: Lenny unbearably close, Marian illuminated and hovering behind him like a guardian angel. As the dialogue stopped the room seemed to shrink. Even Marian Westwood was reduced and unexpectedly human. Only a few feet separated them, the two spirits that haunted Gillian Gilbard, until Lenny stumbled his way into the aisle and let himself be hustled out of sight.

6

Marian Westwood fled to her dressing room and tore off her costume. She sat in her underwear and started removing her make-up in quick, hard swipes. One stray lunatic in the audience and she'd gone to pieces. They'd say she couldn't hack it. What did *she* know? No training, no credentials other than Billy Smith and one winter in *Mother Goose*. A tart from the docks who'd slept her way into the clubs and then slept her way out. She slammed her hands onto the dressing table, scattering brushes and pansticks, spiralling into furious rebuttal of imaginary recriminations. There was a tap at the door. She got up to lock it but there was no key, so she kicked it instead. Then she kicked the chair and the wall. A rising, questioning inflexion outside made her yell: 'GO AWAY!' Her face was slippery with tears and mucus. She couldn't leave the room: she couldn't open the door to their pity. She would stay here until morning, until everyone had given up, and if necessary she'd find a way out of the window and down the guttering. In preparation she went to the window and grabbed the rusty metal bar that held it shut. After failing to force it free of its anchor, she gave up and collapsed against the filthy glass. Cobwebs hissed and clung about her head.

'Alec,' she moaned, 'Alec . . .' trying it again for effect. She turned back to the room and kicked at the air, flinging off one high-heeled sandal, which crashed against the full-length mirror and left a starburst crack. Marian Westwood squeezed and scrunched her face to produce a few hard sobs. She crawled into a corner, folded herself into the foetal position, and waited for everything to go away.

After some confusion and delay Marian's understudy was hamming her way through the part. During the hiatus, the pregnant woman, victim of the lunatic's tirade, had been helped out of the auditorium. Sympathetic hands touched her fleetingly as she passed up the aisle. Out in the foyer she was given a glass of water she didn't want, while somebody hailed a taxi. Meanwhile, the audience rallied round, cheered the understudy's first entrance and gave the play a standing ovation before heading home, intoxicated with incident.

The curtain fell; the cast and crew muttered, consulted, listened at Marian's door. Someone suggested ringing the police; someone else said they should have asked if there was a doctor in the house. The assistant stage manager, fresh out of college and giddily infatuated with Marian Westwood, took charge. He would enter her room, assess the situation and fetch any help that was necessary. Relieved, the others gradually filtered away.

The ASM eased the door open and peered through the hairsbreadth of space. Seeing Marian rolled up in her corner he feared the worst, but kept his cool. He shut the door carefully behind him and approached her, on the alert for empty bottles or strewn pills. Her hair, silvered with cobweb, had fallen across her face; he saw it stir against her mouth. She was fast asleep. He squatted beside her, unsure whether to try and wake her, aroused despite himself by the sight of her, curled up, soft and unaware, in only her bra and pants. His hand hovered over her hip, her waist; he made a decision and very gently touched her upper arm with his knuckles. She jolted and tensed without altering her position. Under the black strands of hair her eyes opened. He said, 'Don't worry. Everyone else has gone.'

And that was how my father won my mother.

7

My father. Harry Scott. Say those words, that name, and feel the calm descending. Gentle, reliable, dependable Harry Scott. Steady as a rock.

That's why he was good at his job. He was the kind of man referred to by his surname alone. Let's get Scott. Scott's your man. One of my father's greatest strengths was knowing what he could do and what he couldn't. He knew he could organise random happenings into a routine and keep the routine ticking over. He knew he could cope in a crisis. He knew he could take all the bullshit, the tempests and tornadoes of other people under pressure. He knew he could lurk in the shadows, arranging the right props in the right places, keeping the engine running, and he knew when to pause and watch the action, the backs and profiles of those in the spotlight, throwing their voices away from him, doing what he could never do.

My father was tall, thin, balding and bland. He was a shy man, not given to flattery or flirtation. He knew he couldn't snatch Marian's attention in the ordinary course of events. If he caught an offhand greeting it was only by standing in its way. He wasn't devious. There'd been no cunning plan to make Marian notice him. He would have been contented with a private passion and, in time, a more realistic love life. But Lenny's outburst and its consequences presented a golden opportunity and Harry Scott made the most of it. He crept into Marian's dressing room and quietly took charge.

In a moment of high sarcasm my mother once told me: 'Your father will sort it all out. That's what he does. From the first time I clapped eyes on him, that's what he did. He's a *fixer*.'

That was when their divorce was cranking through. She'd just slammed the phone down on her lawyer. She tore up a letter-the latest cause of umbrage. I can't remember the details now. What I do remember is the distracted, frantic movements of her head and hands. And I remember that, although at 14 I despised Marian Westwood and sided with my Dad, I was engulfed, then, by a rush of sympathy, and wanted to embrace my mother, convince her, as Harry Scott would have done, that everything was going to be all right.

I didn't embrace her, naturally. The moment passed. She sensed the tipping balance of my emotion and, as usual, overplayed her hand. Tears. Streaming mascara and quavering red lips. I left her to it and stayed the night at my father's.

8

Everything seems inevitable in hindsight. Looking back at
my parents' marriage as a complete event, with beginning,
middle and end, I can't conceive of it any other way. I'm
even a little envious: a marriage fully formed and complete;
a marriage to pick up and admire or despise, turning it this
way, that way, to catch the light. It has its attractions. They
were married; then they weren't. At least they knew where
they stood.

This is how it goes: hot-headed wildcat Marian Westwood
tries her hand at happy-ever-after, but eventually pushes
her luck once too often with the parties, the screaming
abdabs, the flings. Pushes a good man out of her life. After
his passionate interlude, cool Harry Scott comes to his
senses and settles into domestic harmony with the practical
woman he should have married in the first place. If it
hadn't been for me, he could have written off the whole
episode as just one of those fabulous flights. A parable, or a
fairy-tale, depending on his mood.

On these evenings of tale-swapping at Gill's, as the broad
sky blackens over us and the security lights clunk on at the
four corners of the perimeter wall, I find myself considering
alternative versions of my family history. When Marian
feels the touch of a hand in 1959 and sees her balding
saviour on his haunches before her, I find myself seeing
through her eyes. I've tried to put this across to Gill.

'Actually,' I said, 'it must have seemed like everything
falling into place, when my mother met my dad. She must
have thought: here it is at last. Safe harbour. End of the
forced jollity, the panicky parties, the one-night stands . . .
Real life starts here.'

Gill grunted. She doesn't care about Harry Scott; he was
an aberration. But why shouldn't it all have gone to plan?
They were together for 16 years, after all, Marian and Harry.
Why not 20? Forty? Why not the golden anniversary and

confounded critics? Marian's affairs only really resumed in
the last, disillusioned dog-days of their relationship. Until
then Harry had dealt with her tempers, her adrenalin, her
attention-seeking and selfishness, and she had added highs
and lows to his landscape; she'd given him energy and
laughs. Why not carry on as before? In this revised version
of events I find Marian mellowing with age, subsiding into
grey elegance, choosing – under Harry's guidance – canny
character parts, playing against type, managing with no
more pills or booze than most. In this version she earns
respect, wins awards, loses the edge of hysteria, makes us
chuckle, makes us love her. In this version she dotes on her
grandson and treats my husband with distant and strictly
maternal affection. It works that way for other families,
thousands of them, all the time. It could have worked for
us. Just for an instant I share Gill's impatience with my
father. Why did he have to throw in the towel? He'd
tolerated her that long – why not stay the course?

Gill said: 'You wouldn't be here now, if Lenny hadn't had
his episode that night.' She squirmed again at the memory
of Marian Westwood drying on stage. Breaking the spell.

Marian was given a hard time in some of the papers, and
the play folded sooner than it might have done. Work fell
off for a few months. She turned her attention to films – a
terrible mistake, according to Gill. Oh, Marian was too big
for films. They made her look a fool. Besides which, cinema
is so free with its favours. Everyone can see you for two
bob, even when you're dead. Everyone can stake a claim.
Gill preferred the fleeting intimacy of theatre, the shared
roof, the unique quality of every line spoken anew. The way
Gill sees it, Marian Westwood's foray into films was the
start of a downhill slide. The way Gill sees it, she and Lenny
helped ruin Marian Westwood's career. Well . . . it's her
story. I don't want to spoil it for her. It allows her the
pretence of a role in my mother's life. The more mundane
truth is that Marian gave her carping reviewers the finger.

She relished the prospect of making films. She was busy, anyway, enjoying her short courtship and planning her long, lacy wedding. By the time I arrived in 1962 she was talking of leaving the business altogether, to play permanent happy families. There's a picture of her holding me when I was two days old. Her hair's tied back; her eyes are puffy and looking at me, straight at me, nowhere near the lens. She smiles that new-mother smile. She's beautiful. I'll never hang that photograph on the wall for everyone to see; I'll never have it printed off and sold. That's one photograph of Marian I keep to myself.

9

Gill and I have established a regular pattern. I take a break
from the computer at three and she comes round for tea and
an hour or so's work on the garden. She leaves as Gareth
slopes up the path. After feeding Gareth I reclaim the
computer for an hour or two while he does his school work.
That's the theory, anyway. In fact I get a phone call two or
three evenings a week to say he's working at Hannah's and
will get a lift back.

'He won't let me go and fetch him,' I tell Gill. We're on our
hands and knees, clearing room at the back of the garden for
a border. 'It's getting a bit awkward now. I mean, Hannah's
parents can't be expected to taxi him back every other night.'

'What do you think of them?' asks Gill, without lifting
her head from her task.

'That's the other thing. I haven't even met them. They
just drop him off and drive away, and it's usually fairly
late . . .'

I can't bring myself to admit that I hide behind the
curtain when I hear their car. Gill says, 'Oh, well. No loss, if
you ask me.'

We work away in peace. A pigeon flaps into ascent; a dog
barks in one of the other gardens. Our trowels bite and spit
in the earth. I stop to wipe my nose and say,

'That Patrick's a character, isn't he?'

Gill laughs but doesn't comment.

'Struck me as quite old-fashioned, if you know what I
mean.'

'Oh . . . that's all show.' She stops digging and sits back
on her ankles. 'He's from Newcastle originally. You'd never
know, would you? Quite a tough childhood, I gather.'

I concentrate on my tissue to cover my interest.

'Had other problems too, I believe . . .' adds Gill, wiping
her hands on her jeans. 'Depression. That sort of thing. Then
decided to turn his life around.'

'Just like that,' I say. My back's aching. I try and keep her talking. 'Why the posh accent, though?' I ask.

'Oh, you know . . . Smart clothes, smart accent – you're less likely to spot a man's insanity among the trappings.'

She's digging again.

'They *are* all mad in there, then? Staff and all?'

Gill turns her flushed face and cocks a patronising eyebrow. 'What do you mean, *they*?' She jams her trowel violently against a stone. 'Madness is a continuum, Jayne. We're all on it somewhere.'

How odd, I think: Patrick striving to adopt a posh accent and Gill striving to cover hers up.

'Anyway, Pat's no fool,' says Gill, hoarse with effort. 'He knows what he's up against. White, well-spoken, affluent male – all speaks of sanity, still, despite evidence to the contrary.'

'Natalie really took to him,' I say. Gill blows out noisily between her lips in fake surprise.

'No! You think?' Then adds 'Hard cheese for Natalie, I'm afraid. Pat's gay.'

My cheeks fire up. I'm grateful to Gill for applying herself so diligently to the trowelling. What a fool I am. *A male friend, you understand*. He wasn't clearing the way for Natalie. Or for me. He was warning us off. I titter with disappointment and relief.

'What's up with you?'

'Nothing. Just Natalie's luck, that's all.'

To hide my embarrassment I shift to the hedge on the opposite side of the garden path and start work there. It's already bursting its banks again, despite all Gill's good work with the strimmer. I squat down to see what's lurking under its torrent of new shoots and creepers. Behind me I can hear the chock-chock of Gill's trowel. The sun rests on my back. For a long time I squint into the gloom, starting at every scuttling beetle or hissing leaf. Gradually something begins to claim my focus. Something blurred and motionless.

A spiral. A question mark. I reach into the shrubbery, wincing as spikes of dead wood snag at my arm, reminding me of the wasp stings. Carefully I lift away a dense curtain of growth. Wedged into the soil and up behind the hedge is an iron gate, its bars and flourishes furred with rust and bindweed. Forgetting my caution, I burrow in towards it, grab it with both hands, wrestle and shake it until the soil loosens and the weeds begin to tear.

Gill is standing over me when I crawl out backwards, ripping through mud and hedge as I heave my discovery into the open air.

'What the hell are you doing?'

'Look what I've found!'

Gill looks at the gate as though it's blown a raspberry.

'Lot of these houses used to have gates like that,' she says. 'Better off with the nice wooden ones if you ask me. Good and solid. Put it aside and I'll take it to the dump some time.'

At seven o'clock I realise that my lower back is throbbing and I'm ravenously hungry. Gill has gone home; Gareth has phoned from Hannah's. I've forgotten to finish off my day's editing and I'm not going to bother now. I discard another corner of Brillo pad and nurse my torn fingers. The gate's ironwork is emerging, slim and graceful, from its cocoon of muck. Gill was right, of course: it's just a garden gate, nothing special. I don't know why I'm so fascinated with it. Someone, somewhere, designed this object, a postscript to daily life; someone laboured over it, coaxed the malleable metal into swoops and tails. I struggle to my feet and stretch. Slashes of grey and pink cloud are extending across the sky, lugging in the twilight. It's growing cold. Before going back in I stoop for another look at the gate's former hiding place. A white gleam catches my eye. An old saucer, perhaps. I crouch down again and brush away the grass. A mushroom! I've never found a wild mushroom in my life. I make a mental note to tell Bobby, next time I get a chance.

Next day Gill arrives to find an iron gate wedged in place in the middle of the lawn. She contemplates it with a cynical air and strokes her chin. 'But is it art?'

'I don't know,' I say, 'but I know what I like.'

Gill shakes her head, but doesn't comment. She produces her trowel and gardening gloves from her carrier bag and takes up position at the base of the hedge.

'Let's skip tea today,' she says 'and get on with it.'

There's something on her mind.

I'm doing the heavy work today, breaking new ground to continue the borders. We take up our rhythm: the slow gnash and tear of my fork; the quick background scrawl of Gill's trowel as she worries the soil. Every now and then she pauses to hurl a snail over the hedge.

'Poor creatures,' I say. 'Lifted from their hidey-hole and thrown into the abyss.'

'It's us or them,' says Gill curtly. 'They'll scoff every plant down to its stem. They're like vultures.'

'Well, I only hope Gareth doesn't find a trail of snail remains along the pavement. You'll be marked down forever as a mass murderer.' I try not to sound too gleeful.

Gill sits back.

'Sometimes,' she starts, 'Gareth reminds me so much . . .'

Her body subsides with the sentence.

'Of Lenny,' I say. It comes out with more aggression than intended. I wait, one foot poised on the bar of the fork.

She says, 'Lenny's trouble . . .' Then changes her mind and tries again, more assertively, using her professional voice. 'It's that ruthless consistency,' she says. 'Refusing to skim over the details, picking you up on every damn thing, demanding you follow through your own logic. No fudging, no making allowances. It's a kind of intolerance, in a way.' She looks at me and adds, 'It's all part of adolescence.'

Reassuring me. 'Putting the lessons you've been taught to the test. Applying the theory. You know – if killing is so wrong, why is it OK to gas a colony of wasps? If a life is more important than a colourful border display, how can you justify smashing a snail? Oh, I can just hear Lenny giving me the third degree . . .' She recalls herself. 'But then he was a grown man. And a grown man needs to drop the detail sometimes, in order to survive.'

She goes back to work. I can see from the violence of her movements that she's upbraiding herself for mentioning them both in the same breath. My son and crazy Lenny. Gareth and his real grandfather. His flesh and blood.

10

Lenny's tirade at the theatre was a minor incident with long-reaching results – quite apart from bringing my parents together. For a start, Robert laid down the law. He paid a visit to Lenny's den, upstairs at the Vita Nuova. It must have been a bizarre encounter: Robert in his city-worker clothes, refusing to take off his mac and bowler hat, standing in the middle of the virtually empty room, brandishing his brolly to emphasise his point. Lenny, small, skinny and scraggy, almost completely swamped by Mr Tambini's hand-me-downs, fighting off that devilish giggle. Robert told him that Gillian's distress after their last meeting had almost made her ill. He reminded Lenny, unnecessarily, that she was a mother-to-be. He asked Lenny to think of the child. He avoided possessive pronouns with scrupulous diplomacy.

Lenny was shaken, and not a little impressed. He rather liked this large, sturdy, self-contained man. He admired his tact, his way of furling up difficulties in his black umbrella and tucking them out of sight. Lenny asked, 'Are you telling me to stay away from Gillian?'

It was a straightforward question, with no hint of defiance. He wanted to know what was required.

Robert said, 'I'm suggesting that you seek help. Treatment. Before seeing Gillian. Before seeing the child.'

And so Lenny's moods gained a title, became a condition, a problem with a solution of sorts. This was in the days before lithium; instead he was given uppers and downers, like an overworked movie star, and avuncular advice about health regimes, daily strategies, when to eat, when to take a hot bath. When Lenny came to see Gillian and her brand new baby in the nursing home, he sat and spoke with measured words and pauses, and was almost like any other visitor. Perhaps he stroked the boy's head more tenderly, and held the tiny fist with a more inscrutable expression on his face. If he was a touch absent, it was probably a side-effect of the drugs. They hadn't quite perfected the dose yet, he explained. They made him dozy.

Gillian watched the jerking and floating of her baby's arms, listened to his grumbles and squawks. She said 'We're calling him Robert. Well – Bobby. To avoid confusion.' Lenny nodded and smiled and repeated the name, almost like anybody else.

Gillian had decided very soon after their theatre trip that if she had a boy he would be named after her husband. It was a typically efficient way of sorting matters out. A necessary cruelty – like smashing snails. There was no clearer way of conveying her resolution to Lenny, short of shutting him entirely out of her life. And by this time Gillian knew she could never do that.

11

I'm beginning to feel trapped by the parallels in our past. Our stories seem to have manacled us together, me and this grey-haired woman kneeling in the garden beside me, pestering the soil while my fork stamps and levers. And yet, watching the rounding of her shoulders, the squareness of her hips, I'm overcome with the sense that she's a total stranger: that I'm no closer to my annoying mother-in-law than I am to the Gill of 40 years ago. I picture her in the maternity ward, holding Bobby in her arms; I try and picture Lenny, whose face I've never seen, and these characters are as unconnected, as harmless and unreal and insignificant as the black-and-white figures in a musical chorus line.

I stop to take breath and let the fork take my weight. Gill is leaning forward, now, rump in the air, wobbling gently with every thrust of the trowel.

'Why were you so sure,' I ask, 'that Lenny wouldn't . . . make trouble?'

'Trouble?'

Her reply is muffled by the undergrowth.

'About his son.'

She reappears with a hairnet of dead leaves. She seems bewildered.

'Well, actually, he never established . . .' But she knows that won't do. She shrugs. 'I just knew.'

'Did you want him to?'

'What?'

'Make trouble.'

I return to work before she can answer. Stamp, lever, gouge. Another peeling of turf curls away from my fork. I don't want to see the look on her face, but when she speaks I can hear a smirk.

'Bit of an amateur brain-doctor on the quiet, aren't you?'

Nettled by her tone, I snap back.

'All this business about Bobby's name. Making a point of telling him—'

'I didn't make a *point*. I just *told* him. He had to know what to call the child, didn't he?'

The child. Your beautiful son, you mean – my lover – and husband-to-be. I dig more forcefully and my voice shudders.

'Yes, but you could have chosen any other name. Matthew. Mark, Luke, John . . .'

'Oh, for Christ's sake!' she explodes, with a shower of twigs and bits. 'It was 40 years ago! I had a baby and a husband and a normal life to arrange for them both.'

Stamp, lever, gouge. Stamp, lever, gouge.

'Yes, OK,' she adds, more calmly. 'I suppose I *was* making a point. It needed making.'

Stamp. Lever.

'Seems rather a brutal way to do it,' I say. 'That's all.'

She removes her glasses and wipes the sweat from the corners of her eyes. I wait for a blast of righteousness. But Gill says, 'You're right. I wanted to provoke Lenny. That's the truth.'

'*Why*?'

'Because he'd given up without a bloody fight.'

I'm not entirely sure what she means. Given up his son? His life with her? Or something else? Maybe Lenny without his madness just wasn't Lenny any more. She waggles a thumb over her shoulder.

'Are you going to leave that revolting old gate there forever? It looks ridiculous.'

Her words are scraping against her throat. I decide to keep the rest of my questions to myself.

12

When I was born Bobby Jr was two years old and already showing a talent for unravelling complexities. He inherited his mother's fair hair and blue eyes and made them pretty. He provided his own sweet, accepting nature and a knack for avoiding discomfort of any kind. He adored his mother, obeyed his father, charmed his grandparents and treated Uncle Lenny with amiable indifference. Gillian watched for glints of danger in his eyes, but there was only a cheerful sparkle, acknowledging the treats and diversions that every day provided. By the age of three Bobby was calling his mother 'Gill'. By the time he was four they were friends and confidantes, chattering away to each other on more or less equal terms. He started school with his usual buoyancy, immediately making new friends and enchanting the teachers.

Gill felt vaguely let down. She went back to work, chiefly to fill her empty days, but the sense of vocation had waned. She approached her caseload now with weary resignation. She trudged from client to client, ticking them off as so many tasks. There was little hope of improving their lives and little point in understanding them. Poverty, neglect, crime, infirmity – she watched the traps slam shut, one after the other; she watched the clock slice away the minutes until she could hold Bobby Jr again, ruffle his hair and fill her hands with his chubby cheeks.

On a winter's afternoon in 1965 Gillian's father clamped his hands to his head, gave a shout of pain and splashed forward into the papers on his desk. Elvira stooped over him, clasped his shoulders, called his name. Their final vignette.

Gill and Robert organised the funeral and worried about Gill's mother.

'There's plenty of room for her here,' Robert offered. 'You don't want her rattling around that house on her own, do you?'

Another case to tick off, thought Gill; another half-baked, provisional solution to supply. She went to deliver the invitation, steeled against her mother's misery. She let herself in to her childhood home, heard the familiar scrape and creak of the front door as it opened, saw her mother, small and silhouetted at the end of the hall. Small but not frail. Gill had expected watery helplessness; instead her mother was stern and dejected. She greeted Gill bleakly; rather than widening to receive Gill's compassion, her eyes slithered away into exclusive grief. Gill followed her into the sitting room and almost asked, automatically, 'Where's Pa?' Checking the question in her throat, she felt the first real, dismal weight of loss. Her mother sat heavily in the armchair and put a hand to her chest; the absence behind her chair threw the picture out of balance.

'How are you, Ma?' asked Gill.

'I've got a pain,' said her mother. Then, without affectation, 'I think my heart is breaking.' She stated it as a fact about a piece of faulty machinery. Gill stood over her. She didn't know what to say. Presently she repeated Robert's offer. Her mother shook her head, uninterested.

'I'll be staying here,' she said.

Three months later, before Gill had the chance to assure her mother that time would heal, Elvira's heart stopped. Gill found her deflated in the same chair, her head tilted sideways and her mouth open in an expression of exhaustion and relief.

So the clearance men came and priced the chair, the desk, the books, the curtains. Gill stood in the study and gave directions, suffered an aching constriction in her own chest, and told herself it would just have to mend. She didn't pause to finger bookspines or examine notebooks or photographs. Everything was carted away. Gill loaded clothes into cardboard boxes to take to the charity shop. The smell of her father's tobacco hung around his jackets. Gill brushed the graffiti of white hairs and dandruff from her mother's collars. She took a hairbrush clouded with hairs from the bedside table and chucked it into a bag reserved for rubbish. She went from room to room and opened the windows. The furniture had left shadows of unfaded carpet and a low mist of dust. In one long day the sweet, musty air of decades, the air that had once threatened to choke the life out of Gill, was freshened, diluted, blown away. The house was just a house, already recovering its neutrality as Gill closed the door behind her and strode away.

13

Meanwhile Marian Westwood was accumulating gifts and toys, baby teeth and outgrown clothes and keepsakes, storing them away in the flat she'd refused to give up, while Harry issued mild complaints.

They called me Jayne after Harry's late mother. Plain Jayne. A monosyllabic whine. I grew into it. Maybe if they'd chosen something more energetic and glamorous I might have been more like my mother. I was never much to look at, even at a very early age – that much is obvious from the photographs, and even if it hadn't been, my mother left me in no doubt. She wasn't vicious about it: just honest.

'You're no oil painting, Jayne,' she'd say. 'But it's character that matters, remember that.'

She was a doting mother at first. She took all the dirty nappies, squawling nights, drool and vomit in her stride. She showed me off to her friends. She hardly gave Harry a look in. But boredom began to set in as soon as I took my first steps away from her. When I threw tantrums and wriggled free of her grasp she regarded me with shock and disgust. She felt tricked. Cornered. Harry told her all children went through this phase, that it wouldn't last, and she said,

'Well, let me know when it's passed, then,' and marched out of the flat.

She went back to work. I had a part-time Polish nanny and a place in a nursery. Marian brought friends home at the end of the day and held court. She and Harry had a big row about her parties. Harry accused her of 'infesting the place with false friends'.

'*My* place,' she answered. '*My* friends.' She stubbed out a fresh cigarette on the plate he was trying to clear away. She was drunk.

He said, 'Right. There's clearly no room for me here.' And he left the flat.

Marian used to tell me that as soon as he'd gone I came howling out of my room, waddling along with my comforter, calling daddy, daddy, as if the world would end. 'A right little drama queen' according to my mother. 'I was mightily impressed.'

He only walked round the block, of course, but Marian marked me down as a daddy's girl, from that time on.

She was wrong. I was as captivated by her as my father was. When she became herself-that is, when she performed herself, on stage, on camera, surrounded by a group of hangers-on – she lit the sky. She was exciting, funny, sexy, and so was everything and everyone within her orbit. The difference between the private and public Marian Westwood was the difference between a cardboard tube stuffed with explosives and a fanfare of fireworks in the night. I loved her and resented her, craved her admiration, wanted to be her . . . I was her greatest and most unwilling fan.

During the morning break in school we used to congregate in a corner of the playground where weeds and wild flowers poked through the railings from a piece of wasteground next door.

'Who likes butter?' we'd say, picking a buttercup and waving it under a chubby chin.

'You do!' – as a smudge of yellow was mirrored on pale flesh. 'You do!' But when it was my turn there was no reflection; all the light disappeared into my sallow skin. I was quite proud of this distinction and announced to my mother, at home, that I couldn't eat butter.

'Flowers don't show up on me,' I explained.

My mother twizzled a loop of my hair and said, 'That's because you're such a little grey-face.'

Harry gave her a look.

'It's true,' she protested and turned my face towards him. 'Look at her. A little old lady before her time.'

Harry was terse. 'Nonsense' he said, for my benefit, adding 'Look at her lovely, curly hair . . .'

'That's not what I'm saying,' interrupted my mother, baffled by his evasion. 'I'm talking about her pasty skin.'

Many years later, when I was chewed up by acne, she would sigh: 'Poor Jayne. You look like a bowl of porridge.'

And my hatred of her was laced with gratitude for her unrelenting, childlike truth.

14

I now have two presentable borders planted by Gill and one iron gate, a broken coal scuttle, three hefty, cleaned bones and part of a bedstead planted by me in the middle of the lawn. Gill has temporarily withdrawn her gardening services until I decide what to do with 'that junk'. I'm all alone, scrubbing at the bedstead, when I hear my name. Pat is leaning over the back gate, intrigued.

'Going into the antiques business?'

I struggle to my feet, aware of the sodden grass patches on my knees.

'Gill thinks I'm off my head.'

'Well, Gill should know.'

I invite him in. He stands over my collection and casts an uneasy look at the bones, which are balanced against each other in a relaxed pyramid.

'The last owners had a dog,' I explain. 'I keep digging these up, and I thought I'd give them a clean . . . It wasn't very pleasant.'

'No, I don't suppose it was.'

That's not entirely true. In fact I was absorbed in the task for hours, out there with my rubber gloves and bowl of soapy water, whittling away at the gristle and flesh. I forgot to be disgusted and concentrated on working towards that satisfying rasp of release as a clod of meat was shucked free of its frame. I turned the finished bones around and around, admiring their purity, the pared-down sketch of a life after all that transient stuff of identity – features, hair, flesh, muscle – had finally fallen away. The dog's teeth have left cryptic marks along the shaft of each bone, pits and curves and zig-zags. To me they're like symbols, a message in some lost language. To Pat, judging by his expression, they're the chewed-up remains of a dead dog's dinner.

He refuses tea. He's planning to pop in and see Gill, he says, on his way home. Then he says, 'How's your friend?'

'Natalie? Oh, she's . . . well, I haven't really spoken to her since, but I'm sure she's fine.'

I'm flustered.

'Do give her my best. I had such a good time. Surrounded by beautiful, amusing women. We must do it again.'

He smiles knowingly. I wonder whether Gill has reported back to him.

'What will you do with . . .?' He nods towards the junk.

'Oh . . . I don't know, really. I just thought they looked . . . interesting. I'll think of something.'

'You're either an artist or barking mad,' he says, 'and that's a professional opinion. Listen – I must . . .' He looks at his watch, and moves away.

'Sure you don't want tea?'

'Another time would be wonderful. Maybe I could drop in when . . .'

The gate slams and Gareth glares at us like the jealous lover in a bad play. I gibber introductions; he grunts and lollops into the house; Pat makes further excuses and leaves. I'm very angry with Gareth. I find him scavenging in the kitchen.

'Can't you even summon a polite "hello" these days?'

He gives a muffled swoop of indignation through a mouthful of crisps.

'You *know* who that was. Yes, you do. It was Gill's friend, Patrick. Natalie and I—'

He shrugs and turns away.

'You're not a child, Gareth. You have to learn to engage with the outside world at some stage in your life.'

He boggles at my hypocrisy and heads for the stairs.

'And you don't have to panic every time I exchange two words with a man, and anyway—'

He gulps with shock and faces me. 'Talk to whoever the fuck you like,' he yells. '*I* don't care.'

My mouth opens and shuts. He takes the stairs two at a time and slams his door.

He doesn't come downstairs till 10 o'clock. I'm sitting in front of the news. A child missing in Northumberland. A suicide bomb in Israel. Gareth goes into the kitchen, butters a piece of bread and leans in the doorway to eat it.

'You haven't had any supper,' I say. On the TV a politician mouths euphemisms.

'Neither have you.'

'I'm not very hungry.'

'Neither am I.'

'What will your friends say, when you tell them you had bread and butter for your evening meal? What will Gill say?'

'Won't tell 'em.'

Then, with the composure of a man scoring a point, he says, 'Hannah's mum and dad are coming to tea on Sunday.'

At 10.45 we're both on the landing, slanting towards each other, eyes bulging, throats straining. I'm in my dressing gown. I've got a bath running. I was planning a soak and a fret about the prospective guests. Instead I'm hollering at my son.

'Why couldn't you just *tell* them—'

'Christ, Mum! All that crap about engaging with the outside world—'

'That's different!' I lie. 'Are *you* going to clear this place up and make it presentable to—'

'It doesn't *have* to be presentable. Jesus! They're just going to this thing, Hannah's coming over in the morning, they're picking her up in the—'

'Fine! Fine! Let them pick her up! They don't have to come nosing round here to do that!'

'Christ!' He towers over me. 'They're picking her up, and they want to meet you – what am I meant to say? Sorry, Mum won't let you in? Ah, ffff . . .'

He casts his eyes and hands up, in one of his grand-mother's gestures. In the heat of the fray I'm still gratified by his return to self-censorship. I suddenly remember my bath and lunge back into the bathroom to slam off the taps. The water's run stone cold. Gareth skulks on the landing, waiting for an answer, waiting for his chance to go and log on and e-libel his mother.

My voice drops to a wounded pitch: 'If you don't mind, I'd like to have my bath while there's still a bit of privacy round here . . .' I shut the bathroom door, then fury bubbles up again and I yank it open.

'So what we're saying is, Hannah's parents want to check me out. Sniff round the boyfriend's parental home. Make sure it's all good enough for the likes of them.'

Gareth scowls and I bang the door shut again. When did he overtake me on the road to the moral high ground? And when did my mother's spirit take possession of my body?

I'm propped against the bathroom door, contemplating a bath full of icy water. Then I'm crying. I trundle a wad of loo-roll off the holder and blow my nose hard. I'm feeling thoroughly, fabulously sorry for myself. As the tears and snot flow I ask myself why this is such a big deal. Hannah's parents are popping in on Sunday afternoon for a cup of tea and a quick butcher's at Gareth's mother. That's all. And isn't that reason enough?

15

Over the past few days I've let the housekeeping slip. On Saturday I spend four hours reclaiming the house. I bin all the meal-trays, chocolate-bar wrappers, junk mail, empty carrier bags, six-month-old TV listings and biro tops and retrieve stray socks and pullovers. I vacuum floors and ceilings. I scrub the bath, the basin, the kitchen sink; I wash most of the mouldering mugs and plates queueing on the worktop. I clear the fridge of congealed-milk cartons, wrinkled veg and the worst of the sticky puddles. The house has now been brought back to ordinary levels of disorder and dirt.

I'm making amends for my strop the other evening. And I'm putting two fingers up at my mother's ghost. After weathering her storms for so many years, I refuse to start whipping them up in my own middle age. I am not a mad-woman. I take after my father, Harry Scott, the appeaser. I learned from him how to batten down the hatches, how to steer clear of risks. It wasn't always easy, especially when parts were thin on the ground, or when her latest picture or play had flopped. It could be something as simple as deciding what to do about supper.

'Shall we go out?' she'd say, lounging across an armchair, one listless leg swinging to the beat of her timebomb.

'If you'd like to, yes,' Harry would say.

'Don't *you* want to go out?'

Tick, tock, tick . . .

'Yes. We'll eat out. Where shall we—'

'Forget it. I don't want to be humoured. Just tell me what *you* want to do.'

Harry the Man of Peace would put away his newspaper and change his tactics. 'All right. Fine. I don't really feel like it this evening. Let's eat in, and I'll—'

'Right. So we're eating in. Again. Bloody marvellous.'

My flesh would shrink in readiness for another scene. It

would take a good 20 minutes to persuade her that, yes, we truly did want to go out for a meal. Then the wail would go up: 'But it's far too late to book a table now!'

In the early years Harry found it funny. But then, in the early years she was petulant rather than poisonous, aimless rather than bored out of her skull.

On the rare occasions when she demanded my opinion I slipped a glance at my father and said I didn't mind. She insisted: I *must* have a view. Didn't I have a mind of my own? I kept my head down and said I didn't care. I was lumpen and mulish, hoarding my secrets, driving her mad. I can see, now, how infuriating I was; I'm shaken by the force of her frustration, all these years down the line. Nevertheless. I refuse to become my mother.

I shove some of the videos back into their boxes and hide them under the bed: *Kid from Spain, Daddy Long Legs, 42nd Street*. I find an A4 envelope there full of Bobby's postcards and cuttings. I pull out a sepia photograph of a tousle-haired brunette, nuzzling her fur collar, all pencilled eyebrows and wheelspoke lashes. Then a newspaper article, photocopied askew so that the words, already grainy and hard to read, peter out altogether at the end of each line. The headline stands out: 'Queen of the Screen'; underneath it, a picture of an old man in drag. No – it's an old woman, hideously made up in a pantomime version of her younger self. There's a smudgey date at the top of the page: 1986. There was a flurry of stories like this in the 1970s and '80s about former silent stars, mainly women, who were rediscovered languishing in nursing homes or slums and dragged out blinking to face the public. Bobby, of course, was enthralled. I turn the envelope upside-down and tip out a sheaf of other pages, all with similar photographs of aged women, some still pretty and vivacious, still exuding the old seductive powers; others grotesque and sad in blonde wigs and scarlet lipstick. The undead. I'm half tempted to chuck out the lot. But Bobby might want to look through them again, when he comes home.

On Sunday morning I survey the cottage. I'm disappointed. Even after all that toil there's disorder in the lie of the rugs, in the paint on the walls, in the seats and legs of the chairs. There's a knack to tidying and clearing, and I don't have it. Bobby was the tidy one, filing and folding and stacking with his surplus nervous energy at the end of each trading day. Odd that after 20 years together, 20 years of lending and borrowing traits, compromising and changing, I snap back to type as soon as he's gone. As though the real me had been biding her time all along. I can see that the living room is still untidy, but I see it in a general sense, without being able to separate it into individual items and requisite storage places. It's going to take another two hours at least to untangle it all. While I'm trailing round the edges of the room, picking up a shoe here and a cushion there, Gareth appears. He pushes the dining chairs under the table, and I take that as a token of assistance. He says,

'They're not coming till six.'

'Six,' I say. 'Right.'

'They won't stay long.'

'No. OK.'

I take it that we don't want to kill each other any more, and congratulate myself on being my father's daughter after all.

16

Well, it's over and done with and I've ruined my only son's life. I heard him. He was just outside the front door, saying goodbye to Hannah as her parents revved the engine. The door was narrowly ajar; he probably thought I was safely out of range, nursing my shattered pride in a dark corner of the living room. As I passed, creeping towards the stairs to collect a musical, I heard him say: 'I know. But she's my mother.'

It couldn't be anything good, that, could it? I've gone over every possibility. Not one of them is encouraging.

I know she's mad, but she's my mother.

I know she's unbearable, but she's my mother.

I know I should leave home, but . . .

Maybe I'm reading too much into it. At face value, it's not necessarily such a hostile phrase. Five short words, none of them inimical in itself. In fact the only emotive word there is 'mother'. Not usually a benevolent word on my own lips, it's true, but normally resonant with compassion and love.

Sudden inspiration: I know she seems lost and hopeless. But she's my mother: she's strong. She'll pull through.

This cheers me a little. I focus on the movie again.

'I'll get some self-assurance,
If your endurance is great . . .'

Fred Astaire's wistful voice and bony face are making me tearful. He's a gambler; Ginger is a haughty dancing teacher.

'Listen,' she says, 'no-one could teach you to dance in a million years.'

But he leads her onto the floor, and they hop, sway, spin and stride in a ballet of deceit, convincing us that any thoughtless movement can be grace, that any pathetic loser can dance.

I know she's spoiled everything. But she's my mother.

Concentrate on the positives – that's what Gill would say. There was no violence. No rows. No impoliteness. Hannah's parents are civilised people who make sure their opinions aren't overheard.

From about 3.30 every car that passed threatened to be Hannah's parents. Gareth had changed his plans, met Hannah at Berriford and spent most of the day there, bringing her back with 15 minutes to spare before the visit. They disappeared immediately into his sanctum. So I was alone in the hall when the car drew up and sounds of opening doors and mild argument floated up the path. I couldn't swallow. The banister and the front door and the photograph of my mother assumed a malevolence of their own and willed me to disgrace myself. A melting in the gut sent me dashing to the loo just as they were approaching the house. They had to knock three times before Gareth and Hannah finally emerged and let them in. All four of them were crowding at the door as I came hurtling back downstairs, fumbling at my zip. Gareth watched my progress, glumly.

Mrs Hannah came in first, hand extended. 'Bridget,' she announced. A big smile and something else going on behind the eyes. The smile exposed both rows of teeth, upper and lower.

She turned to Hannah and said with jocular severity, 'Well, madam, I won't ask what *you've* been up to since last we met.'

Gareth set his features with an obvious effort, but if Hannah was embarrassed she didn't show it.

'Mum,' she said brightly, 'don't be appalling.'

Somehow, 'appalling' was an unexpected word from a girl who thinks life began in 1985.

Bridget was very tall and straight. Smart-but-casual. Her jacket held its line without interruption from bumps and ridges. She wafted into the living room and said,

'Oh, it's very *light*, isn't it!'

Mr Hannah, who didn't give his name, ducked forward as he walked and seemed shorter than he was. His large, bald head loomed over a thin cloud of gingery hair. As he followed Bridget he winked at his daughter.

We had tea. I couldn't seem to stay seated: I was in a faster time-frame than everyone else. I thought of Lenny and tried to pace myself.

Bridget was a real pro, yacking away about the house, the hospital, how many local farmers have gone bust, how overworked she and her husband are . . .

'Aren't we?' And he inclined his head and crinkled his eyes, which could have meant 'yes' or 'no' or 'who cares'. I gathered that she was a lawyer; I still didn't know his occupation or even his name. I was trying to sneak a look at my watch when Bridget risked a direct question.

'What's your own line of work, exactly?'

'Oh, I . . . just . . .'

I longed for a real profession, a label that she would recognise and finger and admire.

'It's only . . . I just do, sort of, publishing sort of work . . .'

Her smile expanded; her eyes registered an internal whirr of conclusions.

Gareth spoke. 'You're an editor,' he muttered, studying his tea. He sounded angry. I picked up my cue.

'That's right. I've gone back into publishing . . .'

'Oh,' her voice leapt, 'did you take a break from it?'

'Well, we ran an . . . er, an outlet . . .'

A snarl from Gareth. 'Not for long.'

I was at a loss. Was he bolstering my image or grinding it underfoot? I'd noticed Bridget's contrived, wide-eyed interest at the word 'outlet'. Maybe Gareth was steering me away from a wrong turn? Bridget helped us out.

'I expect it's been quite a culture shock, coming here from the Smoke . . .' She simpered at her husband and pressed her point: 'I know *we* found it all rather strange, when we came up from Highgate. One adapts, though.'

Here the husband piped up for the first time, in an unexpectedly rich voice. 'Not so strange for me, of course . . .'

'Not so strange for you, of course, no . . .'

She was about to divulge his name but he headed her off at the pass.

'I'm from Norfolk,' he said, 'originally. So I'm used to the flatlands.'

'Very flat, Norfolk,' she added, inevitably. Then leaned towards me, with a kindly frown: 'Where are you from, Jayne? Originally?'

'London,' I said. More seemed required, so I added, 'My mother was from Cardiff. My father was Scottish . . .'

She nodded slowly, and I could see her trying to assess my history, my place, my sensitivities. We lapsed into paralysis.

Finally, Mr Hannah rallied round.

'Do you know Norwich, at all?'

'Oh, yes!' I yelped, and nearly dropped my tea dregs. 'It's lovely, isn't it!'

I could feel Gareth looking at me, and tried to calm down.

'Haven't been there recently,' said Mr Hannah. 'We *should* go though, shouldn't we, Bridget?'

He took a sip of cold tea and flared his nostrils. Then he said, 'Very well-preserved, the centre. Medieval. Lots of churches. Do you know the cathedral?'

I was nodding wildly; Bridget had stopped smiling and glazed over.

'Beautiful,' I said. 'Beautiful city. All the . . .' And then it occurred to me that the cityscape opening up, clear and sharp, in my mind-the needle spires soaring over hobgoblin roofs-wasn't Norwich at all. In fact it might not be anywhere. It could quite feasibly be a dream I'd had. Or a film I'd seen. Or a combination of both. I half turned away, screwing up my eyes to concentrate on the view, but I couldn't give it a name or a status. There are so many imaginary settings, as familiar as the real streets and interiors of my life, revisited in dreams and fantasies, distorted and rearranged. I was guiding myself through a street, along a series of hairpin bends in the canyon formed by overhanging houses. Past a row of shops, with stalls set up on the pavement, and names that I could almost read . . . if I could just try hard enough . . .

'Mum!' said Gareth. I came to myself in time to catch Bridget slipping a new smile over a troubled gaze.

'Sorry – I was miles away, then . . .' (those shop signs were still on the blurred edge of my thoughts) . . . 'But I'm not sure, now, whether I'm in Norwich or not . . .'

Did I really say that? Probably not. Anyway, there was no point explaining that my version of the city might be an amalgam of *Goodbye Mr Chips* and *Murders in the Rue Morgue*.

After that we all gave up for a while and sat in the reddening light, occasionally contributing indistinct humming noises and little laughs. Gareth put his mug on the floor and gave Hannah a sideways look. He said,

'Just going on the computer . . .' and hauled himself to the edge of the chair ready to get up. Mr Hannah waved an urbane hand.

'Ah, well – we've got to be off soon. You all set, Hannah?'

Gareth slumped back into his seat.

'Anyway,' said Bridget. 'You spend enough time ogling that computer up there . . .'

'Mum,' protested Hannah, 'we're just going to . . .'

I could see more excruciating wink-wink comments coming from Bridget's direction. Sure enough: 'We don't want to know, thank you!' She doubled her chin and raised knowing eyebrows at me. 'All these urgent appointments with the computer . . . a likely tale . . .'

To my relief, Hannah was now provoked.

'Mum, you're *obsessed*! Anyway, it's not like we're *alone*, is it? With seven or eight other people in the chat room? We're not exhibitionists, you know.'

Bridget made conciliatory lip shapes at her, and Mr Hannah muttered,

'Fact remains . . . Time's pressing on . . .'

Bridget asked her daughter, in an entirely different tone, 'Is this your animal rights chat room?'

'*Yes*,' said Hannah, ready for a fight. 'Any objections?'

She's more feisty than I thought. I was beginning to like her.

'Just think before you act,' said Bridget. 'That's all I ask.'

Hannah and Gareth sulked, and so did I. How come everyone else but me knows what Gareth's doing?

At last, Bridget embarked on a conversational coda.

'Well.' She searched for a place to put her tea and then set it carefully on the hearth. 'It's been lovely meeting you. And I love your cottage – *so light*!'

We both got up, nearly cracking skulls, and I said, 'It's a shame Bobby isn't here-maybe next time.'

I don't know why I said it. It seemed the appropriate thing to say.

She nodded, regarding me closely. Then she touched my arm.

'I'm *sure*,' she said. Behind her, Mr Hannah added heartily: 'He'll be back before you know it, and then you'll wonder . . .' But he decided against his little quip. I was sorry: I could have agreed, and ushered them out, laughing. Bridget seemed to think I'd shared a confidence, and deserved a more solemn response.

'You're coping so well,' she said. 'It must be a terrible strain.'

Hannah chipped in, trying to redeem herself after the sulk. 'You're bound to find him,' she said. 'I mean, there's CCTV everywhere these days. It's not like, say, in the past, when people could go off and nobody knew where they were.'

Gareth had his hands in his pockets. He said to the floor, 'He's not a *criminal*. He's on *business*.'

Everyone but Gareth looked at me. I wanted to back him up, without mortifying his girlfriend. I said,

'Yes . . . He . . . It . . . Bobby's still very keen on, on this . . . it's the nostalgia business, really . . . He's hoping we can open another out- . . . shop, all, all to do with . . .'

It was going horribly wrong. We were stuck in the living room, with no comfortable way of getting to the front door. Mr Hannah turned idly towards the back window. If he wandered over he'd have a perfect view of my exhumed collection of rubbish. I started waffling loudly to Hannah.

'Because,' I said 'the thing is, my mother was involved in films. In her heyday – I showed you, remember?'

'Yes,' said Hannah, robotically.

'*Out in the hall* – there's a photograph . . .'

There was a minor stampede into the hall. Only Gareth stayed behind.

Bridget led the field and peered at my mother's signature.

'Marian Westwood . . .' She stepped back. 'Oh, *very* glamorous. That's so very . . . Isn't it?' Her nameless husband pressed his lips together and nodded. 'So very *Hollywood*.'

'In fact,' I said, carried away with my success, 'while Bobby's looking for a new site, I'm thinking of . . . of researching . . .' I cast around for a suitably impressive word. 'A, a *biography*. A biography of Marian Westwood . . .'

'Really?'

Bridget kept her incredulous eyes fixed on the photograph.

'Yes, I've been preparing the ground, putting out . . . feelers . . .'

Too shrill. Too blatant. Gareth was now standing in the doorway behind me; my lies may have been reflected in his face. They all left soon after that, and Hannah lingered on the doorstep to say goodbye to my poor son, and he probably shook his head and raised his hands in despair as he said,

'I know. But she's my mother.'

17

'Well, why not?' says Gill, ladling out home-made apricot crumble. 'I think it's an excellent idea.'

I give her one of Gareth's scowls and she holds out her hands, splatting apricot mush on the floor. 'You're better placed than anyone else to do it, after all!'

'Gill, it was a bare-faced lie. I said it to fill a gap. There is no way on earth that I am ever going to write a biography about anybody, alive or dead, and least of all my mother.' I start on my pudding and she broods for a moment as she's wiping up the splashes. She sits opposite me at the kitchen table and chuckles.

'I can understand why you said it, though. That awful, sneering woman and her "outposts of the empire" routine. "One gets used to the natives and their primitive ways, doesn't one?" God! She gives me the pip.'

'Don't,' I say. 'They may be Gareth's in-laws in due course.' I shudder, recalling Mr Hannah's drift towards the back window. 'Oh, God . . . if they'd seen my garden collection . . .'

Gill barks with laughter and almost chokes on her crumble. When she's stopped coughing and wiped her eyes she says,

'Patrick thinks it might be a coping strategy, you know. Your . . . archaeological digs.'

'Does he think I *need* a coping strategy?'

She tosses her head. 'Either that,' she says, 'or you're an artistic genius. He hasn't decided yet.'

Do they all think I need strategies? Therapies? Is that really why I'm here, on the outskirts of the asylum? Gill changes the subject.

'Really, though, you shouldn't dismiss the idea.'

'What idea?'

'Of doing a biography'. She rushes on, drowning my moan. 'Think about it. You've got the perfect inside knowledge. And people forget, you know-celebrity is so transient. It'll keep her alive . . .'

I'm not sure I want to do that. I choose my words with caution: 'I wouldn't want to sully her memory. Some of it wouldn't be very savoury, if I'm honest . . .'

'Of course not, of course not – nobody wants a hagiography. But it'll be so much better for *you* to deal with the – the more difficult times, than to have some slavering hack nosing through the dirty laundry.'

'I thought you said everyone had forgotten her.'

'Oh, stop twisting the argument!'

'Anyway, it's all academic. It was a big, fat fib to impress Hannah's mother. That's all.'

'If you need to do any research, you know, make any trips – I could help out with that to a certain extent . . .'

A trip to London. Home. A valid journey with a valid purpose. I could stay with Natalie. Hunt down some of my mother's old acquaintances . . . I picture myself a month from now, beavering away, closeted in some audio-visual booth in the National Film Museum. Six months from now, working on a draft chapter. I picture myself revisiting the flat in Bayswater, enjoying the spaces created by later occupants.

'You don't have to worry about it,' I say, 'because it's not going to happen.'

There are times, even now, when I hear my mother's living voice-like a few bars of cheap song that sit uninvited in your head. A bird's call or an inflexion on the radio might trigger it and for a second she's in the next room, calling:

'Jayn-ey!' Two insistent syllables, packed with irritation, disillusion and demand. 'Jayn-ey!' – always at the same pitch, always with a pause on the 'n' that screws up my muscles and clamps my jaw. Will that be how Gareth reacts in years to come, at the mere suggestion of my voice, my long-gone tics and habits? Will he have to explain to Hannah, as he grimaces at some fragment of sound in his cosy, tidy family home? – 'Sorry. Reminded me of my mother.'

'It would be gratifying', Gill needles on, 'just to show that woman . . .'

' . . . that I'm not a pathetic fantasist?'

'Just to wipe the patronising smile off her face.'

I sit back in my chair and watch darkness thickening within the complexity of branches and shrubs in Gill's garden, while the lawn and the fields beyond still carry a wistful glow. All my best intentions to resist a bitch about Hannah's mother are slipping away.

'She seemed to know more about Gareth than I did,' I complain. 'Animal rights chat room! I had no idea he was in to all that . . .' (Even after rifling through his computer files, I manage not to add.) 'I mean, he hasn't eaten meat for a couple of years, but then he seems to subsist on cornflakes and crisps.'

'Well,' says Gill, 'he did get quite worked up about those wasps.'

'And yet he'll spend any amount of time watching *people* being maimed and mutilated for entertainment.'

Gill busies herself clearing dishes and boiling the kettle, but I can see the crow's feet deepening around her eyes at some thought. Then she says, 'Remember how Bobby used to carry him round the garden when he was a little tot? And listen for bees inside the flower heads?'

I stiffen and sit upright again. I'm not sure I want to indulge in memories of Bobby the Good Father right now.

Gill holds the handle of the kettle, waiting for its tremor to reach a peak. She shakes her head and says, 'So strange. It could have been Lenny and him.'

18

Having fulfilled his conditions, Lenny was allowed to pay visits to the family. Robert Gilbard was a just man. So there's Lenny, a little woozy from his drugs, sitting in the garden with Gill and Bobby Junior while Robert attends to something important in his study. Lenny is showing five-year-old Bobby how to listen for the bees in the foxgloves. Like jazz, he says. Jazz trumpeters, with wings.

Bobby wanders away to inspect the flowers and insects at closer quarters. A howl yanks the adults from their seats. Bobby has seen a fly blunder into old cobwebs in a niche of the garden wall. They watch it struggle, entangling itself more hopelessly; they hear the pathetic fizzle of its wings as it heaves against the sticky threads. Gill tries to pull Bobby away: 'It'll be all right,' she promises, 'if we leave it alone.'

But Lenny nudges her away. 'We'll give it a hand, shall we?' he says. He and Bobby find a twig and try prising the creature free. They drag wisps of silk away with infinite care. Lenny directs and Bobby prods and pulls with a steady hand.

'No!' cries the boy suddenly. 'I'm pulling its leg off!'

He drops his twig and Lenny gives up.

'It's tired, now' he says. 'We'll let it rest.'

Bobby trots after them back to the garden table.

'We'll go back, though, won't we? And we'll save it?'

Gill is pursing her lips at Lenny, warning him not to pursue his logic, begging him to allow the child some inconsistency, some fiction. But Lenny can't help himself.

'No,' he says, quietly. 'We'll let it die.'

Bobby's wail of protest breaks into loud sobs. He's wracked with grief. Gill tries to console him, firing thunderous looks at Lenny.

'You tried your best to help him,' she coaxes. 'That's what matters.'

'No it doesn't, not to the baby flies . . .'

Lenny puts a hand on the back of his son's neck and says to Gill, 'He's right, of course. Come with me, Bobby.'

Helplessly, Gill watches him manoeuvre Bobby back to the garden wall. She dismisses an involuntary image of herself at 17, propelled into the staff wash-room in the Vita Nuova. Lenny is leading Bobby by the hand, now, talking to him, preparing him to watch the fly's last exertions, describing what it will be like for the fly as its life slips away. Bobby, intrigued, forgets his distress. He sniffs violently and wipes his nose with his sleeve. They disappear from view behind a chrysanthemum bush.

A yelp makes Gill leap to her feet again and Bobby is cantering back towards her, victorious: 'It's gone! It's got free!'

Behind him comes Lenny, shrugging, hands in pockets, grinning a muted version of the old grin.

Typical that Bobby's first brush with harsh reality had a happy ending laid on.

19

Bobby touching branches and petals, Gareth on his hip, clutching fistfuls of his shirt.

'Hear that? Hear the bees? Like little trumpeters, aren't they?'

It may be a genuine recollection, or I may be grafting Gill's memories on to my own. Lately I've been wracking my brain, sifting through past conversations with Bobby, searching for mentions of Lenny. But Bobby was so careless about his past, shedding tiny scraps of it here and there; anything I do retrieve is probably sloughed off my own imagination. Gill can make all the connections she likes, but the truth is that Uncle Lenny's visits seemed to make no lasting impression on Bobby. Not as a charming playmate, not as a kindly teacher – as nothing more, in fact, than a slightly odd grown-up who took up his mother's time. Sometimes that was Gill's fault. Sometimes she monopolised Lenny, drew him away from the boy, partly from an instinct of defence, partly so that she could offload her plans and preoccupations, talk and talk as she once did in his room above the café. She wanted to confide in him about her new career path, her decision to re-train as a psychiatric social worker. Fresh challenge. Pastures new.

Lenny seemed highly amused.

'So,' he said, 'you're still defying mummy and daddy. Breaking the rules of privacy. Rummaging in people's minds.'

His speech was stilted and a little slurred. Gill tutted and turned in her chair to check on Bobby, who was writing his name in the condensation of the window-pane.

'Are you having suicidal thoughts?' Lenny asked, suddenly leaning forward with artificial earnestness.

'What are you talking about?'

'That's what you'll have to ask people. That's what they're always asking me – haven't I mentioned that?'

He gave a laboured laugh, a guttural sound: one of his new, chemically produced characteristics. 'Check, check, double-check,' he said. 'Have I brushed my teeth? Washed behind the ears? Kept up my doses? Had any suicidal thoughts?'

Gill ignored him and kept her eyes on Bobby.

'Who the hell doesn't have suicidal thoughts?' Lenny muttered after a while.

Gill looked askance at Bobby, but he was too intent on his task to hear.

20

I've had another dream about Pat. Now that I can put a name to him I'm all the more embarrassed. The narrative was confused but the atmosphere was erotic and mysterious, and we were on the inside of the wall. Again I was pressed against it but without urgency, without force; I moved along it in semi-darkness, feeling a landscape of moss and crumbling brick. In my dream the wall was ancient and benign. I caressed its damp growth with my cheek. There was a profound sense of intimacy, surrounded by Pat's unseen presence. There were others, too, unseen and unnamed, watching behind windows, but I knew that as long as I concentrated on the wall itself I could avoid confronting them.

Gill has resumed her gardening visits, determined to press on with the ferns and flowers while I continue my excavations. I've found a thick, clay bottle dated 1902 and a long, rusting spear that's probably something for the coal fire. I sit cross-legged on the grass and clean them up, Gill kneels in a far corner and extends the borders. There are clumps of colour, now, along the back of the lawn and halfway up the side of the path: little regimented rows of unassuming flowers, kept at a safe distance from each other by black shreds of mulch that Gill assures me is peat-free and organic.

Actually, I'm quite pleased to have her here. Gareth comes home as little as possible nowadays. I've taken to looking at his e-mails on a regular basis, between sessions of cutting and adding text. Apparently he's starting to think about university. He and Hannah have had a soul-searching exchange across the ether about it. They want to be together. They've discussed applying to Glasgow, Hannah to do French and Gareth to do Politics. Gareth wants to go somewhere new, somewhere that'll give him breathing space, as he puts it: a clean break. Well, thank God for e-mails. At least if anyone asks I can tell them my son's future plans, for all the world as if he's let me know.

I've been trying to prepare my lines, in case Bobby rings and Gareth isn't there. I know asking for a contact number would frighten Bobby off, but I must make sure he speaks to Gareth before it's too late. Before Gareth doesn't live here any more. Personally, I look ahead to that time with as much relief as misery. The sooner Gareth can escape into a normality of his own, the better. And the further away he gets, the more chance he'll have, I'm sure, of brushing off his disastrous inheritance.

As Gill and I are working I casually mention my dream, in an edited version.

'I was stuck behind that wall,' I say, 'and I think Pat was there too. But it wasn't scary at all—'

'No. It's not,' she interrupts.

'But, I mean . . . There are some dangerous people in there, aren't there?'

She tilts her head in concession, but adds: 'And there are people in there who would never wittingly hurt a soul.'

21

'Gay? Are you sure?'

'That's what Gill said.'

'Well, he gives all the wrong signals, then.' Natalie struggles to sound nonchalant. 'Are you *sure*?'

'You've asked me that already.'

'Yes, but how would Gill know?'

'I suppose he told her.'

'Or she made up her mind in advance. No – come on, Jayne, you must admit she's like that. "Gill knows best". She's probably told herself he's gay because she lusts after him herself and it's some kind of denial.'

My throat snaps shut in outrage and I hack down the phone. Natalie changes tack.

'OK. Well, how about this, then: she's *told* you he's gay to stop *you* lusting after him. Making sure you stay true to her boy Bobby.'

'Stop it, Natalie.'

'Stop what?'

'Stirring. Making trouble.'

'Plausible theory, though, isn't it?'

I move on to another subject. I talk about the work she's been sending me, about deadlines and house style. Then I tell her about Hannah's parents.

'They sound like tedious old farts to me,' she says, dismissively.

I try and tell her about my treasure-trove in the garden.

'Good God, Jayne,' she interrupts. 'Are you out of your mind? Digging up old rubbish? It might be *diseased*. High time you got out of that godawful weird place, my girl. I *told* you not to go fannying around doing the garden. Leave it alone.'

So I don't mention the scheme I've been drawing up. I've decided to place my hoard around the garden, with the gate, my first find, as the centrepiece, and the rest of my freakish statuary arranged at suitable intervals. I ponder the best way to anchor each item, the most effective spacing and positioning; I mark it all out on a sheet of A4 paper while the musicals are running their soundless course at night. I forget to watch; some nights I forget to play them altogether.

Natalie has manoeuvred us back to her original topic.

'You'll just have to find out for yourself.'

'How am I supposed to—'

'*Ask* him, you ninny. Just to be quite sure.'

'I can't. I *can't*. And anyway, why should I? It doesn't make the slightest difference to me whether he's gay or straight.'

She splutters disbelief. 'Do some detective work, then,' she insists.

'No.'

'Ask around.'

'I don't know anyone to ask. Except Gill. And she's told me.'

'Have a nose round. See if you can spot him with anyone. Follow him round the . . . the yard, or whatever it's called.'

'The estate. Absolutely not.'

'Oh, come on. Bit of harmless stalking – we've all done it.'

'Speak for yourself.'

'Well, it's got to be a better way of passing your sentence than digging old doggy-bones out of the lawn.'

OCTOBER

1

Summer's over. I've been watching it go, swept away with the clouds and shadows, surfing over fields raw from the harvest. I never really noticed, living in the city, the progression of colours that marks a passing season. There were minor changes: the blush of leaves, the closing sky, the mottling of flesh. But here every shade on the canvas is altered. Headache-yellow swathes of rape-seed vanish; chalky-brown ploughfields wheel into life. Come the winter, everything will resolve into silver and gold: the pebbledash of Gill's house; the bare trees; grasses and reeds, low clouds. Just for a second, before it's all blotted into dull slush – just for a second, there'll be the lustre of possibility. A paring down. Charcoal and sepia, as beautiful as an old photograph.

This is Gareth's last year at school. His last year at home. He's doing well – on course for Glasgow, which as far as I can tell is still his first choice. There was another phone call from Bobby two months ago. He rang the cottage, this time, and luckily Gareth was there. Bobby said he was well, everything was fine, he had some new ideas, yes, he was still in Liverpool, or 'thereabouts'. I said, 'Talk to Gareth,' and he squeaked self-consciously.

'Yes, yes, Gareth, put him on.'

They didn't say much. Bobby must have remembered to ask about school work, because I heard Gareth telling him his exam results. At one point Gareth shot a glance at me and said, 'OK, I think. Yeah. Coping.'

After a while he said, 'OK, Dad. See you,' and held the phone out, but I heard the click and purr before taking the receiver.

'Did he . . .?'

I didn't quite know what to ask. Gareth shook his head and shrugged.

'He said there's a cheque in the post.'

'I see.'

Neither of us can muster much conviction. There hasn't been a cheque or anything else in the post from Bobby for months.

My archaeological garden is coming along. A fortnight ago I drove to Berriford and bought sacks of concrete and sand. I faced out Gill's dismay and told her she could either help or not, but I was going ahead with my plan. Every morning I looked out through the front window, half expecting a skip to be parked outside and Gill to be loading it with my treasures. But she gave in. She even recruited Pat, and together we made foundations for the gate, for the pyramid of large bones, for the broken bedstead and for the spear. Gill persuaded me to widen the hole at the bottom of the coal scuttle and plant a tomato bush through it. I've still got plenty of other bits and pieces to arrange, but they can wait.

In return for accepting my junk garden, Gill has demanded that I go for walks with her across the fields. She thinks I need to stir my blood. So as soon as Gareth's gone to school we set off, trudging over stubble and stripped earth to the village, where we do a turn around the churchyard before coming back. The churchyard is an unexpected place, with a grand stone entrance, not unlike the hospital's, and a few very ornate gravestones humbled by the weather. Gill has pointed out a couple of more recent stones marking the graves of patients. She showed me one engraved with an oriental script – Mandarin, maybe – and an English postscript: 'Joe Cheng, RIP, 1902-1937'.

'A long way from home,' Gill murmured, stroking the curve of the stone. 'What a strange place to end up, poor sod.'

In the evenings, once or twice a week, the stories continue. I have the sense that we're approaching a conclusion of some kind. Gill has let me take the lion's share of time and narrative. She encourages me to root out more memories, dwell on marginal details; she says it's good practice for that biography. I think she's putting something off. Maybe she's waiting for Bobby to come home. Maybe her stories were meant for him to hear.

2

I've officially reached the decline and fall of Marian Westwood. Not that Gill needs me to tell her about it: she can follow it the same way everyone else did, by watching her films. By about 1971 or so the theatre work had dried up completely. It was a dip, said Marian. It would pick up in due course, she insisted, tapping ash on to her plate, muscles ridging her neck. Normal service would be resumed. In the meantime there was plenty of work, more than plenty, very busy indeed, no rest for the wicked. She'd appeared in a succession of *Who Needs . . .* pictures for Johnny Dunville, he of the Saturday Minstrel Parade. *Who Needs Love?* was the first. Then there was *Who Needs Girls?*, *Who Needs Money?* and so on. Even Marian's dwindling band of hangers-on referred to them with open contempt as 'Who Needs a Script'. Marian certainly didn't need one. She vamped across the screen in a variety of tight dresses, with her flashing eyes and increasingly ragged cleavage, growling at the leading man's double-entendres. She referred to her early appearances as 'cameos'. It was healthy to satirise oneself, she said, and it was a privilege to work for a great man like Johnny Dunville, who did so much for charity and had made an anti-fascist film in 1935.

By the turn of the '70s there was no disguising the desperation, as titles and plots grew more sordid. In *Who Needs a Quick One?* she was demoted to the lascivious older woman, thrusting scaffolded boobs at a reluctant young buck. She refused to watch the final cut, but she acted up to the part on and off screen: an overpainted parody of her youth.

She blamed Harry. He was still working in the theatre; he could have pulled strings. Alec had, after all: he'd been there when she needed him.

'But then Alec,' she spat, 'gave a toss about me and my career.'

Alec was still around for his Baby Girl. As he coiled into an almost circular old age he continued to make himself useful. He hadn't lost all his contacts yet. When booze, fags and company weren't enough my mother knew where to go. Sometimes she didn't come back.

I worried for my father, monitored his silences with concern, but if truth be told Harry was already removing himself from the marriage and – at least partly – from me. He met sweet Amanda in 1973. She was ushering at a matinée and brought him an ice. He sat out another 3 years in Bayswater and then he bailed out. He came to meet me from school one afternoon, took me to a truckers' caff and bought me a fry-up, and as I fed slimy egg white down my throat he explained that he was going to have to leave.

'You're pretty grown up now,' he said. 'You've got a good head on your shoulders. You won't let this throw you.' He was almost pleading.

'No,' I said, obligingly.

'You'll carry on with your school work, won't you? Don't let her distract you, and whenever you need peace and quiet come to us.'

I nodded. I tried to slice my fried tomato but it sank into a red pulp, swimming with pips. I wasn't sure what to say, so I offered lines from American TV shows:

'As long as you're happy, Dad. Don't worry. You can rely on me.'

At 14 Harry Scott had left school and started his apprenticeship miles from home. At 14 Marian Westwood had accepted a drink and a chance of freedom in the Ship's Tits in Cardiff. No wonder they both had my childhood signed off.

3

After Dad had left I preferred to spend my weekends with him and Amanda, but Marian had hysterics every time I suggested it.

Saturdays weren't too bad. Sometimes she took me shopping. If she was working, I was left to my own devices all day. In the evenings my main dread was that her friends would come over, and I would be sent around topping up drinks and lighting cigarettes ('Don't take anything naughty in front of my little princess, darlings – she's still pure and innocent'), before slinking into my room and locking the door against the racket. I was too old, now, for cosy bedroom visits and girly chats. I wouldn't have let her if she'd tried.

By Sunday we couldn't wait to get rid of each other, but the farce dragged on until I could escape to school the following day. As props for our domestic scene Marian would buy a stack of newspapers, and there we would sit, me and my mother, trapped in mutual exasperation, with the smell of stale booze and ashtrays and newsprint, and the tinned jollity of 'Family Favourites' in the background. She would hide behind each paper, one by one, pretending to read, exclaiming and tutting, exchanging one supplement for another when the time seemed right. To this day I refuse to buy Sunday papers. They make me ill-at-ease and guilty. At 15, though, I found a way of using them to annoy my mother even more. I would read every word of every paper. Every single word. Right down to the small ads and the tiny disclaimers at the back. If I reached the end of a paragraph and realised that some of the sentences had skimmed by too easily, I had to go back and register each word and each punctuation mark separately, consciously, to myself. My mother understood that it was an obscure dig at her. She registered her disapproval with exaggerated foldings and flappings and a menacingly thin mouth. I kept to my task, concentrating all the harder. If we had a meal, or if she summoned me out for a walk, I noted my place (page, column, line) and carried on as soon as we'd finished.

If she had a dinner date or a phone call to make she left me to it; when she returned I would still be at my task. She turned the lights off and went to her room, knowing that as soon as she'd shut the door I'd put the lights back on again. Eventually I'd hear her erupt into an incoherent, high-pitched, tearful frenzy. Then I closed the paper, got to my feet and waited for the blood to flow back into their veins before going to bed.

4

'You know who this is, don't you? This is Marian's girl.'

'Jeee-zuss wept!'

The woman stepped back for a better view. She was short and top-heavy; her square face was gouged with acne scars. An older, desiccated version of me. The man at my side tightened his hold on my shoulders, keeping me in place while her scrutiny ran its course. I frowned into my glass of sweet sherry, acutely aware of my own pus-heavy cheeks and chin. The woman delivered her verdict.

'Nothing like 'er.'

My captor gave me an encouraging shake.

'This,' he said to me, 'is your Auntie Sal.'

'Jesus, don't call me that,' bellowed Auntie Sal, moving away. 'Makes me sound like a fucking old maid.'

She waddled off. I noticed that her hair, dyed black like my mother's, was wispy and thinning at the back. Her skull gleamed under the pub lights.

'Is she—'

'Wassat?' Without releasing my shoulders, my host brought his ear to my mouth.

'Is she really my aunt?'

'Aye! Oh, aye.' He drew away with a look of surprise. 'Marian's big sister. Didn't she say nothing about Sal?'

Nothing about Sal, nothing about this man – apparently my Great Uncle Jed – and nothing about any of the relatives milling around the snug, swapping sentimental condolences, cracking jokes, raising a glass to my grandmother's name.

The news had come by post. No late-night phone call, no mournful visitor on the doorstep – just a one-page note in awkward handwriting, which Marian read over her morning toast and Irish coffee.

'Oh, shit,' she said.

There was a smear of cream around her mouth, peppered

with toast crumbs. Her hair was pulled back into a pony-tail, revealing grey roots.

'Your grandmother's dead,' she announced, and her eyes flicked up at me in terror.

'Well *I* can't go,' she wailed, answering an unspoken challenge. 'They can't expect . . . I've got too much on, for God's sake . . .'

It was 1977. The film work had withered away. She'd lined up a walk-on part in some dire TV sitcom and had the half-promise of a celebrity panel game.

'You'll go, won't you Jayney?' she wheedled. The letter was shivering in her hand. 'Next Tuesday. The funeral. You can miss school – compassionate leave, or whatever. We'll find you something nice to wear. Something elegant. You'll go, won't you, sweetheart? Pay our respects. For both of us.'

So here I was, in the iron grip of Great Uncle Jed, sipping my disgusting drink, staring through the smoke drifts at Auntie Sal as she levered herself on to a bar stool and cackled at some aside from her companion. There were about 50 people at the wake; there'd been around a dozen at the funeral. When I got out of the taxi at the chapel, cramped with shyness in my tailored black dress and lace-up shoes, there was no-one to be seen. I stood on the steps and tested the door, allowing myself the wild hope of the wrong address and a quick escape back to Central Station. But the door rasped and there was a stirring in the half-light, and Great Uncle Jed hobbled towards me in a brown suit at least a size too small.

'All right, love? Too early, are you? We're seeing off my sister now – just.'

The minister hovered behind him.

'I'm Marian's daughter,' I gasped. I had to repeat it three times, while Jed fastened his hand about my wrist and lowered his head to hear. Then he understood and his head sprang back up—

'Oh, Christ, it's Marian's girl!' and to the minister and the scattering of guests, now shifting round in the pews, 'See this? It's Marian's kid! The movie star's little girl!'

The words ricocheted back from here and there, and all eyes were on me as Great Uncle Jed led me down to the front pew and sat me next to him. A couple of minutes later the coffin was carried in, followed by two old women and a much younger woman, soon to be introduced as Auntie Sal. Jed writhed in his seat, getting a good look at the procession, then offering me his comments in a stage whisper that blotted out the feeble organ music.

'They did ask me to follow in, like,' he hissed. 'But I didn't want to. At my age you puts your arse on a seat every chance you get.' He wheezed with mirth, then squirmed round again to see the coffin placed on its plinth.

'Dear me,' he said. 'Not much left of the old mare, was there?'

He was right. I didn't remember my grandmother as a small woman, but it only took four slightly built men to carry her in. She must have shrunk over the eight or so years since our last visit.

Great Uncle Jed took charge for the rest of the afternoon: frogmarching me into the pub across the road, buying me the kind of drink he reckoned I'd like (my request for an orange juice was dismissed with a rumble of catarrh), pointing out the relatives I'd never known existed. The two older 'coffin-chasers', as he called them, were my grandmother's sisters. Great Aunt Bella and Great Aunt Bridie. I learned that my grandmother's name was Bess.

'I never knew her name,' I confessed to Jed.

'Bit late now,' he remarked.

Bella and Bridie sat together on one of the benches against the wall, brandishing their drinks and swaying gently from side to side, heads together, singing: 'I don't want to set the woooorld . . . oooon . . . fi-yer!'

'Bella, Bridie and Bess,' said Jed. 'The busy bees, we called 'em. Aye, and they was bloody busy, an' all. Going from flower to flower, sucking what's there, like!' His chest heaved and a wave of phlegm bubbled into his throat.

I tried to connect the tortoise-necked old woman who'd sat toying with the tablecloth in her tiny house with Bess the Busy Bee, swinging her hips, licking her lips, taking her sips of nectar.

Jed wanted me to stay on.

'Sal!' he roared. 'Marian's kid can stay with you and Trev, can't she?'

Sal gave me a short, unsmiling look from her bar stool. 'S'pose so.'

Desperation raised my voice.

'Wassat?' Jed's face loomed next to mine, fuzzy with stubble and smelling of pipesmoke and beer. 'Oh, aye, all right love – She've got to go back, Sal. Marian's expecting her, like.'

Sal shrugged and I caught the beginning of a sneer as she turned back to the bar. I was sick with shame and humiliation – for my mother, the ghost at the banquet, and for me, scuttling back to the familiarity of the flat, its heaps of clutter and neuroses, as eager to flee from the family as she had been three decades before.

I caught the 6 o'clock to Paddington and stopped at a Spar to buy us a Fray Bentos pie and frozen peas. Marian was in high spirits when I got back. She'd been offered Widow Twankie in the Basingstoke Haymarket that winter.

'Panto,' she sighed, examining the rings on her pudgey fingers. 'God, that takes me back. Should be a laugh and a half. So, how did it go?'

We cleared room for our plates on the little round table and sat mashing peas and steak-and-kidney. I told her about Jed and the Bees and Auntie Sal.

'You never told me I had an Auntie Sal,' I accused her. She giggled.

'Auntie Sal! God, I bet she loved that.'

'She said not to call her "auntie". Made her sound frigid, or something.'

My mother flung herself against the back of her chair. Her laughter made me join in. Then something occurred to me.

'I don't think anyone asked me what my name was,' I said.

Marian dabbed her eyes with her sleeve. 'Oh, sod them, Jayney,' she said, using my name as a reward. 'Jed's all right but the rest of them . . .' She took a mouthful of food and narrowed her eyes as she swallowed. 'Sal was always a hard bitch, always. She gave me a bad time from the day I was born.'

She released her foot from its shoe and lifted her leg, pointing the toe out at an angle.

'See that?'

A stubby pink scar sat between the ankle bone and the back of her heel.

'Sal did that with a corkscrew.'

'On purpose?'

I was suspicious. This had all the hallmarks of a Marian Westwood drama. But she nodded without affectation. 'Oh, yes. It was always on purpose. On the sly. My mother was shit-scared of her too. She never done a thing to stop her.'

Never done a thing. The child's complaint rang through her carefully constructed accent.

I munched at soggy pastry for a moment, considering this other Marian, as unknown as all the rest. Then I said,'Tell me about the Busy Bees.'

She gurgled, and her eyes glimmered with memory and mischief.

We sat there for hours among the letters and bills, ashtrays and dirty glasses, discarded jewellery, pots of nail varnish, bottles of aspirin and anonymous pills, and Marian repeated the scandals she'd heard about the Bees and their various lovers, the stories about Jed running off to join the merchant navy and getting kicked out in Ceylon, about her grandfather and his parents, about the neighbours, about her mother's GI, and about meeting Alec Blessing in the Ship's Tits. She drank vodka, prompted me to taste some, patted my hand when I screwed up my face in disgust.

'Good girl, Jayne,' she said. 'Don't you follow your mother's wicked ways.'

She was sparkling, lively and young, performing as she used to with her cronies – but that evening I had her all to myself.

5

'Gill, look at this!'

Bobby was lying on his side in front of the telly on his parents' expensively faded rug. He'd been watching the Sunday matinée, *Babes in Arms*, stretched out in a lanky, shallow curve, head on hand, and was lingering in the hope of a cartoon before the God Slot. Instead there was an overweight comic, mugging to camera over playfully crooked letters: 'Work for Idle Hands'. As Gill came in, wiping her hands on a teacloth, Marian Westwood was sashaying towards her, into a studio sitting room.

'That's wotsername, isn't it?' said Bobby. 'Who brought you and Robert together?'

Bobby had grown up with the romantic comedy version of his parents' courtship. Gill stood over him, aghast. In her pretend house, Marian wobbled and puckered and patted her too-black hair at the bemused comic star.

'From what I hear,' she was purring, 'you're a very handy man indeed.'

Canned laughter clicked on while the comic did a double take, then clicked off again. Bobby grinned up at his mother.

'How are the mighty fallen!' he said, then bit his lip. Gill had tears in her eyes.

Gill was like that in those days. Anything could set her off into rage or tears: items on the news, films, newspaper stories, a sharp word from a colleague at work. It was wholly out of character. Robert privately put it down to the Change and said nothing, but Gill's menopause wasn't due for another 10 years, and when it arrived she dealt with it like a sergeant-major. This was different.

To herself, she blamed the pressures of work. She was particularly bothered about one of her clients, a young man of about Bobby's age, trapped in a world of fear and ritual. He would shower himself over and over again. If the shampoo dribbled down his face, or if water splashed on his arm before it was completely soaped, or if any of his other rules were broken, he had to start again. When Gill asked him what would happen if he broke the cycle, if he didn't counteract the mistake, he said:

'Bad things will happen.'

'What kind of bad things?'

He couldn't tell her; voicing the fear might bring it to life. But he wrote it down, backwards, to maintain his protective spell. The note read:

'ENASNI OG LLIW I.'

He was a bright boy, with a sharp sense of humour that could still occasionally force its way through the fortress of rules. Gill liked him. She liked his defiance and dignity. But this boy was sick at heart, tired of the anxiety that chained him; recently his mother had been shadowing him, sleeping on the floor at the foot of his bed, afraid that he would break the cycle once and for all.

Bobby was 17 and already storing up schemes for a wayward future. He might go abroad after his 'A' levels; he might audition for drama school; he might take up photography. In the meantime he'd agreed to go on holiday to New York with his parents before his last year at school.

'OK,' he'd said, amiably, when Robert made the offer. 'I'd like to see New York. And I suppose it'll be the last time we all go together.'

It hit Gill like a falling brick. She knew, of course, that 17-year-olds didn't generally want to spend their holidays with their parents. At 17, she'd barely had a word to say to her own. But now that Bobby had given their trip a conclusive, ceremonial value, she was confronted with the stark truth. Bobby was leaving her. From now on it would be Gill and Robert. She felt like a jilted lover, left to spend her spinsterhood with a guardian she hardly knew.

And here was Marian Westwood, who for so long had been suspended, familiar and aloof, in the background of

Gill's past, like a royal portrait – here she was reduced to
flabby one-liners in a sleazy teatime filler. For a few
moments Gill watched her idol's degradation. Marian was
bloated and upholstered, and under the thick make-up
looked older than her 47 years.

'When they asked me to call round and look at the old
boiler . . .' jeered the comic. A sexually frustrated, middle-
aged woman: Marian's character was one step down from
villain. The camera pulled in close on her affronted face,
accompanied by another blast of recorded laughter. Gill
turned on her heel and went back to the kitchen. By the
time Bobby had mustered the energy to go after her she'd
mopped up her ludicrous tears and was sitting with
steepled arms, elbows resting on the breakfast bar, fingers
plaited, head bowed as if in prayer.

'Gill . . .' ventured Bobby. 'You're all right, aren't you?'

His questions generally invited reassurance. Gill lifted
her head just enough to see him over her hands. Automatically, she gave the required answer.

'Of course. Nothing to worry about.'

He nodded, immediately satisfied. For once, Gill was
irked. She added:

'It's so sad. Such a waste of talent. If you'd have seen her,
you know, in her heyday . . . She was-*alight*.'

Bobby was bored already. He'd heard it all before. He
said, 'Yeah, well, at least she's working. She's not on the
dole queue yet.'

Gill watched him lope back to the rug and the telly.

A little while later Bobby, lying hypnotised by the
comedy's predictable progress, heard a trickle of keys in the
hall, and Gill calling: 'Just popping out for a few hours.
There's a shepherd's pie in the freezer-tell Robert, if he gets
back before midnight.'

Robert was spending his Sunday as he usually did,
catching up in the office so that Monday wouldn't take him
by surprise.

The front door slammed. On the screen, the overweight comic backed away from Marian's advances and sat on his toolbox. He jumped up again with a yelp. Bobby tittered half-heartedly, and said: 'OK. See you later' – too low and too late for his mother to hear.

6

She hadn't been to Lenny's room for nearly 18 years. Not since that spring in 1959 when she'd wondered whether to share the secret of her pregnancy. When she and Lenny met – less and less frequently over the years – he visited the Gilbards' home, admitted at the owner's discretion. Gill had trouble finding a place to park, and had to walk through the maze of Soho from the car. She got lost, and asked directions from a couple of girls in the doorway of a strip club. One towered in platforms and a tiny skirt; the other was in a flowery dressing-gown. Gill followed their instructions but could find no familiar landmarks. It was hard to tell whether some shops were abandoned or well-covered. She passed windows patched with pictures of disembodied breasts, splayed thighs, glistening tongues. Like a battleground, she thought. Like a butchers' shop. She turned a corner and was brought to a halt with shock.

The Vita Nuova hadn't changed. Or rather it *had* changed: it had aged and sagged and faded along with its clientele. The brown-and-cream letters on the fascia, so young and cheeky in the 1950s, so free of war and formality, now seemed naïve. The 't' had disappeared from 'Vita'. Gill approached cautiously on the opposite side of the road until she could see through the fume-stained window. She made a whimpering sound, half sob, half giggle. Lenny's mural was still there, still – she was sure – unfinished under the strategically placed mirrors and yellowing posters. For a few minutes more she watched, and then someone appeared behind the counter, fussing with crockery. No-one she recognised. This gave her courage and she crossed the road. The door croaked and jangled, as it always had. There were only three customers there-an old man rumbling in the corner and a young couple, the girl heavily coiffed and made up ready, Gill guessed, for the evening's first show.

'Is Lenny in?' she asked, breezing past the counter. 'No, don't worry – I know the way.'

He didn't look pleased to see her. He was disconcerted, and so was she. Lenny's hair was cut short. His clothes were plain but clean, well-fitting and – the word popped into her head with her mother's emphasis – 'respectable'. He was politely welcoming; she was politely apologetic. He offered tea. 'It won't take a minute,' he said, 'I'll just nip downstairs . . .'

She refused.

The furniture was sparse but ordinary: a leaf table, two chairs, a single bed against the wall, a small chest of drawers with a small black-and-white TV on top. He waited as she conducted her mental inventory and then said: 'No camp stove. I cook downstairs nowadays. Or Mrs T keeps something aside . . .'

'Mrs Tambini! Is *she* still going?' Gill's surprise sounded false and self-conscious.

'Still going. The old boy died, though. Couple of years ago now.'

'Oh dear, I'm sorry to hear . . .' Gill surveyed the room again in desperation. Lenny's voice relaxed.

'Sit down,' he said. 'I'll go down and get us a bottle of wine.'

Gill sat tentatively on one of the chairs, then changed her mind and sat on the edge of the bed. She noticed that the only decorated area of wall was a corner by his pillow, filigreed with intricate doodles. She felt the push of tears again and drove her fingers hard into her palms.

He came back with the wine and glasses. She caught a flicker of the old amusement when he saw her there, on his bed. After pouring their drinks he sat at the table.

'How are you, Lenny?' asked Gill.

He nodded dreamily. 'As you see. Fine. Job's fine. Still in the library. Everything's . . . yes. Fine.'

He chuckled awkwardly. Gill pictured him at work, slotting books into their places, stamping dates and writing out catalogue cards, becoming a fixture, a museum piece, an ageing oddball. This was how solitary, scratchy old men evolved; the sort of men who used to queue for soup in the church hall.

As an afterthought, Lenny asked: 'How about you?'

This was terrible. She shouldn't be here, in the home of this mild, subdued stranger. She took a gulp of wine and her eyes roamed round the room again, trying to recreate the scene of her 20th birthday. What had set him off that day? she wondered. Something usually did; someone was usually to blame. Maybe he'd been nervous. Maybe it had mattered to him more than she ever understood – making her happy. To distract herself from this train of thought and the threat of more tears, Gill said, 'Oh, you know, I'm . . . I'm muddling . . .'

Her answer trailed away. She hadn't elbowed her way into this room full of ghosts to sit here exchanging platitudes. Gill affected an intimacy she didn't feel.

'Oh, Lenny,' she said. 'I've had enough. I'm very fed up. It's all so, so bloody . . .'

Lenny's face clouded, but it was too late now. Overcoming the impulse to leap up and run downstairs and back to the car, Gill laboured on. She avoided mentioning Bobby, and moaned about work instead. At first she stuck to office politics, resources, difficult colleagues, but the dam was breached; soon she was breaking confidences and telling tales. She named names. Simon – the boy who couldn't stop cleaning himself. Mr Turnbul – the retired teacher, shattered by grief and alcohol, who fought the urge to drink by sliding pins under the flesh of his arms and legs, and who resisted that urge by hollering obscenities from his window. Sadie – once a formidable political activist, now approaching 90, confused but ferociously indepedent, who left food to rot in the corners of her beloved house, and who defecated in her front garden after dark.

Gill said, 'You accused me of meddling in people's minds

– remember?' Lenny's face was blank. 'I don't even do that, you know. I just fend off one crisis at a time. Keep my fingers crossed behind my back.'

Lenny examined his glass thoughtfully.

'Put four walls around Sadie,' he said, 'and she'll have an outside loo.' The corners of his mouth fluttered. 'Front garden – it's a fairly sensible place to go.'

'Except it's all crazy paving,' said Gill, and was treated to a lop-sided grin. She pressed her advantage. 'Fair play, Lenny, you can see her neighbours' point. You wouldn't want Mrs Tambini leaving her droppings outside your door.'

They smiled at each other. Gill leaned against the wall. The knots and loops of his doodles hovered in the corner of her vision.

Lenny said, 'Following the rules. That's what it's all about. You can stick pins in your nose and in your ears but not in your arms-unless fashion dictates.'

'Lenny, he can barely move his fingers now . . .'

'Put your bones and crusts in a bag or on a heap in a field and they can rot to high heaven. Defecate into a porcelain bowl and wash it down a big pipe . . .'

'No, Len. Too easy. Mr Turnbull's a desperate man. Simon, Simon's mother – they're profoundly unhappy. They're scared.'

'Well, who isn't?'

Gill shifted irritably and caught her breath. Lenny, seeing her riled, sat back comfortably in his chair.

Two hours later Gill was lying on his bed, flinging her arm out to jab a finger in his direction.

'Glib,' she said, with a shower of spittle. 'Glib and facile. If it's just labelling, if it's just conventions, why do they come to us for help? People want help. They want to be released from this . . . this . . .'

Lenny was sitting cross-legged on the floor. He bared a

clamour of wine-blackened teeth as she cast about for the missing word.

'Ever heard of drapetomaniacs?' he said. 'They were slaves who tried to escape from their masters. That was a form of madness, in those days. A madness that makes you want to run away. Wait a minute—' He cut across Gill's slurred protest. Lenny was sober; most of the wine had been poured into Gill's glass. 'Homosexuality,' he said 'was a mental disorder. I dare say a good few sufferers were pretty depressed about it, and desperate, and scrambled their brains with whatever they could get, and wanted release. Kleptomania – taking what you want. Nymphomania—'

'Taking what you want,' said Gill, turning her head to look him in the eye. Lenny glanced away like a guilty schoolboy. He paused, then struggled on: 'Once upon a time . . . if a woman wanted a divorce – that was a form of madness too . . .'

'And a woman who left the man she loved?' Another voice said the words that were in Gill's fuddled head. She heard them recited from a stage, far away. Sentimental nonsense, she thought, and closed her eyes. Bloody fool. After a few seconds, which could have been an hour, she registered Lenny's silence and realised that she had, in fact, said those words herself. She opened her eyes. He was watching her; she couldn't tell whether he was angry, or hopeless, or sad. With a spasm of pity she hoisted herself onto one elbow and said, 'Oh, Lenny . . .'

He moved forward, onto his hands and knees, crawled to the bed, and she placed her hand on his head and kneaded the cropped hair, remembering how thick and soft it had been. She smiled with nostalgic desire.

'Gillian, oh Gillian . . .' she sang, prompting him. But Lenny hadn't sung his songs for a long time. He shook his head and touched her mouth with his fingers. As they kissed Gill put her arms around his shoulders, and felt the ripple of fear.

7

Incidentally, Gill shouldn't have wasted any sympathy on Marian Westwood. She went off that winter to play Widow Twankie as happy as Larry. I saw her off at Waterloo (my mother never learned to drive). There she stood, swathed in scarves and her poncho-style coat, surrounded by the heaped geometry of her bags and cases – lozenges and circles and oblongs and squares – playing to the circle with cries of 'Whatever happened to *porters*?'. All she needed was a waft of steam and she'd be the grande dame in a 1930s film. Another passenger helped us load the luggage and then asked for her autograph. When they'd shut the door I could see her asking him, with delicate, girlish movements, to pull down the window for her. My hands delved further into the pockets of my duffle coat. She was perfectly capable of opening the window herself.

'Straight to Daddy's, now, Jayney,' fluted my mother. *Daddy's*? I cringed. 'I'll phone you as soon as I arrive,' she lied. 'And don't forget to check on the flat, will you?'

I closed my fist around the two spare keys in my pocket: one to Bayswater, one to Dad's. The train moved off and relief welled up, lifting my heels as I strode back to the concourse. I could go anywhere I liked, now. I could do anything. I was on my own and free until 6 o'clock, when I was due at my father's house. I walked across Waterloo Bridge, down the Strand, the length of Charing Cross Road and had a coffee in Oxford Street. I decided to walk all the way to Bayswater, collect my bags and then catch the train to Dad's. That was all I did, that afternoon: walk, sit, watch the world. But I relished those hours. For the first time I had an inkling of adult life, of making decisions, of controlling my own fate; for the first time I believed this might be possible, and it seemed like a cell door opening.

Amanda was a home-maker. She and Harry lived in a little house in Bromley which contained no human smells.

Lemon in the kitchen, sea-breeze in the bathroom, pine in
the loo, magnolia in the sitting room. No furtive, cabbagey
underlay, no stale meat or sweaty feet. All traces of personal
gas were sucked out by extractor fans, blasted away by fizz
from the cistern. I was taken in like a feral creature from the
Bayswater wilds, cleaned, fed, tucked up and civilised.
They didn't talk much; Harry read his paper, Amanda
watched the telly, did her mini-tapestries, occasionally
disappeared to fetch hot chocolate or home-made biscuits,
and the evenings lounged ahead with no threat of quarrels,
pyrotechnics or half-pissed visitors. But it wasn't my home.
I was a loved, tended and cosseted guest, a tourist treated to
the near-authentic family experience. I still asked permission
before taking off my shoes.

Harry and Amanda took me to see Widow Twankie towards
the end of the run. It was the first time I'd ever seen my
mother on stage, and it was a revelation. When she made
her first entrance I didn't recognise her: she was decked out
in a bell-shaped gown hung with all kinds of grotesqueries,
and a vertically spiralling lavender wig. But I knew it was
her – I *felt* that it was her, as the audience braced itself
around me. We were in safe hands. My daft, drug-blown,
self-obsessed, battling, bewildered mother strode downstage,
put her hands on her hips and took command of us all.
    'Oh, woe is me' she boomed, 'My palpitating heart, oh –
do you mind, Madam? Yes – put away the hipflask and pay
attention, there's a dear . . .'
    We guffawed ecstatically. She insulted us, teased us,
treated us to knowing looks, hauled us in and out of the
plot with ease, and we squealed and gurgled and revelled
in her confidences. My father was vibrating next to me, taut
as a wire; I sneaked a look at him and understood more
than I ever had before. I wondered whether Amanda was
seething in the shadows, and leaned forwards to check as
another crash of laughter buffeted the auditorium. Amanda's

eyes were wide, her hands suspended above her lap; she was hooked.

After the show we went backstage and waited to be admitted to Marian's dressing room.

'Are you all right, Jayne?' asked Amanda, touching my arm. 'Got a headache?'

I found that I was grinding my teeth. Please, I was thinking, please don't let Marian spoil everything. I wasn't sure what to expect – sarcasm, frosty silence, downright rudeness . . . Poor Amanda, I thought; poor, innocent Amanda, about to see the magic shot to smithereens. Harry rapped on the door and walked in and we heard their voices mingled with others. Then we were ushered in. Marian was still made up, except for the wig; her hair was combed back and plastered down with a skullcap. Several other people were lolling around the room, including Stinki Pu The Evil Chopstick, who was in his vest and pants, lighting a pipe. Twisting round in her chair, Marian extended an arm through the fug to take Amanda's hand.

'Did you enjooov?' she cooed. I half expected Amanda to curtsey. Then I was steered to the royal presence and she draped her arm round my waist.

'My Jayney,' she announced, 'my little princess!'

I tolerated her embrace and avoided the view in the mirror.

It all went so smoothly; they all played their parts. Harry and Amanda were the captivated fans, Marian the magnanimous star. We stood around and listened to them discuss the evening's cock-ups for a while, and were then dismissed. Marian blew a kiss into the air.

'Shan't inflict my warpaint on you, darling. Off you go, then, thanks so much for coming, glad you enjoyed it, all to do again in 16 hours' time . . .'

She rolled her panda eyes and the other cast members groaned. Sixteen hours, 21 hours, matinée, evening – for another eight weeks they knew where they'd be, what they'd be doing and what they had to say, and they were all on top of the world.

On the drive back to London Harry and Amanda chattered in the front like children. It had rained while we were in the theatre and the streetlights cast a sheen on the road ahead. I sat in the back, lulled by the hiss of passing cars. Every so often Harry and Amanda raised a chant, some daft line from the panto:

'What's the magic word?'

'Look out – there's a villain about!'

We left the main road and drove through a softer pulse of light and dark. Amanda's voice was still primed with excitement as she said,

'Oh, I hope they have pantos in Australia . . .'

She faded into unconvincing laughter, but there was no mistaking the sudden tension in the air. I sat forward.

'When are you going to Australia?'

My father slowed the car to negotiate a curve in the road. He swore under his breath; I thought he was cursing the parked cars that narrowed his route.

'Oh, it's just an idea,' said Amanda, without looking at me.

'Nothing final,' said my father.

'It's a bit of a fantasy, really,' said Amanda.

'On holiday?' I asked, growing suspicious. They didn't reply. I was leaning between the front seats, trying to read their expressions. 'Are you moving to Australia?' I asked. Harry became brisk and businesslike.

'It's only a discussion we've had, Jayne, just a possibility, that's all. For the future.'

'Just a dream, really,' said Amanda.

'Can I come?'

I didn't mean it. I was calling their bluff. Amanda turned to Harry with a searching look, so reluctant to say no that she might even say yes. Harry cut in quickly.

'We probably won't even go, love. Like I said . . .'

Only a few weeks before this I'd wandered through London intoxicated by the prospect of independence. Now I was on the edge of panic. At the same time, I was enough of my mother's daughter to see the potential in this situation. I produced a tone of stoic martyrdom worthy of Widow Twankie herself.

'Never mind,' I said. 'You don't have to take me with you. I'll be OK.'

I refused to let them raise the topic again. Amanda was almost unbearably attentive and wracked with guilt. Occasionally I caught Harry regarding me with a pensive, anxious look. In the event, they didn't emigrate for another four years, and I like to think that was at least partly down to me.

I waited until Marian's return before breaking the news with solemn relish. She was disappointingly phlegmatic.

'That man's a fucking coward,' she remarked. 'He just can't take the pace.'

Nothing could take the wind out of her sails. She'd been phoned by a director, had a sniff of work and was euphoric. She wasn't about to let Harry and Amanda burst her bubble. She waved aside my complaints.

'Well, you can always fly over and see them if you're that keen. Anyway, you're a bit old to be Daddy's girl now. You've got your own life to lead, your own friends. Haven't you?'

Doubt dampened the end of her sentence. She'd never actually seen my girlfriends and probably doubted that I'd ever manage a boyfriend. In fact I did have my own little crowd at school – assorted misfits who came together to make up the numbers. Between ourselves we divided our contemporaries into categories: the good, the bad and the ugly. The good did their homework and passed their exams, kept to the rules, joined the choirs and clubs and were set to be prefects, student leaders, chief execs and members of parliament. The bad were the girls who'd leapt into womanhood at 13, whose breasts burst the buttons of their school shirts, who made the male teachers twitch and clear their throats and cross their legs, who smoked in the loos and terrorised the boys with sullen, arrogant eyes. Those of us who were left over – we were the ugly. We congregated in corners – the fat and the skinny, the big-nosed and the buck-toothed, the acne-ridden, the bottle-glass bespectacled – and gossiped about more interesting lives. A motley Greek chorus, commenting on the plot through Portakabin classroom windows.

8

Gill, Robert and Bobby were watching the departure board at JFK. They had the weary, shut-down air of delayed travellers. It was three o' clock in the morning and they'd had just three days in New York before the phone call. One of the Tambini daughters, barely coherent, babbling apparently random words: attack, mother, suicide – Lenny. Hurled down the line over 3,000 miles, his name speared through Gill's brain in her hotel bed. She was up, disentangling herself from the sheets, waving away Robert's muggy questions, scrabbling for underwear and shoes.

Hoarse with tiredness, Robert sat up in bed and said, 'Lenny again. How the hell did he find—'

'It wasn't Lenny.' Gill shook her head and released a smattering of angry tears. 'Cara, or Carla, or – I don't know who, a Tambini girl, they found the name of the hotel . . .'

Robert watched her stringing clothes from her suitcase.

'Found it where?'

Gill didn't answer. She hardly knew. She remembered telling Lenny where they'd be staying, but couldn't arrange her mind around the question of why he'd written it down. Anyway, it didn't matter any more. She sat on the bed and started hauling on her trousers.

'Lenny's dead,' she said, and repeated it, testing its reality. 'Lenny's dead.'

She was glad of their presence in the hollow, small-hour tedium of the airport, although she'd told them not to come.

'Of course we're coming with you,' Robert had said, getting up to summon Bobby from his room. Bobby shambled in, tousled and childlike.

'Why do we have to go back?' he asked. He was sorry about Uncle Lenny in a distant way, but this was a marginal event for Bobby, and he saw no reason to pretend otherwise.

Uncle Lenny was just another of his parents' friends, a thin man with funny teeth and hesitant speech, who sat on after coming to meals, arguing with Gill and hogging her attention while Bobby lost himself in musicals and film magazines. 'Can't we just send our condolences?' he croaked.

Robert aimed a look at him and indicated Gill with a faint movement of his head.

'You *don't* have to come,' Gill conceded. '*I* have to go because . . . well. I just do.'

Bobby put his arm round her shoulders, forcing her to come to a pause. 'OK. We're coming too, then. We can do New York another time.'

So now here they were, watching for the plane that would take them to an absence. Robert went to make enquiries and came back growling.

'Some kind of strike at the other end' he said. 'It might be a long wait.'

He shoved his hands into his pockets and paced around in the harsh light.

'Strikes,' he muttered. 'It never used to be like this.'

'Oh, no . . .' said Gill. 'You're wrong. It's always been this way.'

Suddenly everything seemed quite clear to her. She understood what Lenny had always tried to tell her: that chaos and the unexpected are the natural state of things. We delude ourselves with routines and the belief that they'll last: with the faith that our home and family will always be there, in their usual places; that planes will fly and cities will stand.

She thought of the trite lines in a dreadful play, many years before: 'Faith survives even death itself. Faith in life. Faith in renewal.'

She'd been prepared to believe it all: answers. Progress. Faith. She cast a look at Bobby as he retreated to a bank of chairs and folded himself up. She had tried so hard to give him faith – learn by your mistakes, she'd taught him, see the best in everyone, hope for the happy endings. But surely, deep down, right down on the sea floor, even Bobby didn't believe in his technicolour fictions. Nobody believes them. But only Lenny had been ready to admit it. Everyone else shied away from the truth. Truth is dangerous. Lock it up.

All Gill's omens, all the signs which had directed her life – just accidents. Coincidence. Invention. Now, for the first time, she felt this in her heart, and was overcome with tiredness, with the waste and pettiness of it all.

Sick with jet-lag, heavy with dread, Gill sat in a taxi with her husband and son while London's afternoon life hurried past the windows, incongruously gawdy after their flight through a fragile dawn. Despite her state of mind she'd slept for a few hours on the plane, and dreamt of a client, a child of 16 who was already a mother – an unaccountably disturbing dream which had left a lingering flavour. Gill clasped her son's hand and he returned the pressure. Gill tried to focus her mind on the fact of Lenny's death. The sense of him was strong, but Gill had no belief in afterlife. Her atheism was her greatest consolation. Any notion that a part of him, his soul, his spirit, had survived, was unaccept-able. Survival and suffering were indissoluble to Gill.

Robert sat forward to give directions to the driver as they entered the tangle of streets approaching the café. Then he sat back and patted his wife's leg.

'Nearly there now,' he said, as if she wanted to arrive, and in a way he was right. Gill felt his bulk beside her, squashed into a corner of the seat, and was grateful. After all, after everything, she had chosen a husband who would shield her from madness and despair. She had brought up a child to know only lightness and hope. She cursed herself for that idiotic, half-drunk comment in Lenny's room. She cursed herself for believing her own lie. Because now, drawing up in this taxi outside Lenny's home, Gill knew that her marriage was not one of convenience. She knew that when Robert shaped her days with his little rituals, when he sat at his desk tidying figures into columns and spaces, the gratitude she felt was also a kind of love. Over the years, one had became the same as the other. She hadn't had the courage, before, to admit that to herself. Or to Lenny.

Two of the Tambinis' grandchildren were waiting for them at the Vita Nuova. One of them, a young girl with hair plaited down to her waist and a crescent of gold studs outlining each ear, introduced herself as Theresa and apologised about her mother.

'I told her not to phone,' she said. 'But she had your number and she was in a right state.'

It took a moment for Gill to realise that she was referring to Carla, who'd babbled the news down the line to New York. The girl was about to go on, but Gill was already on her way to the stairs, rattled by her own heartbeat. She could hear their calm voices – Robert and Theresa; she was vaguely aware of Bobby following her to the bottom of the stairs and calling her name. The door to Lenny's room was open. She had an impression of havoc, of calamity. She took a couple of deep breaths before going in.

Both hands shot to her mouth and clamped it, stifling a cry, or even a laugh. The walls reared up at her and the ceiling plunged, making her shoulders hunch instinctively. It's OK, she assured herself. Take your time. Piece by piece, she examined each foreign element in this well-known room.

A step-ladder was sprawled, legs apart, in the middle of the floor. Dotted everywhere were saucers and cups – the tough, transparent plastic ones that had always been used in the café. Each one contained a different colour – pools of crimson, midnight blue, bottle green, heavy purple. Here and there they were echoed in lighter, whiplash splashes across the carpet. Another colour, of a different quality altogether, began as a wide blot on the bed and formed a diminishing, broken trail, draping across the ladder and disappearing towards the far corner of the room. It was the charred, almost black red that could only be blood.

After registering all this she allowed herself to study the most oppressive part of the scene. She looked at the wall on her left, then at the wall to her right. Gouged and chipped into each one was a massive eye, covering all the available space; each iris was painted in a kaleidoscope of dark, jewel colours, merging and deepening towards the centre so that the pupils were a thick, impenetrable, nameless shade, each one reflecting a circle of light from the ceiling's bare bulb.

And now Gill looked up, flinching; she shielded her eyes and, behind her, someone turned off the light. Lenny had started work on another eye, had completed the upper lid and part of the lower and scratched an outline around the lightbulb; a wild slash vaulting away from it suggested an accident, a fall, catastrophe.

'Shit,' said Bobby. 'What was he on?'

'Nothing,' said Gill through the muzzle of her hands. 'That's the trouble.'

Robert was coming upstairs, calling her. He reached past Bobby to hand her a note in Lenny's handwriting. It had the address of their New York hotel in the top left corner; the letters were squared off as if he'd used a ruler to line them up. Beneath the address he'd written 'Tuesday', and 'Dear Bobby'. Gill glanced up and, taking a silent cue from Robert, scrunched the note into a tight ball. Bobby, still stunned by the ceiling decoration, didn't even notice.

Then Robert said, 'I think we'd better go on to the hospital. We seem to have got our wires crossed, somehow.'

9

Mrs Tambini had been given six stitches in her arm and sent home with her daughter. She was shaken and confused, but fit enough to contradict her daughter's frantic allegations. No attack, she insisted, no stabbing, just an accident which – she persisted, through Carla's indignation – was mainly her own fault. Nobody had attacked anyone, and nobody was dead.

So Gill mustn't worry, Robert repeated as the taxi turned up the driveway of the psychiatric hospital. Gill sat up stiffly at the edge of the seat, her hand already on the door-handle. Robert was saying that there would be no criminal charges. He and Theresa were quite sure of that.

When the taxi drew up Bobby had to be prodded awake.

'He doesn't need to come in,' said Gill to her husband. Robert dealt a sheaf of fivers into Bobby's hand.

'Take the taxi home. We'll be back as soon as we can.'

As the cab swivelled round for the next leg of its journey Bobby settled back with contentment, glad to be free of all the hassle, of his mother's anguish and his father's restrained concern. He allowed himself a twinge of self-pity: if he really wasn't needed, why couldn't he have stayed on in New York? But the afternoon sun was warm on his closing eyes; the taxi chuntered unhurriedly up to the next traffic queue, and all was well enough in Bobby's world.

Robert brought two plastic cups of coffee from a machine. The waiting area was quiet, apart from a woman who was talking urgently into a pay phone at the far end of the lobby, and occasional hurrying footsteps and greetings from behind the inner doors. There was a strong smell of disinfectant and an underlying putrid sweetness. Gill had established that she knew the Mental Welfare Officer on Lenny's case, and had sent word that she was here. Her eyes darted about like a bird's. She took a cup from Robert, sucked at the muddy liquid and made a face. Then she jumped to her feet, spilling coffee on the floor.

'Penny!' she called. 'Penny!'

A matronly woman approached them, clutching a plastic bag full of folders to her chest.

'Gill. They said you were here.'

Penny took a seat opposite them, drew a folder out of the carrier-bag and considered Gill's distraught face.

'You're a friend of Leonard Hall's?'

Gill gave a nervy giggle. 'Yes, I'm on the other side of the fence for a change . . .' She faltered. 'Valuable experience, I suppose . . . grist to the mill . . .'

She glanced from Penny to Robert, aware of the emotion in her voice. She seemed to have stumbled into some other identity. All her professional control, all clarity of thought had deserted her.

'I don't suppose you can help me trace his next of kin?' asked Penny.

Gill shook her head. 'His parents lived in Norfolk, I think . . . I'm not even sure they're still alive.'

'And what about his wife?'

Gill heard a crackle of plastic as her hand tightened around the coffee-cup. She said, 'No. No wife. Not married.'

Penny was reading something in the folder with pursed lips. She nodded, slowly.

'Oh-kaaay . . .' she said.

Gill recognised the tactic. Playing for time. Don't try that with me, she thought, and said sharply, 'Why's he been transferred, Penny? There's been a nasty accident, everyone's fine, end of story.'

'Mmm. You may be right.' Penny looked up and met her eye at last. 'Thing is, he was in a bit of a state.' Her tone was measured, the pitch low. 'Quite . . . agitated. He's been on medication for a while, hasn't he?'

'Years, Penny. *Years*. This isn't a—'

'Yes, well, I'm afraid he came off it a few weeks ago, and he's refusing to consider going back on. And . . .' she shifted her shoulders. 'He also made a few threats. Mainly against himself. Probably just the heat of the moment, you know, in quite a fraught situation. But you can't be too careful . . .'

'Can I see him?'

Gill jerked away from Robert's cautionary hand on her arm.

'Not quite yet. He's . . . he's not ready yet, Gill. Doesn't want visitors.'

Doesn't want *me*, thought Gill. That's what she means.

Penny let her voice drop further, beneath its official level.

'With a bit of luck,' she said, leaning away from imaginary eavesdroppers, 'he'll settle down before Major Tranquillizer comes on duty tomorrow afternoon.'

Gill smiled weakly. Major Tranquillizer was a psychiatrist notorious for his abrupt treatment of patients. It would be a red rag to the bull. Penny straightened and re-adjusted her voice.

'I'll keep you posted, you can be sure of that. Mrs, er . . . ' she checked a note in her file. 'Mrs Tambini is sticking up for him, I gather, and that should calm things down no end.'

The plastic seat squawked as Gill slumped back. Robert put his arm around her and gave Penny a few answers and assurances. Presently Penny had gone; the waiting room was empty. Stray sounds filtered from the depths of the building. Doors opened and shut. Names were called. When Robert judged the time to be right, he brought Gill to her feet and, supporting her weight with one arm, led her back into the open air.

10

I wake to a tapping and lie for a while, listening, wondering whether this is the sound of my paranoia. A lazy sound, regular but slow, with long, languorous spaces in between, longer than the swing of a pendulum.

Tap . . .

and I lie there, vacuous and patient.

Tap . . .

and a possibility begins to nag.

Tap . . .

Maybe it's only in these dead hours that I hear it. Maybe it's there all day, muffled and crowded out by other worries, tasks and conversations.

Tap . . .

Now I reach a point of decision. Now whatever I do must be a conscious effort. I can accept it, settle into its rhythm, close my mind over to its lullaby beat. Or I can get up and find out what it is-at the same time, inevitably, giving form and words to the fear it represents.

Tap . . .

Decision made. I kick off the duvet and heave my legs over the side of the bed. I let my head hang for a moment while my next move evolves.

Tap . . .

I dig the heels of my hands into my eyes and the noise assumes an identity.

Tap . . .

There's a leak in the roof. Water is falling in measured portions on to a beam or a board above my head.

Tap . . .

Simultaneously, as I knew it would, my percussive notion reveals itself as a clear, unavoidable question.

Is Bobby with somebody else?

As I pull on my jeans and a sweatshirt the room shucks off a degree of darkness. I've never tried to get into the roof before. I plot my course. Stepladder from under the stairs. Torch from box under bed. Meanwhile the question which for so long has resisted recognition is flowering into a whole soap opera of characters and storylines. Bobby's mistress. Bobby's other wife. Younger than me. Thin, clear-skinned, with a finer intelligence and a cleverer humour. A child toddles in to tug Bobby's trouser leg and grows a soft headful of fair curls. A baby pings into the crook of his arm and another settles on the hip of the second Mrs Bobby Gilbard. Hang on . . .

I've found the stepladder and have trouble extracting it from the cupboard. Gareth stirs in his room and I call up: 'It's OK. It's only me.'

Hang on . . .

The second Mrs Bobby Gilbard? Or the first? Her children fast-forward through puberty and tower over husband and wife: three poised, independent adults. An extra 15 years drag at her skin and add grey to her hair and I'm calculating furiously as I hobble upstairs with the ladder. Before I met Bobby – where was he? India, London, office, university – strolling among an endless cast of characters, meeting, touching, telling secrets, making declarations. What promises did he make? Has he finally gone back to redeem them, now that his alternative life has failed? Why did I imagine that his real future began with me?

As I grapple with the ladder there's a tumbling from inside Gareth's room and his door opens half an inch.

'What the hell are you doing?'

'It's OK,' I whisper, unnecessarily. 'The roof's leaking. Just going up to check. Go back to bed.'

'Can't it—?'

He shuts the door on his question. No, it can't wait. I've got to deal with this now. I climb the ladder, reach up and manage to slide the wooden board aside. Then I realise I've forgotten my torch. Back we go again.

A younger woman, definitely. Wavy, dark hair and a slightly hooked nose. Taller than me – maybe as tall as Bobby. Taller. A self-possessed, firm-fleshed woman who looks down indulgently on his fantasies and fibs. A woman who can take care of herself and of him. And of their . . . (the children disappear one by one. Pop! Pop! Pop! Her belly swells) . . . and of their unborn child.

As I tread back up the wavering ladder, directing the torchbeam above my head, I make one last calculation.

How long has Bobby been away?

Her belly expands a little more. She must be quite near her time.

I don't usually like confined spaces. I have a horror of spiders. I've inherited that from my mother, who recoiled from any living thing without a recognisable face. Spiders, beetles, daddy-long-legs, anything wholly inscrutable. Today, though, it doesn't seem to bother me at all. I haul myself up into the loft and swing my torch around the darkness, uncovering a blandness of wood and tile, cobwebs and tufted strips of lagging. In fact, once I'm accustomed, it's surprisingly light in here, even without the torch. There's a musty smell, not unpleasant, and a sense of being halfway to the outside world. I don't feel oppressed as I scuttle, troll-like, across the sturdier struts, ducking under beams and crouching into the pitch of the roof.

Tap . . .

There it is. Teasing me. My torchlight sways round and up, searching for a quivering of water. Something scuffles just above my head. A bird, finding its foothold just a tile's-width away. I switch off the torch and catch a scribble of early light. There it is: a gap, barely more than a hairline, between two tiles. That must be where the rain's been getting in.

Tap . . .

I crawl to the sound and inspect the source. By pressing

the side of my face to the gap and looking downwards I can see the shadowy accommodation buildings and the top floors of the hospital villas in the security lights' beam, waiting for the night to lift clear. One window glares yellow in the doctors' block. Someone else is up, then, or afraid of the dark. A few smatterings of birdcall float across the estate and the bird on the roof shuffles in response. By swivelling my eyes to the side I can see the outer edge of the garden and my bone pyramid, splayed in a skeletal star, smoky and mysterious in the widening light like a prehistoric henge, an undeciphered message.

Suddenly I'm elated. Half-squatting, already aware of the cramp in my legs and back, my face damp and gritty against the roof, I feel a rush of happiness and hope. I think of Bobby, warm in his other bed, turning to embrace his other wife, with passing goodwill. All the security lamps go off at once, with perfect, computerised timing. I watch the hospital and houses assume their daylight solidity. I float alone above my home and my son, invisible, invincible, capable of flight.

11

Next time I go to Gill's I'm ready to pounce with a question.

'Did Lenny have a wife?'

'What?'

She's startled. I lean across her kitchen table, keen-eyed, and she leans back, keeping the same space between us.

'The woman at the hospital – Penny, was it?'

'Penny Foster, yes, a very good—'

'She asked if he was married. Was he?'

I wait for her reply as if it will provide all my own answers. She looks at me and looks away. She licks her lips, thinking.

I'm not completely out of my mind. I know that Lenny having a secret wife, unknown to Gill, all those years ago, would have no bearing at all on me and Bobby. But if she says 'yes', if a man can love and be loved, can haunt a woman's life, and yet can keep a share of himself for some other, anonymous family – well, it would be something. A clue, perhaps. A vindication of my small insanities.

Gill says, 'It all depended what Lenny chose to claim and what we chose to believe.'

'What does *that* mean?'

She glares at my aggression but doesn't comment on it. She says, 'It means, nothing was ever straightforward where Lenny was concerned. Anyway,' – she makes an effort to lighten her tone – 'you're skipping ahead, now. I'll tell you in good time.' Then her head droops, and her finger and thumb are working at the ridge of her nose, making her glasses bob up and down. She seems to be struggling with indecision. Finally she takes a long breath, sits up and looks at me, directly, resolutely. There's just a hint of moisture shining in the corners of her eyes. She says, 'OK. Let's get on with it. Next chapter.'

12

Waves of breathing broke across the ward. It was dark. Not like his room above the café, where the walls and furniture gave out their own milky shimmer in the night. Here, the dark was unrelieved, smothering, filling Lenny's eyes and mouth. In a far corner, a red pinprick, a warning light, hovered in the blackness.

Lenny was trying to concentrate. If he could only isolate one strand of thought, the rest might fall into place. But it was difficult to know where to channel his efforts. He was in hospital, among strangers; didn't want to be there, didn't know how to leave; couldn't go back to his room, where blood had been spilled. For three days he had refused to take his medication or to answer any more questions. Her name had been mentioned, and he had refused to hear it. He coughed to block out the sense of shame and failure that her name carried with it. He wondered what Gillian had heard about the accident, and a sudden surge of rage turned him in his bed. He was not a problem for her to solve. He would not accept their easy chemicals; he must keep his mind clear and keep track of events. Lenny had been in these places before and he knew that in order to prove himself and his sanity, he must establish precisely what information was needed, what he should ask and what he shouldn't. His thoughts were still racing too fast for him to attempt a written record or a chart, so he decided to commit everything to memory until they slowed down. He rehearsed it all constantly, point by point, losing his way, returning to the beginning. The bustling of nurses, the rambling of patients, the ceaseless irrelevance of washing, dressing, eating – all this got in the way and tripped him up. Sometimes he had to stop, razor against chin, or halfway through buttoning a shirt, and put his mind to the task in hand. Sometimes it seemed wiser to go back to bed and start again. At night he redoubled his efforts, but this darkness was flooding his brain.

One: blood was spilt in his room. He remembered a cry, Mrs Tambini motionless with shock and then stumbling, her cry rising uncontrollably, like a child's. He may have injured her badly; he knew it was vital to recall every detail of this incident but the gush of blood drove him beyond it.

Two: he was brought to hospital and given a physical check-up but told no results.

Three: he may have made a rash threat; when he was ready, he must try and remember the words and make them harmless.

Four: medication had been offered and refused. He needed to know exactly what these drugs were, what their purpose was and what their effects would be.

Five . . . five . . . A patient moaned in his sleep and Lenny twitched angrily. He returned to the top of his list.

One: blood was spilt in his room . . .

How does she know all this? I listen to Gill with increasing doubt.

'How do you know all this?'

Her words trail away while she continues to watch the scene and Lenny's mind.

'I know,' she says, dreamily, 'because he said so.'

'So he *did* agree to see you in the end?'

She winces, trying not to let the images slip, and says,

'Stop jumping ahead. Shut up and listen.'

'Leonard . . .'

Lenny stirred from a dream of jumbled lists and stray words sprouting bizarre shapes and meanings of their own, refusing to be corralled.

'Wakey-wakey, Leonard,' sang the nurse, and a helpful voice from somewhere else on the ward added, 'Pill-popping time!'

'Dr Caine says you're to have this'. As Lenny sat up the nurse handed him a fold of thin, printed paper. He opened it carefully and scanned the tiny paragraphs of print.

'What is it?'

'Manufacturers' information. So – happy now?'

Lenny regarded the nurse from the corners of his eyes. Suspicion quickened his heart, but he was determined not to surrender to it. He crackled the paper straight and tried to draw sense from the print.

'Drug trolley's on its way,' said the nurse casually. 'So you'll be all right to take your dose today, then, won't you, Leonard?'

Lenny forced himself to breathe steadily. He was trying to pace his reactions, measuring them against the expressions on the staff's faces. When his frustration seemed about to break the surface, when his speech was speeding into a tumult or when he'd been quiet and morose for too long, he recognised the response: the slide from cheery briskness to blank purpose; the loss of even fleeting eye contact; the tightening of voices into short, slapping statement. During the daily occupational therapy sessions he observed other patients, became familiar with their mistakes. Anna, with her neat grey bobbed hair and imperious profile, a Hungarian emigrée who had crossed the border curled up in the boot of a car: her mistake was loud disdain for the hospital routine. 'This is crrap!' she would bark, rolling the 'r' immaculately. 'I will not!' – when asked to write descriptions of her friends and family. 'Personal information is none of your crrap business!' And Ted, the retired bus driver, who relapsed into a droning mumble whenever he lost interest. Lenny watched and learned. This was how he discovered his own tendency to mutter his list of points aloud. Now he kept it to himself.

'Happy then, Leonard?' The drugs trolley had clattered to a halt by his bed. The nurse put a hand on her hip in tired anticipation of an argument. Lenny peered again at the piece of flimsy paper in his hand.

On the last ward round he'd recited his usual question, flushed with the effort of slowing it down: 'What's the medication? It's not my usual medication. What's it for?'

The consultant psychiatrist had flashed him a white smile. 'Just something to calm you down a bit, Leonard.'

'But it's not my usual medication. What's it for?'

The psychiatrist had moved on. 'I'll see you get an explanation,' he said, and left Lenny weak with achievement.

The manufacturers' leaflet meant nothing to him. A voice in his head, Gillian's voice maybe, told him that it mattered: count this as a moral victory. Pretend it's enough. Take the drug, speak carefully, at reasonably frequent intervals, and get yourself discharged. Earn yourself a promotion to sub-sanity. Lenny chuckled and the nurse started to measure out his dose.

'Well, glory be!' she said. 'Good for you, Leonard.'

He took the solution and beamed at her; as she turned her back Lenny opened his overcrowded mouth and let the solution dribble back down his chin and onto his chest.

The only option left now was to get out. At 5 o'clock the next morning, as soon as the darkness had lifted and the corners of beds were visible, the duty nurse slipped out, as usual, for a fag. Lenny had often gone to the toilet early in the morning, just for some peace to rehearse his list. This morning he shuffled past the toilet, pushed open the fire door and padded down the cold concrete stairs. When the stairs petered out he put his weight against the security bar and opened the emergency exit. Somewhere behind him an alarm sounded. Lenny put his hand to the top pocket of his pyjama jacket and felt the outline of his biro. His body contracted against the bleak morning cold, stopping him momentarily in his tracks. Steeling himself, he padded on through the yard and along a pavement striped with faint light from the streetlamps. By the time he reached the park and the tennis courts, Lenny was warmer. He stood in the middle of the courts, near the limp tennis net, and shut his eyes. Now: to deal with this situation. He must keep his mind focused. He must try and stem the rush of thoughts. Lenny bent his knees slightly to stop the shivering.

One: blood was spilt in his room . . .

When the nurses found him he was squatting on the concrete, bent almost double, eyes and mouth shut, one hand hugging his ribs, the other pushing a biro nib hard through his pyjama trousers and into his thigh.

Lenny sat up in his bed and thought about the breakfast trolley – what time it would arrive, what food there would be. He worked constantly to divert his mind from the locked door. This was worse than it had ever been before. He had never been on a locked ward, had never known the thundering desperation that made him kick out at the nurses when he heard the words 'secure unit'. Now he was driven and exhausted by the sense of his own body. He needed to feel the sheets against his legs, his feet against the lino floor, his hand on the wall – surface to surface, blocking and soothing this terrible, flowing consciousness. And when people addressed him – 'Good morning, Leonard. How are you feeling today?' He needed to meet their words with his – 'Fine thanks!' – to touch the surface of their sentences with his own, capturing and confirming their existence. He washed, dressed and shaved in a rush. Blood had been spilt. Threats had been made. He had refused his drugs, absconded, harmed himself, lashed out again. These were bad mistakes, and Lenny knew that every mistake counted against him. He knew he must follow the rules and pass the test; he battled with the impulse to make fun of the psychiatrist, to spit out his medication, to sing obscene rhymes. He hugged himself to repress these impulses, but now and again the effort made him cry, as though his energy had to leak out. Maybe it wasn't too late. Maybe he could start again, say and do the right things, and if he held out long enough this mania would pass, the drugs would take effect, and everything would be all right again. Maybe the process could be reversed. He heard a commotion at the door as a shift changed; the lock would be released, the door would open, and all he wanted on earth was to get out of this place. Before he could establish control his body had catapulted itself from the bed, throwing aside a member of staff, kicking a jug and a glass off one of the bedside tables. No Mrs Tambini now, to usher everyone away and let his terror play itself out. No-one to blame it all on his moods or explain that it would pass, given time and patience. Now he hurled himself into a wall of braced bodies which collapsed around him, leaning, pressing, holding him fast to the ground.

13

'Emmett Park.' Gill was aghast. 'Why in Christ's name are they sending him there? It's bloody miles away.'

'I suppose there's no room anywhere else,' said Robert, reasonably.

'I need to speak to someone. I need to see him. I need to get this sorted out.'

'But if he doesn't want to see you, darling . . .'

Gill flinched at the term. Robert had only started using it since Lenny's crisis.

'Apparently he's asked to see Bobby.'

They stared, each waiting for the other to respond. Finally Gill said,

'He will *never* see Bobby in *that* place.'

Robert studied her face. Over the past few weeks it had been pulled and creased into a triangle of grief, the outer edges of her eyes and mouth slithering towards old age. He said, 'Maybe *I* could go,' and was rewarded with a widening of hope in her expression. That was all Robert intended: to lift her misery, for five minutes, for an hour. It never occurred to him that Lenny would agree.

The drive from London to Berriford took five hours. Robert had booked them bed and breakfast in a house a few miles from the town. It was a ranch-style 1950s house faced with boulders and strips of rotting timber. They asked about places to eat and the owner, a barrel-chested man with a white beard and a soft, falsetto voice, told them there were plenty of places in town. So Robert drove them into Berriford and parked behind the Co-op, and they strolled the empty streets, trying to assume a holiday air. Three youths jostled by, on their way to some place with lights and music and noise, hidden from view to anyone over 20. As they passed Robert and Gill one of them mumbled something and the others snorted in agreement. There was no other sign of life except for a pub on the corner. Gill wanted to go back.

'No,' said Robert. 'You must eat something or you'll feel worse. We'll try the pub.'

There were only three other customers, all ranged along the bar; one of them was delivering a long and sodden monologue, awash with expletives so blurred at the edges as to lose all impact.

'Lizzendomee, vugginwell lizzen,' he was saying, and the others lowed in affirmation. 'Lemme vuggin tellyazumminya vuggingunds . . .'

From behind the back of their settle Gill and Robert heard a murmur of rebuke from the barmaid, and the word 'visitors'. For only a moment the monologue dipped into an undertone.

They ate a good, hot meal of roast chicken and chips. A huge TV screen hanging in the opposite corner was playing an action movie without sound. The hero's square mouth yapped urgent instructions to his cronies.

'An' thazzanuther thing, ya vuggin lizznin?'

Gill sat close to her husband, thankful for this interlude of satisfied hunger and mindless images and the liquefied speech of a drunk. Tomorrow she would find somewhere else to sit and wait, while Robert found out the worst.

14

Russell Mitchell phoned after Marian's triumph as Widow Twankie. Russell Mitchell, who'd given her a break a quarter of a century or so earlier, after a superfluous night in her rooms above the High Kicks Revue. One of Russell's grandchildren had been taken to see her at the panto. It had put him in mind of old times. Could he take her out to lunch?

She spent four days deciding what to wear, demanding and then rubbishing my advice, having her hair re-dyed and her legs waxed, slapping the underside of her chin in the mirror. She presented herself for inspection before their appointment. Tight red dress, stoked-up chest, earrings that jingled whenever she moved, spangles glittering on the toes of her shoes.

'You look gorgeous,' I said. She was very nervous. I blotted a mascara smudge from her cheek with my thumb and adjusted her collar.

She said, 'There'll be work in this, you mark my words,' and tottered off towards the lift.

She was right. Russell Mitchell had a play for her. A one-hander. As soon as he'd heard her name again he'd known she was perfect for the part.

But Marian came back flustered and foul-mouthed. She plucked out her earrings so violently that she tore an earlobe. Blood ran in busy streams down her neck, over her hand and onto her sleeve.

'Oh, fuck! Fuck that arsehole! Fuck them all!' She stood over the kitchen sink, squeezing kitchen paper against her ear and barking at me as I tried to wipe her neck. In the flat opposite someone paused to watch.

'Why are you cross?' I asked. 'I thought you *wanted* more work.'

She slammed her hands on the edge of the sink and turned to face me. A wedge of blood-soaked paper fell to the floor and a red globule immediately blossomed on her ear.

'Do you know what that prick wants me to play? Oh, this *blood*, how does so much of it get *in* there?' She tore another square of paper off the roll, clamped it to her ear and leaned over me with a leer and crinkled, patronising eyes. She touched my arm, caressed it. She became Russell Mitchell.

'"A hasbeen, darling, a fallen star. Drinking herself witless. Helluva part. Sour grapes and pathos. Sweetheart, it's *you*."'

Marian drew away sharply, rising into a wail. 'Oh, this bloody blood!' One hand shot up in an obscene gesture, and our spectator in the opposite block pulled down his blind. I hadn't even realised she'd seen him.

I led her into the living room, sat her down, mopped her up and poured her a drink. She unbuttoned the back of her dress.

'And I feel like a netted whale in this bitch.'

Her eyeliner had spread and wandered, spinning dark webs around her eyes. She said: 'I can't breathe. Help me out of my stays.'

She stood up and let the new dress crumple round her feet, while I heaved at the hooks of her armour. Then she returned to her drink, billowing gratefully over her underwear, and I tidied away her party clothes.

'He wanted me to grow the colour out,' she whined, pulling at a strand of blackened hair. 'He actually *said* that. "Let it grow grey, darling", he said. "There's no disgrace in it, sweetheart, it comes to us all". Comes to us all! Just because *he's* turned into Mister Fucking Magoo.'

I topped up her gin.

'And,' she added, 'he was useless in bed, as I remember.'

I felt very sorry for her. She looked up at me with outraged eyes.

'He wants me to do it *without makeup*!' She checked my reaction. 'It's just unprofessional, isn't it, Jayney?'

I weighed my words before answering, then knelt at her feet.

'Mum,' I said, and that alone made her blink. 'He obviously admires you as an actress.'

Her mouth opened narrowly, revealing a dark glint of liquid.

'A one-woman play,' I said, impressively. 'And he wants *you* to do it.'

'With grey hair and no pancake!' she squeaked.

'Because he reckons you've got the courage, as well as the talent.'

I braced myself for the eruption, but none came. She sat there drinking her gin, and eventually I got up and went to clear a space for my homework. Much later, when I was sitting in a circle of lamplight, making notes on the Salic Law, her voice emerged, small and bewildered, from the sofa.

'I must go and pay Alec a visit,' she said.

She went to Alec Blessing and I went to see my father. I thought he might be able to persuade her to take this part. I saw with the clarity of youth the alternative paths that Marian might take: one to a boozy decline, gradually disappearing into the heap of Bayswater garbage; the other to praise and acclamation, a revived career of decent character parts – Beckett, Pinter, Shakespeare – a matron of honour, Dame Marian Westwood, one of our national treasures.

Harry and Amanda greeted me together at the door, radiating news. Amanda was pregnant. Harry had the dazed, smug look of a man who hadn't known he still had it in him. Amanda clutched my arm, nuzzled my shoulder, tried every girlie, matey trick in the book to make me feel included. Unfortunately every coo and giggle and coy, playful touch only frayed the connection between us. I had Marian on my mind, and there'd obviously be no help from this quarter.

Harry sensed my discomfort and offered solace: 'This does mean that we won't be moving to Australia, or anywhere else, for that matter, for at least a year or two.'

'I thought you said it wasn't decided anyway,' I challenged.

'No, but . . .' He glanced helplessly at Amanda, who rubbed her flat stomach and said, 'What names do you like, Jayne? You'll have to help us choose. We're absolutely *hopeless*.'

Marian didn't return from Alec's that night and still wasn't back when I got home from school the following day. I heard her key in the lock as I was opening tins in the kitchen. She was ragged and tired and sat down hard on the arm of the sofa, letting her coat drop. I stood in the kitchen doorway brandishing the can-opener, ready to kick her with my information.

'They're having a baby.'

'Who?'

'Dad and Amanda. She's up the junction.'

It was a phrase I'd heard Marian use in exaggerated Mockney. She drew in her cheeks as if she'd eaten a lemon. I wasn't sure whether she'd laugh or scream, but presently she relaxed and just sat there, turning her hands about and about, fingers outstretched, studying the bony ridges and rucked flesh and the smooth, shiny rings.

Deflated, I said, 'What were you doing?'

'What?'

'At Alec's.'

'Oh.' She snickered and said, 'Looking through old photographs.'

At the time I thought she was being sarcastic. I turned away and shut the kitchen door.

DECEMBER

1

For a week or so now Gill and I have been avoiding each other. When we spend an evening together we talk about Gareth's schoolwork, about Hannah, about the garden. If we do embark on another round of story-telling, the narrative is slow, and we tinker with it in a desultory way before giving up. We're too tired, it's too late, there's always another time. The final chapters are approaching. What do we do after that?

So generally I make excuses about work and Gill accepts them, and if Gareth is out – which he usually is – I might watch one of Bobby's musicals, or climb into the attic and watch the darkening estate. The ladder is kept folded and ready on the landing, against the wall. I told Gareth I was thinking of having some kind of flooring laid up there, so that I could store the videos and theatre programmes and other salvaged rubbish.

'Eventually,' I said, 'we might get Gill to help out and convert it into an office. That would get me out of your way, at any rate.'

He frowned. 'What's the point of that? I'll be moving out before long.'

Ten months, to be exact. Ten months left for Bobby to come and wish his son goodbye.

Once, I spotted Pat from my vantage point in the roof. He was hurrying towards the main block, files under his arm, briefcase in hand. I remembered what Natalie had said about a little harmless stalking. It struck me that I could, quite easily, monitor his movements, learn his routine, note the best times to catch his progress, his visits to the accommodation block, his meetings and stolen chats with friends. Not for any particular reason. Like a birdwatcher, I'd set no goal beyond the sighting. No pounce, no kill; just the thrill of power, of observing without being seen. To know and to see. That would be enough.

Power has its drawbacks. When I hear Pat calling from the garden gate on a Friday afternoon I'm stupefied with guilt.

'More exhibits?' he asks. I'm in the process of digging out a massive, neogothic bedstead. I make a cretinous noise in reply.

'Mind if I come in?' and he's already crossing the lawn, treading carefully around my excavations. He knows. He knows. He's about to confront me with my nefarious activities, accuse me – no, worse, prompt me in the gentle, sympathetic way that classes me as a patient. A woman who sits in the roof to spy – how can that be sane?

He stands with his arms folded, assessing my latest find in the winter gloom.

'A bed?' he asks. With an effort I pull myself together and concentrate on sounding normal.

'Amazing, isn't it!' I say. 'People used to bury all sorts of things. There could be a whole household under there . . .'

'Is that what you're doing?' he asks. 'Finding out what people bury – is that the . . . the concept?'

I pick at the rusty bedstead and wonder what I'm supposed to say.

'Sorry,' he says. 'That probably sounds very prosaic. It must be a pain in the butt to be quizzed about your art by passing philistines.'

Now I'm really stumped. Does he seriously think I'm an artist? This may be a clever ploy to put me at my ease, but it's working. I'm beginning to take command. My sessions at the peep-hole take on new profundity: the artist at work. Watching. Conceiving.

'That's OK,' I say, wiping my hands on my lap, and there's a hint of condescension in my voice. A soft, cold rain begins to form, hanging in the air and prickling my face and forearms. 'Foul weather,' I say. 'Fancy a cuppa?'

To my surprise he accepts. I lead him into the living room, hastily plucking bits of clothing and papers off the floor and sofa. With an effort of will I resist apologising for the mess, hoping he'll see it as part and parcel of the creative life. We sit and natter over tea and I find myself noticing details – as any artist must. His eyelashes. The way his forehead corrugates as he talks. The precise shape of his lips. I waffle on about Christmas, how we'll celebrate it, what I'll try and get for Gareth. Turning it into small talk makes it marginally less daunting, though it's been crouching at the end of the year, casting its shadow backwards since the autumn. I'm determined not to rely on Gill to sort it all out. Last year she provided giftwrapped parcels for me to give Gareth and while he opened them I struggled to remember what they were. She brought us a miniature plastic tree, pinned up our cards, noted the names inside and handed me fresh cards to sign and send in return.

I don't tell Pat any of this. I search for standard phrases and say, 'It seems to come earlier every year,' and 'It's all such an expense,' and sigh, like any normal person.

When we've run out of clichés about Christmas Pat says,

'Gill's told me about your mother. She was famous, wasn't she?'

He sounds like a schoolboy. I take him out to look at the photograph in the hall.

'Oh, yes . . .' he says, standing close to the picture, examining her black and white face. 'I didn't know the name, to be honest, but she does look familiar . . .' He steps back again. 'She's beautiful,' he says. He sees me grinning. I'm thinking that Marian would have enjoyed being a gay icon.

Then I realise that he's comparing me, looking for similarities and finding only differences. He says, 'Aren't you writing a book about her or something?'

Thanks, Gill. I can see my face changing shades in the reflection of the frame.

'Oh, I don't know . . . You couldn't put her in a book . . .'
I'm burbling. 'Anything I wrote wouldn't tell the half of it
about her. And it would probably say too much about me.'

'Well,' he says, 'that must be a problem with all biog-
raphies.'

'I'd have to put in a big disclaimer: any resemblance to
persons living or dead is purely coincidental.' I'm laughing
like an idiot, and he's humouring me. If only I could stop
blushing. I try and shift the subject. 'You must hear a lot of
family stories, I suppose. Professionally.'

'Mmm, a fair few.' He carries on gazing at my mother, his
expression closed and polite. That must be the expression
he wears at work, while he's sitting at an angle to his
patients, not too close, not too far, asking cautious questions
and jotting down answers, hour after hour, behind that
perimeter fence. Tell me about your father, mother, brother,
sister, uncle, grandma. How did you get on? How did you
feel? Scribble, scribble in the notebook and tick, tick off the
mental checklist of disorders: disorder of thought, of
attention, perception, mood . . .

'How do you know,' I ask, and my face cools as the blood
ebbs again, 'that your patients are telling you the truth?'

'They might not be,' says Pat. 'But what they say can still
be . . . helpful.'

I feel a stab of resentment on behalf of his subjects. Truth
or lies, speech or silence, nothing will free them from the
questions, questions, or the judgement waiting at the end.
And all that time Pat is giving nothing away. Does he hate
his parents, does he pray to God, believe in aliens, check the
cooker five times before leaving the house? Has he ever
fantasised about casual acquaintances, nursed an obsession
with someone else, is he straight or gay? He's not telling. I
call that a cheat.

'Well, I wish you luck with the book,' he says smoothly,
stepping towards the door. So he doesn't listen, either – not
in his free time, anyway. 'It's a stunning portrait.'

'Bobby loved it,' I say. Why suddenly mention Bobby

now? I start telling him how Bobby had this photograph blown up until only the eyes, nose and mouth could be seen, and then displayed it in the window of our shop, how he had a special drawer for her theatre programmes and posters, and discouraged customers from buying them, and all the while Pat sidles into his departure.

As I'm seeing him out through the garden, he gestures towards the bedstead.

'If you need any help digging it up . . .' he says.

'Thanks. I might just leave it as it is.'

He nods earnestly. He's a man practiced in diagnosis and classification, and evidently I have been classified as an artist. Everything I do or don't do is art, and should be taken seriously.

I wave him off down the street towards the hospital drive. Did I make a hopeless fool of myself? Is he, at this very moment, drawing portentous conclusions from my gabbled comments about husband and mother? Oho. So Bobby and Marian adored each other. Aha. She felt redundant in their company. Uh-huh. When Marian wasn't around any more, Bobby opened a shop that was more or less a shrine to her memory, and then dumped wifey and disappeared. Case closed.

But it wasn't like that at all. This is how it was: one minute Bobby was happy, really happy, with our marriage and our life. Then he wasn't. There's no suppressed frustration to trace; no dissonant underscore, adding irony to every scene of domestic contentment. Bobby was doing fine, until one day he wasn't, and he ran away. And that's that.

Returning to the house, I pause to reconsider the bedstead. Define a woman as an artist and that's what she becomes. It's only halfway out, stapled into the lawn. Four of the rails are clear of the soil, pointing towards the house. Maybe I *will* leave them as they are, then. I'll polish them up and leave them here, like standards frozen on the battlefield.

2

There was no Leonard Hall in the world that I entered, when Bobby first took me to the Victorian terrace with the tarty accretions and high-ceilinged rooms. No funny Uncle Lenny, no poor, tragic friend of the family. Nothing.

'You know who this is, don't you?' said Gill, waggling her aubergine head. And Robert lowered his newspaper with the pages open.

'This is *Marian Westwood's daughter.*'

'Good God! Marian Westwood? Good grief! Now that takes me back . . .'

They reminisced, and Gill kept a firm hold of my arm, and I thought the intensity in her eyes was something to do with her husband, with nostalgia for their youth and romance and dressing up for the theatre. She asked about my mother's career and I told a few white lies. She said 'Who'd have thought it?' several times. In spite of everything she'd learned from Lenny, Gill never could resist an omen. So here she was, presented with another sign, trying to understand what it meant.

By that time, 1980, Lenny had been in Emmett Park for about two years. Robert was travelling up every couple of months to visit him. I knew nothing of this and why should I? I was just a spotty girl in love with Lenny's son.

After that first visit, when Robert drove back to Berriford and found Gill waiting for him in Beech and Maystick's café, they both thought it would be the last. Robert edged round the table to sit next to Gill and looked about, at the resentful waitress, at two elderly ladies in a corner.

'Quite nice, this,' he said. He fiddled with his stone-coloured lapels. He was vaguely bruised around the eyes, as though he'd witnessed an accident and was staving off the shock.

Gill waited, let him order a coffee, asked nothing until Robert felt obliged to speak.

'Well,' he said, 'it's a pretty grim place. But we knew that.'

Gill's breathing grew heavier and Robert hastened on: 'But he's in reasonably good spirits. Reasonably good. I'm sure he'll be . . .'

The coffee arrived and he forgot to finish his sentence.

The visitors' room had reminded Robert of school. It was a large hall with a rudimentary stage at one end and people sitting in groups here and there around low tables. Their conversations rang briefly in the air, collided and faded away. Robert was led to a corner where Lenny sat smoking. He looked smaller than usual.

Robert took his place on the chair opposite and Lenny laughed. He kept up a suppressed giggle all through Robert's first, prepared questions.

'Are you all right? Is there anything you need? Is there anyone I can contact on your behalf?'

From across the hall came a noise that might have been a sob or a cough, immediately blurred by the acoustics. There was an institutional smell here: disinfectant, polish, a hint of sweat.

Lenny ignored Robert's questions and asked one of his own. 'How old are you, Robert?'

'I'm 55.'

'Congratulations. A decent age and a decent life.'

'Thank you,' said Robert, not knowing what else to say.

'Successful career, beautiful home, and oh, what a wife . . .'

Surreptitiously, Robert eased his watch from under his cuff to check the time. Another hour of this, he thought, and I can go back with a clear conscience, take Gill home and never see this lunatic again.

'And Bobby – how is the boy?'

'Doing well, thank you.' Robert cleared his throat and sat back, trying to spread his balance evenly over the chair. 'Making plans, you know. Soon be flying the nest.'

As he spoke Lenny's face and body drooped. After a moment he said,

'I'm 50.'

'Really?'

'Five years to catch up on your life achievements. Do you think I'll make it?'

He tensed suddenly, arms stiff, hands clasped, as a burly nursing assistant passed their table. Robert eyed the man with alarm and Lenny leaned forward. 'He's not too bad. The worst ones have been kicked out now, they tell me. But you still have to be careful.'

'What do you mean?'

'Keep your head down, do as you're told.'

Robert said, 'You're here to be helped, Lenny.'

Lenny smiled. 'That's right. Quite right, Robert. That's why I'm here.'

He raised his voice for the assistant to hear.

'And I'm doing rather well, don't you think? Haven't popped like a cork yet. I'm even taking my medication. *Just a spoonful of sugar . . .*' He started singing, then slapped his mouth shut and whispered: 'Mustn't sing. I keep forgetting. Gets on people's nerves.'

Robert was suspicious. He'd seen Lenny play the fool before.

'Why don't you stop all this nonsense?' he said quietly. 'Then you can go home.'

'Home?' Lenny's eyes widened, then he smirked. 'I suppose you've been to my room? Seen my little work of art, then. I don't think Mrs T was very pleased.'

He screwed his eyes shut to block out a memory. Blood was spilled in his room.

'Out of *here*, at any rate,' said Robert.

'Yes . . . not very salubrious, is it?' said Lenny, his eyes still shut. 'My life's crowning glory. Graduate of the University of Raging Mania. Well . . .' The eyelids relaxed. 'It's done. I can't change it now. This is who I am. Husband without a wife, Father without a son. That's me.'

They sat in silence for a while, but Robert didn't check his watch. Eventually he said, 'Why did you come off the drugs, Lenny? We had an agreement.'

Lenny looked up at him sharply. He thought of an afternoon in another life, of Gill and the promise of change. He said, 'I needed to think. I needed the fog to clear. My mind was pulling all the time. Straining at the leash. I had to let it go.'

On the long drive back to London it began to rain. They listened to the windscreen wipers slashing across the radio reception. Gill was biting her nails. Robert trawled through his recollection of the visit, searching for comfort.

'He does seem calmer,' he said, eventually. 'He seems to know what's required of him.'

'Required of him,' echoed Gill, bitterly.

'Keeping his head down. That's what he said.'

Robert remembered the current that had passed from the nursing assistant to galvanise Lenny's limbs. He heard again the implications that lay in the wake of his words. Rewards. Retribution. *Be careful. Do as you're told.* Robert fought down a tide of nausea and said, 'If you're worried I'll go up and visit him again.'

'Will you?' Gill's's shredded fingertips were poised at her mouth.

'As soon as I can make the time.'

3

Lenny kept answering people back – that was his problem. He graduated from toilet-scrubbing duties to sweeping and decking, but was demoted twice after making wisecracks to the wrong nurse. He soon learned to tell wrong from right – on the staff and among the patients.

'It's pretty democratic here,' he told Robert. 'There are good guys and bad guys on both sides, in all ranks.'

'This is absolutely scandalous. I'll put in a complaint,' said Robert on his second visit. Lenny warned him with a look. 'Don't do that,' he said. 'It won't help.'

There was a hierarchy of wards. Luckily Lenny managed to stay clear of the worst places – side-rooms where the windows were painted over and 'unofficial interviews' took place. Robert developed the habit of studying Lenny's face for marks, noting his posture and movements for signs of pain.

'Try and keep your tongue in check,' he advised him on the fourth visit. 'Do what's required to get out of here. That's all that matters.'

Lenny made two friends in Emmett Park. He hadn't intended making any. All his energy was focused on containing his hurricane of anger and panic. He had nothing to spare for anybody else. But in this place a civil word, an unprompted enquiry or a scrap of sympathy had too much value to ignore. He was learning to recognise allies. A charge nurse who let him rest in the dayroom when a new drug made him feel queasy . . . A psychiatrist who laughed at one of his nervous jokes . . . A social worker who brought in a chess set for him and another inmate to use after tea. Walter, Lenny's chess partner, was a large and diffident man with a tendency to walk into furniture and knock things over. His clumsiness and his crime had earned him the boot on more than one occasion, and he'd perfected the art of stillness, standing in a corner or sitting in his chair until he was told to move. At the chessboard, by contrast, he was all grace and dexterity, his fingers bunching to a point, darting between the pieces, moving and removing them in quick, clean swoops, arcs and turns.

Walter and Lenny took their places at one end of the dayroom, ignoring the TV in the corner and the arguments and idle chat of other patients and the duty nurse. Walter spoke very little, but when he did it was in a tender monotone, repeating the news about his eccentric mother and hard-working daughter and the new job his grandson had started. All his news came from letters written by his ex-wife, who had kept in touch all these years despite not clapping eyes on him since 1942. Walter's mass was a useful deterrent against some of the worst bullying, and he acted as bodyguard to a couple of more vulnerable patients. Lenny liked him. He found his anodyne recitals and stationary presence soothing. He did his best to avoid the gossip about Walter's past. They had played four matches before someone told him Walter had killed a child. He'd been a soldier and he'd killed a little boy, all those years ago, when Lenny had been hardly more than a child himself. Lenny didn't want to know, but for a few weeks the child kept him company, plaguing him with questions as he watched Walter scoop up another pawn.

'He's assistant manager,' droned Walter, tracing a web of future moves on the board with half-shut eyes. 'Assistant manager, white goods, and the pay's better too, she says . . .'

And Lenny wondered how old that child would have been now, and who would have been in his family photographs, which names listed proudly in his letters to old friends, whether he'd have had grandchildren of his own.

'And he's paying for my daughter to go to Spain next year, he's a good lad . . .'

Lenny wondered whether this child's face, in his last moment of terror, had been fixed in Walter's brain for the past 35 years, merging with the features of living relatives whose photographs occasionally arrived in the post. Lenny began to fidget during their matches, and grow agitated again. He thought of cancelling the games. But instead he developed a knack for calming himself. He dressed Walter in a uniform, surrounded him with war, remembered his own dread of it, of being caught up by it, of the thud and crump and shaking walls at night and the scree and skid of collapsing buildings by day. He muffled the boy's cries in this din, hid him in flame and rubble. He reminded himself that during war children were killed all the time, in a variety of different ways, and he lost the boy among their numbers. He taught himself to cast Walter as a man entangled in war, and gradually forgot altogether to link this big, boring man with the child who'd died at his hands.

Nathan was one of the patients taken under Walter's wing. He was a scraggy, limp lad, his body warped and skewed in permanent self-defence. He was prone to violent fits during which he sometimes soiled himself. He was immediately earmarked and suffered badly when Walter wasn't around. His face was ploughed with scars where he'd slashed himself in the past, and a broken nose, contributed by other hands, added to his generally crooked appearance. He'd spent many hours in 'deep litter', doped and knotted into a canvas shirt in a locked side-room. He could have been anything between 25 and 45; his ruined face gave no clues. Nathan would lurk behind Lenny or Walter while they played their matches, and laugh uproariously at everything Lenny said. Once, when Walter was relating his grandson's progress, Nathan suddenly interrupted.

'White goods,' he said. 'Is that food?'

'No, Nathan,' said Walter, without altering his inflexion. 'White goods is machinery. Washing machines. That sort of thing.'

'I thought it was like bakery,' said Nathan. He ducked his head to the left and the right, checking that he wouldn't be overheard. 'That's what I want to do,' he whispered. 'It's my ambition. Open a baker's shop'.

4

Lenny looked forward to Robert's visits with ambivalence. They were his link with the outside world, a promise that might not be fulfilled. There were no deadlines here, no set dates of release or parole; hope might not be the wisest strategy. Lenny was slipping into routines, learning rules; Robert, with his suits and formality and whiff of car fumes and city air, was a disturbance.

Robert introduced working methods to his visits, making the best use of time and identifying goals. The main aim, he assured Lenny, was to get out; injustices could be tackled at a later date, in a safer place.

'You've changed your tune,' muttered Lenny.

'Needs as needs must,' said Robert, taking a notebook from the inside pocket of his jacket.

Lenny quite liked one of the doctors. He had an easy-going manner, remembered what Lenny told him from one session to the next, and spoke to him as though they were both there by accident and had to make the best of it. He was an amateur watercolourist. Sometimes he put aside his notebook and asked Lenny about painting techniques, and Lenny allowed himself to believe it was out of genuine interest, and not some professional trick. Once, as they were getting up at the end of the session, Lenny saw the doctor sigh heavily and rake his hair off his forehead and said,

'You must be worn out with interrogating crackpots.'

'What's wearing me out,' said the doctor 'is always being seen as the enemy.'

Lenny wondered whether this was an unprofessional thing to say, but for the first time he felt sorry for the man. Walter was always telling Lenny to try and accept 'their' help. 'They're not all bastards,' he'd say. 'You might reckon they haven't got a clue, but it's only polite to let them try.'

The following week Lenny's doctor broke the news that

he was leaving. His replacement was a brisk man with a beard so close-shaven that Lenny couldn't think about anything else.

'Now, then, Lenny,' he started in their first session together. 'Let's go back over some old ground . . .' and he stroked his suede moustache and scanned Lenny's notes, his eyes skipping left to right, left to right, as he spoke.

Robert's visits became increasingly businesslike. Together they reviewed all Lenny's discussions with psychiatrists, psychologists, social workers, analysed the answers he'd given since the previous visit, and identified his errors.

'Don't fire the questions straight back,' said Robert. Lenny chuckled.

'But I want to know about *his* suicidal thoughts. We might be able to compare notes.'

Don't crack jokes.

Don't tell lies.

Don't tell the truth.

They rehearsed his replies.

'How are you feeling?' Robert would ask.

'Bloody marvellous, how do you think?' Too sarky.

'Great'. Too manic.

'Like shit.' Too depressive.

'"Up . . . Down . . . Spinning around,"' sang Lenny, then chorused with Robert: '*No singing*.'

They agreed on the best wording.

'I feel quite calm today.'

'I feel fairly positive today.'

Lenny was moved into a villa and given kitchen work.

'I'm getting away with it,' he confided to Robert. 'I don't know what they're writing down, but it must be good. Even though anyone feeling calm and positive in here *must* be deranged.'

5

About a year after I first met Gill and Robert, Lenny was discharged from Emmett Park to a rehabilitation unit. He said his goodbyes to Walter and Nathan. Walter shook his hand, and Nathan stifled a laugh with his fist. They hadn't been meeting as regularly since Lenny's move into the villa, and they already treated him with embarrassed detachment, as the living might speak to the dead. Lenny wasn't sure which side of the divide he was on.

As the car slowed down between Emmett Park's pompous gateposts Lenny turned in his seat to look down the driveway.

'One last glimpse of the ancestral heap,' he said.

The social worker driving and the nurse in the passenger seat laughed.

'Think yourself lucky,' said the driver. 'We've got to go back in tomorrow.'

'Yeah, and you make sure it *is* your last glimpse, too,' added the passenger.

The rehab unit was in two converted houses 17 miles north, in the grounds of a psychiatric hospital. Lenny was given a bed in one of the dormitories. As he unpacked his bag a young man came in and sat on the opposite bed. Lenny recognised him as a former Emmett Park patient. He watched as the young man took some coins from his pocket and counted them carefully onto his bedside table, making meticulous notes in a pad that was open there. Lenny hadn't seen anyone handling money for three years. Judging by his solemn care as he counted and documented his small change, this boy may never have handled it in his life.

'Been to town,' said the boy, haven given no sign of noticing Lenny at all. Lenny wondered what to say.

'Long day parole,' explained the boy. 'First time.'

'Good for you,' said Lenny. 'How did it go?'

Without meeting his eye the young man nodded, encouraging himself. 'OK,' he said. 'OK. Bought lunch. At a pub.'

He was striving to sound indifferent. But the hollows of his face were dark with awe. He'd bought lunch at a pub. And it was OK.

6

I'm sitting in front of the telly, half-watching troops being mustered on the late news. I'm aware of the sound of someone opening the back door. The kitchen light goes on. A voice says, 'Why are you sitting in the dark?' and I look up and see Bobby standing in the doorway.

No. It's Gareth.

'Are you OK?' he says.

'Fine.' I pull myself into a tidier position and wipe a trickle of saliva from the side of my mouth. 'Fine. Just thinking . . .'

'Has Gill been here?'

He's looking at the bottle and glass on the floor. I start gathering things feebly together.

'No. I was just . . .'

He hasn't moved from the doorway. He's watching me.

'Have you had any supper?' he asks, spikily.

'Nothing much,' I say. 'I sort of forgot . . . I was lost in thought.'

'What about?'

I'm taken aback. He hasn't quizzed me like this since hitting his teens.

'Oh, about . . . I don't know. About Dad.'

I heave myself up, glass in one hand, bottle in the other.

'Has he rung?'

'No.' I look him straight in the eye. 'I would tell you if he did.'

He lowers his eyes and turns to let me pass. I deposit the glass and have to lean on the sink for a moment to steady my mind.

'Want something to eat?' I ask.

'No thanks.'

'Sure?'

'Sure. I'm going up to pack. I'm going to Hannah's tomorrow for a few days.' At the sitting room door he pauses and adds, grudgingly, 'If that's OK.'

'Well . . . when are you coming back?'

I force down the tremor in my voice.

'It's just a few days.' He sounds exasperated. 'To do some coursework and stuff. So you can have the computer as much as you want.'

Next morning I give up after an hour's work and go over to Gill's. I catch her railing at the papers.

'Come on,' I insist. 'Let's go for a walk. You're the one who likes walking.'

'Don't you need to get on with your . . .?' She's wary.

'I can do that later. Come one. Fresh air and exercise.'

Gill searches the sky for an excuse.

'The weather's coming,' she says. 'We'll get bogged down.'

'Well, get a move on, then, before it arrives. And bring a brolly.'

We make it across the field, stepping from ridge to ridge of crumbly earth between the crops. As we reach the path that winds round to the village the rain hits, lashing at our backs. Gill shakes her brolly into action and we let the gusts steer us towards Peccam.

'What happened to Mrs Tambini?' I ask. It's the first time either of us has spoken since leaving her house. 'Did she ever see Lenny again?'

Gill wrestles with the umbrella handle.

'Oh . . . she wrote to him a couple of times, I believe. But after the accident she grew quite frail. She went on living with her daughter. As soon as she was out of the café the grandchildren gutted it and turned it into a video bar. Needed doing, I suppose. Business decision.'

We turn into the village and all at once the wind drops and the rain eases and, after a final, sulky spray, moves on.

'That's all it was,' says Gill.

'What?'

'An accident.'

Beyond the village houses we can see clouds dragging the rain along the horizon.

'What *did* happen?'

'In Lenny's room? I don't know . . . She tried to pull him down from the ladder, I reckon. He was cutting her ceiling to shreds, after all. He overbalanced, fell . . . that's my impression. Lenny would never have hurt her. Even in his most frantic episodes he never deliberately hurt anyone else.'

By silent consent we head for the churchyard's over-blown portico. Gill shuts the umbrella and pumps it a couple of times, showering the graves. We walk to Joe Cheng's plot and stand staring at the pictograms. Gill traces a couple with her finger.

'Like flowers,' she says. 'Diagrams of flowers.'

We walk on and she suddenly turns away from the path and across the wet grass. I slush along behind her, struggling to draw level and hear what she's saying.

'Yes, she was never the same again, apparently, poor old Mrs T. She died, oh, must be 20 years ago. About 1982 or 3, I think it was. I'm sure you and Bobby were up to your ears revising for finals at the time.'

I'd never heard of Mrs Tambini or the Vita Nuova and had no inkling of the life that was ending while I immersed myself in Ancient Civilizations and Pre-Feudal Societies and European Neolithic Structures. These were my only preoccupations: these and Bobby Gilbard. Bobby Gilbard, warm beside me in a narrow bed in a cold, rented room. Bobby Gilbard cooking porridge while I read out revision notes, squatting in front of a single-bar electric fire on a chilly May night. Beyond the heat of that fire, outside the grubby orange curtains – nothing. My mother might be cracking open another bottle and cursing the soul of Frances Dee, who'd made such a success of the one-hander Marian had turned down. Harry and Amanda might be packing and writing their farewell cards, finally making their escape now that I'd found a new safe haven. Bobby's mother might be paying her respects at an old woman's funeral. It was all just a sketch of life, compared with the reality of exams and Bobby Gilbard.

7

Mrs Tambini's funeral was teeming. Ranks of family, toddlers padding up and down the aisles, refusing to acknowledge the gravity of events, cousins embracing across the pews, tears from Carla at the front. Behind them, towards the back of the church, Gill sat among a clutch of loyal Vita Nuova customers, flanked by a couple of old men with thick white stubble and charity suits, one of whom hawked into his hanky all through the priest's address. Three women slipped into the last pew, two of them in late middle age and orange with foundation, another pale and no more than seventeen: girls from the local clubs, who'd bought their daily meals from Mrs T between shows. After the service everyone crammed into the café – now called 'The V'. Salami sandwiches, crostini, spicy sausage, anchiove fillets, wine and weak tea were served among silver and electric-blue tables. Above them, a bank of slanted screens remained respectfully blank. Lenny could have come to the funeral, but decided not to. He'd been at the rehab unit for 11 months and was looking for a job and a flat. He asked Robert to pass on his condolences to the Tambinis and said, 'Tell them I won't be there. They'll be relieved to hear it.'

Gill delivered his message and watched Carla set her jaw. Theresa, the granddaughter with the gold-edged ears, was concerned and eager to hear about his progress.

'He's doing well,' said Gill, parroting Robert's phrases. 'He'll be back on his own two feet before long, as soon as he can find somewhere . . .'

'But there's no room here, you know,' Carla cut in. 'We've refurbished now. There's no room for a lodger.'

Gill's mouth opened and shut without an answer. Carla was becoming tearful again.

'It was the shock that killed her, I still say it, never mind it was years ago, the shock did for her in the end . . .'

'All right, mama,' murmured Theresa, hooking her arm through her mother's.

'No, but I don't say he can help it, he's wrong in the head, I know that, and it's a shame, but here they are putting him back on the street, free as a bird . . .'

'Mama,' said Theresa. 'Don't get upset. Lenny's not dangerous.'

Carla's voice soared as she unhooked her arm. 'Not dangerous? You stand here after seeing your grandmother put in her grave and tell me he's not dangerous? Never mind what the doctors say – you know better? If he wasn't dangerous why did they lock him away?'

8

We've reached one of the older gravestones, washed almost clean by the elements. Only the round suggestion of an angel survives, with a ripple of hair and a featureless face, and the last, dissolving wisps of inscription. All trace of identity has vanished before the bones have had time to rot. Gill strokes the angel's buffed head.

'I like this one' she says. 'It's my adopted stone. A sort of unknown warrior.'

She places both hands on it, embracing it, and presses forward, looking round at the cemetery, the church, the broad sky beyond the ivy-muffled wall. She says, 'I first came here after Robert died.'

'After . . .? You mean, when you got the job at Emmett Park?'

She shakes her head. 'Before that. A couple of days after Robert's funeral. I came up here to see Lenny.'

'I didn't know . . .' I cast my mind back but without any clear grasp of the sequence of events. I remember the phone call after Robert's death, Bobby stiffening, self-aware, searching for the correct response. I remember him cajoling her, begging her to come to us, or to let us come and stay with her, and I remember that dismissive phrase he used: 'He was so much older than Gill'. Life had taken an unexpected turn, and Bobby found a reason to explain it away.

'No, well . . .' says Gill. 'I must have mentioned that I was paying Uncle Lenny a visit, but it probably didn't register much at the time.'

He'd been out of the rehab unit for five or six years by that time, living in a flat in Berriford and working as a night-watchman at a shoe factory. Gill broke the news about Robert by phone. She rang the number written in Robert's diary; it was answered by a woman, who tutted and yelled

Lenny's name. Gill heard the echo of a hallway and hard footsteps before he arrived. She thought he sounded older, more brittle, but maybe that was the shock. She asked him whether he'd like to attend Robert's funeral.

'I could come and pick you up,' she offered.

He was awkward, blundering along the verge of several excuses. In the end he said, 'I don't like to travel too far. You understand.'

There was a long silence. Gill didn't want to hang up. This was too final. After Robert's death she needed a sense of continuity. She said, 'Can I come and see you?', and heard the fragment of a sigh. Suddenly she was in despair. 'I won't stay long' she pleaded. 'I'll book a B&B. Just an hour, just a quick chat. You and Robert grew quite . . .'

'Quite close, yes,' said Lenny. After a pause he added, 'I expect he told you, I don't live in luxury.'

'When did you ever?'

A snippet of his old laugh, at last. Gill said, 'I'll ring some time after the funeral. Give you due warning.'

'Late afternoon is best,' he said. 'Before I go to work.'

9

Lenny's flat was on the first floor of a fume-blackened terraced house on the approach road into Berriford. Gill searched the labels next to the doorbells and found one marked 'LH', with a doodle of a fanged face next to it. There was no noise when she pushed it, but as she pushed again she heard commotion from inside and Lenny's voice calling, 'Yes, I can hear you!' as he clattered down the stairs. She put her head back and sucked in the roadside air. She clutched her overnight bag with both hands. She hadn't seen him for 11 years.

The door opened. A brightness caught her eye immediately and she stared at his closely cropped, white hair. Lenny was staring at her bag.

'Don't worry,' she said. 'I've booked a B&B. Haven't checked in yet, that's all.'

Her tongue had trouble dealing out the words. Lenny gave her a look which she couldn't fathom. Rebuke, affection, compassion. His eyes were bloodshot, had a yellowish tinge, but the old slyness, the old darkness – or the memory of it – held her fast. He took her arm to guide her into the hallway, then put the other arm around her in a cautious, polite embrace.

'I'm so sorry,' he said. 'Robert was a good friend.'

He stepped away and, having established the rules of conduct, gave her a slow, sad grin. One of his teeth was missing, at the side; the rest still crowded against each other, avoiding the gap.

'Come up and see my stately pleasure dome,' he said.

As they passed the payphone he lifted and replaced the receiver in a quick, automatic movement.

'They leave it off the hook,' he explained. Gill glanced at the numbers jotted on the wall around the phone – fat black ones, thin, scrawny ones, the occasional name and a fanged face, twin of the doodle on Lenny's doorbell label.

The wooden steps were bare and dark at the edges, bordering the spectre of a stair-carpet. Here and there the stubs of carpet-pegs remained. There were doors along the hallway and leading off from the landing, all blue, all identical except for the number painted in cream over the letterbox. Lenny's flat was Number Four. He'd left it on the latch and reached past her to nudge it open.

'Go on through,' he said. An interior door, half mottled glass, divided a passage from the main room. Gill opened it and glanced involuntarily at the ceiling. No evil eye. The walls were bare, too, apart from the worn hints of a wallpaper pattern. Under the window, which was coated with city dirt, there was a trestle table. A curtain was pulled across one area, probably the kitchen; a sofa-bed took up one side of the wall. Not very different from the Vita Nuova room, thought Gill, in theory. But in fact it had a life about it that had been scoured out of the old café lodgings. There were clothes piled in a corner, a book on the table, a shelf with ashtray, mug, small stacks of coins, a coat draped over a chair. She put down her bag and wandered to the window. Through the murk she could see the endless movement of cars and, on the opposite pavement, two youths gesticulating in some argument or joke. An iron security bar formed a simple cross on the outside. Behind her, Lenny said,

'Bars on the windows. Makes me feel at home.'

She turned and caught the tension working in his face before he could quell it.

'How are you, Lenny?' she asked.

'I'm doing well. I'm feeling fairly positive,' he said, then chuckled at a private joke. 'As you can see,' he said, with a curtsey, 'I'm pretty stable. They've got me on a good combination at the moment. Not too much of the old vomiting and falling over with this lot. Bit of bother with the waterworks, that's it. And I've kept down my job for four years, you'll be proud to know.'

Proud to know. Despite herself, Gill bridled with annoyance and pleasure at the intimacy that suggested.

'What about you?' Lenny said. 'Are you coping? You must be feeling . . . rough.'

Gill's head dropped. She was caught in one of those sudden freefalls of grief and fatigue, and had to hoist herself back to her plateau.

'Coping,' she said. Then, answering another, tacit question, 'Bobby's coping very well, too.'

Lenny went through the curtain to make tea. Gill went to the bathroom. His clutter was here, too-ordinary clutter: razor, soap, towel, a box of sticking plasters. The litter of an ordinary man. When she was washing her hands she examined herself in the narrow mirror over the basin. What did Lenny think when he looked at her? Deep folds pulled at her eyebrows, a ridge of old worries marked her forehead above the nose. Pull yourself together, she told herself, and tried to produce some lather from the cracked oval of soap. You're a middle-aged widow and he's got other things to think about.

Lenny didn't want her there. Apart from Robert he hadn't welcomed visitors since leaving the rehab unit, though there were a few he had to endure as part of the deal. He preferred to be alone, to stay in his flat by day and to work in darkness. His main aim in life, nowadays, was to escape notice. He'd done well enough at the unit, trying his new drug combinations, attending his regular sessions on employment, finance and relationships, learning computer skills and meeting the multi-disciplinary team to discuss his future. He kept it up until his last day there: behaving like a sane person getting well, reining in his indignation, minute by minute. The boy who had counted out his money on Lenny's first evening there didn't make it. Overwhelmed and frightened on one of his days out, he'd leapt in front of a moving car, and was now in intensive care, waiting until he was healthy enough to return to Emmett Park. Lenny's diligence increased. He never risked a wisecrack, never lost his temper, never grabbed anyone by the collar to demand they return his lost years. The prospect of passing back between the stone pillars and up the long drive, of seeing Walter's lightning chess moves and Nathan's ravaged face again kept Lenny's moods in check – so tightly in check that once he left the unit he hadn't the energy or the courage to move very far away.

He brought tea: one in a stained Charles and Diana mug, the other in a green plastic cup from a flask.

'I don't do much entertaining,' he said, apologetically. 'You can have the royals.'

He didn't mention sitting down so they stood. Gill found it a relief, after hours in the car seat. She asked him about his job and he told her what she'd already heard from Robert: that he worked from 9.30 at night to 6 in the morning, that he sat in a kiosk by a close-circuit screen checking and identifying unexpected blots of movement.

'Sometimes,' he said 'there's a fox. I leave it scraps. I probably shouldn't.'

She knew that too.

'I expect you get to read a lot,' she suggested. He beamed, lifting his skin into delicate lines around the cheeks and eyes.

'I've never been much of a reader,' he said. 'You know that.'

Gill wondered why it was that she hadn't found it odd, in the past, that he had no books in his room.

'I used to find it hard to concentrate,' he explained, as if to someone he'd just met. 'So I haven't developed the habit. I read the paper now and then. It's quite cosy out there in my kiosk,' he added, as compensation.

Gill said, 'It sounds rather tedious.'

He laughed out.

'I hope you don't denigrate your clients' achievements this way, Gillian!'

'Never,' she said, stung by the use of her name. 'Never. I have never treated you or thought of you as a client.' She was unaccountably cross.

'Well,' said Lenny, 'maybe that's where we went wrong.'

For a while they said nothing more. Lenny leaned against the opaque glass and Gill slowly circled the room. She knew he was remonstrating with himself. Here she was, old friend, ex-lover, recently bereaved, driving all the way up here to see him . . . he should be kinder. But he didn't know how. Gill felt herself dragged again by an undertow of dejection and sat on the sofabed. With considerable effort of will she broke the silence.

'Bobby's doing well.'

Lenny watched her from the window. She raised her voice. 'I expect Robert showed you pictures of the baby?'

Lenny moved to a built-in sideboard under an alcove in the corner of the room. His shoulder had left a smear in the dirty condensation, letting in a little more drab sunlight. He opened a drawer and produced two photographs. He held them up to peer at them.

'He must be very different now,' he said.

'Full of beans. I'll send you more up-to-date pictures.'

Lenny continued to examine the snapshots of Gareth a few hours into his life, tucked into the crook of my arm in a hospital ward.

'Lenny,' said Gill suddenly. 'Are you married?'

He gave her a quizzical look.

'You told a welfare officer that you had a wife.'

'Did I? Oh, yes . . .' His mouth buckled in distaste at the memory. 'Stupid.' He returned to his scrutiny of Gareth's scrunched face. 'I was, actually', he said. 'A very long time ago. Before I met you. Didn't last long.'

'You were *married*?'

'I suppose so. You could call it that.'

Gill squeezed her eyes hard shut against her rising irritation.

'What does that *mean*, Lenny? Were you or weren't you?'

'Very fond of your straight answers, you professionals.' He sniffed abruptly and put the photographs back in the drawer. 'That's not what I had in mind, though. When I said I had a wife. If I remember rightly I meant you.'

He had his back to her now, bouncing the drawer along its sticky runners. Gill studied a broken ring of brown tannin on the inner rim of her mug. Lenny said,

'Caused me no end of bother, that particular bit of clowning. Embellishments, porky-pies – not a good idea when you're trying to stay out of the madhouse. Remember that.'

'I'll keep it in mind,' muttered Gill.

Lenny turned to face her and rested against the side-board. 'Robert told me that, as a matter of fact.'

'I'm sure you knew quite well for yourself.'

She wanted to lie down now, to drift off, but the recollection of their last meeting, in another sad room, kept her upright. Lenny cleared his throat and pondered over his tea. He seemed to think a tribute was required.

'You and Robert did a great job . . .'

Gill's face lengthened in mock dismay and he giggled and assumed a Hollywood drawl. 'You must be *very proud.*' Then he dropped to a natural, intimate pitch. 'Gillian,' he said. 'Don't worry. You made the right choice.'

She stayed for another two hours. They talked about Bobby, even about me and Marian Westwood. Gill told him about Bobby's schemes and Lenny said, 'He was always full of ideas, I remember that. Even as a kid.'

He recalled conversations he'd had with his son. Gill said,

'You told him bees were like jazz players, buzzing away inside the flowers. He still says that. I've heard him say it to Gareth.'

'Have you really?' Lenny's face shone like a child's. He said, 'I hope I didn't frighten him too much. I remember telling him about all the noises we can't hear. I hope he wasn't upset.'

'I don't remember that . . .'

Lenny swilled the last of his cold tea in its cup.

'He was always interested in wildlife, wasn't he? A little naturalist. I think we were discussing worms and insects – why they don't make a noise. I said, imagine if you could hear everything. Tiny cries and calls, among the roots, under the earth, in the ponds and rivers.'

'Sounds like the sort of thing you'd say.'

'I can't help it. I can't pretend it's not there.'

Gill pictured Lenny stopping his ears against the Earth's clamour of love, death and labour. A howling, screaming mass, hurtling through space – that was Lenny's world. 'I couldn't lie to him, could I?' pleaded Lenny. Gill was stony-eyed. He pouted. 'I hope he wasn't upset,' he said again.

Gill chewed her lip, and wanted to say: yes, of course he was upset. You scared him. He was just a little boy. She wanted to punish Lenny. Instead, she sniffed and made a gesture with her hands, sweeping the subject away.

'He's got this daft saying,' she said, for no particular reason. 'When something's tickled him. He says, "It's enough to make a worm laugh."'

Lenny flashed his chaotic grin and as usual she had to smile back.

When Gill left, having missed her booking-in time, they hugged without passion or embarrassment.

'What will you do if your B&B room's been taken?' asked Lenny. She knew he wasn't offering a solution.

'Oh, I'll find somewhere else. If the worst comes to the worst I'll drive back.'

'Give my love to Bobby,' he said, seeing her off from the inner door of the flat. 'And to his family.'

She was fumbling for her car keys in her bag, grappling with the unfamiliar latch to open the flat door, and by the time she turned back to answer him he'd retreated into his room again. She saw him, fractured and puddled through the glass, moving away. She was already working out the route to the B&B. She didn't call goodbye.

10

In nine years of sporadic visits Bobby grew closer to my mother than I had ever been. After that first charm offensive on Boxing Day 1984 she took to summoning us for 'special occasions' – some spurious, some genuine. We had drinks to celebrate her birthday, two months adrift of the actual date. We drank to the memory of some actor whose name she kept mispronouncing, whom she never could abide, and who'd died the previous year. We also raised a glass to Johnny Dunville in a restaurant, in the company – to Bobby's great delight – of a couple of old *Who Needs . . .* regulars. They were even snapped in mid-toast by a tabloid photographer, who issued a curt instruction to me and Bobby to move out of the frame. We lingered at the next table, where a young family gawped at the proceedings and asked us who those people were. And of course there was a gathering to celebrate Gareth's birth, though it didn't take place until he was 3 months old.

The day Gareth was born, while I was still marvelling at this warm, strange, crumpled, wriggling creature on my chest, Gill and Robert arrived at the hospital, Gill wide-armed and misty-eyed, Robert pleased and shy, with his hands in his trouser pockets.

'Take my chair, Gill,' said Bobby, leaping up, 'and give me some change. I'll go and phone Marian with the news.'

Gill fussed around in her bag but I could see her colour rising, I could see her biting her lip like a lovestruck teen. She sat by my bed and stroked Gareth's downy head with her finger and answered his crackling noises with comforting hums and hahs, but I knew her mind was elsewhere. Marian Westwood would soon be here. Here, on this ward, by this bed, tossing her magnificent hair, cooing over their shared grandson, exuding perfume and fame. I knew better. It was no surprise to me when Bobby returned a little crestfallen, bearing Marian's excuses and congratulations and a sugary speech about how dear we all were and how proud she felt. Gill was clearly disappointed. And yet in all the years that Marian was alive and accessible, Gill never once made any effort or request to meet her. She had the true fan's instincts; she knew how to keep the illusion intact.

Three months later Bobby answered one of my mother's peremptory calls: why didn't we drop by? It was high time she was introduced to her little prince. ('Grandson' was not a favoured word.) Within two hours we were rattling up to Flat 7a, bracing ourselves and Gareth against the hiccough at her floor, hurrying to get through the doors with Gareth's baggage-train of nappies, bottles and what-not else before it was reclaimed by the lift and shaken back down to the entrance hall. The door to her flat was flung open as we struggled to gather our bags and not to drop our bemused son.

'How wonderful!' she bellowed, arms above her head like a flamenco dancer. I straightened and Gareth, balanced on my hip, opened his eyes and mouth at this painted apparition. All at once she changed gear. Down came the arms for a restrained, almost timid embrace; down came the voice with a muted 'Oh!' and her stage face subsided into tenderness. She took Gareth from me with infinite care, held his gaze with infinite benevolence, and I saw for the first time how she must have been when I was a babe-in-arms. I was touched. When Gareth needed changing I tended to him quite happily while Marian switched her attention to my husband.

'He's *so* like you, my darling boy,' she was saying, hand firmly clamped around his thigh. 'What a heart-breaker he'll be when he grows up, just like his gorgeous dad.'

'Behave yourself, Marian,' said Bobby, covering her hand with his but showing no signs of moving it away.

Occasionally, when Gareth was very young and I was very scared, I would take him up to Bayswater while Bobby

was at work and let him float in Marian's arms above her
flotsam and jetsam. She didn't bother with the set-pieces for
me, of course, though I always made sure she was sober
before setting off. For an hour or two I'd sprawl on the sofa
among cigarette packets and sweet-papers, dozing while
Marian jiggled Gareth and sang to him and told him bits of
nonsense, just a stout and doting grandmother in moth-
eaten sweater and jogging pants, with her chipped nails and
broad band of grey at the scalp. Sometimes, if she wanted to
give an audience and I wasn't in the mood, Bobby would
take Gareth along. Or I'd stay at home with Gareth and
Bobby would go on his own. As Gareth grew older and
more like me, Marian lost interest. Once he'd started school
and I'd gone back to work it was generally Bobby who
answered the Bayswater call. Once or twice he went straight
there from work, stayed for a meal and then called in
on Gill with his report before coming home. It was understood by everyone that spontaneous visits were out of the
question, whoever might be involved. I thought then that
these randomly timed invitations were just another way of
giving us the runaround. It didn't occur to me until after
Marian's death that she was taking advantage of her better,
more intelligible days while she could. Well, I was a busy
working mother. I had a lot on my plate. I couldn't be
expected to realise just how much of a state she was in,
especially when she'd been in some kind of state most of
my life. She hid it from Bobby, too, for a long time.

In the end it was Alec Blessing who alerted us to the
impending crisis. By that time he was in his 80s and living
in a nursing home, but Marian still went to see him for
occasional reassurance and useful contact numbers when
she needed an extra boost of something or other. At about 7
o'clock one Wednesday evening I was shooing Gareth into
the bath when the phone rang. I could hear Bobby talking,
his voice dipping and rising with startled concern. A few
minutes later he appeared at the bathroom door. I was

washing Gareth's hair and he was squirming and protesting that he could do it himself. We were both covered in suds. Bobby sang, '*Lovely, Just the way you look tonight!*', then continued in a cheery enough tone,

'That was someone called Hilary.'

'Who?' I was annoyed, trying to rinse Gareth's hair while he dodged and splashed.

'Apparently she works at a nursing home. Alec Blessing asked her to track us down.'

'*Alec Blessing?*' I stopped. Shampoo dribbled down my arms and splatted onto the floor.

Gareth squeaked himself round in the bath and said, 'Who's Alec Blessing?'

'He must have got the number from your mother,' said Bobby.

'Who's Alec Blessing?' shouted Gareth.

'No one. A friend of the family.' I tipped a jugful of clear water over Gareth's head and while he was spluttering asked, 'What did he want?'

'Thinks we should go and see Marian.' Bobby made a dramatic face to imply that things were worse than he could say. 'Saw her yesterday, and thinks she may be a bit . . . frazzled.'

So Bobby took over bath-time and I drove over to the flat. I took my key, this time, and let myself in, knowing she'd be furious to be caught unawares. As soon as I stepped through the door my foot crunched against something on the floor. I couldn't see what it was; the place was in semi-darkness. Just a slice of low light from the gap of her bedroom door.

'Mum,' I called, and recoiled from the vinegar stink of alcohol and something worse – old vomit, maybe – catching at the throat. 'Mum?'

An animal grunt from her room. I pushed the door to a fanfare of bottles clinking and rolling on the floor. The

stench in here was overpowering. I ran back to the bathroom and retched in the sink. There were stubbed-out
fag-ends in there. The loo hadn't been flushed and was dark
with urine. The sour air made me retch again, but I managed
not to throw up. I was livid. I should be in my own, clean
home, reading my son a story, and instead I'd been hauled
out by a dirty old man to shake my own mother out of her
stupour. Back in the bedroom, I yelled at her, and the hump
in the bed shifted. Shards of light bounced against the
empties. I switched on the main light and roared: 'Marian
Westwood! Get up!'

A bloated, white paw moved the bedclothes and revealed
a face that wasn't hers. It was a face without form, an
inflated bag stained with yellow. Her hair was a mass of
filthy netting, spidered around her cheeks and forehead.
There was a movement, and one hoarse word emerged:
'Christ . . .'

I didn't want to be there. I wanted to turn and run, fetch
someone else, fetch my dad from across the world. After a
moment my panic resolved itself into action and I phoned
for an ambulance. Then I went back into her room and said,
'It's all right, someone's coming.'

But I couldn't bring myself to approach her bed.

11

They drained her of excess poison, leaving only the stuff that had already settled into her skin and bones and veins. They dosed her up to clear the infections and warned her that her pickled organs would fail if she didn't clean up her act. She came out of hospital alive, unnerved and full of resolutions. While she was in there Bobby and I had tackled the flat, flushing out and carting away bottles by the bag-load, chucking the fag-ends and sweet-papers and receipts and empty food cans, checking discarded bills, working our way back to a manageable boundary of possessions: magazine back-issues built into low walls, pens and rings and matchboxes banked up along table edges, shoes stacked around the skirting boards.

'She must have made one hell of an effort,' he commented, 'when she knew we were coming to visit.'

While I washed up the backlog of dirty dishes, Bobby sat in the living room sorting through some of his finds from under the sofa, the chairs, the bed, from the bottom of the wardrobe.

'Hey,' he called, 'she's got some fantastic stuff here. Theatre programmes . . . "After Silence" – good God, Gill would love to see this. Take a look at this cast!'

He recited a series of half-forgotten names with increasing amazement.

I emptied a bowlful of greasy water, piled in the next batch of plates and glasses and turned the tap on full. Across the way I was aware of movement from one of the windows. They probably think she's dead, I thought. They probably think we're emptying the place and getting shot of it. I directed a violent jet of washing-up liquid over the dishes.

'You know,' Bobby prattled on, 'you could open a museum with this lot. Or a shop. People love this kind of memorabilia . . . Look at *this* . . .'

'*You* love it, you mean,' I called back.

'Well, so do you, and we can't be the only ones, that's all I'm saying . . .'

I thought: you seem to be in a hurry to divvy up her belongings, and the poor old bag's not dead yet. I nearly said it, but changed my mind. I plunged my hands in to the bowl. The water was much too hot. The first touch was like ice. Pincering the stem of a wine glass, I felt a loosening under the surface and lifted the glass from the water with blotched fingers. A perfect semi-circle was bitten into the rim. I swore and tipped up the bowl, catching the broken piece by its rounded edge as the soapy water slapped into the sink.

'Have you seen this one, Jayney?'

I came to the kitchen door, slipping the half-moon of glass into the pocket of my jeans. Bobby was peeling one picture from a sheaf of others. Marian Westwood, 1954. It was cracked from one edge and he handled it like china.

'Oh, yes,' I said. 'I've seen it. And all the rest.' I knew where all the pictures were – heaped into old grocery crates, gathered into wicker baskets. Sometimes, as a child, I would escape from the parties to my parents' room and spend hours cross-legged behind their bed, looking through the photographs and making up characters for all her different faces.

'This is wonderful,' said Bobby, husky with reverence. 'We should get this re-printed or something. They can do miracles with old prints nowadays. Do it as a surprise for her. A present, when she comes home.'

We'd been told to collect her at the end of that week. She could have done with another week of ward discipline and regular food, but they needed the bed. One of the nurses had told me pointedly that Marian needed someone to 'keep an eye on her'. She shouldn't be left alone, said the nurse, to get low and start turning to the bottle again. I knew exactly what was implied: she wouldn't need the bottle if she had a proper daughter instead. 'Everyone,' said the nurse 'everyone needs a bit of care and attention once in a while.'

'She won't come to us,' I assured her. 'She wouldn't want to come to us,' I said to Bobby, inviting agreement. 'She'd hate our little place in Archway. There just isn't the room . . .' I said. 'She'll never shift from that flat,' I said. And at her bedside, under the nurse's citric gaze, I said to Marian, 'You wouldn't want to move in with me and Bobby, would you, Mum?'

'Christ, no,' she spat, and I had to stop myself turning to the nurse with a wide smile of triumph. 'Take me back to Bayswater,' Marian commanded. 'I know where I am there. My friends know where I am.'

Her friends. There were one or two who dropped in every so often, the one or two who'd ended up as aimless and washed-up as she was. There was noone else. My father sent her a get well card and insisted, on the phone, that I let him know if he 'needed to catch the plane'. Alec Blessing had gone into an accelerating decline after conveying his SOS, as if that final good deed had blown his system. When we phoned the nursing home to let him know Marian's progress Hilary promised to pass on the news – 'but whether he'll take it in or not is another matter, I'm afraid.' But friends or no friends, I knew I could rely on Marian not to budge from her den.

On the day of her discharge we had to bring Gareth with us when we picked her up and took her home. Gill couldn't look after him; she'd gone up for her job interview in Emmett Park. Gareth squeezed himself into a corner of the back seat while we helped Marian in through the other door. She was like a waxwork, her skin sallow and dense, her movements constrained and inflexible. She tried to smile at Gareth, and said something that none of us quite understood.

In the lift up to the flat Gareth hid behind my leg, doing

his best to vanish, as we squashed ourselves in and held
Marian firm against the jolts. Bobby unlocked her flat door
and waved her in with a flourish.

'Madame,' he said, 'your palace awaits.' Under the layers
of sickness, she grew slightly fluttery.

'Oh, my dears,' she said. 'You *have* been busy.'

She lowered herself gradually on to the sofa. Bobby sat
next to her, and from under it drew out a box of the photographs and programmes he'd found most interesting.

'These are incredible,' he said. 'Talk me through them.'

I grabbed the opportunity to take Gareth out of the
chamber of horrors and into the kitchen.

'Can I get anyone anything?' I called.

'How about a drink?' came Marian's reply. In the pause
that followed I could see Gareth registering the pulses of
consternation and closing his body against them.

'Mum . . .' he whimpered, and then we heard Bobby and
Marian's laughter from the other room.

'My little joke, Jayney,' said Marian. 'Don't get your
knickers in a knot.'

In her last few years Marian established more of a pattern
than she'd ever known before. There'd be the usual summons
for good days, then the midnight call from a worried neighbour, or from Marian herself, if she was conscious enough
to take fright. Back onto a ward or into a clinic to be drained
and dried and then home, adamant that she'd never take
another drink again. Gill had moved by then, had sold the
high-ceilinged house and bought us a new home with
plenty of space for an alcoholic mother, but Marian wouldn't
come. Even if I'd made more than one offer, even if I'd
made it with sincerity, I know she wouldn't have come to
live with us. Think about it. Marian Westwood, shambling
around in a smooth-walled family house with her boring
daughter and a lively little boy? I thought about it, and I
thought about Gareth clinging to my jeans, and the look on

his face as he shadowed me in the Bayswater kitchen, and I didn't issue a second invitation.

Maybe I could have kept a closer eye on her. Maybe I didn't always have to work late or take Gareth to mini-rugby instead of popping in to inspect her flat for bottles. But she'd have found a way.

As she said to Bobby, 'I love a drink. I come alive with a drink. You're meant to admit there's a problem – and I do. I'm just not that bothered about solving it.'

Oh, yes, Bobby was still the golden boy, still cancelling meetings and rearranging school runs to answer the call to her side. But he came back from their sessions a little more jaded than I'd seen him before, a little more worn down, and I'm ashamed to say that gave me a certain grim satisfaction. Then, in February 1993, she was found in a heap at the lift door by a neighbour, went into hospital and didn't come out. When they recognised the signs, they wheeled her bed into a private room, lugging all the equipment that was tapped into her, ushered me in and shut the door. I sat beside her. Nobody explained this change of scene; no one provided a timetable of events. I knew there was a downward feeling in my chest and the pit of my stomach; I knew I'd become jittery and self-conscious. Afterwards I assumed this to be natural foreboding. There we were, me and Marian Westwood, basking in the winter sunshine that filtered through a large, net-curtained window. I'd brought an *Evening Standard* in case she was unconscious and started to read it, unsure what else to do. She lay there hissing and clicking through an oxygen mask, suspended by a network of wires and tubes. Every so often she would say something inaudible, and we'd go through a performance of pulling off the mask, misunderstanding each other, exchanging pointless comments and resuming our wait for God knew what.

Once, when we'd grappled the mask away, she turned out to have been saying, 'I feel like Frankenstein's fucking monster.'

Another time we managed quite a conversation.

'Where's Bobby?'

'He's at work, Mum.'

'What about Gareth?'

'Don't worry about Gareth. Bobby's picking him up from school.'

'He's an angel.'

I wasn't sure who was meant and didn't ask. After a hiatus, while she pawed again at the mask, she said, 'Don't let him see.'

I helped her fit the mask back comfortably.

'OK,' I said. 'I won't.'

She drifted off now and then. I watched her, listened to that rhythmic breathing-hiss, click; hiss, click – and wondered what would happen when it changed. Above the mask the flesh of her nose was pocked; her eyelids were swollen but the lashes were still dark along the familiar, slanted curve. Her hair, cut short, was grey and wiry. It was hard to believe she was only 63. I touched her hand and noticed the wedding ring embedded into her finger, imprisoned there as she had fattened around it.

Time passed. I spoke to Bobby from the phone in the corridor; a nurse replaced Marian's catheter; I started on the crossword. An interruption in her breath made me look up, heart pounding, but she was trying to speak again. She was quite aggravated. I pulled the mask aside.

'What's the baby's name?'

'Gareth,' I said, with a thrill of alarm.

'No, no, you idiot,' said Marian, quite lucidly. 'Harry's baby. What's Harry's baby's name?'

'Laura,' I said, bridling. 'And she's not a baby. She must be 16, at least. Why?'

She shoved me away with a grimace of impatience. I sulked over the crossword, embarrassed at my mistake, suffering the same humiliation I'd known as a child who didn't get her friends' jokes. Then she said, 'Tell Harry not to come.'

And because I was still sulking I didn't answer. I don't suppose she noticed, though. An hour or so later I suddenly realised the rhythm had altered, and her breathing was slower, longer, more distant, less and less distinguishable from the bustle beyond the door or traffic brushing the motorway in the distance. I was still waiting, brandishing the *Evening Standard* in bunched fists, when the nurse came in, performed some mysterious rite of inspection and whispered, 'I'll fetch Dr Bannerman.'

I stood up, aware of some momentous development, sure I could still see a hint of movement under the covers as my mother breathed in, breathed out. The doctor arrived, bent over her, removed the mask and performed some rite of his own, mumbled to the nurse and nodded sadly to me. The nurse said, 'Maybe you'd like to make a phone call or something, while we just tidy her up. We'll call you in, then, to say goodbye.'

It was only then that I finally understood. Idiot.

12

There were obituaries in *The Guardian* and *The Times*, both written by Russell Mitchell. She would have been pleased, in an aggressive, told-you-so sort of way. *The Guardian* printed a copy of the 1954 shot. It was odd to see it there, in furry newsprint, faintly marred by text on the other side of the page. Odd to realise that this picture which had always been part of our home and our private past was actually public property. Of course, that was its sole purpose.

We gave her a simple send-off in the crematorium chapel. Harry came over, defying orders, and stayed with us for 10 days. Great Uncle Jed turned up, but none of the others. His frame had collapsed further over the years and his phlegmy cough was worse, but apart from that he looked more robust than my mother had for many years. I was sure he was wearing the same suit he'd worn at my grandmother's wake, now a much better fit. He made a wheezy fuss of Gareth, smuggling him mints during the service. Gill came down from Emmett Park and insisted on leaving straight afterwards to drive back up, despite Bobby's almost hysterical protests.

'You've got Harry to cater for,' she said in her conclusive way. 'You can do without me.'

I'd expected her to be more upset, perhaps sentimental. But she sailed through the proceedings with serenity. I thought maybe it was an act put on for Bobby's and my benefit. Or her new and demanding job on the women's wing, preying on her mind.

Three years after Marian's death a large, bulky, brown envelope arrived in the post. Gareth hung over my shoulder as I tipped a pack of black-and-white photographs on to the dining table, all the same size, all with the same unused sheen. He started to finger through them as I tried to decipher the letter that slid out last of all. It was written in a long-tailed, elaborate hand in old-fashioned purple ink. A hand-typed name sat under the illegible signature: Perry MacPherson Esq, Executor. I read the letter again and decoded enough to tell me that Mr MacPherson was forwarding the enclosed on the instructions of the recently deceased Alec Blessing. I was mildly surprised that Alec had lasted that long. As I picked up one of the photos I became aware that Gareth was staring at another with the breathless discomfort of a child encountering the forbidden.

'Put that down, please,' I snapped, as if the pictures were his fault.

'Is that Gran?' he asked, replacing the photo and backing away from it.

'I think . . . I think it was for a film. A . . . a sort of historical film. As I remember.'

I flipped rapidly through the photographs, had a fleeting impression of splayed limbs, hair and gauze, then slipped them back into the envelope. Gareth was standing behind my chair, monitoring my reactions. These were the old photographs Marian and Alec would examine during their nostalgic get-togethers. And presumably that had been Alec's main function: to remind Marian of her youth and beauty; to remind her of the camera's lust, and of the fact that she was, after all, just a slut from down the Docks. I felt uneasy, but not because of the images themselves. The notion of Alec Blessing leaving us his soft-porn memories was faintly threatening. Yet it had probably seemed to him a kind, even touching gesture. A reminder of his love for Marian Westwood.

'Mum . . .' said Gareth, shakily.

'It's OK,' I said, and turned to cradle his round face in my hands. 'I was just thinking, that's all. About your grandmother. About what a good actress she was in all those films.'

13

It's dark outside, but Gill hasn't turned on the lights. We're
sprawled in her sitting room, too tired to take off our coats.
The kettle boiled 10 minutes ago but neither of us has the
strength, yet, to go and make tea, though I'm parched,
chilled to the bone and ravenously hungry. Our short walk
developed into a two-and-a-half-hour hike. From the grave-
yard we set off in the opposite direction from the hospital
and headed for the next landmark – the power station's
smoke stacks on the horizon. They were elusive as rainbows,
those stacks, seeming to retreat as we approached, sometimes disappearing altogether as we trudged along the
margins of fields and empty roads. Then all at once they
were there, filling the sky, but no more approachable – set
back behind a complex of low, ambiguous buildings and
fenced-off yards. There was no industrial din, no metallic
stench, no procession of workmen. It was all very quiet,
apart from an indefinable murmuring from one or other of
the blocks, and not a soul was in sight.

'Another place that keeps itself to itself,' I said.

We walked on to a scattering of houses, an embryonic
village forming around the station boundary. A board at the
gate of one house had 'Dell's Cattery' painted in gothic
lettering, over a silhouette of a prowling cat. At the end of
the row the landscape extended again into an endless sheet
of golds, browns and dusky greens. Gill indicated the houses
we were leaving behind.

'Great view from the back windows,' she said. 'From this
side of the road, in any case. Why would you live on the
other side? Chimney stacks behind you, neighbours in
front. All this space and they box themselves in like that!'

We must have covered a good 7 or 8 miles in all. My muscles
are already starting to nag. I haven't bothered to pull up my
socks, which rucked up uncomfortably when I heaved off

my mud-caked boots. Gill's eyes are closed. My stomach grumbles.

'I'll make the tea, shall I?' I offer, unconvincingly.

'Mmm.'

Neither of us moves.

'And stay for dinner,' says Gill, without opening her eyes.

I go back home for a bath while she's cooking. I soak in bubbles, then cover myself in moisturiser and dab on the perfume I've been keeping by for five or six years – expensive stuff that Bobby bought me to celebrate our first takings at the shop. I apply eye-liner. I wear the orange skirt I wore for our meal with Pat – the only decent skirt I possess. When I arrive Gill's wearing a silk blouse, Japanese-style trousers and a haze of musky scent.

Gill's laid a tablecloth, and there's a candle in a bottle at the centre. We clink glasses. The wine is smooth and slightly spicy. I'm completely enveloped by the pleasure of the first mouthful as it warms my skull and throat; by the kitchen's deliciously savoury air; by the anticipation grinding my stomach; by the occasional bark and car engine that divides the silence outside. I wish we could forget the story-telling tonight, but the moment passes and I say the first thing that comes into my head.

'There was a time when I thought I'd never have a drink again.'

'Scared of following your mother's footsteps?' asks Gill.

'Not exactly. Just something about the smell of alcohol – something I could detect in it, something rotten. At the back of it. Anyway, that phase didn't last. This wine is lovely.'

Gill laughs and turns the stem of her glass in her hands. She's subdued. Reticent. I carry on talking.

'Well, I'd say I've finished my biography, pretty well.'

She looks up at me, puzzled and distracted.

'Marian's life and times,' I prompt. 'I'd say that's the draft version more or less done.'

She nods. I try again.

'At her funeral,' I say, 'you were very . . . self-possessed. I remember thinking that.'

She considers this for a while, then rouses herself.

'I suppose I knew,' she says. 'I was facing the inevitable. Most of us are fairly self-possessed, when the doubts have gone.'

I realise, with a jolt, that Marian's death was transmuted into another of Gill's signs. First her whole life and then her extinction – which should, surely, have been a personal affair – was swallowed up into the black hole of Gill Gilbard's superstition.

'How do you mean, "facing the inevitable"?'

She smiles at my sharpness.

'Believe me, I know how off-the-wall this sounds,' she says. 'But . . . to me, they were twin spirits. That's the only way I can express it. Not that I've ever tried to express it before. Twin spirits.'

Gill had been living at Emmett Park for about four years when my mother died. Four years of getting on with her job at the hospital, four years without seeing Lenny or even hearing his voice. She called the house now and then, but either got through to another resident who claimed he wasn't available, or received no reply at all. She couldn't risk turning up out of the blue. Any show of spontaneity would disturb the new, rehabilitated Lenny, who guarded his routines with such care. All the same, she didn't fret.

'The job took up most of my time,' she says. 'The job and getting this house, doing it up, planting out the garden, that sort of thing. Time went by in the usual way. I reckoned I'd make contact with him sooner or later. Or he'd make contact with me.'

Then came the news about Marian Westwood. Gill duly changed appointments, filled the car, packed her funeral clothes. And before setting off she picked up the phone, obeying the instinct that she'd regularly tried to stifle for over 30 years: I must tell Lenny.

'I could hear it ringing at the other end,' she says, 'and I knew.' She straightens her back with the kind of smug conviction that makes me want to scream. 'I could feel . . . his absence. I knew he wasn't there any more.'

14

The day after Marian's funeral and Gill's long, late journey home, she drove to Berriford and parked outside the grime-encrusted house. Lenny's name was still on the label, along with the cartoon face, but she didn't ring his doorbell. Instead she tried every other bell in succession until the door was opened, by a large woman with slippers moulded around her misshapen feet.

'Does Mr Hall still live here? Flat number 4?' asked Gill. The woman propped herself against the door-jamb, chest heaving with the effort of standing up.

'No one lives there, now. Council came and cleared it out.'

Gill was rooted to the spot. She looked past the woman, up the stairs.

'Go and knock if you don't believe me,' said the woman, adding without emotion, 'Council came and emptied it after he passed on.' She obviously assumed Gill was someone official. Nobody who dressed and spoke like Gill would be making personal enquiries after Lenny Hall.

'I see,' said Gill. 'Well, thanks anyway.'

The woman stayed put, gathering strength, while Gill went back to her car. As she was unlocking the door, she heard her say,

'Sad, really. Strangers coming to chuck out your stuff. Noone else to come asking.'

I've come asking, thought Gill. But she raised her hand to the woman and said,

'Yes. Very sad.'

Gill drove home and made calls, as she did every ordinary working day. Berriford Social Services. The district hospital. She left messages, gathered facts and took down notes. Lenny Hall? Let's look at his file . . . hadn't turned up for work. Hadn't responded when the social worker called. In the end they broke the door and found him half covered in a single blanket. They could see his breath in the cold room. He'd caught a bug, that was all. Something unremarkable. Flu, something like that. Didn't eat. Didn't take his drugs. Didn't do anything to fight it off. Pneumonia had set in, and Mr Hall wasn't a strong man. People she'd never met spoke gently and cautiously, apologised to her, commiserated with her, offered her other telephone numbers. Lenny hadn't left many clues, they explained. So they hadn't known who, if anyone, to contact. No address books or diaries or letters. Just unlabelled photographs of a young woman and her child. There'd been some confusion about his notes. His records had gone astray. Naturally they would have tracked her down when they'd come to light. In due course.

'I think Lenny would have approved, in a way,' says Gill, getting up from the table to serve food. She's become businesslike and clipped. I imagine that's how she was, as she tracked down the truth.

'It was all so . . . anonymous. Sneaking out when no one was looking. By the time I'd cottoned on, the bed was stripped, remade and full of someone else. Ashes scattered in a corporate garden. Flat cleaned out and ready for the next on the list. Nobody around to interfere.'

She sits again and we eat for a while. The food is wonderful. I relish its flavours and textures and fend off a feeling of disappointment. What did I expect, after all? A final manic outburst, a whirling dervish of resentment lashing out at everything around him. A suicide of Jacobean gore. Or perhaps that Lenny was still alive, still watching over his close-circuit screen through the night, or even burning the light in his villa room on the other side of the wire.

I'm not sure what to say to her. After numberless evenings of narrative and confession, it's all a bit of an anti-climax. When I've nearly wiped my plate clean I say, pointlessly, 'You had a tough time of it, those few years. First Robert, then Marian, then Lenny. Death comes in threes, don't they say?'

Gill beams. 'Lenny would have told you that's a statistical likelihood, not a golden rule.'

That's rich, I think, coming from the arch-priestess of augury.

'Plum and honey layer-cake for afters, OK?'

'Sounds perfect.'

As she deals with the next course I study her rounded shoulders and bowed head, and the tiny, dry white hairs at the nape of her neck. Suddenly I want to put my arms around her, this bossy, infuriating, lonely woman, abandoned by all her men. I think of Lenny tiptoeing out of her life, just as his son would in years to come, without apology, without a backward glance. An idea reveals itself. It must have been sitting there, waiting to be noticed, for quite a long time.

'Gill,' I say.

'Yes?' She doesn't turn round.

'Does Bobby know Lenny was his father?'

'No.'

The answer is blunt and final. She brings our pudding to the table, picks up her spoon and twists it between her fingers.

'But I have wondered . . .' she says, then shakes her head at her own folly.

'Go on.'

'Well, I've sometimes wondered whether he could . . . just *know*. Without anyone telling him. But that's nonsense.'

'What if Lenny told him? Wrote to him, maybe?' I'm getting worked up, now. Soon, if I don't take care, I'll be weepy. 'What if that happened, and Bobby's been brooding about it all this time, and then when the shop folded . . . and we moved up here . . . and he thought – he might have to face up to it, and you know Bobby, he couldn't . . . *Were* you? Were you going to tell him?'

Gill finishes her mouthful placidly and says,

'No, I wasn't.'

She can see from my rapid blinking that this isn't enough to reassure me.

'I would never have done that to Robert,' she says. 'And neither would Lenny.' She lifts her eyebrows. She might be about to laugh.

'Listen. Even if Lenny came back to haunt us all. Even if he's a poltergeist somewhere, creating havoc right now. Even if he could still tell his secret, Lenny would keep it safe.'

JANUARY

The first day of a new year. I'm wearing Gareth's anorak under Bobby's overcoat, and an old pair of woolly gloves, and I can see my breath dissolving against the roof tiles. The cold seems to start in my bones and work its way out. Through the fog I can see lights on in the villas. I wonder whether they celebrate the change of year in there. Somewhere close by a bird is warbling in the false heat of a streetlamp. It's a comforting, lulling sound. No doubt Lenny would point out that it could be a shriek for help or a wail of anguish, but it doesn't sound that way to me. That's the great advantage of birdsong – so alien. I can hear whatever I like.

Last night we toasted the end of the old year here, before Gareth and Hannah set off to see in the new one at a friend's party in Acreston. Gill brought a bottle of cheap champagne.

'Well,' she said, 'here's to a year of happy revision and first-class grades!'

Gareth and Hannah groaned, but they were in high spirits.

'This time next year,' burbled Hannah, 'we might well be celebrating Hogmanay on the streets of Glasgow!' She started to sing – '*I belong to*—' then caught a cautionary look from Gareth and slurped at her drink. I was gripped with an unexpectedly powerful affection for the girl, a kind of gratitude for her indiscretion.

I said, 'I'll rely on you to keep Gareth out of trouble, then, Hannah,' and she beamed at me with relief.

When their lift arrived and they were fussing with coats at the door Gareth turned to me and said, in a rapid undertone,

'Will you be OK?'

I patted his back, resisting the impulse to hug him, and said, 'Of course I will. Gill and I are planning a right old knees-up at midnight. Have a great time. But be sensible.'

I could hear their shouts and laughter as I shut the door, and then the car doors slamming and the rev and whine of the engine as they sped off between the dark fields. Too late, Bobby. They've gone. You missed your chance.

Gill and I turned on the telly for Big Ben's chimes. Revellers in the city and in an unseen studio yelled a hoarse countdown. 'Twelve! Eleven! Ten!' No surprise knock at the door. No dishevelled, sheepish first-footer clutching a lump of coal and an armful of fresh schemes for the coming year. But we knew that, Gill and I. As her story unravelled with the seasons, we had grown more and more certain that Bobby wouldn't be coming home.

Gill reached over to touch her glass against mine. From the television came a mournful, tuneless drone of Auld Lang Syne.

'Happy new year,' said Gill.

And I said, 'To absent friends.'

She echoed my toast without taking her eyes off the swaying crowd on the screen.

'Absent friends.'

By the same author . . .

The Pier Glass

"We are all in search of a story. If none presents itself, we invent our own."

Different lives . . .
Different time frames . . .

One Story

Published 2001
ISBN 1-870206-44-4
£7.99

James is a university history lecturer who lives in South Wales. His girlfriend lives and works in Italy. Do they have a future? And what has a medieval bard got to do with James?

Nia Williams' compelling first novel interweaves different lives and different time frames as characters from the 15th Century, the 1890s, the 1950s and modern-day Cardiff are brought together by a skilfully plotted story of epic dimensions.

Honno Welsh Women's Press,
Canolfan Merched y Wawr,
Stryd yr Efail/Vulcan Street, Aberystwyth,
Ceredigion, SY23 1JH
01970 623150
post@honno.co.uk
www.honno.co.uk